# A
# LAND TO
# CALL HOME

# Books by Lauraine Snelling

*Hawaiian Sunrise*

## A SECRET REFUGE

*Daughter of Twin Oaks     Sisters of the Confederacy*
*The Long Way Home*

## DAKOTAH TREASURES

*Ruby*

## RED RIVER OF THE NORTH

*An Untamed Land     The Reapers' Song*
*A New Day Rising     Tender Mercies*
*A Land to Call Home     Blessing in Disguise*

## RETURN TO RED RIVER

*A Dream to Follow     Believing the Dream*
*More Than a Dream*

## HIGH HURDLES

*Olympic Dreams     Close Quarters*
*DJ's Challenge     Moving Up*
*Setting the Pace     Letting Go*
*Out of the Blue     Raising the Bar*
*Storm Clouds     Class Act*

## GOLDEN FILLY SERIES

*The Race     Shadow Over San Mateo*
*Eagle's Wings     Out of the Mist*
*Go for the Glory     Second Wind*
*Kentucky Dreamer     Close Call*
*Call for Courage     The Winner's Circle*

# A LAND TO CALL HOME

## LAURAINE SNELLING

# BETHANY HOUSE PUBLISHERS

MINNEAPOLIS, MINNESOTA 55438

*A Land to Call Home*
Copyright © 1997
Lauraine Snelling

Cover illustration by Dan Thornberg

Published by Bethany House Publishers
11400 Hampshire Avenue South
Bloomington, Minnesota 55438
www.bethanyhouse.com

Bethany House Publishers is a Division of
Baker Book House Company, Grand Rapids, Michigan.

Printed in the United States of America

**Library of Congress Cataloging-in-Publication Data**

Snelling, Lauraine.
    A land to call home / Lauraine Snelling.
       p. m . — (Red river of the north ; 3)
    ISBN 1–55661–578–7 (pbk.)
    I. Title. II. Series: Snelling, Lauraine. Red River of the north; bk. 3.
PS3569.N39L36    1996
813'.54—dc21

                                               97–4652
                                              CIP

To my mother,
who loves unconditionally
more than anyone else I know.

LAURAINE SNELLING is an award-winning author of over forty books, fiction and nonfiction, for adults and young adults. Besides writing both books and articles, she teaches at writers' conferences across the country. She and her husband, Wayne, have two grown sons and four granddogs, and they make their home in California.

### Dakota Territory
### September 1884

D ear Hjelmer."

Penny Sjornson dipped the tip of her quill pen into the ink-pot, then tapped the tiny black bead back into the bottle. What could she say to him that she hadn't already said many times over? Why did he never write back? He had promised he would. In that first and only letter, he had pleaded for her to wait for him.

She brushed a feathery strand of sun-gold hair back from her forehead, now wrinkled in thought. She stared up at the tendril of smoke rising from the chimney of the kerosene lamp. Behind her she could hear the sounds of children going to bed, the boys to the bunks in the lean-to and seven-year-old Anji to the bed she shared with her aunt Penny in the soddy.

Here it was the end of September, and Hjelmer had already been gone for two months—two of the longest months of her life. Granted, it wasn't terribly long compared to eternity, but then she wasn't one of the angels yet either. She studied the freckles on the back of her slender but work-worn hands. Kisses from God, her mother had called them. Penny thought so often of the mother who had died in childbirth the winter her eldest daughter reached ten. When their father disappeared not long afterward, the three children had been split up between the relatives. Penny wanted them all back together again someday almost as much as she wanted a letter from Hjelmer.

Her aunt Agnes Baard laid a gentle hand on the young woman's shoulder. "Having a hard time of it, eh?"

Penny nodded. "But I promised to write Hjelmer one letter a week, and Joseph said he is going to St. Andrew tomorrow and will mail it for me. Tante Agnes, why doesn't he write?"

Agnes settled wide hips on the chair at the end of the trestle table. "I wish I knew." She shook her head. "Never did trust that young man myself. Trouble seems to follow him like chickens will the corn."

"It's not his fault that Mary Ruth took it in her mind to—"

"To get that young man for her own, I know. But she must have had some reason to feel she could accuse him like that. I know he says he never even kissed her, but—" Agnes clamped her lips over the rest of the sentence.

"But what?" Penny leaned forward. "You've heard something and you didn't tell me?"

"Uff da. Me and my big mouth. You want a cup of coffee with Joseph and me before we go to bed?"

"Tante, you are changing the subject. What did you hear?" Penny could feel her jaw tighten. "I want to know. What did you hear?" She tamped down the urge to slam the table or shake her aunt. "I am not a child anymore to be kept in the dark and only told what is good for me to hear." She closed her eyes for a moment, then took a deep breath. "Please, Tante Agnes, tell me what you've heard."

"I don't hold with gossiping."

"Please."

The sigh heaved Agnes's ponderous bosom that swelled above the belly protruding under her apron. "Ingeborg said she saw Hjelmer kissing Mary Ruth Strand out behind the haystack. And you know as well as I do that Ingeborg don't make up stories."

Penny stared at the yellow-orange flame burning the edge of the wick in the lamp. Weeks earlier something inside had warned her to be ready for such a telling. She had ignored it then but could no longer. "He lied to me then?"

"Well, I heard tell of women kissing men, you know, and maybe them not wanting it but being too polite to push the hussy away," Agnes offered by way of comfort.

"She's a hussy all right, and that's being Christian charitable." Penny pushed the tip of the pen into the table so hard it broke off. She sighed. Now she'd have to sharpen the quill again, and it was already getting down to the finer part of the feather shaft. She pushed the cork into the inkpot and gently placed the precious piece of paper back in the carved wooden treasure box, one of the last things her father had given her. If paper didn't come so dear, she'd do what she wanted—crumple it up and throw it in the stove along with her promise to Hjelmer Ivan Bjorklund, that . . . that . . . She couldn't think of a name she dare utter aloud. But one of those she'd heard the threshing crew say would surely be useful right now.

Agnes heaved herself to her feet, grunting in the process.

"No, Tante, you sit down and I will get the coffee." Penny looked down at her aunt's feet, closely resembling sausages stuffed into a casing. Her elk-skin moccasins were already the only shoes she could wear. Penny didn't remember her aunt having trouble like this when she'd been in the family way before.

"There's a good girl." Agnes settled back into her chair with a sigh. She glanced over to see her husband, Joseph, in the rocker with his head rolled back, snores puffing from his open mouth. "Don't think he wants any, so just bring for you and me. Them sour cream cookies you baked today would taste right good now, don't you think?"

Penny used her apron for a hot pad to lift the blue granite coffeepot to the hot side of the stove. She lifted the iron stove lid with the coiled-handled lid lifter and dropped a couple pieces of kindling on top of the glowing coals. When those flared, she added bigger sticks that would burn quickly. She set the lid back in the hole and pulled the coffeepot over the now crackling fire. It wasn't cold enough yet to keep the fires burning at night, but before she went to bed, she would bank the larger coals in ashes to keep them for the morning. Going to the shelf, she fetched cookies from the jar and set them on the saucers with the cups. All the while, thoughts of Hjelmer leapfrogged through her mind.

Where was he? He had said he was going down to Fargo to get on with the railroad laying track to the west. He'd mailed his one half-page letter from there. "My dearest Penny," he had written and signed it "Yours, Hjelmer." She'd done what he said, sent her letters to the Fargo post office. He'd pick up any mail there. Had he even received any of her letters? Had he been injured after that and not able to write? She shuddered at the thought. Was he still alive? Death came easy on the unforgiving prairies of Dakota Territory, and she'd heard horror stories of terrible accidents. In the fall of 1884 the big push was on to web the country with railroad tracks.

"I'm sorry, child, to have brought that up," Agnes said when Penny sat back down. "Hjelmer just has some growing up to do, I think, and maybe this is God's way of making that happen. Sometimes men are still boys, only wearing bigger clothes, until God takes them by the suspenders and gives them a good shake. When

He sets them back down, they've learned a thing or two and make fine men. If Hjelmer is half the man his brothers were, he'll be a good husband someday."

The two looked at each other in the lamplight, knowing they each thought of the terrible winter that took the lives of the two Bjorklund brothers, Roald and Carl, along with Carl's two little girls. Others in the area had died, too, from both influenza and the killing blizzards.

After she was finally in bed, Penny tucked the covers under her chin and stared into the dark. She could hear Joseph snoring in bed and Agnes puffing in the way she had lately. The seven-year-old beside her turned over and sighed in her sleep. "Dear heavenly Father," Penny whispered, "I can't believe the bad things I hear about Hjelmer, for if I do, how will I manage? Please watch out for him and bring him safely home again. I want to do your will, dear Lord, and I always thought when Hjelmer came here from Norway that he was the one I would marry when I grew a bit older." She paused, the dog barking outside catching her attention.

*What if it were Hjelmer coming now?*

But when the barking stopped and the dog settled back down, she knew it was probably nothing more than a passing coyote or some such curious animal. "Please take care of Tante too. I'm so afraid something is wrong, no matter how much she tries to tell me she's fine. Thank you for our house and the farm, and thank you for your loving care for all of us. Amen." She turned on her side, the corn husks in the mattress rustling beneath her. The tightly strung ropes that held up the bed creaked, and she heard a clump of dirt drop from the sod roof. Joseph had hoped to build a house of wood this year, but it didn't look to happen now. They would probably just add another lean-to onto the soddy.

* * *

"No letter then, girl?" Her uncle, Joseph Baard, already had the horses harnessed and hitched to the wagon before the sun peeked over the horizon.

Penny shook her head as she loaded a box packed with eggs to trade at the Mercantile in St. Andrew. "It's not ready yet. Tante says for you to ask Kaaren and Ingeborg if they want to come over for some quilting on Saturday."

"That I will." Joseph turned and lifted one of the smoked elk haunches from the shelf in the smokehouse, nestling it into the straw that lined the wagon bed. "Agnes going to send any garden stuff?"

"I'm getting it now," Penny called over her shoulder on her way to the root cellar. "Come help me, Knute. There's butter to get out of the springhouse." Knute was her ten-year-old nephew. When she returned with a sack of carrots dug the day before, Penny slung it into the wagon, and Joseph settled it in the corner in the front. He'd be picking up more goods from the Bjorklunds, so he needed plenty of room.

With everything loaded, he entered the soddy to fetch the dinner Agnes was just finishing packing into a basket. "Surely does smell good in here." He inhaled a deep whiff. "Got any of that coffee left?"

"Ja, and I sugared some pancakes for you. They're rolled in a cloth on top so you can eat them midmorning." Agnes tucked a cloth over the top of the food. "Don't forget to pick up the mail."

He looked at her with sorrow lining his narrow face.

She playfully slapped his shoulder. "Now, don't try getting around me."

"Just because I forgot one time. You know MacDonald and I was talking, and—"

"And you just drove off, I know." Concern darkened her eyes. "You be careful now, you hear?"

Joseph shook his head. "Women, always worrying." He poured a cup of coffee and turned to leave. "Make sure those two rapscallions of yours help Petar out in the field. They like to slack off when I'm not here."

"Uff da. Talk about women worrying. Don't forget to ask Kaaren and Ingeborg—"

"I know. Come for quilting. Those horses will be peaceful companions after all these instructions." He grinned at her, tipped his hat, and left.

Agnes joined Penny in the yard and watched her husband drive off. They could hear his whistle floating back over the jingle of the harnesses. The rooster crowed in the barn and a cow bellered. "Well, we better get to the chores," Agnes said. "Those animals all want feeding. I'll set the bread to rising while you milk the cows." They turned toward their respective duties, and the never ending daily work began.

Joseph returned after dusk had darkened to night. The dog barking at the jingling of harness heard long before human ears announced his return to the family. The boys burst out the door and ran up the dusty road to the east, shouting, "Far, far, glad you are home!"

Penny wanted to do the same. Two years earlier she would have, but now she kept reminding herself to practice being a woman beyond girlish ways. But the run up the road beckoned her. When she heard Joseph whoa the horses, she strolled out the door, her casual actions belying her tripping heart. Surely there would be a letter today.

"Sorry," Joseph said after handing a letter to Agnes. "That's all there was."

Penny blinked hard and waited for him to hand her something to carry. Why, oh why, hadn't she heard from Hjelmer? She thought of the letter she'd written that afternoon, planning to add more as the week progressed just like she usually did. As far as she knew, she'd never broken a promise—but she was surely tempted now. Tempted to throw the letter in the fire and forget all about that young, lazy, lying—handsome, laughing, loving Norwegian. She thumped the sack of flour down on the table. Prayer didn't seem to be helping, and her aunt Agnes assured her that swearing wouldn't either. But banging pans did.

"Mercy, child, whatever is going on?" Agnes laid a brown wrapped package on the shelf along the wall. One look at Penny's face and she nodded. "I understand. Sometimes churning butter is good for moments like these, or kneading bread. One time I cleaned all the manure out of two stalls in the barn, first time after the winter pileup. Stalls looked good and I felt better."

"It's not fair!" A smaller pot slammed into a larger. "I could . . . I could tear all those blond curls off his head."

Agnes nodded, turning so Penny couldn't see her smile. Ah, the trials of young love. She didn't wish to ever go back to that time of life. Joseph, while not perfect, was a good God-fearing man who did his best for his family. One couldn't ask for much more. Praise be to God.

"Kaaren and Ingeborg said they'd be glad to come. They said perhaps the next time they would invite several others, like you did before." Joseph handed Penny a tablet of paper. "Thought you might like this."

Penny tried to blink the tears away, but one out-raced her effort and trickled down her cheek. "Thank you, Onkel Joseph. You are so good to me."

Joseph cleared his throat and nodded. "You are welcome, child. Little enough for all you do around here." He dug a sack out of his coat pocket. "Brought one of these for everybody. Thought maybe we all needed some sweetening up."

"Candy!" Anji grabbed the sack and started handing the red-and-white sticks around.

When everyone stuck theirs in their mouths, Agnes said with a chuckle, "All we need is a tree to make it look like Christmas."

"And thnow." Anji was having trouble with her s's, especially since she'd lost her left front tooth.

"That'll be here soon enough. We'll butcher on Monday if the temperature drops. Not normal to have such a warm fall." Joseph yawned and stretched his arms over his head. "Time for bed, everybody. We put in a long day."

On Saturday the quilters arrived before nine, with Thorliff and Baptiste leaping out of the wagon as soon as they saw Knute and Swen Baard. Eight-year-old Thorliff's porkpie hat hit the ground about the same time as his feet. He picked up the faded flat hat and clapped it back on his head with both hands, covering straight hair more white than gold from the bleaching of the long summer sun.

"You two behave yourselves now," Ingeborg Bjorklund called to the backs of four boys racing out of ear range as fast as possible.

"We will." She heard the faint answer. What she could hear well was three-year-old Andrew's wail from the back of the wagon.

"Go with Tor! Me go, Mor."

She turned in time to catch his skirts as he started to climb out of the wagon and onto the slowly turning wheel. "No, Andrew, sit down."

"There's no stopping him." Kaaren Knutson, Ingeborg's sister-in-law, turned in spite of her bulging stomach and snagged a flailing arm. "Come on, Andrew, come to Tante Kaaren."

"No-o-o!" His cry echoed across the flat-as-a-stove-top Red River Valley. High overhead in the bright blue sky, a prairie hawk screeched.

"Look, Andrew, a big bird." Grunting, Ingeborg lifted him to the seat beside her and tilted his chin up to see the hawk soaring on the rising air currents.

When the child followed the pointing of her finger, a smile instantly dried his tears. "Big bird."

"That's a hawk." Ingeborg kept him in the circle of her arm, knowing well he could still make a flying leap for the ground. Andrew was nothing if not brave. Keeping up to Thorliff made him try many things that should have been beyond his abilities, like sliding off the haystack and riding the mule. One day she had found him playing under the bellies of the harnessed horses. Thank God, Bob and Bell seemed to understand he was a young'un and watched out for him too.

"Hawk," he answered, laying his arm across his mother's shoulders. He turned to face her, a grin appling his cheeks. "Big bird." When she smiled back and tickled his tummy, he chortled with the most infectious laugh in all of Dakota Territory.

"Those boys are so brown, the only way to tell Baptiste apart is his dark hair." Kaaren shifted on the high wagon seat they had padded for her with a quilt. Although her baby wasn't due for another two months, she looked ready to deliver any minute. "Uff da," she murmured, using both hands to move her abdomen into a more comfortable position. Pointing to her ponderous belly, Kaaren asked, "Are you thinking this is twins as much as I am?"

"There were twins in the Bjorklund family. Bridget told me so a long time ago. She warned me in case it happened."

"I know. Carl always thought having twins would be a wonderful gift from God." A cloud flitted across her eyes at the memory of her first husband, who had died of flu one winter. She sighed. "Lars says two for one ain't a bad return."

"Ja, but he don't have to nurse and diaper them. Diapers for one baby is hard enough, especially in the winter. I remember taking them off the line frozen stiff and finishing the drying over the stove in the soddy."

"Not so long ago either. I've been hemming flannel and knitting soakers, but if I have twins, I won't have enough." They stopped the horses at the hitching post in front of the barn.

"You wait and I'll help you down." Ingeborg wrapped the reins around the brake handle and climbed over the side, using the spokes of the front wheel as a middle step. She lifted Andrew down and hung on to his hand to walk around the wagon. "Just you be patient, son. You cannot go after Thorliff. Remember, Gus is in the house waiting to play with you." She reached up to give Kaaren a hand.

"I'm going to have to sit back in the wagon bed from now on.

This climbing up and down from the seat is getting to be too much."
Kaaren gripped the wagon seat while she felt for the spoke with one
foot. Ingeborg placed the searching foot on a spoke and reached to
give leverage for Kaaren to sit against if she felt weak. Once they
both had their feet on the ground, Kaaren shook her head. "Two
more months. How will I ever manage?"

"Like women everywhere. One step at a time." Ingeborg slipped
the bridles from the horses and tied the ropes from the hitching post
to their halters. "Those boys better come back and take care of the
horses or they'll get whatfor from both me and Agnes."

They retrieved their quilting baskets from the rear of the wagon
and walked toward the soddy that lay dozing in the sun. The air
wore the crisp dress of Autumn, with the sun valiantly trying to
warm it. After a frost that blackened the gardens, Indian summer
settled in for an extended visit.

"My land, I never even heard you drive up." Agnes bustled to
the door at their knock. "Come in. Come in." She ushered them in,
then stepped outside. "Knute, Swen, you two come take care of the
horses now!" Her holler could be heard in the next township.
"Boys!" She shook her head when she came back in the soddy. "How
they can get that far away so fast is beyond me." She shook her head
again when Kaaren removed her shawl. "Merciful God, please don't
let her have that baby right here today." She clasped her hands
against her bosom. "Are you sure you figured right?"

Kaaren nodded. "Lars thinks maybe I should go down to Grand
Forks to the doctor there, but other than needing a wheelbarrow in
front of me, I'm fine. He said we should take bets on whether there's
one or two in here." She patted the huge bulge as she spoke. "If it's
two, we'll need the money." With a sigh she sank into the rocker.
"Maybe what I should do is put my rocker in the back of the wagon
for traveling."

Ingeborg and Agnes exchanged looks. "What a wonderful idea.
Why didn't we think of that earlier?" Ingeborg gave Andrew, who
had buried himself in her skirt, a gentle push. "You and Gus go play
now. See the blocks?"

"I fixed them up a pen in the back of the house with hog wire
from the edge of the lean to to the back of the soddy. That way they
can dig in the dirt and not head out across the prairie." Agnes went
to the door. "Penny!" She turned back to her guests. "She can leave
off with the churning and help Anji get these little ones settled. We

got something to discuss before she comes in to help with the quilting."

Penny wiped a strand of hair from her sweaty forehead with the back of her hand as she came through the door. She greeted the two women, took the hands of the little ones, and led them out the back door.

"Now, quick." Agnes seated herself in the chair she pulled away from the table, making a triangle of the two rockers and the chair. She leaned forward and dropped her voice to a whisper. "I thought maybe we could make the next quilt for Penny and Hjelmer."

"She's heard from him then?" Ingeborg asked.

Agnes shook her head. "No, only that one letter, and it is worrying her some awful. That scalawag. When I catch up with him, he's going to wish he'd been faithful about putting pen to paper. I keep telling myself it's only two months since he's been gone, but I got a bad feeling about this."

"We haven't heard either, and I'm sure he hasn't written home. His mother asked about him in her last letter."

"Be that as it may, and knowing how long it takes us to get something finished, I'd like to start a wedding ring pattern for them. Every bride needs that quilt on her wedding bed, and maybe the stitching of the quilt will bring Hjelmer home sooner."

"Fine with me. I just thought maybe we could quick piece up another baby quilt, just in case." Ingeborg nodded toward Kaaren. "We could work on that today while Penny is helping us. I'll ask around at Sunday meeting tomorrow and find out who else wants to join us."

"Good." Agnes nodded. "We could do the baby a nine patch or a four square and plain." She rose to go to her trunk under the window. "I have some scraps in here. We could do a crazy quilt."

Penny came in just as her aunt knelt in front of the chest. "Here, let me do that. You know Onkel Joseph said to—"

"Don't care what he said. A woman's got to get in her trunk now and again, and you can see I'm not climbing on anything." She tempered her words at her niece with a gentle smile. "You go ahead and pour us all a cup of coffee."

Penny started to say something, thought the better of it, and flashing a grin that asked "what to do with her?" went to the calico-skirted cupboard for cups.

Before long the women were taking turns cutting pieces, laying the squares out in a pleasing color pattern, and stitching them together. Their conversation flashed as fast as their needles. The fragrance of beans baking with salt pork and molasses, the laughter of the children outside, and the comfort of one another's company made the morning fly by. As soon as they'd served all the men and children, they ate quickly and returned to their stitching. Penny washed up the two small children, tucked them into bed for a nap, and returned to the job at hand.

"I have some of the head and leg wool from the spring shearing carded for quilt batting," Ingeborg said, smoothing her latest square out on her knees. "There now. Don't that look nice?" They all admired their handiwork and kept on stitching. "Don't seem like we should wait a month to tie this. Might be needed before then."

"Inge!" Kaaren shifted in her chair, grateful for the footstool Penny had placed beneath her swollen feet. Sitting for more than a few minutes in one position was becoming increasingly difficult. "Uff da."

"What is it?" Ingeborg leaned forward, as if ready to leap out of her seat.

"Those little feet are beating a tattoo on my ribs. There must be more than one in there. Sometimes I think it's a whole army." She rubbed the upward curve of her belly. "Hush now, little one, hush."

"Ones." Ingeborg kept her gaze on her stitching, but everybody could see her mouth twitch.

With the squares of nine patch stitched together, Agnes sorted through her store of cloth. "I have blue for the solid squares or yellow. Which would you like?" She held up the cloth in the colors mentioned.

"I think the blue—no, the yellow." Kaaren shook her head. "Making up my mind even over little things is a big chore."

"The yellow it is." Agnes cut one square and used it as a pattern for the next. When Penny gently but firmly took the scissors from her hand, the older woman straightened and dug her fists into the curve of her back. "I don't remember being so stiff and tired with the others." She rubbed her back again. "Must be getting old."

Back in their chairs to finish the final seams, the women turned the talk to the new people who had moved into the area during the summer.

"I know someone who will be at the service tomorrow. Someone who's been asking after our Penny." Ingeborg nodded and winked at Agnes.

"Who could that be?" With innocent wide eyes and smiling

mouth, Agnes looked up from her handiwork.

"That nice Mr. Clauson, that's who. He said he was looking for a wife, and when he saw Penny, he was sure he'd found the one."

"Of course. She's the only unattached female for five square miles," Kaaren added.

"Or ten." Ingeborg finished the sentence.

Penny could feel the heat staining her cheeks, making her wish for a cold wet cloth. "But you know I'm promised to Hjelmer. He's *your* brother-in-law, after all."

"Ja, well, who knows about Hjelmer, and Mr. Clauson is here with land of his own and an itching for feet to meet under his table. Not that I wouldn't mind being that woman, 'twere I but a few years younger."

"Tante Agnes!"

"Just teasing, my girl, but nonetheless, there's wisdom in those words."

*But what about Hjelmer?* Penny could hear the wail echoing and re-echoing in her mind.

**2**

Thunderheads darkened the westering sun.

Hjelmer Bjorklund looked up from the iron bar he was hammering into a coal scoop and watched lightning fork through the black expanse above. In spite of the chill fall wind, he wiped the sweat from above his eyes and thrust the flattening bar back into the bed of white-hot coals. He nodded to the boy whose job it was to pump the bellows and switched to a broader hammer. He wanted to get the coal scoop done before dark, and with the storm, darkness was almost upon them. The cook had been badgering him for it, threatening no supper unless Hjelmer brought the finished product with him.

"Could snow. It's almost that cold," shouted Leif Ransom, his friend since Hjelmer joined the James J. Hill company as it pushed the tracks of the St. Paul, Minneapolis and Manitoba Railway toward the Pacific Northwest. The two met one night in the chow line, lined up bunks one above the other, and soon developed a reputation as hardworking, honest young crew members who stuck up for each other and for those who needed a champion.

"Ja, it could." Hjelmer waved at the jovial young man carrying a sledgehammer over his shoulder and then went back to his coal scoop. He thinned the metal even more at the open end and bent it up first on one side then the other. Thrusting the formed piece into the water bucket, he watched it sizzle and steam. Just as he pulled it out, the steam whistle echoed across the flatland, announcing the end of the workday and time for chow. Hjelmer's empty stomach rumbled in response. He banked the coals in the forge and shed his apron, making sure his heavy leather gloves were tied to the apron strings, then he folded the equipment in half and stuck it in his wooden chest. If things weren't properly stowed, they had a habit of disappearing. He rotated shoulders nearing ax-handle width and rolled his grimy white sleeves over arms corded with well-formed muscles.

Arnie, his bellows boy, finished dropping all the tools into their proper slots around the forge bed, and the two leaped to the ground. "See ya tomorrow, Mr. Bjorklund." The boy sent Hjelmer a grin, showing one front tooth missing. The way the boy talked, Hjelmer had an idea the gap was compliments of the father the boy had left behind in Minnesota.

Away from the sweltering heat of the forge, the cold wind knifed through Hjelmer's black wool coat. He wished he had one of sheepskin like some of the other workers. The leather outside and the wool turned in made for better wind protection, and with nothing between the camp and the northerners howling across the prairie, he knew he would soon need added protection. He pulled a black wool watch cap farther down over hair that had deepened over time from tow-colored to the amber of honey left late in a bee tree.

Thoughts of the snug soddy he'd so reviled last spring when he arrived from Norway made him shake his head. So much he had learned in the last six months. Those at home in Nordland would never believe half of it if he told them. That thought prompted a twang of guilt for not writing his mother, and that one reminded him of an even worse sin. He hadn't written a second letter to Penny. Asking her to wait for him had taken all the gumption he possessed, and now he'd let her down again. Visions of her sparkling blue eyes and curls that captured the sun made him sigh. He fingered her letter he kept in his pocket, so worn at the folds that he cradled the paper in his hands to read it again lest it fall totally apart.

One letter. She had promised to write every week, and while he hadn't traveled that far, he did say he would answer, that he would keep in touch. He would come back for her, and they would build a building by the school to house their home and their store, with his own blacksmith shop set right next door. He wondered if they had built the school yet. And who was the father of Mary Ruth Strand's baby? One thing he knew for certain, it weren't him, accusations by her or no. He knew what it took to make a baby, and he had never gone that far, not with her or any woman.

"You look like you lost your last friend." Leif clapped him on the shoulder. "And I know you din't, 'cause I'm right here." As short and stocky as Hjelmer was tall and broad of shoulder, Leif laughed at his own joke. Life, according to the gospel of Leif, was one long, continuous joke, the kind that if a man didn't laugh he might never quit crying. When he threw back his head and laughed, summer mink curls bounced on his forehead, the combination attracting broad smiles from anyone present, especially those of the women, young and old alike.

"Ja, you are." Hjelmer broke into a jog to outrun his biting thoughts. "If we don't hurry, the food will all be gone." They dodged in and out of the line of men plodding toward the cook car. Kerosene lanterns hung from the box cars to light their way. Just as they stepped inside, a peal of thunder shook the sky and the clouds let loose a deluge, as if they'd just turned a heavenly bucket upside down to drench those foolish enough to have dawdled.

"Just in time," Hjelmer said, whipping the hat from his head and stuffing it in his coat pocket. Rosy lantern light softened the bare tables lined with benches and the life hardened crew taking their places. With the workday finished, laughter bounced from the smoke-gray wooden walls to meld with voices loud enough to be heard above the noise. It was nearly impossible for anyone to carry on a conversation lest they be side by side. Young boys toted steaming bowls of vegetables and platters of meat from the cook car to the front of the dining car—if it could be given such a dignified name. Most called it the cookshack. Serving only two meals a day, the cooks fixed enough food to feed twice as many men as the crew, and the food always disappeared before the late arrivals got enough.

The two were just scraping the last of the apple pie off their plates when the foreman stopped behind them. "You two boys want to join the poker players tonight? Big Red over there asked me to invite you." He nodded toward a man at the far trestle table who laughed just then at something his neighbor said. The laugh rolled over the tables, bounced off the walls, and caused more than one man to turn to look, hoping to get the joke too.

Hjelmer never failed to wonder how such a deep laugh could come from such a narrow chest. The man stood just over five feet, his hair flaming in the lamplight. Red at least suited him, but *big*? The reputation that rolled outward like waves toward shore said otherwise. Big could possibly refer to his temper. Soon as anyone came to camp they were warned to stay on the sunny side of the banty Irishman. No one, on pain of severe injury, made remarks about his size or lack thereof.

All these thoughts raced through Hjelmer's head as the desire to

LAURAINE SNELLING

feel the cards in his hands again made them tremble. Could he play just one or two hands, have a few laughs and a beer or two, then leave it alone?

A rippling up his spine reminded him of giant Swen from the foundry in New York, the man who threatened to kill him for supposedly cheating at cards. Hjelmer knew he didn't have to cheat to win. And he hadn't.

"Thanks anyway, but I better not. You go ahead, Leif, if'n you want to."

"The men are gonna think you're scared," Leif whispered behind his hand. "You get invited here, you play."

Hjelmer studied his friend from under sandy lashes. He shook his head. "Thanks, Mr. Hanson, but if it is all right with you, I'll come another night. Tell Big Red thanks for the invite."

Hanson cocked an eyebrow. "You know, if you're scared or don't know how to play, we can show you how it's done."

Hjelmer half turned on his bench. "That's right kind of you. Maybe another night."

Hanson studied them a moment more before turning to make his way back across the trestle-table-and-bench-clogged room.

Hjelmer watched him go. A feeling down in his gut said he'd just made a big mistake. The look on Leif's face said the same. Should he tell his new friend what had happened in New York? That he'd made a vow to never gamble again? Instead, he said, "Come on, let's get out of here."

The two ducked their heads as they strode through the slanting rain that bore a mighty close resemblance to sleet. Reaching the door to their home on wheels, they pushed it open and quickly stepped inside. The remodeled boxcar looked as if someone had plunked down a one-room house that was too large for the wheel bed, so it hung over two to three feet on both sides, and then built portable steps up to it. A potbellied stove in the center of the car radiated heat for about five feet around it, an inviting gathering place for those not ready to hit the straw-stuffed sacks frequently referred to as louse houses. A pot of coffee strong enough to pound into spikes steamed on the flat surface.

Hjelmer dug his carving sack out from his pack and brought it to the circle. One of the other men moved over so the carver could use the dim light from the hanging kerosene lantern. In the close quarters, the reek of burning kerosene almost disguised the odor of hardworking, unwashed bodies.

"Watcha makin', son?" a black man with shoulders about as broad as Hjelmer's asked in a gentle voice that still echoed his southern beginning.

Hjelmer took out the bird he'd begun carving a week earlier when he found a chunk of elm wood that had been cut off a railroad tie. Trees, branches, anything of a near size made up most of the ties, but when one was too big, they split it or cut it for firewood. He'd wanted to salvage the entire piece but grabbed a chunk small enough to keep in his sack.

He held the half-formed creature up to the dim light. He'd debated carving a flying eagle like he'd seen soaring over the Red River during the summer, but unless he inset the wings, the piece was too small. Instead, he'd shaped the bird sitting on a post or snag, not sure yet which it would be. He'd gotten it roughed out, so the shape was evident.

"An eagle?" At Hjelmer's nod, the grizzly-headed man flashed a smile so bright against the darkness of his face that his teeth glistened in the light. "My pappy used to carve, but his tweren't nothin' like this." He raised a long finger to touch the bird's head. "We had eagles back to home so big they'd take your breath away. Old tales said eagles done carried bad chilluns away, so we was best we could be. I see'd one take a lamb right outta the field. Took him some flappin' to get into the air again, but he done it."

"That must a been some sight." Hjelmer spit on his whetstone and commenced to sharpen his knife blade, using the circular motions his father had taught him long ago. The action always brought back thoughts of home in the Valdrez region of Nordland. He still had trouble calling his homeland Norway in the way of the Americans, but here on the crew he was picking up the strange language faster than he thought possible.

When the knife was sharpened to his liking, he dug into the wood, bringing wing feathers to life with each minute stroke. The voices of men swapping yarns around him lulled him into a near dreamlike state. A stream of tobacco sometimes rang in the spittoon, but mostly it missed. A laugh burst out once in a while, or a curse, when two men got to arguing over the relative merits of one cook over another. Rain drummed on the roof, sometimes leaking down around the stovepipe and sizzling on the black metal.

Penny strolled into his mind, and with a pert smile over her shoulder, she beckoned him to follow. What was she doing now? Had they finished the harvest? Were they able to build the school?

Haakan had been promising Ingeborg a wood house before winter, but she wanted a new barn instead. What of Mary Ruth Strand, the lying chit who got him in this fix? Why had he ever paid her any attention when he knew from the first that he'd follow Penny to the ends of the earth and beyond if necessary? He flinched at the vow he'd made to Penny, the one that said he'd never even kissed the Strand girl. He hadn't lied—exactly. Mary Ruth kissed him out behind the haystack that day they were leaving. But then, if he were honest, he knew he had kind of kissed her back, and somehow his arms had found their way around her slim waist.

But that was all. He didn't give her any reason to accuse him of getting her in the family way, and deep in his heart he felt sure no one else had either.

He was tired of running.

When he left the land of dreams and returned to the smoke-filled sleeping car, most of the men had gone to bed. A few still smoked their cigarettes, and another licked the paper on the one he finished rolling. Leif's chin bounced on his chest when he snored. How he kept upright on the chunk of wood for a chair was more than Hjelmer understood. He put his knife and carving things back in the sack, wrapped the eagle in a piece of leather to protect it, and after slipping it in the sack, too, he poked Leif.

"Bedtime, before you take a header off that stool and crack your head on the stove." He'd said the same thing every night for the last week.

Leif blinked and yawned, stretching his arms over his head and yawning again. "I weren't sleeping, ya dolt."

"Ja, and my bestamor can't bake lefse." Hjelmer made his way between the narrow bunks, which reminded him strongly of the bunks in steerage on the voyage over. None were built for comfort, only to see how many people could be crammed into the least space. He shivered when he stripped off his outer clothes and crawled under the covers. He needed another quilt or blanket before winter came or he'd freeze to death. He listened. The rain had finally stopped. He heard Leif turn over on the bunk above him and resume his puffy snorts. Full-blown, deep-throated snores came from other parts of the car. Hjelmer turned on his side and closed his eyes resolutely. Morning came much too soon for lying here awake.

He'd not been surprised to see puddles everywhere in the morning, but there weren't enough to slow down the laying of track. By noon, mud coated all the workers to their knees. Some slipped and cursed the gumbo, as the black muck was called. It clung to boots and tools like a hundred-pound second skin. Grateful that he worked above it all, Hjelmer bent steel rod and bars into the shapes needed to repair broken tools and forged parts for the track-laying equipment.

Arnie pumped the bellows for the two forges that stood side by side—Hjelmer's and Gunther Mueller's. Gunther was a stout German who had come directly from the old country without a lick of American to pass his lips. Of course not many other words passed that rigid mouth either. When Hjelmer tried to talk with him since he understood some German, and Norwegian and German were much the same, he got an icy stare and a guttural "nein." *No* sounded the same in many languages.

When the supper whistle blew, Hjelmer joined the line of plodding, mud-slathered men on their way to the cook car. Just when he turned to look for Leif, he felt himself sail through the air and land splat in the mud. He rose to his feet amid the hoots and hollers of those waiting in line.

Wiping mud from his face and brushing it off his clothes only made it smear worse. Snickers rippled farther down the line when he stepped back into his place. "Did you see who did that?" he asked the man behind him. The fellow shook his head but kept his eyes anywhere but meeting Hjelmer's. "What about you?" He tapped the shoulder of the man in front. Without turning, the man shook his head.

"What happened to you?" Leif roared when he saw Hjelmer.

"I took a ride through the air." Hjelmer spoke from between clenched teeth.

"Ja, he been flying like ta birds." A man in front of them a couple of spaces flapped his arms and grinned, showing teeth rotted at the gums. He spat a quid to the side, mute testimony as to what happened to his teeth.

"And you didn't see who shoved you?" Now Leif spoke for Hjelmer's ears alone.

Hjelmer shook his head, wondering who he could have made mad enough to do such a thing? "Shoved me? No! Had to be someone pretty big to pick me up and toss me like that. These men know who it was. They just ain't talking."

They finally reached the door to the cook car, but when they tried to find a seat, none seemed available unless they sat at the far end of the car. Frequently there was little food left on the platters by the time it reached the latecomers.

But they hadn't been late.

"We shoulda gone to the poker game last night when we was invited." Leif grabbed a full platter from a passing server and was glad they at least still had meat. When the young boy howled, Leif smiled and handed the platter back. "Mange takk," he said with a grin. The boy shot a look laden with fear over his shoulder.

Hjelmer tried to follow his gaze, but far as he could see, no one glowered in return. "You really think this could be coming from Big Red?" he asked after the boy scrambled out of earshot.

Leif nodded. "I heerd about things like this before. Just never been on the receiving end. That man has *some* power in this camp."

The two had lapsed into Norwegian, as if hoping they could talk privately. When Black Sam, as everyone called him, sat on the bench across from them, both young men flashed him smiles. "Y'all gwan ta play poker this night?" His soft voice could only be heard by leaning forward.

Hjelmer shook his head. "You don't really think that's what this is all about, do you?"

Sam nodded his head. "Dat Big Red, he bad one to cross. He say jump, most men say, 'how high.' "

Hjelmer sighed. "Just because I turned down a poker game. That don't make no sense."

"Dey like to fleece the new hires. He gave you time to ask to join, and you din't. Now he invite, and you say no. Now he get ugly."

"Did they do this to you?"

Sam nodded. "Don't leave nobody out."

"What did you do?"

"Lost all my money. Den dey not care." Sam stuffed half a roll in his mouth and chewed thoughtfully. "Now I make myself scarce after payday and send all money home soon's I get it. Dey know I don't got nothin'."

Hjelmer rested his elbows on the board slab table. Repeated scrubbing had worn the wood smooth and bleached it near white. He sipped at his coffee mug and thought hard about a way out. Like mice being chased by a cat, his thoughts flew everywhere. He could send the money home to Penny, but what if she didn't get it? To Ingeborg? Certainly she would save it for him.

"Are there any banks near here?" He knew the question was stupid soon as he asked it. Sam and Leif shook their heads. "So how come they don't bother you?" He looked over his shoulder to his friend.

Leif ducked his head but a glint in his eye gave him away. "They decided I was too stupid to learn and threw me out of the game."

"Ahhh." Hjelmer nodded. Could he pull that off too? He loved the thrill of beating others at their own game, and the cards always loved him. Could he fake it? He found himself thinking about the toss in the mud while he fell asleep that night. Surely that little warning, if that's what it was, would be enough for them to leave him alone. Maybe it really had been an accident. He turned over with a snort. A man his size didn't fly through the air by accident.

The next morning at breakfast before the sun did more than gray the eastern sky, Hjelmer managed to sit at the same table as Big Red, albeit a few seats down and on the opposite side. When Leif came in, Hjelmer held up a glove with a hole in the finger and shook his head.

"Now what am I going to do? Ain't got no money till payday."

Leif looked at him blankly. "Well, then you go charge a new pair of gloves at the store car."

"Then I'll get even less money." He slapped the glove on the table. "Ain't fair." Hjelmer snuck a peek out the side of his eye. "And here I thought to go join those fellers with the card games. Can't win if you ain't got money to start."

Leif shook his head in commiseration. "'Pears that way."

"Maybe I can patch this thing. You got any leather?" Hjelmer studied the ragged hole.

Leif nodded. "You can borrow a needle and thread from Sam maybe. He's got about everything in his kit."

"Ja, everything but money." Hjelmer scraped the remainder of three fried eggs up with his biscuit. Munching on his last piece of bacon, he covertly studied Big Red and the two giants on either side of him. Obviously the man had found a way to make up for his lack of brawn. You never saw him without at least one of the men by his side.

Hjelmer had yet to discover what Red did on the rail laying. But he knew the man must have a job of some kind or he wouldn't be allowed in the cookshack. What would it take to get on the man's good side rather than his bad?

The whistle blew and all the remaining workers chugged the

dregs of their coffee mugs and headed for the door. The dawn-to-dark workday had begun once again.

While Hjelmer kept his eyes open, even to watching over his shoulder, life settled into a rhythm that suited him well. Other than the train whistle dictating when he awoke, ate, or slept, his reputation as not only a repairer of things metal but a creative shaper of useful items grew and spread among both the crew and the bosses. Sometimes he thought longingly of the Bjorklund farm in the Red River Valley, where a rooster crowed instead of a train whistling to arouse the hands, and where the food flowed plentifully from Ingeborg's and Kaaren's capable hands. And where five miles west lived Penny Sjornson. When would he see her again? Would he ever?

One night, tossing on his bed to the wind soughing around the corners and plucking at the crevasses, thoughts of Penny twisted his heart to the point of pain. If it hadn't been for the Strand chit, he and Penny might have been married by now. All the neighbors would have helped him raise a soddy after the school went up, and in his own shop by the side of the house, he could be repairing plows and all the other kinds of machinery that farmers, aided by avid salesmen, were moving into the valley. Perhaps by now he would have designed some new pieces that he could sell to a manufacturer or make himself. He finally fell asleep to the music of Penny's voice lifted in song, as he remembered hearing it at the worship gatherings.

By the next afternoon the wind had warmed and a second Indian summer settled over the land. The pace picked up even more, if that were possible, with the crew laying track as though Father Winter were biting at their backs. Which in truth he was. They would only work until the snow got too deep, and then they'd disband for the winter.

One night a rumor buzzed through the camp. New washer-women had arrived. While Hjelmer had heard tales of the joys and delights of visiting the tent camp that followed the train, he had done his own laundry, usually after dark because that was the only time available. The tales he'd heard had nothing to do with clean clothes.

"So, you been south of the camp yet?" Leif asked one night, a droll, innocent expression raising his eyebrows just a hair.

Hjelmer left off sopping his beef gravy with a thick slice of bread and looked at his friend, the sound of his voice raising suspicion just by its tone. The men across the table paused in the speed of fork to mouth and back to the plate again. Even the chomp of chewing ceased for a moment. Only someone being played the fool caught their attention so completely.

Hjelmer let himself be set up. "Naw, can't say that I have." He bit off half the slice of dripping bread, chewed, and swallowed. "Why would I want to do that?"

"Ain'tcha got no dirty laundry?"

Snickers rippled outward from around them.

Hjelmer shook his head. "Can't say that I have."

"No sheets to wash?"

Snickers grew to chuckles.

"Nope."

"Not even wool underwear?"

Chuckles exploded into guffaws.

Hjelmer kept a sober look on his face and stared at each of the men across the table, one of which slapped the table with callused palms, setting tin forks to dancing on the dented metal plates. Empty coffee mugs added their peculiar thump-a-dees to the simple band.

"Now, what's got you fellers all in a twist about something so ordinary as dirty clothes?"

"Leif, you better show your friend how easy it is to get washed down south of the track in them tents there." The burly man wiped spittle from his beard, he'd laughed so hard.

"That I will. Fact is, we better hightail it down there right now, soon's we gather up our laundry."

Hjelmer ignored the winks and digs in ribs and finished his supper. When the serving boy came by with the coffeepot, he held up his mug. "I ain't going nowheres till I get another cup of coffee. My long johns waited this long, they can wait some longer." He ignored the snorts and splutters his comment caused and sipped his coffee. Across at another table, he could see Big Red and his cohorts looking their way, question marks all over their faces.

The aroma of steaming coffee overlaid the stench of unwashed bodies, sweat-soaked wool, and spluttering kerosene lanterns. Hjelmer cradled the cup between his hands. If he could tune out the rumble of conversation and the shouts, both obscene and otherwise, perhaps he could envision Penny. But when images of the auburn curls of the Jezebel, Mary Ruth Strand, her sea-green eyes, and her laughing lips replaced Penny's Norwegian blondness, he shook his head.

"Come on, let's go see about the laundry," Leif said, clapping him on the shoulder.

Hjelmer rose willingly. Thoughts of Mary Ruth had gotten him in trouble in the first place. Amid the suggestive comments of the other laborers, they left the cook car.

"Go get yours and I'll meet you back here."

They returned in a few minutes, each with a bundle tucked under his arm.

"Glad I could oblige you with such sport in there." Hjelmer stuck his hands in his pockets and hunched his shoulders against the wind whistling down his neck. Each night turned colder earlier than the last. At this rate winter would soon be on them.

"Ja, you gave those men some good laughs." Leif looked over at his friend. "You . . . you do know about the washerwomen, don't you?"

Hjelmer raised an eyebrow. "Know about the washerwomen? Is there something I should know? Tell me." At the look of consternation on Leif's square-jawed face, he thought, *Let's see how he likes the shoe pinching the other foot.*

"Well . . . ah . . . you see . . . ah . . . the women . . ."

"Ja, I know, they are women."

"The women, they . . . ah . . ."

"Spit it out, man." Hjelmer could barely keep a straight face, but he knew Leif could see his expression in the brilliant moonlight, so he covered a cough with his hand.

"The . . . the ladies are not of the best reputation. They sell . . . you can get . . ."

Hjelmer couldn't stand it any longer. He hooted at his friend's discomfort. "Say no more, my friend. I used to work on the fishing boats from Norway—remember, I told you about my Onkel Hamre? I'm not some young boy fresh off the farm."

Leif punched him in the shoulder. Up ahead they could see dark shadows moving around in the tents lit by lanterns burning inside. They knocked on the first tent that had a "wash" sign on the side and waited.

"Coming," a musical voice answered. The head that peeped through the opening did not belong to a woman who'd been used hard and left. A kerchief barely covered springy dark curls, and her smile caught and held a bit of moonlight. "Now, how can I help you fellas?"

Hjelmer held out his bundle. "You do wash?"

"I do. Don't let my age fool you. I can scrub with the best of them and still come out on top." She thrust out a hand. "I'm Katja. Leave your bundle tonight and pick it up tomorrow. Or I can deliver it if you need."

"No, no. That's all right. I'll pick it up." Thoughts of the remarks he'd get if she showed up looking for him warmed Hjelmer's cheeks. He handed her his bundle and touched the brim of his fedora. "Mange takk." The look in her eyes stayed with him all the way back to camp.

3

*Mid-September 1884*

olveig is coming, Solveig is coming," Kaaren Knutson danced
around her kitchen as much as her enormous girth would allow.
The words could be set to any music she wanted. As she sang, she
spread the crazy quilt over the sheets covering a newly filled corn-
husk mattress. The ropes strung on the bed frame that held the mattress creaked when she knelt to tuck the quilt in at the bottom. She'd
thought of using straw for filling, but it packed down so, and she
liked the smell of corn. At the rate Ingeborg brought in geese from
the flocks that honked their way south, they would soon have
feather beds of soft goose down.

Smoothing strings of hair off her sweaty forehead, Kaaren
paused to knead her fists into the small of her back, if any part of
her could be called small at this point in her pregnancy. Everyone
in the area was betting she would have twins.

"Or one baby big enough to plow the fields already," she'd told
her husband, Lars, when he teased her about her girth.

While she hated to take the time, she sat down in her rocking
chair and put her feet up on the stool. She shook her head at the
sight of her swollen feet. Setting them up on the stool was the only
way she'd been able to see them for some time. Looking like freshly
stuffed goose down pillows was near as she could come to a de-
scription. She hated the thought of comparing them to sausages,
overstuffed ones at that. Hard to believe she still had over a month
to go, at least.

She rocked gently and let her head rest against the chair back.
Solveig, known as the prettiest of the four Hjelmson sisters and the
second youngest, had been but a girl when Kaaren and Carl left Norway four years ago. Now she wrote of finding a strong, hopefully

handsome young man in Dakota Territory. One who loved the Lord as she did and needed a wife. She had sent a telegram from New York when she arrived, so when the paddle-wheeler on the Red River tooted three times, Lars would take a horse to the river to pick her up. They now had a floating dock and a sturdy raft to pick up passengers, mail, and small items ordered from Grand Forks. For things like machinery, they still drove to St. Andrew, where the townspeople had rebuilt the dock to make it sturdier for unloading heavy equipment. Last time she'd taken a wagonful of produce to the Bonanza farm in Minnesota, the dock had looked more like a real wharf, with heavy pilings driven deep into the mud and solid planks for the deck.

So many changes she'd seen in the time since they'd trekked across half the world to get to their new farmland.

Kaaren removed the hair pins that held the loosening golden bun at the base of her head and combed her work-roughened fingers through the long tresses. She shook her head, then reformed the bun and secured it again with the pins she had held between her lips. Lars liked her hair streaming down her usually slender back, but that was not seemly for one of her advanced age of three and twenty. She pushed herself to her feet, feeling as though she could explode any minute. "Uff da." She arched her back, kneaded the spot that ached, and headed out the door to beat the triangle of iron rod that Hjelmer had bent for her to call the men from the fields. The venison stew that had been simmering all morning was ready, and she knew the men's stomachs had been talking to them for some time.

A few minutes later she heard Lars whoa the horses and the sound of the jingling and squeak of harness as he pulled it off the team. He would use the oxen for the afternoon sod-breaking to give the horses a rest. Paws' barking announced the arrival of the boys and Ingeborg, and Haakan wouldn't be far behind. Often Kaaren cooked for them all when Ingeborg was hunting or, as today, cutting up a deer she'd shot two nights before. Ingeborg had wanted to let it hang longer, but while the nights were cold, the unusually warm days made that impossible.

With all of them gathered around the table, Lars said grace. "And dear Lord, take extra care of Kaaren right now and the babe she carries. I thank thee in advance for your protection over all of us. Amen."

Kaaren swallowed an extra time or two and sniffed. This gentle man she had married caught her off guard so often with his tender concern for her.

"You sit down and I will serve." Ingeborg didn't ask, she just did.

Kaaren smiled her gratitude and reached over to give her little nephew Andrew a pat on the cheek.

"Tante 'Ren," he called her, with Bjorklund blue eyes dancing above a sunny grin. "Good food." He waved the crust of bread she'd spread with jam and set at his plate.

She knew they'd probably have to wash a sticky mess out of his blond curls, but his joy at the treat made the extra effort worth it. "Can you say thank you?" She carefully enunciated the English since he was already picking up Norwegian. While they all had decided to use their new language as much as they could, Norwegian still came so much easier to their lips.

"Tank oo," he obliged.

"We saw Wolf when we were out with the sheep," nearly-nine-year-old Thorliff said as he took his filled plate from his mother. "Baptiste said he hadn't been around for a while."

The boy beside him, about the same age but with the black eyes and matching hair of his French-Canadian and Lakota-Indian ancestry, nodded. His people were called Metiz, the name they all used for his grandmother, with whom he lived in a tepee on the riverbank during the warm season.

"Is that usual?" Kaaren asked, passing him his full plate.

Baptiste shook his head. "Grandmere was afraid he might have gone to the Great Spirit. He never goes away for more than a day or two."

"Was he hurt?" Haakan swallowed his mouthful of stew before asking.

Baptiste shook his head.

"It's still hard for me to believe a wolf is one of our guardians here. Those in the North Woods were feared, probably more than they deserved to be." Haakan had walked across Minnesota at his mother's bidding to assist the two Bjorklund widows in their farming, never dreaming he would marry one and become a flatland farmer. And the Red River Valley defined the word flat, for sure. On the trip he'd slept in a tree one night to stay safe from the wolves he heard howling nearby.

"Wolf saved our sheep one night from a whole pack of wolves,"

Thorliff answered. "He killed some of the wild ones, and the others ate them."

"Thorliff, that's not a good thing to talk about at the dinner table," Ingeborg said, then took her place after having served everyone and refilled the coffee mugs.

"Well, he did."

"I know, but just because it is true does not make the subject good for talking at mealtime."

"Would you rather talk about the barn raising?" Haakan asked with a grin.

Ingeborg flashed him a raised right eyebrow.

Kaaren smiled and forked a piece of meat to her mouth. This discussion had gone on before and got plenty heated when Haakan said he wanted to build a wood house before winter. Ingeborg said if they were going to build anything, it should be a barn. The four of them had gone back and forth for several meals, until Haakan had finally thrown his hands in the air and shook his head in defeat.

"I thought you hated the soddy in the winter and wanted light. I'm trying to give you light, woman."

Ingeborg flinched and swallowed the words she'd obviously intended to add to the argument. "I'm sorry, but the barn is so much more important. I can endure another winter in the soddy when I know we have room for the animals."

Kaaren knew that was as close as Ingeborg would come to a real apology. Here the man had been trying to do something nice for her.

"That's your choice, then. How about tonight we figure how much lumber we are going to need and have it brought to the train station at Grafton? Faster to get there now than to St. Andrew."

"Ja, and no river to cross hauling the loads home." Lars nodded and reached for another slice of bread.

"Can we go with and see the train?" asked Thorliff, sharing a look of excitement with Baptiste.

"We will see."

"Me see train." Andrew banged his spoon on the table. "See train."

"You don't even know what a train is," Thorliff said.

"Thorliff." At his mother's remonstrance, the boy ducked his chin. "Maybe we could all go with one load and see the town. I heard the general store there has far more things than the Mercantile in St. Andrew."

"Yes, thanks to the railroad. You mark my words, we're going to have a line even closer before 1890 rolls around." Haakan waved his fork for emphasis.

"So, can we go?"

"We will see."

"I will flag down the paddle-wheeler tomorrow on its way up-river and give the captain our order. We should have the lumber within the week. We got enough timber along the river to cut our own if we just had a sawmill. Hope to heaven we can get a steam engine and the saws before the cold sets in. What a business we could do over the winter."

"You got plenty to do with cutting wood for the steamship, don't you?" Ingeborg asked.

Kaaren didn't say anything. If the men felt there was a chance to make money on this new scheme, she wouldn't argue. But then she agreed with the creed of most women—let the men make the decisions about the land and machinery. Ingeborg still struggled with that.

"We don't need to make two big decisions right now." Ingeborg took the spoon away from Andrew and used it to dip stew into his mouth. "I think I let you have too much bread, den lille guten."

"Jam." Andrew tried to duck away from the spoon and pointed to the jar on the table.

Ingeborg turned to the two older boys. "This afternoon I need you to bring in more of that green maple so we get plenty of smoke for the venison. Then you and Baptiste can keep the fire burning."

A grin lit the boy's tanned face. "No school?"

Kaaren shook her head. "School. Right after dinner as usual. You can get the wood, then run back and forth to keep it stoked. If you take turns, you'll each get to read more aloud."

Baptiste groaned. Reading aloud was not his favorite subject, but when it came to natural science, he excelled. He and Thorliff had a pact. Thorliff would help him read, and Baptiste would teach his friend the way of the woods, the prairie and river, and his friends the animals.

The adults laughed. "You boys," Kaaren said. "You'd think I beat you every day."

"Me read?" Andrew looked up from the bread he'd pounded flat, then ate.

"Not today." Ingeborg spooned more of the stew into his mouth. "You get a nap so I can get something done."

"Inge, he can come here." Kaaren laid a hand on the mound of her belly. At the look of concern on the others' faces, she shook her head. "No, the baby is not ready to come. Just dancing the pols in there, I swear."

"Did you lie down for a while yet?" Lars asked. When Kaaren shook her head, he looked at her sternly. "You promised."

"Ja, but the day isn't over. After the lessons I will." She leaned back in her chair. "Just think, I will soon be teaching all the children in our own schoolhouse. Won't that be a dream come true? God is so good."

"You *look* like you should be teaching a roomful of restless children," Lars muttered into his coffee cup.

"I won't look like this much longer." She grimaced again as the baby kicked so hard her apron bounced.

"Did you see that?" Thorliff's eyes grew huge and round, the Bjorklund blue showing even more than usual.

"Ja, and I felt it too." Kaaren knew she shouldn't talk about the baby around the younger children. It just wasn't proper. But with all of them here in one room, proper didn't seem to be so important any longer. The boys had seen sheep, calves, and even a foal born. A baby wasn't that much different.

"Grandmere said she was coming this afternoon to see how you are." Baptiste wiped the milk mustache off with his sleeve. "I'm done. You want I should start on the wood?"

"There's egge kake for dessert." Kaaren was well known for her egg cake. "I have applesauce for frosting."

Baptiste flashed her one of his rare grins. "I'll wait."

Over the cake, Haakan again picked up the discussion they'd been chewing at for the last several days. "When do you think we should go look for a steam engine and lumber mill? We could get it set up before the snow comes and use it during the winter."

Ingeborg shook her head. "How can you do that and a barn too?" She ignored his muttered "house." "As I've said fifty times, all those extra cattle we bought need a place out of the cold."

"Ja, but we could do that with a roofed corral." He looked up at Lars, the look clearly saying "help me."

"I'm thinking we should set the boys to splitting shingles, and we could help them in the evenings. The barn will give us more room for indoor work this winter. We could keep one end of it for a workshop." Lars winked at Ingeborg. "Maybe even build you two women a loom."

"So you agree with me, then?" Ingeborg shot a triumphant smile at her husband. She waited for his answer.

Haakan threw his hands in the air. "I give up. Try to give you something you want so dearly and you refuse. There will be no more discussion about building a frame house—this year."

"The cattle are more important. They bring in money." Ingeborg pointedly ignored his last statement.

"And you don't?" Both eyebrows disappeared under the shock of wheaten hair falling on his forehead. But the smile they shared buried their stubbornness in love.

After the plates were soaking in an enameled pan on the stove, Ingeborg picked up the now nodding Andrew and nestled him against her shoulder. "I'll be going after geese again this evening, but Thorliff can watch him." She laid a hand on the drowsy child's back.

"No, bring him over." Kaaren smiled at the picture they made, with Ingeborg dressed in her britches and a shirt she'd cut down from the clothes of her first husband, Roald, who had died in a snowstorm during the blizzard and flu epidemic of 1882. Even though Kaaren hated to see her sister-in-law dressed like a man, she'd come to appreciate the greater freedom it gave her, especially in the woods and fields. Ingeborg's golden crown of braids made her look like a queen in spite of her man's clothing.

"You know, after the baby is born, I might think of making some britches myself."

"Kaaren!" The shock on Lars' face made the joke well worth-while.

"Just teasing." She gave him that special smile she reserved just for him. His return smile, accompanied by a wink, made her breath catch in her throat. *God, thank you again for this man you sent me. Thank you for healing his foot and for the babe we share.* When she caught her breath the second time, it was for an entirely different reason. That baby had more kicking power than Jack the mule.

"I will see you later, then." Ingeborg strode out the door, her broad-brimmed man's hat clapped on her head.

"Mange takk for maten," Haakan said as he leaped to his feet and, grabbing his hat off the peg by the door, followed his wife out-side. "Here, Inge, let me carry him." The two older boys scampered out the door yelling "thank you" over their shoulders. Thorliff's "Far, wait for me" floated back on the breeze as the screen door slammed.

Kaaren smiled again at her husband. "Life surely is different around here, thanks to you two."

Lars reached above and behind him to bring her face down for a kiss. "I thank my God every day for my life here." He kissed her again, inhaling deeply. "How come you always smell so good?"

"It's the egge kake you smell."

"No, it's you. Soap and roses and fresh air and you. Only God can make a perfume like that."

Kaaren could feel herself blush. Every once in a while this man talked like a poet or a dreamer, making her heart ache with the joy of it. Sometimes she felt she could burst from the sheer wonder of loving him and his loving her. "God is good," was all she could say around the lump in her throat.

"Make sure you listen for the riverboat. Solveig should be here either today or tomorrow. Remember, if you need me, ring the triangle." He rose, drained his coffee mug, and reached for his hat all in one smooth motion.

"Listen to you. Every day you tell me the same thing. While this might be your first baby, it certainly isn't mine." Memory of her two daughters lying in the graveyard with their father caused an instant flooding of her eyes. Sometimes she scolded herself for the tears, but they always caught her unawares. "Go on now. I will know when to call you. I do get some warning, you know."

"You're sure?"

"Lars, we talk of this every single day. I am fine, and I will be fine. Besides, the boys will be back in a minute or two. You want they should catch you still in the house in the middle of the afternoon?" She gave him a playful shove and stood at the door to hear him whistling his way back to the sod barn. Flies buzzed at the screen door, demanding entrance, and Paws barked from the other house. She listened to hear if it was his announcing company bark or if he was just playing with the boys. Geese sang their way south, a haunting melody of freedom. Sometimes the sky seemed almost dark with the waterfowl heading for their winter quarters in the Southland. Warm as it was, she could still smell the fragrance of fall in the air. Wishing she could go out and dig the remaining carrots and turnips from her garden nearly drew her outside, but she knew if Lars caught her at it, the look of a wounded boy that covered his face would make her feel as though she'd been the one delivering the injury.

She sighed. Some women would call him too protective, but she looked on his way as cherishing her like the Bible said. It also said for women to obey their husbands, and that she was determined to do.

"Those dishes aren't going to wash themselves," she muttered, turning from the outside that called to her. The boys would be back before she knew it. Picking up her song from where she left off, Kaaren poured boiling water out of the kettle and into the dishpan. She shaved several thin curls of soap from one of the last bars she and Ingeborg had made the year before, and dropping the bits of soap in the hot water, she gave it a moment to soften before sudsing it up. Good thing it was nearly time to butcher the pigs they'd kept for their own use. After she rendered the lard, she could add some of that to the fat she'd saved, and they could make soap again. Getting all the fall chores done with a new baby in her arms would take some doing.

With the dishes dried and put back in her gingham-skirted cupboard, the boys set to their lessons, and one of the geese baking in the oven, Kaaren took advantage of the quiet to settle for the ordered nap in her rocker. She looked longingly at the bed. Perhaps later.

"Tante Kaaren, I'd best go check on the smokehouse." Thorliff stood at her side, concern knitting his eyebrows. "Are you all right?"

"Of course, why?" She blinked to clear the fog from her vision. Hadn't she just sat down?

"You were moaning."

"I'm sorry. Sometimes the baby makes me do that." She stretched and yawned. "You go. Baptiste, you come sit by me so I can help you with your words as you read."

A groan from the boy huddled over his slate gave his opinion of her request.

The boys were nearly finished with their history lesson when Paws yipped outside the door. The screen door creaked its way open, and a wizened apple face preceded a body bent only slightly by the age evidenced in the old woman's nearly white hair. The remaining black strands wouldn't line a robin's nest. Metiz nodded at the two boys grinning at the interruption and crossed the room to lay a hand on Kaaren's bouncing abdomen.

"Baby, he busy."

"Could be a she." They'd had this discussion several times before.

"Come soon." The woman's gnarly fingers gently probed Kaaren's belly.

"Metiz, I have more than a month left, remember?"

"He not think that." She laid her head against the fluttering apron, holding her breath to listen. "Maybe two in there."

"I know. I am so huge. Bigger than that barn Ingeborg and Haakan are talking of building." She flinched at the impact of a particularly hefty kick from within. "He, she, they—whatever—sure are busy."

Metiz reiterated her earlier statement. "Come soon."

Kaaren bit her lip, studying the dark eyes that shone with knowledge. Metiz had yet to be wrong. "They, if there are two, would be so tiny. If they come now, they might die. . . ." The last word trailed off. Surely God wouldn't allow her to lose a child again. *God, please don't ask that of me. I couldn't bear to bury another. And Lars wants children so much. This is one gift I can give him. Please.*

"Great Spirit not leave." Metiz' soft words fell like a soothing spring rain on parched soil.

"I know that." Kaaren tried on a tremulous smile. It still fit. "Our God is mighty and always here." She knew she was saying words meant for her own ears as well. "He's here." She crossed widespread fingers around her belly, as both brace and protection. "Don't be in such a hurry, little one. Finish growing first, for out here you need to be strong." So often she'd found herself talking to the babe, as if she already held him in her arms. She looked up to see Metiz nod.

"I go now."

"Would you like a cup of coffee first? There is some egge kake left from dinner."

Metiz shook her head. With a pat on Kaaren's belly, the old woman turned and left, whistling for Baptiste as the screen door slammed behind her.

⚜ ⚜

"I still wish we'd bought lumber for a house." Haakan and Ingeborg stood in the moonlight by the piles of lumber that had taken five days and four wagons to bring from Grafton. Getting the order from Grand Forks to Grafton had been the easy part. All but Kaaren had taken their turns driving into the town. After Andrew got over screaming at the size and noise of the train, he'd had a good time too.

Ingeborg sighed. "I know, and I thank you for that. Windows surely would make the dark days more tolerable, but we can put windows in the barn."

"Ja, and the animals will live better than we do." He walked over to the plot he'd staked off for the barn. "Tomorrow I'll cut this sod. We can use it for the lean-to on the house."

"Three more days and our barn will begin to rise on the prairie." Ingeborg couldn't keep the satisfaction out of her voice. Just like over at the Bonanza farm, she would have a huge wooden barn with a place for the hay up above, stanchions for the milk cows, stalls for the horses, and a place to fence in the pigs at one end. The sheep could take over the sod barn they had put up before any other buildings.

"It means a lot to you, doesn't it?" Haakan finished his pacing and rejoined her.

"Ja."

She couldn't begin to tell him how she'd dreamed of wooden barns and increased livestock the long months after Roald disappeared. The dreams had kept her going at times when her body screamed for rest and her mind couldn't. Only half a year until the homestead was proved up, and the deed of ownership would be hers. She amended the thought—theirs. Belonging to all four of them, she would make sure hers and Kaaren's names were on the deeds, too, even if that wasn't the way most things were done out here.

Haakan took her elbow and steered her toward the house, where the children lay sound asleep. Paws greeted them, tail wagging, when they entered.

"Paws, were you on the bed?" Ingeborg tried to sound gruff. The dog hung his head and, tail drooping, sank to his belly.

"Sure be that he cannot tell a lie." Haakan dropped a kiss on Ingeborg's cheek, then turned her face for another. "Let's forget about the dog and the barn and everything for a while, what do you think?"

Ingeborg felt the quickening of her heart. She knew what he meant, for she'd thought much the same herself. She wrapped both arms around his neck. "Would you rather have a cup of coffee first?"

"No, thank you." He nuzzled the side of her neck, sending shivers down her spine. "Think I'll just blow out the lamp."

✕❦ ❦✕

When Ingeborg woke in the morning, she felt a sense of peace. Peace that flooded her whole being, making her want to laugh and shout. *God is so good. How can I ever thank and praise Him enough?* She turned her head to see Haakan blowing on the banked coals so they would nibble at the kindling he'd shaved into the firebox and flare into heat that would warm both the house and their meals for the day. She should be doing that, but lying in bed and watching her husband work gave her a special thrill and deepened the immense feeling of being loved and cherished. She wrapped her arms around her middle, trying to keep it all inside so she wouldn't lose the precious moment.

"I'll bet we have thundershowers before the day is over." Haakan's soft voice let her know that he knew she was awake. He came over and sat down on the pole side of the bed. "I'll do the milking this morning and check the smokehouse on my way out. You lie there for a while longer." He ran his fingers through her long hair, which for a change was not confined in braids. "Feels alive, like you, silky and soft."

Ingeborg smiled up at him. She touched the cleft in his chin with one finger. "Mor said this was caused by the kiss of an angel."

"Ja, well, my far got kissed, too, then, and his far before him." He nibbled the end of her finger. "Mange takk, Mrs. Bjorklund."

"Velbekomme, Mr. Bjorklund."

He closed the door without a squeak that might wake the boys.

Ingeborg hummed as she went about preparations for breakfast. She took the potato water she'd set on the warming shelf of the stove a couple of days earlier and inhaled the yeasty smell. Saving part of it to set again, she stirred in an egg, buttermilk, molasses, a scoop of butter, salt, and flour. With the wooden bowl nestled in her arms, she beat the mixture to work in as many air bubbles as she could. When it got too thick to beat, she flopped it out on a towel on the table and began kneading in the remainder of the flour needed. Now they'd have fresh bread for the barn raising on the morrow. She set dried beans to soaking, too, and once she had finished kneading the bread and set it to rise again on the warming shelf, she went about cutting up salt pork to add to the beans.

When the boys awoke, she sent Thorliff out to help Haakan. After dressing Andrew, who now thought he should do everything himself, making the process twice as long as usual, she tied a dish towel around his neck and set him on his box with some dried June-berries for a treat.

By the time Haakan brought in fresh milk for breakfast, she had the oven full of baking beans and a smoked venison haunch.

"Smells wonderful in here." He set the strainer over the milk can and slowly poured the warm liquid through the cloth. "You set much to cheese lately?"

"Ja, as much as I have room for. We should use those sod bricks to enlarge the well house. If I had more shelves, I could cure more cheeses at the same time." She pointed to the washbasin for Thorliff to wash his hands. "Think I'll smoke some of those cheeses that are nearly ripe. It'll give them a different flavor."

"Ja, it will. We need to make a run to the Bonanza farm soon. Snow could come anytime now." He finished his task and joined the boys at the table. After saying grace they fell to, the stack of pancakes disappearing as quickly as Ingeborg brought them to the table from the stove.

"Don't take the sheep too far today," Haakan said.

Thorliff nodded. "Grass is growing everywhere again after that last rain we had."

Ingeborg watched her son trying to act like the man he was becoming.

"And remember, if you see lightning on the horizon, you make a beeline for home."

Thorliff nodded.

Ingeborg watched them walk out to the barn, Haakan matching his steps to those of his son. Maybe for his birthday the end of October, they could buy Thorliff a wide-brimmed hat like Haakan wore. That would please him no end. She smiled at the thought of the joy on Thorliff's face when he would open the box. Ja, that would be just the thing. She shook her head at the thought that her eldest would soon be nine years old. "Uff da, where has the time gone?"

The storm held off until after dinner. Haakan hurried back out to the field to take advantage of every moment to break new sod.

He had yet to find time to break any on his own piece. It had taken all summer to repair the mess Polinski had left behind. He'd almost left his family behind, too, but something finally made him come back for them. Haakan had had to tear down the roof of the soddy and start with new rafters because the lazy man had burned some of them during the last winter.

"Uff da." Ingeborg drove away the thoughts of Polinski and turned to kneading her bread again.

Thunder rolled in the distance. She finished forming the loaves and set them to rise for the last time. Honey on bread still warm from the oven would give the boys an afternoon treat when they brought the sheep in.

Thunder rumbled closer, but still no rain fell. Perhaps the storm would blow over them.

She lighted the lamp and sat down with her Bible to read for a few stolen moments before Andrew woke up. Turning to the Psalms, she read aloud to better appreciate the music that came with the words.

A sharp crack brought her out of her chair, the thunder crashing before she could get to the door. Andrew let out a wail, his face screwed up in terror.

"Oh, son, easy now. It's just thunder and lightning. Sounded right over our head. Let's go look for Thorliff and Far. They should be coming in." Carrying him on her hip, she stepped outside. The smell of cordite caught her by surprise. The lightning had struck somewhere, but a walk out by the barn revealed nothing until she rounded the corner and saw the haystack. Bright red flames already licked the hay, blackening the stack as it devoured the dry grass.

"Oh, dear God above, our hay." She ran back to the house and beat the triangle with all her strength. Then rushing inside, she set Andrew on the bed with a warning to stay put and grabbed the rifle from its pegs by the door. Three times she shot into the air, sending the call for help the neighbors had used since they first arrived.

Lars came running back first. He needed no instructions. By now the black smoke was rising and beginning to billow. "You winch, and I'll carry and toss. Fill all the buckets you have while I see if I can fork most of it off the stack."

Ingeborg prayed her way through turning the handle at the well and dumping the water into buckets. Haakan arrived on the back of one of the team, dragging the other by a rein. With the sod on the roof of the barn, it was in no danger, but the hay . . . if they lost it . . . She refused to contemplate the enormity of that. They had to save the hay.

The flames flared high enough to see from the well now. Lars hadn't been able to slow it, let alone put it out.

4

"What can I do, Mor?" Thorliff asked as he pelted into the yard.

Ingeborg wiped away the sweat already streaming into her eyes. "Where are the sheep?"

"Baptiste stayed with them. I heard the shots and saw the smoke." Thorliff dumped the bucket cranked up from the well.

"Take Andrew over to Tante Kaaren." The crank spun around until the bucket hit water again. She could hear Haakan and Lars shouting at someone else arriving at breakneck speed.

Thorliff took off as though a wolf was hot on his heels. She could hear Andrew screaming.

Turn, dump, spin, and crank again. She kept up the pace, trying to keep ahead of the growing line of bucket passers. The Baard tribe arrived, and Penny took over the handle.

"Tante's in the house making coffee. She brought some bread and such to feed everyone." Penny cranked, and Ingeborg dumped the buckets.

A cry went up. "Save the other stack!"

"Oh, dear Lord, the lumber." Haakan's shout ripped up her spine.

"Douse it!" a voice yelled.

More teams with wagons and riders pounded into the yard.

The smoke burned eyes and throats.

Someone dropped a second bucket on a line into the well. Ingeborg looked up to see Metiz on the end of the rope. Tears, sweat—she wiped them away again and kept on dumping.

Her arms felt as if the sockets had loosened. Someone brushed at her hair.

"A spark. Can't let you burn too." Mrs. Johnson patted her shoulder. "Here, Penny, you join the line, and I will crank."

Ingeborg only nodded. Bits of burning hay rode the breeze to breed new flames. When had the wind come up? She could hear shouting, the roar of the fire, and now the snapping of dry wood. *Dear God, the lumber for the barn, our hay, how will we make it through the winter? If only . . .* She stopped that thought aborning. *If only* would only slow her down, and she'd learned in the last few years what time and strength that useless game devoured.

*Please, God, keep anyone from getting hurt. Please save the animals. Please, God* kept time with the dumping of buckets. Her skirts, heavy with splashed water, dragged at her waist.

"Here." Agnes handed her a cup of water and a soaked dish towel. "Drink the one and let me tie the other over your nose and mouth. You'll breathe easier."

Ingeborg kneaded her screaming back with one fist, drank, and then let Agnes tie the wet cloth behind her neck. While her throat still felt as if she'd been swallowing flames, she could breathe easier.

"Mange takk," she whispered, but Agnes was on to doing the same for others.

Heat like that of the worst imaginable August afternoon burned her back and arms. Knowing how she felt, she took a bucketful and dumped it on the backs of those around her, then turned while Metiz did the same for her.

*How long, oh, Lord?* She glanced up at the smoke-filled sky. It should be dark by now. Had time stood still? Wasn't this just a taste of what hell would be like?

"Enough. You stop." Metiz laid her hand on Ingeborg's shoulder. "Fire done."

Ingeborg straightened to find others setting down their buckets. The smoke had indeed let up, the west wind blowing it away. She untied the still saturated cloth, thanks to the sweat and splashing water, and wiped strands of hair back from her forehead. She forced herself to turn and look toward the damage. Only a few humps of charred hay lay where a fine haystack had stood that morning, a mute testimony to the fierce heat. The next stack, half burned, still smoldered, with Lars and Haakan forking off any blackened or smoking remnants. The rest would be so water soaked no self-respecting animal would eat it. She couldn't see around the corner of the barn and corral to where the lumber had been stacked.

She knew she didn't want to see.

Thorliff came to stand beside her, so blackened by soot that if she didn't recognize his eyes, she might not have been sure whose boy he was.

"We saved one stack." He coughed and wiped his mouth with the back of a grimy hand.

"And the lumber?"

"Some. All that behind the barn is water soaked, but it will dry." He shook his head. "But that pile between the hay and the barn . . ." Another headshake. He looked up at her. "One of the cats had her kittens in the stack. Far wouldn't let me find them."

She could see his chin quiver. Two days earlier, he'd shown Andrew the squirming little tiger kitten, eyes only half open. There were four kittens, the mother cat allowing the boys to see them only because Thorliff squirted milk from the cow's teat directly into her mouth. Seeing the cat licking her whiskers free of foaming milk always made Andrew laugh.

"Ja, those things happen." She laid an arm across his shoulders. "She or the other cats will have more kittens. Are the rest of the animals all right?"

Thorliff swiped the back of his hand under his runny nose. "Ja, me and the other kids took the young steers and calves over to Lars' corral. We threw water over the pigs. The chicken house was far enough away to be safe." He wiped his nose again. Ingeborg handed him a soaked handkerchief from her apron pocket and he blew. "Those were good kittens."

Ingeborg only nodded. What more could she say?

Coughing and snorting, most of the people gathered looked down at their feet when she walked by and thanked them all for coming. Haakan was doing the same, and they met at what used to be the corner of the corral, posts and poles either charred or burned entirely.

"This won't beat us." Haakan looked deep into her eyes.

"Ja, I know. It's only a setback." Ingeborg tried to clear her throat, but the raw flesh only made her gag. One thing she knew with a certainty undimmed by fires or floods or whatever the land might send: God had delivered her from the darkness after Roald died, and if He could bring her through that, He would bring her through anything. "Good thing we hadn't built the barn already. The lightning would have struck it instead."

Was that a laugh? Haakan's voice was so hoarse she wasn't sure.

But the smile that showed white teeth against a smoke-blackened face let her know.

"Oh, Ingeborg, only you could look for the good in this . . . this . . ." He swept a hand through the air, encompassing the entire smoldering mess. His laughter caught on a cough, and he bent double with the force of it. His clamped grip on the pitchfork handle kept him upright.

"Kaaren taught me that, her and the Scriptures." Ingeborg heard others laugh and cough as the story spread. If he only knew what price the lesson had cost her.

"Food's on." Agnes rang the triangle just in case anyone hadn't heard her booming voice. The mound growing under her apron might swell her feet, but it wouldn't stop her from doing for others.

Later, as the wagons headed for home, friend after friend assured them that if winter was harsh that year, they would deliver some of their hay by sled. The Bjorklund animals would not go hungry.

"I put up extra, you know," Ingeborg heard more than once.

"You want we should start with the wood we still got and get as much of the barn up as we can?" Joseph and Agnes stopped their wagon for one more spate of questions. "Or ain't you got enough to do even that? I saw the big timbers was on the other side of the barn. Mostly siding went up."

Haakan rubbed the cleft in his chin with one still grimy fingertip, shifting his mouth to the right and massaging his left cheek with his tongue. He shook his head. "Think we better hold up. I haven't really looked it all over yet."

"If cash for the lumber is a problem, I could—" Joseph stopped when Haakan's hand came up, flat out.

"Mange takk, but we ain't so poor as to borrow from our friends. If we need more money for it, we will go to the bank."

Ingeborg tried to hide a smile, but Agnes caught it and sent one back. These proud men of theirs.

"Ain't so much a loan. Call it repayment for all you do for us."

Haakan shook his head again. "Joseph, the owing side is all ours. Now git on home to your chores. We'll raise the schoolhouse on Saturday like we figured."

Joseph spat a glob of tobacco over the wheel of the wagon.

"Uff da," muttered Agnes, shaking her head.

"Now, woman, a man's got to have a weakness of some kind."

Joseph touched the brim of his hat with one finger, winked at the Bjorklunds, and slapped the reins on his team's backs. "Hup now."

Ingeborg waved again. Surely another gift of today was the knowledge that they didn't have just neighbors. They had good friends, the kind that would last for all eternity.

A cow bellered from the pasture and then another.

"Milking time." Haakan turned to Ingeborg. "Kaaren sent over that she will have supper ready after chores. Lars said she was feeling a mite blue since she couldn't come and help fight the fire, so she said she was doing what she could."

"I could milk so you and Thorliff could count the boards we have left."

He put an arm around her shoulders and hauled her into the spot under his arm where she just fit. "Lars and I, we will do that tomorrow. You think we have enough in the bank and the money tin to buy more?"

"We could wait till next year."

"Ja, I know. But next year I am building you a house—with plenty of windows." He looked up at the sky, the clouds purpling as night triumphed over the setting sun. "I think we should go ahead."

"It's up to you."

Haakan stared into her face. "What did you say?"

"You heard me."

"Lord above, the fire must have affected her mind." He raised both hands skyward. "Thank you, heavenly Father."

Ingeborg elbowed him in the ribs. "Uff da, the way you carry on." But this smile she didn't try to hide.

Lying beside her sleeping husband that night, Ingeborg shifted from side to side, trying to find a comfortable spot for all her aching places. Words of praise continued to flow through her head. Perhaps the fire *had* affected her mind. She wrapped an arm around Haakan's rib cage and snuggled next to his back, spoon fashion. *And most of all, Father, thank you for this man you sent me.*

⚬⚬ ⚬⚬

Saturday morning found them all in the wagons by daybreak, chores already finished and food packed in quilts to keep warm or cold. Two sod cutters lay in the back, a clanking testimony to the labor ahead. Today was the day Kaaren had been longing for—the raising of the schoolhouse. The two outfits followed each other down the road to the five-acre plot fenced off on the southwest corner of Bjorklund land for a cemetery. Roald had planned from the first to donate land for the school and church, his dream of a town rising there at the corner of his property on its way to becoming reality. First the school that would double as a church, then they would build a real church. Now with Hjelmer—if and when Hjelmer returned—there would be a store and blacksmith shop. And if the railroad did indeed stop here, the town would grow farther than even Roald had dreamed.

"You really think the railroad will plan on a water stop here?" Kaaren asked as they neared the cemetery.

"Good a place as any. They need a water tower about every twenty miles, and we're at nineteen. That's if they come this way at all. Sure wish we knew what their plans are." Lars studied his wife's face, looking for any sign she was wearing out.

Kaaren smiled up at him. "Now, don't look at me like that. Today I feel wonderful, as if I could race you across the prairie."

He quirked an eyebrow. "Really? Now that would be a sight."

"Oh you." She slapped his knee, her playfulness evident for the first time in days. She shrugged. "I wouldn't miss this for the world. My own school, and today the walls go up."

"Brought enough froes and mallets, along with tree butts, so all the boys can split shingles. We might even get half the roof up. Did you hear Joseph say he would donate a stove? And Johnson is building you a table for a desk."

"I heard you and Haakan volunteered to make desks for the children."

"That was supposed to be a surprise." Lars wrapped the reins around the brake handle.

"Then you shouldn't have told Mr. Anderson. His wife can't keep a secret for more'n a minute, if that."

"That'll learn me. You kind of keep an ear cocked after dinner for the riverboat. If she comes today, Solveig can meet half the county." Though they were the first ones there, other rigs could be seen plodding their way across the prairie.

Kaaren waited for Lars to help her down from the high wagon seat, sharing a smile with Ingeborg when she stepped lightly onto the wheel spoke of the wagon parked beside them and down to the ground. Soon now, too soon if Metiz was right, she would be able to move like that again.

"You sure you should be here?" Ingeborg reached in the back of the wagon and swung Andrew to the ground. "Now, stay by me," she ordered in the tone that even Andrew knew meant he'd better obey.

"Had to be."

Ingeborg nodded. "Thought as much. You could take a lie-down here in the wagon later."

"Ja, I thought of that."

"Andrew!" Ingeborg spoke sharply in her no-nonsense voice.

The youngster, still in the dress of babyhood, looked over his shoulder, with Bjorklund blue eyes pleading for freedom. "Find Tor." He looked around the end of the wagon, then back at his mother.

Ingeborg shook her head. She moved to the rear of the wagon and assisted Haakan in unloading the tree trunks cut in two-foot lengths, just right for shingles.

As soon as the Baard boys arrived, they pitched in, and before long, Haakan had his shingle-splitting class all set up. Each splitter sat on a stump with the butt in front of him, grasping a froe in his right hand and setting it at a slight angle on top of the butt. With the mallet in his left, he tapped the top of the metal froe and the shingle split away. It sounded easy and Haakan made it look that way. But if the froe wasn't held just right, when hit with the mallet the steel blade bounced or fell flat, neither of which action split a shingle.

"You got to hold on to that handle." Haakan adjusted the upright handle for Swen. "Now, you don't have to hit hard, just enough to drive the blade into the butt. The wood will split by itself."

The tip of Swen's tongue showed between his clamping lips. When he hit the froe just right and the shingle split away, a grin to dazzle the eye creased his face. "I did it!" He set the froe again and repeated the action.

"You got it, son. Keep on, and when you have a stack of about ten in front of you, pick them up all at once and lay them in the frame there. That will help form the bundles, and then you can tie them so it is easy to carry them to the roof."

He walked between his eager pupils, all of whom now had the rhythm —most of the time.

As others arrived, the boys joined the splitters until ten lads were busy splitting shingles, and two others tied bundles and carried them from the three-sided square frames to the growing stack of bundles. They traded off jobs, and soon laughter and joking punctuated the slam of mallet on froe and the screech of wood splitting into shingles.

With each boy set and producing to his satisfaction, Haakan unhitched his team and drove them to the site Lars and Joseph had already marked out with pegs driven into the corners. They would use four teams or more to cut sod, and the men could rotate laying the strips, hauling, and cutting.

Some people brought wood for the fire, others brought hams and fried chickens, baked beans, the last vegetables of the season from their gardens, and pies and cakes for dessert. Tools appeared alongside the men, and soon the walls of the schoolhouse began to rise. Joseph ran the crew laying the three-foot-by-eighteen-inch sod blocks, overlapping the ends in the manner of bricklayers the world over.

After agreeing not to discuss the fire at the Bjorklunds anymore, the women got the cook fire going, the coffee started, and hauled out the water bucket and dipper. They assigned Penny to trot water to the workers and two of the younger girls to oversee the small children. Agnes arranged quilts for Kaaren to lean against on a stack of small tree trunks that would eventually become the rafters.

"I don't need such babying," she said with a laugh.

"Sit!" Agnes tried to look and sound stern as she pointed to the impromptu chair. "You can tell stories to entertain the youngsters, if you like."

"But I . . ."

As two women lined up on either side of Agnes, all with matching crossed arms and frowns, Kaaren did as told.

"Uff da." But leaning against the padded logs felt good, and with the breeze lifting the strands of gold from her forehead, she beckoned the children. They gathered around her, one little girl laying her head on what remained of Kaaren's lap and another snugging up against her side. She stroked the white-gold hair of the child at her knee and began. "Long time ago in the northern part of Nordland, an old troll lived in a cave right beside a beautiful stream that danced and sang its way from the snowfield on the mountaintop to the valley below. Now, the old troll was so-o-o old that he helped build the mountain."

"How old was that?" asked Gus, the youngest Baard boy.

Kaaren shook her head. "No one knew how old he was."

"They couldn't count that far?"

She nodded. "That's a wonderful answer." As the story continued, she kept an eye on the rising walls of her schoolhouse. When
she finished, the children begged for another. By the time the
women had dinner ready, she'd fought the battle of Jericho, visited
Daniel in the lion's den, and staggered across the desert with the
Israelites.

Penny came over and handed her a cup of water. "You sure tell
a good story, Mrs. Knutson. Makes me wish I could come back to
school just to hear you."

While the children scampered off to take the plates their mothers had filled, Penny took a place on the quilt. Tracing the colorful
patches with a fingertip, she sighed.

"I take it you haven't heard from Hjelmer."

The younger woman shook her head. "Not a word. Makes me
not want to write to him, but I promised, and as Tante Agnes has
drummed into my head, a promise is a promise no matter if the
other person keeps their part or not." She looked up with swimming
eyes. "Do you think something's happened to him?" She swallowed
hard, "I mean, what if—?"

"My mor always said the Bible tells us to 'let the day's own troubles be sufficient for the day.' Worrying never does us any good. She
had a habit of adding to her favorite verses. 'What if' is a useless
pastime if I ever saw one." She studied the downcast face. "Do you
really want to get more schooling?"

Penny nodded.

Kaaren shifted on the quilt and stretched her back. Getting up
was going to take three men and a team of horses. "Mange takk."
She took the plate handed to her and rested it on her shelf. At
Penny's grin, she smiled back. "Good for something it is, but you
can be sure I won't miss it."

"You think there is a way I could go on to school?"

Kaaren nodded, catching her lower lip between her teeth. "Just
let me talk to Ingeborg. We might be able to work something out."

Penny rose to her feet, eyes sparkling like sun-kissed wavelets.
"Thank you, oh, thank you."

*The young pup nephew of mine, if he were here, I would . . . I would
. . .* Nothing punishing enough came to mind. If he didn't watch out,
he might let this beautiful young woman get away from him. And
it would serve him right.

She tried to stretch out another twinge in her back. Laying a hand on her belly, she thought, *This baby sure has been quiet today*.

After dinner she settled the little ones about her for naps, and letting her eyelids drift halfway closed, she listened to the men laughing and joking as they hoisted sod shoulder high. Two men climbed up in the wagon bed to position the latest load of sod bricks. They switched around again so the taller men were unloading the wagons and hefting up the new layers of sod as the walls grew higher. They'd already laid the thick boards over the door and window spaces and had stretched another layer of sod over those.

*Whitewash*, she thought. *If I whitewash the walls the children will feel brighter. It will be like having another window.* How she wished for a wall of windows to let the out-of-doors come in, but with a soddy, that wasn't to be. She shifted, discomfort making her squirm. A cramp started at her back and worked its way to the front.

A child sat up and rubbed her eyes, looking around for her mother, who sat with the other women on quilts nearby, talking and laughing over the chorus of clicking knitting needles. The little girl smiled up at Kaaren's gentle voice and lay back down, dropping again into sleep before the sigh ended.

"You better get that fiddle tuned up, Baard, we're that close to done." She heard the male voice as if from a great distance.

"Ain't we putting up the rafters first?" someone asked.

"Ja, that been our intent."

Laughter out at the bare plot where the sod had formerly lain caught her attention. "That's it!" The cry echoed from the men to the boys, who broke into cheers.

"You keep splittin' them shingles. We got a lot of roof to cover."

Groans rose from the young splitters.

The men gathered around the soddy with its seven-foot walls. Agnes rose from her knitting to stoke up the fire and moved the coffeepots into a hotter spot. Kaaren stifled a whimper.

Ready to lift the center beam into place, the men formed two teams, each taking a side set to raise. When the beam thudded home, the teams slammed the rafters and sheeting into place, and like weeds sprouting when the sun warms the rain-drenched earth, the hip roof took shape.

"Come on, Far!" Young Swen Baard yelled from his shingle-splitting post.

"Aw, Baard, your side goes any slower, and we won't be outta here till tomorrow morning."

The women added their cheers as the pounding increased in speed.

Lars limped over to his wife and extended a hand. "Come, you will be the first to walk through the door and look up through the rafters. Should have the roof on by the end of the week if those young sprouts keep going like they are."

"Mange takk." Kaaren let him pull her to her feet and wrap an arm around her back when she staggered. She clenched her teeth and forced a smile for his benefit.

"Are you all right?" Concern made him stop and turn to look at her more closely.

She nodded. "Ja, just show me the new school building, then I think we better not stay for the dancing and supper."

"Kaaren!"

She shook her head. "No, I want to see my school from the inside."

He led her around the wood scraps and in through the doorway. The workers paused, and a hush fell.

"Do you like it?"

Kaaren stood in the middle of the room and looked up at the blue sky now fading toward sunset. She stamped the dirt beneath her feet and crossed to lay a hand on the rough surface of the wall, pulling loose a green stalk and tossing it over the beams. "This is the most beautiful school anywhere." Her voice rang for everyone to hear.

Cheers erupted from all around. Joseph Baard nailed the last rafter in place.

Kaaren sagged against her husband. "I think you better get me home now."

"Are you sick?"

"Not really, but your son or daughter seems a mite impatient to enter this world."

"Oh, good Lord above." Lars dropped her hand and tore out the door. "Harness the wagon . . . ah . . . load up the horses." He shook his head and spun around. "Kaaren, where are you?"

Her laughing voice came from the soddy. "Right where you left me."

Lars darted back in the school building. "We're having a baby." He started back out, turned, and hooked an arm around her middle.

"Come on, what are you waiting for?"

Haakan drove the quilt-padded wagon up to the door. One look at Lars' face and the man on the wagon seat shook his head. "Think I better drive."

**5**

*She is early, so early.* Ingeborg kept her fears from her face.

Karen groaned against another spasm.

"Easy now. We have a long time ahead of us." Ingeborg knelt in the bed of the wagon beside her sister-in-law, who after all they'd been through together was closer than a sister. They were more like pieces of the same heart. "Would you feel more comfortable sitting up?"

"I think so." Kaaren rotated her shoulders and took a deep breath. Letting it out slowly, she used her elbows to raise up while Ingeborg stuffed two folded quilts behind her.

"If this jolting didn't bring on the pains, nothing else could."

"Sister, this is so early." Kaaren looked over the mountain of her belly to the wagon following close behind them. Thorliff sat straight on the wagon seat, the lines held gently but firmly in his hands as he'd been taught. She waved at him and he nodded, shooting Baptiste beside him a grin of pure pride.

"Are you doing all right?" Lars leaned back from the seat above. "You want I should prop you up?"

"That would be good." Kaaren clenched her teeth, feeling the cramping starting at her spine and encircling her belly.

"Easy now. Just breathe deep and let it all out. My mor used to say that babies come when they are ready, whether the mother is or not."

Sighing, Kaaren blinked her eyes and felt her body return to whatever was normal for now. Dust tickled her nose and made her sneeze.

Ingeborg drew a square of white cloth from her apron pocket and offered it with a loving smile. She helped Kaaren sit up for Lars to get behind her, his long legs stretched out to her sides. Folding one of the quilts loaned by a neighbor, she tucked it between the wagon side and Lars' back.

Kaaren leaned back against her husband's chest and sighed again. The rocking of the wagon now felt comfortable, like a cushioned chair. He rubbed her shoulders, kneading the taut muscles to some pliancy.

"You know, the cows, they head off to a quiet place all by themselves and return with a bouncing calf." His words tickled the hair around her ears.

"Ja, and the cat. She, too, goes off and hides. Is that what you want me to do?" She looked up to see his smile bathe her in love. He shook his head.

"No, just helping you think of something else."

"Ja, well . . ." She clenched her teeth again, digging her fingers into the muscles of his leg. "This baby of ours ain't thinking anything else, let me tell you." Her words forced her to breathe in small pants. Her eyes widened. "Ah, that helps."

"What? My leg that might never work right again?" He rubbed just above the knee. "Glad it was my good one."

She slapped his hand playfully away. "You want we should change places?"

"Heaven forbid!" The shock in his tone made both women laugh.

"My mor said scrubbing floors on your hands and knees was good for birthing babies."

"She didn't have packed dirt floors neither." Ingeborg stood to ask Haakan a question. Clenching the board seat for balance, she raised her face to talk. When he turned his head, she caught the look, of what? Concern, worry, or was it fear? His eyes darkened under his hat brim, and lines bracketed his mouth. She laid a hand on his arm. "She is all right. This is the way of babies coming into the world. You haven't been near birthing before?"

He shook his head. "I never knew the hurting was like this. Mor went to the bedroom; we went to the barn, and a while later, she had a sleeping baby in her arms. We would tiptoe in, and she would smile and say, 'Look what the angels brought us.' "

"Ja, well, women been bringing babies into this world in pain and suffering ever since the fall. The Bible says it should be so." She glanced down to check on her patient. "It is never easy, but the work is worth the pain. 'Twill get a lot worse before it gets better." She kept her voice low, meant for his ears alone.

"God give her strength." Haakan clucked the horses a bit faster but knew too much speed would make the wagon jolt even more.

Ingeborg returned to find Kaaren in the throes of another spasm, but this time Lars, in a most gentle voice, reminded her that small breaths helped and rubbed her shoulders and neck.

*Please, dear Lord, get us home quickly. I think this baby is in a real hurry.*

When the wagon finally halted in front of the soddy, Ingeborg and Kaaren shared a look of relief. Haakan wrapped the reins around the brake handle and swung over the back of the seat.

"You want we should carry you in on the quilt?" he asked, tipping his hat back with one finger.

"Nei. I will walk."

"Walk!" Lars shook his head. "Has this thing caused you to lose your mind? I will carry you." He bent to hook an arm behind her legs when Kaaren thumped him on the shoulder.

"We don't need your back broken, and I don't need the quilt. Just help me down from the end of the wagon, and Ingeborg and I will begin the walking."

"Begin the walking?" Haakan and Lars looked from the women with resolution written indelibly on their faces to each other, recognizing they wore the same astounded expression.

"But . . . but . . ."

Ingeborg felt Kaaren tighten again. "Here, Lars, help your wife. Haakan, you get down to the ground and make sure we don't drop her. Walking now will make the baby come more easily later." Her look left no room for argument.

The men did as told and then followed Ingeborg's instructions to go about the evening chores as if nothing were wrong.

Lars blustered, but at the wave of Kaaren's hand, he glared once and led the horses off to the barn to be unharnessed. "You will call if you need me?"

"Ja, we will," Ingeborg called over her shoulder as she and Kaaren paced the length of the soddy. The temperature dropped with the darkening sky, and still they walked. Ingeborg went inside and returned with Kaaren's coat and they walked some more. Lars brought up the brimming milk buckets, and after a headshake from Ingeborg, he went about the business of straining and setting the pans for the cream to rise in the soddy they'd built that summer for a cooling room. A trough filled with cold water held the cream cans until there was enough for butter. Ingeborg turned much of the whole milk into cheeses, but Kaaren churned the butter they sold to the store in St. Andrew and to the Bonanza farms across the Red River.

"You want we should go in?" Ingeborg asked, glancing up at the stars that now dotted the cobalt sky. Lighter blue still lined the western horizon.

"Ja, I guess." Kaaren stumbled once and bent to cradle her belly. "They are coming closer together." She stood and sucked in a deep breath. "Oh my."

"What is it?"

"The water broke. I'm drenched." She looked down at the front of her dress. "Uff da, such a mess."

They found Lars sound asleep in the rocker, his head tipped back and gentle snores puffing his lips. A loaf of bread missing several slices and cheese still on the table said he'd fixed his own supper.

"I should have come in and heated something," Ingeborg whispered.

"Or me." Kaaren tried to smile around the pinched lines at the edges of her mouth.

"You been busy enough. You want he should go to stay with Haakan and the children?"

Kaaren shook her head. "Maybe that is the right way, but he will help me later. I could tell in the wagon, he . . ." She doubled over again, her gasp waking the sleeping man.

Lars leaped to his feet, the rocking chair banging back against the chest. "Are you all right? How can I help? Is the baby almost here?" His questions rifled the still air.

"You can help your wife continue to walk, and I will make us all some coffee. Then I will run over home and check on the others." Ingeborg rattled the grate and, as the coals flared, added some wood shavings from the box under the reservoir. When those caught, she placed the kindling and added a couple of slightly larger sticks. As she went about the mundane chores, she kept an eye on Kaaren. Lars' arm seemed to calm her and lend her strength. Perhaps it would be all right if he helped. She wasn't about to tell anyone of the impropriety. Like Haakan had said, men were usually banished to the barn or the fields and welcomed home after the baby had made its entrance into the world.

Ingeborg found her family sound asleep in their beds, the boys' faces washed and the supper things all put away. Paws thumped his tail at the side of the bed, his guilty look saying he'd landed there just before she walked in. He liked sleeping with Thorliff, if given half a chance.

"How is she?" Haakan's voice came through the dimness.

"Making do. In the wagon, this baby seemed in a hurry but then must have took a rest. Things should speed up now."

"Do you need me to help?"

"Mange takk, but no. Lars will come for you if . . . if . . ." She turned back to the doorway. "God willing, all will be well."

Thoughts of her own baby born long before its time and buried before she even knew it existed caused her to clamp her bottom lip between her teeth. Those days when they first arrived at their homestead had brought all kinds of hardships, but with God's help they had survived.

Kaaren was still pacing the floor, albeit more slowly, when Ingeborg reentered the northern soddy. She'd changed into her nightclothes and wore a shawl around her shoulders. Four paces, turn, and back. "H-have a cup of coffee. It's hot."

"You want some?"

Kaaren shook her head. "I think I will sit down for a while, though. We are wearing a ditch in the floor." She lowered herself into the rocker. "Lars, please read to me, will you?" She motioned to the Bible in its place of honor on the shelf above the rosemaled trunk she'd brought from Norway.

Lars gave Ingeborg a raised eyebrows look but did as asked, pulling the kerosene lamp closer to his shoulder so he could see. The Norwegian words rolled off his tongue as he began with the Twenty-third Psalm.

Kaaren rocked gently in the chair, the squeak of the rockers adding to the night music.

Ingeborg cupped her coffee mug in her hands and let the beauty of the words sink into her soul. The Lord had surely been their shepherd, and now she knew for certain He always would be.

Kaaren's groan shattered the peace.

Lars leaped to his feet. The table rocked and only through his lightning grab did he keep the burning lamp from spilling over. He shot Ingeborg a terrified look and clasped Kaaren's shaking hands. "What is it? What can I do?" He clasped one hand around her elbow and helped her to her feet.

"I . . . I think it is time to go to the bed."

"Keep her walking." Ingeborg watched for a moment. "I will get things ready." She dug in the trunk and brought out a piece of worn cloth, tearing it into strips as she moved toward the bed. Once they were knotted together, she lifted the corn husk mattress and tied the length to the rail stretching the ropes. Then she folded back the quilt and laid a second sheet, folded square, in the middle of the bed. "Now, Lars, you sit up against the wall, and we'll brace Kaaren against you."

"What are the strips for?"

"You will see." Now that the time was nearing, she could feel herself settle into the rhythm as Kaaren whimpered with pain. "A time to be born," the Bible said, and after the suffering would come the joy. She stuck more wood in the stove and moved the pot filled with water closer to the flame. Going back to the trunk, she removed the packet Kaaren had prepared beforehand. Soft clothes to wrap the baby in, tiny shirts, hemmed flannel squares for diapering, and a folded square with a long strip to wrap around the baby's belly to hold the severed cord in place. Clean scissors to cut the cord. A baby quilt lay underneath the other things.

A cry forced itself past Kaaren's clenched teeth.

"Can't you do something?" Lars pleaded.

"It is just beginning."

"Just beginning! She's been at this for hours. You said the baby was going to come fast, that he was in a hurry." He tried to keep his voice low, but the words hissed between clenched lips.

Ingeborg shrugged. "It was a fast start, and the water broke and . . ."

Kaaren moaned and opened her eyes again.

"How many babies have you helped bring into the world, anyway?"

"Lars." Kaaren tried to look up at his face. "Babies don't come until they are ready." She clenched teeth and fingers against another spasm.

"Inge!" Lars shook his head. "Can't you help her?"

Kaaren pulled against the knotted cloths, a sharp groan matching the grimace of her face.

Ingeborg was glad Lars couldn't see his wife's face. "Lars, this isn't helping her. If you'd rather, go wait in the barn, or better yet, go on over to my house and get some sleep. Women have been enduring this since time began."

"No!" He settled Kaaren back against his chest and rubbed the thigh muscle her clenching fingers had sent into a cramp.

Kaaren screamed on the next one, which seemed to follow right on the back of another.

But an hour later, with contractions rolling through her body, the baby still hadn't come.

*Dear God, what are we to do? The baby should be showing by now. Is it turned? Is something else wrong? Please, you can't let Kaaren lose this baby, or Lars lose them both. Please, I beg of you, tell me what to do.*

"Never again will she go through torture like this," Lars muttered, the words lost in another scream.

Ingeborg understood his fear. *Father in heaven, Jesus, help us please.*

## 6

Y ou'd best be praying," Ingeborg whispered.

Lars shot her a startled look and then nodded. With his chin resting on his wife's sweat-darkened hair, he closed his eyes, his lips moving soundlessly.

Ingeborg knelt beside the bed, taking one of Kaaren's shaking hands in her own. Storming the throne of heaven with her entreaties, she felt tears slip down her cheeks, tears of fear and worry, of a breaking heart and a sorrowing mind. She thought He had abandoned them before, would He do so again? She had prayed at other bedsides, and God took them home anyway. Flashes of Kaaren's two little daughters lying pale and cold, and Carl slipping away from under her ministering fingers whipped through her mind, wrenching her heart.

She gritted her teeth. Taking in a deep breath, she raised her head. There would be no doubting. God said He was with them, and whatever His will, that would be good. He would not let them go. He never had. In spite of her doubts and her rebellion, He had been there waiting for her to turn around and seek Him.

"Kaaren, I am going to see if I can feel the baby's head."

Kaaren nodded without opening her eyes. She lay panting from the strain of the last contraction. Ingeborg wrung out the cloth in the pan beside the bed and wiped the sweat from Kaaren's pale brow and the sides of her face. Then going to the washstand, she took a bar of soap and scrubbed her hands. She held them dripping above the basin, palms up. Her hands were so big and the opening so small. How would she. . . ? She shut off the thought and returned to the bed.

"This will probably hurt." She put every teeny bit of confidence she could muster into her voice. "I'm going to wait until the pain comes and see if I can feel the head."

A slight nod showed Kaaren heard her.

When Kaaren screamed again, Ingeborg slipped her fingers into the birth canal, but where there should have been a round head, her fingertips grazed what she immediately knew to be a tiny foot. She bit her lip till the blood salted her tongue. "God above, help us here. Please, I beg of you."

Kaaren lay back against her husband, gasping and sniffing against the tears that joined the sweat coursing down her face.

*What to do, Lord? What to do?* Ingeborg felt a presence beside her and turned her head. Metiz stood next to the bed, having entered without a sound. Even the screen door kept silent for her.

"How did you know?"

"Baptiste, he find me. You call me, I come."

Ingeborg shook her head. "I didn't call you. God did." She swallowed and nodded toward Kaaren. "I think the baby is breech. He can't be born that way."

"No, must turn." Metiz looked down at her hands. "I wash." When she returned, she nodded to Lars, whose eyes were filled with fear. "You help turn her."

"What?"

"Get her on hands and knees."

"Are you crazy? She can't move."

"We move her." She raised her voice. "Kaaren, you hear?"

Kaaren nodded so slightly that a blink would have missed it.

"We help you to hands and knees. Baby not like that, maybe move by himself."

"Ja, I will." Her voice faded in and out, as if the breath it took was too precious to waste on words.

Between the four of them, they soon had Kaaren in the new position. Lars braced his wife from one side and Ingeborg from the other. When the pain gripped her again, her scream seemed to go on for all time.

"Now, sit back."

Lars propped her against his chest again so that Kaaren reclined, her hands clenched in a death grip on the knotted rope. When she shuddered and began to pull against the rope, Metiz felt for the baby. Her obsidian eyes sparkled when she turned to Ingeborg. "It work. Baby come now."

"Thank you, Father in heaven."

"Great Spirit love babies." Metiz returned to lay her hands on Kaaren's belly. "You push baby out now."

Kaaren raised her eyelids only halfway, letting them fall shut her agreement.

"You be strong!" Metiz' voice rang in the sweltering room, the command striking tremors in Ingeborg's soul.

Lars whispered in Kaaren's ear and grasped her elbows. With a keening as old as womanhood, Kaaren took a deep breath and pushed with a might far beyond her own.

"One more."

Lars whispered again. Kaaren gasped.

"God, give her strength!" Ingeborg brushed the torrents away from her eyes.

The ancient cry set her heart to pounding. She reached down and caught the still little body as it slipped out of its sanctuary. "It's a girl." Hushed tones greeted the reverence of the moment. But only for a moment.

"Baby not breathing." Metiz pushed on the infant's chest while Ingeborg wiped mucus from the tiny nose. Then the old woman grabbed the infant by the heels and slapped her smartly on her peach-sized bottom.

A gasp, a choking cough, and the little one let out a wail that brought smiles to all the faces.

"Help me," Kaaren forced out between lips bloodied from being clamped between her teeth.

Metiz handed the baby to Ingeborg and dropped to the side of the bed again. She looked over her shoulder at Ingeborg. " 'Nother baby."

"Twins?" Lars left off looking at the baby in Ingeborg's arms and wrapped his arms around Kaaren as she pushed again.

"One more." Metiz placed gentle fingers around the emerging head and turned the baby just enough so it slipped into her hands. "Girl." But like the other, the tiny form lay limp.

Ingeborg handed the first child to Lars. "Put her in your shirt front, tight against your chest. We've got to keep her warm."

While Ingeborg did that, Metiz tipped the infant upside down and shook her gently. With still no response, she held the baby cradled in her hands while Ingeborg wiped away the mucus.

"We slapped the other on the backside, and that made her catch her breath."

Metiz nodded. "Get a basin of warm water, not too hot." She

slapped the baby and shook her gently once more, but still the baby didn't breathe. Compressing the tiny ribs also had no effect.

Ingeborg sent prayers shooting upward as she filled the basin from the reservoir and tested it with her elbow. When she set it on the table, Metiz swiftly submerged the still form, brought it up and dunked her again.

"Blow in nose."

Ingeborg did as told while the old woman pressed just above the baby's belly. A shudder, a gulp, and the little one squeaked. With the next breath, she whimpered.

"Thanks be to God," Ingeborg breathed, tears of gratitude, fear, and all else streaming down her cheeks.

"She's breathing?" Lars whispered, so he wouldn't wake Kaaren who still lay against him, sleeping the sleep of the exhausted.

"Ja, she is." Ingeborg didn't add the "barely" said in her mind. "Have you ever saved any babies so tiny?" she whispered for Metiz' ears alone.

A bare shake of the head told of Metiz' concentration as she swished the baby in the water again, now keeping the face clear.

Kaaren groaned as her body began to expel the afterbirth. Ingeborg flew to her side and began massaging Kaaren's stomach. Beneath her hands she could feel the muscles contracting and remembered this stage after Andrew's birth. It still hurt, and she turned to see Kaaren bite down on her lip and clamp her fingers on Lars' knees.

Kaaren opened her eyes when it was over. "Do I remember two babies being born?"

"Ja, you do. Two little girls."

"Are . . . are they alive?"

"Ja."

"I have one right here." Lars took her hand and brought it to his chest so she could feel the squirming body. "I think she would be happier with you than with me."

The sun that rose on Kaaren's face lit the room, even as the window glowed with the sun rising outside. "Can I hold her?"

"As soon as we get things cleaned up here and a fresh nightgown on you." Ingeborg kept about her tasks, afraid to hazard a look at Metiz. The other baby hadn't made any more noise.

Lars staggered at first when he rose from the bed, stamping to get feeling back in his feet and the cramps out of his legs. The babe that lay cradled against his chest whimpered, then cried a lusty wail that sounded far too big for the tiny chest. "Hush, little one," he crooned, stumbling and bumping against the chair. "Come on, feet, you've been through worse than this. Let's get moving."

Ingeborg caught the wince, knowing the needles that were shooting up his feet and legs. "You did well, Lars Knutson."

"Mange takk. Aren't you glad you didn't banish me to the other soddy?"

"Ja, that we are." She finished washing Kaaren's face and arms, then dried them and helped her sit so the nightgown would slip over her head. "There now, better?"

Kaaren nodded, only the flinch of her eyes marking the continuing contractions. "I'd forgotten this part." With Ingeborg's help, she sat on the edge of the bed so the sheet could be changed and, with a sigh, lay back against the pillows. "Inge, you are so good to me. What would I ever do without you?"

"Hush, now. Save your strength for the babies. This one sounds hungry." She turned to look at Lars. The love shining from his face as he gazed at the small bundle in his shirt made her catch her breath. *Would that God would keep these babies alive and let them grow.* "You can bring her to her mor now. I'll get something to wrap her in so she stays warm."

She took one of the larger flannel squares and tucked it around the infant as Lars laid his precious bundle on his wife's breast. Immediately the tiny mouth began nuzzling for sustenance.

"Oh, dear Lord, she is so precious." Tears streamed down Kaaren's cheeks as she arranged the infant against her breast. "Thank you, Father, thank you." Her whispered words of praise continued as the baby began to nurse.

Ingeborg left gazing in awe at the sight and turned to Metiz. "Is she alive?"

Metiz nodded and continued her gentle stroking motions down the baby's back, her arms and legs, then in circles on the belly and chest.

"What are you doing?" Ingeborg asked softly.

"Warming blood. Make it move. You rub hands together and lay on head."

Ingeborg did as told, watching the blue tinge slowly disappear to be replaced with the flush of red. When the tiny head turned, and the pursing mouth with a tongue no bigger than a thumbnail nuzzled her fingers, Ingeborg lost her heart to the tiny girl. She felt it fly right of out of her chest, almost looking to see where it lighted.

She could hear the murmurs from the bed as Kaaren and Lars whispered over the wonder of the suckling babe, but the sounds seemed to come from a far and distant land. Her entire being was focused on the smaller twin before her.

*Dear Lord, let her live. Let her live. Fill her with your strength and spirit that she may live and breathe and grow in grace.*

She stopped the litany of beseeching and asked, "Have you thought of names yet?"

"Ja, we will name this one after Kaaren's mother, Sonja, but I think we should change it to Sophie to sound more American."

"And this one?"

"We had only chosen one name. We really didn't believe there would be two."

"I think Grace. For it is by God's grace she is still living." *And only His grace will keep her through the hours and days ahead.* But she didn't say the rest, only wove it into the prayer that spiraled heavenward like the incense of old.

"Ja, that is a lovely name." Kaaren shifted the now sleeping infant to her shoulder and patted the back that lay smaller than her hand. "Do you think she can nurse now?"

"I pray to God that she can." Ingeborg looked up to catch the slight nod from Metiz.

Taking the flannel square she had draped over the back of the chair to heat from the stove, she wrapped her precious charge and carried her to her mother.

"Here." Lars took the sleeping baby and cuddled her in his arms so Ingeborg could help Kaaren settle the other. But when they put Grace to Kaaren's breast, she didn't begin to suckle.

"What do we do?" Kaaren raised stricken eyes, seeking the answer on Ingeborg's face.

*I don't know! God, what do we do?* Ingeborg's mind raced, searching for any memory that would help them, any thought, any story she'd heard. Nothing. Why hadn't she listened more closely when the women gathered and talked of childbirthing?

"Can she swallow if we get some in her mouth?" Lars knelt by the bed, one hand clutching the bundle he'd secreted back in his shirt front and the other touching the baby's head like a benediction.

"We'll never know till we try." Ingeborg looked up at Kaaren. "Can you bring some of your milk out with your fingers?"

"I never have, but I can try." A smile tipped one corner of her mouth. The gray of utter exhaustion tinged her face and painted dark circles under her eyes. With shaking fingers, she managed to squeeze out a few drops, but they missed the baby's mouth, landing on her cheek.

Ingeborg scooped the precious fluid up with her finger and rubbed it against Grace's lips. *Please God, help her to drink, You of the life-giving water, make this baby drink.*

The tiny mouth opened and closed, and Grace turned her face toward her mother's breast. Kaaren continued her efforts to get Grace to nurse in this manner.

Ingeborg sighed. She stood erect and blinked her eyes, trying to clear the grit from them.

"Look," Metiz whispered. "She drinks."

Sure enough, little Grace's cheeks dented in as she swallowed, suckled, and swallowed again.

"Praise be to God." Lars sat down on the pole that made up the side of the bed. The screech of it sounded loud in the stillness as all held their breath, waiting for the next sign that Grace was feeding.

When it came, they all exhaled in a whoosh of relief.

"She stronger than she look." Metiz rubbed her bent fingers together. "Good. I make food now."

"I will do that," Ingeborg said with a weary smile. "I know where everything is."

Metiz nodded. "Make tea for Kaaren." She gestured to the deerskin pouch she wore at her waist, where she always stored her small cache of herbs and medicinals.

"I should go do the chores." Lars rose, again setting the pole to creaking the ropes holding the mattress. The rooster crowed from the barn and a cow bellered. "The animals are hungry too."

"No, you keep that baby warm. Haakan will send the boys to do your chores or come himself." Ingeborg handed Lars a baby quilt. "Wrap this into a sling to keep her steady."

"She's going to suffocate in there."

"Not if do right." Metiz took the quilt and tied it over his shoulder. "Baby like to hear heartbeat."

Lars shook his head. "I thought to build them a box and set it on the oven door. Done that for baby pigs and lambs."

"Next to heart best."

Ingeborg turned to see Kaaren stroking the head of the child now sleeping in her arms, tears dripping off the end of her chin. To keep from tearing up again herself, Ingeborg took the frying pan off the shelf and set it on the stove. She restoked the firebox and lifted a small pan down from the warming shelf. Ladling warm water into it, she set it on the hottest spot. Kaaren needed nourishment more than any of them, and before that, the restorative teas that Metiz brewed. She reminded herself to set some of the elk she'd shot to boiling so the new mother could drink the broth. Surely elk broth would be the same as beef broth, her mother's all-time favorite for whatever ailed one.

Paws' barking drew her to the window. Haakan and the boys strode into the yard, Andrew riding on the tall man's shoulders. Within moments the clanging of buckets told her Thorliff had fetched the milk pails and headed back to the barn. When Andrew failed to appear at the door, she knew Haakan had kept him in the barn, probably in the oat bin to keep him out from under animal hooves.

She returned to her business of preparing a meal.

Metiz spread her crushed herbs and simples over the top of the now boiling water and set it back to simmer. "I get meat from smokehouse?"

"Ja, the ham by the door. It's been sliced off already. There are eggs in the springhouse." Ingeborg finished measuring flour and lard into the bowl. "Oh, Metiz, see if there is any buttermilk for these biscuits. Mange takk." Ingeborg raised her voice so the woman who padded silently out the door could hear her. How Metiz could leave without the screen door squeaking was beyond her.

A baby's whimper brought her attention to the family at the bed. Kaaren lay sound asleep with Grace still pillowed on her chest and the quilt drawn up for both of them. Lars rocked the infant in his shirt, patting the small mound and moving his lips in what Ingeborg knew to be a soothing murmur. She'd heard him use the singsong tone with the animals, and they always quieted down.

She measured coffee into the pot, making sure there was more water in the reservoir. Thorliff could bring in fresh when he came. Also, the woodbox needed filling. Brushing a floured hand across her forehead, she caught herself in a yawn. They could all do with some sleep, but someone had to cook and care for them.

"Here." Metiz handed her a jug of buttermilk. She set the ham on the counter and, taking a knife from the rack Lars had fashioned, began slicing the meat.

"Mor, Mor." Andrew pounded on the screen door, the banging enough to wake ten sleeping babies.

"Hush." She opened the door and held the screen door open. "The babies are sleeping."

He looked up at her, his eyes round circles of summer sky. "Me see."

"Ja, but you must be quiet." She took his hand and led him over to the bed. Lars unbuttoned his shirt, and Ingeborg lifted Andrew so he could peek in.

"Baby?" He turned to his mother, patting her cheeks with his chilly hands.

"Ja, baby Sonja, or Sophie."

"Sophie?" He looked back at the tiny form now sleeping in her father's care.

"And Grace is sleeping with Tante Kaaren."

"Me see?"

"Later. You come and wash your hands for breakfast." She set him back down and hustled him to the washbasin. "Where's Thorliff and Baptiste?"

"In chicken house." Andrew rubbed his hands together and swiped the backs across his mouth. When he held them up to be dried, he grinned up at her. "Andrew hungry."

"Say, I am hungry."

He nodded. "Me too." Giggling, he let her lift him to the box set on the chair so he could reach his food.

"Uff da, you are getting so big." She smoothed the hair back from his forehead, then hugged him against her apron. "Den lille guten. Mor's good boy."

Metiz turned from the ham sizzling in the pan. "Boys come."

Baptiste and Thorliff erupted into the room, only silencing when Ingeborg frowned with a finger to her lips.

"Can we see the baby?" Thorliff asked, trying to keep his voice down but not really succeeding.

"After we eat. Tante Kaaren and the babies are sleeping."

"Babies?" Thorliff raised dripping hands from the washbasin.

"Twins. Two little girls." Ingeborg handed him a towel. "So very tiny, son. We all need to pray for them."

"Like the runt pig we had last spring?"

Ingeborg and Metiz shared a mother's glance. "Well, not exactly, but kind of. The babies were born early and . . ." She cleared her throat. The thought of burying those two tiny bodies . . . *Oh, God, please not. They want to live. We need them to live.*

"Mor?" Thorliff stood at her side. "I will help."

"And me." Baptiste stood beside his friend, as dark as Thorliff was fair.

"I know, and I can always depend on you both." She turned them toward the table just as Haakan pushed open the door.

"Good morning." He hung his hat on the pegged board nailed into the sod wall. "Froze good last night." He looked toward the bed. "She is all right?"

"Ja, and you were right. Twins . . . girls. Sophie and Grace."

"And?"

She shook her head. "They are so tiny, I don't know how . . ."

"You let God worry about that. We will do all we can." He touched her cheek with the tips of his fingers. "Grace, what a wonderful name." He looked around. "Where are they?"

"Metiz fixed slings so they are cradled against . . . well, Lars has Sophie. She was born first and is slightly larger. Grace is with her mother."

"Well, I'll be." Haakan smiled at Metiz. "You are an amazing woman."

"When get bigger put on papoose board. Keep safe."

Haakan took his place at the table. "I've heard of papoose boards." He waited for all to bow their heads. Lars and Kaaren slept on. "I Jesu navn . . ." The Norwegian prayer rolled off his lips, and before he said the amen, he added, "And, Lord, please bless this family and make these two precious new children of yours grow strong and healthy."

By the time they finished eating, Lars had awakened. He stood and pulled his wet shirt away from his body. "That part of her works."

Ingeborg leaped to her feet. "You sit here and I will change her. I think we need to make a warm place to change the babies. They could catch cold so easily."

"After breakfast I will see to something." Haakan reached for another biscuit. "Thorliff, it will be your job to take care of Andrew while your mor gets some sleep. He can help you in the barn."

Lars transferred the baby to Ingeborg's hands and took a place at the table. Metiz handed him a plate with hot ham and three fried eggs. "More?"

He shook his head, already buttering one of the fluffy biscuits.

Ingeborg tuned out the sounds of eating as she removed the wet diaper, wiped the baby, and rewrapped the diaper around the tiny infant. Sophie started to cry, a mewling sound like that of a small kitten. As quickly as possible Ingeborg wrapped her in a clean flannel blanket and then the quilt. How to keep them warm enough would be the main problem, unless they slept all the time in slings like those Metiz devised. Could Kaaren carry both of them at the same time?

Ingeborg crossed to the bed as the mewlings turned into a wail. "Hard to believe such a sound comes from one so tiny." She smiled into Kaaren's tired blue eyes. "Sophie is hungry again."

"I can tell."

"While you nurse her, I will fix a plate and help you eat. How does that sound?"

"Inge, I can feed myself." Kaaren winced when she tried to sit up.

Metiz silently handed Ingeborg a steaming cup. "She drink first."

Kaaren settled the infant at her breast and made sure the sling holding Grace was still secure. With both hands occupied, she shook her head. "You were right." Like a baby bird, she opened her mouth for spoonfuls of the tea, and when that was finished, she managed to eat a bit of ham and eggs.

Later, leaving Metiz on the first watch as she insisted, Ingeborg set out for home. The sun looked warmer than it felt. The oak and maple trees along the riverbank shimmered in their autumn finery, the leaves casting up like feathers when the wind puffed them away. She should be hunting today. And Haakan had mentioned wanting to butcher now that the cold had come. Frost still lay on the north side of the grass hummocks and on the roofs of the soddies, both barn and house.

She lifted her face to catch every ray of sun. Geese and other waterfowl sang their way south but in much fewer numbers than earlier. They could always use more smoked goose and down for feather quilts. She thought instead of the tiny ones left sleeping on their mother's chest. "Please, dear God, they are so weak and tiny. You who counts the sparrows, please find it in your heart to help these babies live. It is all up to you, I know that. I thank you that you saw us through the long night and brought them safely into their new life. I know that with you all things are possible." She could feel tears gathering behind her eyes and shut off the thoughts that battered on the door of her mind. "And we will give you all the praise and glory. Amen." Sleep claimed her before she could even pull her boots off.

⁂

"Mor, Tante Kaaren needs you." Thorliff's tugging on her arm pulled her from a deep sleep.

## 7

I brought your laundry back."

Hjelmer stared at the young woman who stood on the rough plank steps before the doorway to the sleeping car. He'd said he would get the laundry himself. He looked over his shoulder to see who else might be in the car. Much to his consternation, the ring of men clad in wool long johns, their shirts hanging from the bunks, turned to see where the musical voice came from.

"Mange takk." He dug in his pocket for change. "How much?"

She named her price and handed him his fresh-smelling bundle of clothes, taking her payment in the same motion. "I'll pick up next Monday."

"No, I ah . . ."

"I didn't do a good enough job?" She turned, planting her hands on hips that set her full skirt to swaying. Even when she stopped, the skirt continued to move as if it had a life of its own.

"No, it's not that, I . . ." Hjelmer raised his eyes heavenward. He could hear the snickering behind him catch hold and pass around the circle like a flare in the forge, exactly what he was trying to keep from happening.

Her teeth glinted white in the lamplight that formed an oblong patch of gold on the steps and beyond. "See you Monday." She spun and darted off before he could think of another thing to say. She didn't seem to understand the meaning of his simple "no."

"Ah, so Katja is after ye," one of the hecklers said.

"She don't go for nobody," another added, masking a ribald comment behind his hand. The man next to him nearly fell off his stump for laughing.

Hjelmer could feel the heat begin in his neck and quickly work its way up over his jaw. This he didn't need, not now, not ever. In his heart of hearts, only Penny reigned. If Penny still cared for him. Why hadn't she written? He snorted on the way to his bunk. Why should she write after he never answered the first one? Were all the letters—if she did write—stacking up in the Fargo Post Office, waiting for him to come pick them up?

He flung himself down on his bunk rather than going back to his carving for the moment. What a mess he was making of his life. Big Red's men were after him to join the poker games, and as Leif said, they didn't let up till you gave in and lost every dollar you had earned. He hadn't written home to Nordland, either, let alone to his relatives on the bank of the Red River. Would they think him dead? A few more months and he would have a good stake put by. If only he could go home to the farm on the prairie. But if he did, that Strand would hold the shotgun on him until he married Mary Ruth. He slammed a hand on the post holding up the bunks. That baby was *not* his. He'd never disgraced her or any woman, in spite of the teasing on the fishing boat and now here.

Thoughts of swishing skirts and raven's wing curly hair filled his mind. It wasn't for want of chances, that was for sure. He heaved himself to his feet and rejoined the men around the stove. He might be a gambler, but he wasn't a skirt chaser.

The men passed around a flat bottle, each taking a swig and wiping off the neck. "Here's your turn, ye missed the last."

"No thanks." Hjelmer continued with his carving, fashioning the eagle's eye with the tip of his knife.

"You don't drink; you don't gamble; you don't go after women. Son, you sure are some boring." A glob headed for the spittoon and missed as usual.

Sam chuckled, his grizzly head nodding in delight. "He got principles, he do dat."

"Well, principles ain't gonna protect him from Big Red much longer. After payday tomorrer, you better be ready to play or run."

Hjelmer swallowed. He'd been afraid of that. Walking past a table set up for play was like asking a drunk to not drink. He could make some real money so easy that way. Double his earnings or more. He carefully wrapped the eagle in its soft leather blanket and tucked it into the sack along with his tools.

"Night, fellows." He rose and stretched. "Don't stay up too late. Workday tomorrow."

"Payday, you mean." A cackle followed Hjelmer outside to the privy. When he returned and crawled under his quilt and blanket, he sighed. Tomorrow he would decide. After all, did the vow not to gamble ever again really count when he'd made it only to himself?

*And to God.* He could hear his mother's voice plain as the night was dark. He hadn't said the words to God, had he? And besides, God didn't seem to matter much out here on the prairie where you heard His name mostly as a swear word.

When morning came, he'd made a choice. He would play dumb like Leif had so they wouldn't plague him anymore. He hated losing his paycheck to prove the point.

That evening after picking up his pay, he hustled into the store set up four cars beyond the cookshack and paid off his chit. New gloves and blankets cost dear at the company store, but he needed them both. A sheepskin coat was next on his list. On a whim he laid down the cost of the leather thigh-length jacket.

"You want to buy the coat now?" The clerk shook his head. "Ain't got none in stock."

"I'm paying in advance. Let me know when they come in."

"Waal, I don' know. We ain't never done this afore." He scratched the bald spot glowing under the lamplight.

"So this is the first. Just write it in by my name like you did the other things and mark paid."

Tongue between his teeth, the scrawny man did as told.

"Mange takk." Hjelmer jingled the remaining coins in his pocket. Now if he could just get to his eagle bag, he'd insert some of his remaining pay into the hollowed-out hole in the base of the prairie dog he'd carved earlier. A plug filled in the hole in the meantime.

One day he'd have to take time off to get to a bank. Perhaps after the snow got too deep to work. The foreman, Hanson, had asked him if he'd like to work in the roundhouse at Fargo or maybe St. Paul. He'd not given an answer yet.

"So, you gonna try out my idea?" Leif fell into step with him when he left the bunkhouse.

Hjelmer nodded. "If I can manage this, I oughta go on stage like that actor fellow we saw advertised in the store." Posters told of a handsome man starring in a stage play at the theater in Fargo.

"I'll be a-watchin' your back. They think I'm dumb as a drunk rooster when it comes to cards."

"Just so they don't think we're in cahoots. Got run out of another town 'cause a big guy thought I was cheating." Hjelmer lifted the tent flap and ducked inside. Smoke grayed the tent and set him to coughing after the crisp evening air. Four tables, each with a lantern above and four to six men sitting around it, about filled up the available space except for that set aside for the bar.

His gut seemed to purr. He forced a blank look across his features and strolled over to the table where Big Red presided. If he was going to play, he might as well play in the lion's den.

"I see you finally decided to play smart." Big Red removed the cigar from his mouth and waved it in Hjelmer's direction. "Just in time, right, boys?" Heads nodding around the table warned the young man of what he might have missed out on.

"I told you I don't know much about cards. My far didn't hold with wasting time on such things." He hoped his father wouldn't mind taking the blame.

"Wasting time, is it?" Red's sandy eyebrows lowered. "We'll see about that, yes we will." He pointed to a man two off from his right and jabbed a thumb toward the door behind them. The man near to crashed his chair over in his hurry to vacate his seat.

Hjelmer caught the rocking chair and slid into it. He shook his head at the bartender's offer of a drink and looked around the table.

Most of the chips mounded in front of Red.

Not surprised, he tried to think how he would act if he really knew nothing about cards in general and poker in particular. How much would a greenhorn know? The names of the cards? Surely not the plays or how to count.

"We're playin' Five Card Draw." Red shuffled the deck one more time and began dealing the hand.

"So, what does that mean?"

Snickers came again but died the moment Red looked at the guilty ones.

"You told me you would teach me if I came to play. Now, I ain't playing a game I don't know nothing about." Hjelmer leaned his elbows on the table, making the now silent man next to him look about the size of a yearling compared to a full-grown bull.

"Sorry. I forgot I said that." Red licked his lips.

"Just want to keep everything on the up and up here. I heard about you fellows taking advantage of newcomers and . . ."

Red waved him silent. He laid out a few simple rules and dealt another card.

"Maybe if I could write down some of that, like what a full barn means and . . ."

A look of pain caused Red to squint. "I 'spect that would help but it's called full house."

"Not barn!" exploded on a guffaw across the table.

"Oh, sorry." Hjelmer waved to the bartender. "You got any writing paper and pencil behind that counter? I need to make some notes."

"How about if we play out a hand and you watch."

Hjelmer caught the wink Red sent to one of his friends. "Fine with me. But can I ask questions as you go along?"

Leif covered his snort with a coughing fit. "Smoke." He fanned his face with his hand.

When the paper arrived, Hjelmer stuck the tip of his tongue out between his teeth, gripped the pencil till it screamed, and wrote full house. The cards had all been dealt, and silence hovered, a pall above them like the smoke. He looked up. "Now, what did you say makes a . . . a full house?" He glanced down at the paper, as if needing the reminder.

A sigh to his left cut off at Red's look.

Red smiled like a friendly uncle. "That's three cards of one rank, say the queen, and two of another, like maybe threes or sumpin'. Whatever guy has the highest in the three is the winner."

Hjelmer nodded. He'd never written so slow since he entered school.

By the time Hjelmer had written down all the ways of winning and which cards won over which, the man across from him, who'd been drinking steadily from the bottle by his side, exploded.

"I thought we came here to play cards, not wet-nurse some Norsky kid."

"Ears!" The one word was enough to stop him from further tirade, but he continued mumbling into his hand.

"Okay, now I'm ready to watch you play." Hjelmer leaned to the man on his right. "Okay if I watch your cards?"

Leif stepped outside, presumably for fresh air. Hjelmer could hear him coughing. "Sad the smoke bothers him so much. He might like to have sat in too." Was it "heaven preserve us" he heard from off to his left?

"Play!" Red snapped.

The game proceeded with the drinking man finally raking in the pot.

Hjelmer started to ask a question halfway through the hand, but the look on Red's face said he'd better not.

"You get to keep *all that*?"

The grin failed to reach the man's eyes.

"I think I like this game. Pass me some cards."

Red now wore a pained expression. "We say 'deal me in.' "

"Oh." Hjelmer wanted to look over at Leif, who'd returned to the card party, but he knew he couldn't keep a straight face if he did.

"No! Don't touch that card till they're all dealt." Only a whip in an expert hand cracked with the precision of Red's command.

Hjelmer withdrew his hand. When the other players picked up their cards, he followed suit. Trying to put them in some kind of order, he dropped one and it floated to the floor face up. When he leaned over to pick it up, he fumbled with it. "It's stuck to the floor. Ah, there, I got it," he said, sitting back up and splashing a goofy grin on his face. "Now what?"

"We bid."

Hjelmer studied the paper beside his right hand. "Now, let's see, those two match and . . ." He leaned closer to the man beside him, showed him his hand, and asked, "Would you bid on that?"

"You can." The man edged his hand away so Hjelmer couldn't see the cards.

"Mange takk." When his turn came around, he threw a quarter in the pot like most of the others. Another time around and he did the same. The urge to fold grew in his belly.

"I'm out." The first to fold laid down his cards.

"Pass." Four men remained, including both Red and Hjelmer.

Finally head to head, Red bid him up. He tossed in a quarter. "I'll call ya."

"Call me what? My name's Hjelmer Bjorklund as you well know." He thickened his Norwegian accent, looking puzzled. Then as if he finally got the joke, he laughed. "Sorry. That means you want I should lay down my cards, right?" He spread them out. A mishmash of nothing.

Red cackled and scooped the coins to the pile in front of him. "Well, son, you *are* learning."

Two more hands went the same way but with Hjelmer folding early. "I don't like to give my money away like that."

"You don't bid, you don't win." Red's smile had reverted to that of benevolent uncle.

Down to one quarter, Hjelmer bid on the next hand. When it came his turn again, he whispered to the man next to him. "If'n you loan me a couple quarters, I'll pay you back later."

The man tossed his cards in, scooped up his meager winnings, and slammed out of his chair. "You want me to play anymore, Red, you keep these dumb immigrants outta here." He headed for the bar.

"Here." Leif handed Hjelmer some more change.

"Oh good. I thought to play this hand." Hjelmer stared at the three aces he'd been dealt. He signaled for one hit. Another ace. Now what? Act stupid or clean house? He kept on bidding. The pot grew. It was left to him and Red after the final "too rich for my blood."

Smoke billowed from the cigar clamped between Red's stained teeth.

*Quit reading the other players*, Hjelmer ordered himself. If he followed through on his instincts, he'd have Red by the throat. The stink of taking advantage of a sucker radiated from the man in waves. And there was no way to undo his hand at this point. When it came his turn to bid, he shook his head. "Out of money again." When Leif stepped forward, Hjelmer gave a barely perceptible shake of his head.

"Beat that then, son." Red spread his cards on the table. "A full house." He laid down three queens and two jacks.

"Oh, that means I lost again." Hjelmer laid his hand down. "I only got four ones and this other card."

An expletive burst from Red's mouth, causing the cigar to teeter and drop glowing ash on his hand. A second vile assembly of words trailed the first.

When a titter started on one side of the table, Red squelched it with a glare. "Pick up your money, son."

"You mean all that is mine?" Hjelmer leaned forward and scooped the stack of coins to his place. "I think I like this game. Now what?"

"Beginner's luck," grumbled a man sliding his chair back. "I ain't staying here wet-nursing no baby." Several other men followed. Finally Red nodded.

"Well, it's about closing time, anyhow." He beckoned Hjelmer to his side.

"Mange takk for inviting me." Hjelmer ducked his head. "I come next week too."

"Don't be hasty. Perhaps you better learn to play the game before you return. Makes things more interesting that a way." The benevolent uncle had returned to everything but the man's eyes. "Understand?"

"Ahhh, and I was just beginnin' to have a fine time." Hjelmer shook his head. "You sure about that?"

Red nodded. He signaled to the giants on either side of him, and as one, the three stood.

Hjelmer stepped back so as not to get his feet trodden on. He ducked his head again as if being polite and left the tent. Once outside, he drew in a deep breath and let it out with a whoosh. One good thing, he'd signed his death warrant if he ever tried to play in this camp again. He jingled the coins in his pocket, now feeling heavy since there were considerably more than when he started out.

Leif joined him in the darkness. Together they strode toward the bunkhouse. Visions of Penny lit the back of Hjelmer's eyelids. What was she doing this night? Did she still remember that he said he loved her? And that she'd wait? He *had* broken his vow, but it turned out all right in the end. Surely that meant God didn't count the vow as real.

*But to be safe, I won't play again*, he promised himself.

## 8

"Oh, hurry, Inge, please hurry." Kaaren tried to stop the bleeding, but she had no more rags at hand without getting up from the bed. Moving terrified her. What if she bled to death before Ingeborg could get there? Why, oh why, had she insisted Metiz go home? She'd felt so much stronger, and with Lars coming in soon from the fields, she thought they could all sleep till he came. And Metiz had needed rest too.

She heard feet thudding against the hard-packed dirt, and immediately the door flew open as if by a huge wind.

"Inge, I'm so glad you're here." Kaaren tried to keep the tears from squeezing under her eyelids, but one was more determined than she. She dashed it away and tried to smile, but her lips quivered beyond her control.

"What is it?" Ingeborg crossed the room, her hand to her breast, trying to catch her breath. At the same moment she saw the spreading stain on the sheet. "Oh, dear Lord above, help us now." She turned at the door opening again. Thorliff stuck his head in.

"Go for Metiz!"

"Baptiste already did."

"Oh, please, Father," Ingeborg murmured as she gathered the clean strips of cloth off the line between the stove and the wall. "Then get Lars," she ordered Thorliff.

At that moment the riverboat steam whistle shrieked across the land.

Ingeborg sucked in a deep breath. "That must be Solveig. It is late in the day for the boat to come by. Lars will be coming in on the horse. You run down to the dock and tell them someone is coming."

"I could row out and get her." Thorliff stood a little straighter, as if that might make him big enough to be trusted with the task.

"You help Lars, all right?" She heard the door slam behind him. Packing the strips in place, she massaged Kaaren's low belly. "Metiz said this sometimes helps."

Kaaren flinched and grasped her lower lip between her teeth.

"Feel those cramps?"

She nodded. "S-silly question."

"They're good news. I know there is something I could brew, but I don't remember what. Oh, Metiz, we need you. I should know so much more."

"H-how could you?"

"I don't know, but praying for wisdom, I am." She kept up the rhythmic kneading, massaging deep till it seemed she could feel Kaaren's backbone. While her hands kept busy, she pounded the ear of God with her pleas.

She heard a horse galloping by and knew Lars had heard the whistle too. *Dear Lord, send us Metiz soon.* She checked the packing and breathed a sigh of relief. The flow seemed to be slowing. "Praise God, my dear sister, He led us to do right."

One of the tiny girls lying in the bed beside Kaaren whimpered. Ingeborg kept up her circular kneading motions and nodded toward the miniature bundles. "They are both nursing better now?"

Kaaren nodded. "Twice since you left. Another thing to praise God for." She took in a deep breath, feeling like the millstone that had been roosting on her chest had rolled away. "Oh, Inge, what would we ever do without you? Just the sight of you, so strong and capable, calms my fears."

"Ja, well, I do for you and you do for me. That's what this life is all about. Just think, Solveig should be here soon. Then you needn't fret about the things not getting done."

"How did you know that?"

Ingeborg smiled down at her. "I know you." She glanced around the soddy. The dinner dishes still sat in the dishpan. Metiz must have cooked the meal or one of the men did. "Did everyone eat here?"

"Ja, and Haakan has Andrew out with him. We decided you needed to sleep."

"Me? What about you?"

"That's all I do is sleep." She looked down at the slings by her side. "And feed babies."

"That's about the best you can."

"I shouldn't have sent Metiz home, but she was looking gray around the mouth. I forget sometimes that she is an old woman." Kaaren's eyes drifted closed and she slept again.

A whisper of air moved behind Ingeborg, and she turned to find Metiz crossing the room.

"Bad?"

"Thought so there for a few minutes. What was in that tea you brewed?"

"Brought more." Metiz returned to the stove and, lifting the lid, stuck in several pieces of cut wood. "Need water to boil."

"I must have slept like the dead." Ingeborg stretched, pushing her fists against the ache in her back from bending over the low bed. Even now her eyes felt gritty, as if someone had thrown sand in them.

The wood caught fire and snapped in the silence. The window flamed like a square of fire as the setting sun painted red on the silver of the stove. Ingeborg lifted the lamp from the shelf above the wedding chest Kaaren had brought from home and set it on the table. After trimming the wick, she took a sliver of pitch wood and, lighting it in the stove, set the lamp to burning. Gold flickered and flared, then steadied when she set the chimney in place.

"There, that's better. I should get supper started. The men will be back in a moment. Did you hear the whistle? That means Solveig is finally here." She knew she was chattering, but for some reason couldn't seem to stop. "I'm going out to the cellar." Pushing the door open, she stepped outside and breathed in deeply the chill fall air. With the coming of dusk, the wind kicked up, bringing with it a taste of frost. The way the temperature was dropping, she knew they'd wake to a silver morning.

She hummed to herself as she lifted a haunch of smoked elk down in the smokehouse and filled her apron with carrots and onions from the cellar. She stopped. No, stew would take too long. She would cut off slabs of elk, fry onions and potatoes, and make biscuits. If only she hadn't slept the afternoon away, she could have baked a cake or pie for dessert. No matter what, they would celebrate the arrival of the latest emigrant from Nordland. There would be letters from home, so they could catch up on all the news. Oh, it will be so wonderful. Solveig will know all the answers to her and Kaaren's questions about home. Men never shared the bits of daily life that women did. At least Hjelmer hadn't when he arrived.

Returning to the house, she saw the horse and rider returning from the river. They must have left her trunks down at the river to be picked up with the wagon.

The boys ran on ahead and caught her at the doorway.

"She's not here," Thorliff panted.

"Not here? Then what. . . ?"

"Onkel Lars will tell you. Only a paper came. A . . . a telegram, Onkel said."

"What's a telegram?" Baptiste asked, nudging his friend.

"I read about it in a book. A message is sent over wire strung between poles by something called Morse code. On some kind of machine they tap out the message made of dots and dashes."

Ingeborg caught the look of disbelief on Baptiste's face.

"He's right." She stepped forward as Lars galloped up.

"It's bad news, Ingeborg. Boys, go get Haakan and Andrew. Tell him to hurry so we only have to talk about this one time. You bring in the other horses and unharness them. We'll tell you all about it later." As he talked, he swung his leg over the horse's withers and slid to the ground, handing the boys the reins. "Up you go." He boosted them both on the broad back of the dark gelding and sent them on their way with a slap on the horse's rump.

"Come inside. Kaaren is frantic with worry, I can tell."

"What is it? What's wrong?" The babies started to cry at Kaaren's agitation that made her try to sit up.

"No! Lie still!" Metiz ordered. She removed the sling from around Kaaren's shoulder and gently swung the babies until they settled down again. "You make worse."

"I'm sorry, but what is going on?" Kaaren's hands fluttered like moths around a lamp.

"It's Solveig. She's been in a train wreck. That is why she hasn't gotten here yet."

"Is she . . . is she dead?"

Lars shook his head. "Now lie back and I will read this to all of us. Haakan will be here in a moment, and I thought to wait for him."

"No, tell me now." Kaaren shielded her eyes with the back of her hand.

Lars moved closer to the lamp that flickered in the breeze from the open door.

With Andrew on his shoulders, Haakan ducked through the door, setting the little boy down in one smooth motion.

"Mor, horse go fast." Andrew flung himself at his mother's skirt, his grubby face one huge grin. "Far ride me."

"Ja, Mor's good boy."

"Hungry."

Ingeborg listened out both sides of her head, both to Lars comforting Kaaren and to Andrew demanding her attention. She picked him up and handed him a slice of potato.

"The captain brought this telegram from Fargo. Said it came in yesterday. It reads: 'To Mrs. Lars Knutson, stop.'" He looked up. "They write that at the end of each sentence." He returned to his reading, tipping the paper to get better light. "'Solveig Hjelmson injured, train wreck. Stop. Can travel, needs assistance. Stop. Come immediately. Stop. Dr. Louis Amundson. Stop. Reply requested. Stop.'" Lars looked up from the square yellow paper. "That and the address is all we know."

"Thanks be to God, she is alive." Ingeborg clasped Andrew to her until he began to squirm.

"Hungry, Mor." He patted her shoulder to get her attention.

Kaaren's lips moved in silent prayer. She sighed when she opened her eyes. "What will we do? Who will go?"

"The captain said he'd pick up the one we send on his way back upriver in the morning." Lars sank down on the nearest chair. Metiz continued to sway the sling, comforting the little ones. Haakan took Andrew from Ingeborg and set him on the box tied to a chair at the table.

"Mor will have supper ready soon. You be good and wait."

At the tone of his voice, Andrew nodded solemnly.

Ingeborg released all the air she'd been unconsciously holding and rubbed the back of her neck. "Supper will be ready in a few minutes." Scooping bacon grease out of the crock on the warming shelf and dotting it in the cast-iron frying pan, she dumped in the chopped onions and sliced potatoes. If her hands kept busy, her mind could think better. Amid the clattering of pans and sizzling grease, she waited for someone to say something.

"I stay, care for Kaaren." Metiz broke the silence.

"I can't leave you and the babies." Lars scrubbed his fingers through his dark hair, standing it on end. "But I can take care of the chores. Haakan, you could go."

"She will need a woman to help her." Haakan turned to look at Ingeborg. "You know her."

Ingeborg nodded. "Since she was little." She turned the slabs of elk meat over and shook the pan of potatoes. The screech of pan against stove made her shiver. Or was that the news about Solveig that really sent frissons of fear skittering up and down her back?

"You must go, Ingeborg. We could ask Penny to come help Metiz and me. Haakan, you will go with?"

He looked from Ingeborg to Lars and back again. "There is so much work to do. Could you go by yourself?"

Ingeborg swallowed hard. Taking the boat to Grand Forks wasn't a problem. She'd done that before. She could board the train there for St. Paul. But all alone? Changing trains and finding the hospital? How much help did Solveig need? How badly was she hurt? Remembering the terror of being lost in New York made her hands shake as she set plates and silverware on the table. Could she read English well enough to read street signs now? To tell a buggy driver where to go?

Haakan took the long knife from her clenched hand and set about slicing the bread. "I will eat quickly so I can help the boys with the chores."

"Maybe Solveig will need someone stronger if she cannot walk." Ingeborg kept her voice low, for Haakan's ears alone.

"Ja, I thought of that too." His chest swelled with the breath he took in. "If it would make you and Kaaren feel easier, I will go with you. The barn will just have to wait."

"And if the snow comes?"

"Then we will build on the good days. It will all work out, Inge, but the most important part is keeping Kaaren calm and the babies alive. If my staying here would make that more possible . . ." He shrugged. "I just don't know."

Lars left Kaaren's bedside and came to join them. "I will send Thorliff over to the Baards' first light. He can bring Penny back, and knowing Agnes, she will be here as soon as she can hitch up the wagon."

"But she shouldn't be driving the wagon now." Visions of Agnes's feet swelling out over the moccasins Metiz had made for her when her shoes became too tight made Ingeborg shake her head. "Nei, she must stay home and take care of herself. Perhaps Petar could come to help with the field work for a few days."

Lars nodded. "Ja, he will. You know Joseph. He will have the whole neighborhood here, putting up the barn, adding the lean-to on your house, and sending the others out into the field to break sod." Lars shook his head. "You know Baard."

"Come talk over here so I can hear too." Kaaren's voice held a note of command that was unusual for her.

Ingeborg turned from checking the potatoes and saw Metiz laying one of the twins at her mother's breast. The other whimpered, mewling like a week-old kitten. How would Kaaren ever have enough milk for the two of them?

The discussion continued around the table, but Ingeborg could tell it was all decided. She and Haakan would be rowing out to catch the boat in the morning.

Haakan left, and in a few minutes the boys came in, each carrying a full bucket of milk.

"You want we should put these in the springhouse?"

"No, set them there out of the way and come and eat." Ingeborg cleared Haakan's plate away and set two for the boys. "Go wash first."

"How much more is to be done?" Lars asked as the boys slid into their chairs.

"Far went to milk at our house. We fed all the rest of the animals, let the horses and oxen out in the center field to graze. The horses weren't hot or nothing."

"Forgot the eggs." Baptiste paused in lifting a forkful of meat to his mouth. He started to rise. "I go do that."

"After you eat." Ingeborg laid a hand on his arm. "You boys have done a fine job. Mange takk."

After the kitchen was cleaned up and dishes all put away, Ingeborg turned to Metiz. "I will stay. You go home and sleep."

"I sleep here." Metiz pointed to a pallet she'd arranged on the floor.

"No. You sleep in the other bed, and I will take the floor." Lars looked up from smoothing back the hair from Kaaren's forehead.

Metiz shook her head.

Ingeborg hid a smile behind her hand. None of them had ever succeeded in getting Metiz to do something she was set against. She just acted as if she didn't hear you, like now as she lay down facing the wall and pulling the cover over her shoulder.

"Inge!"

"Don't look at me." She raised her hands in the air, palms upward. "I'm going home to bed." She picked up Andrew, who had curled up on an old coat in his special place behind the stove and was sound asleep. With him nestled into her shoulder, she turned back. "You call me if there is any problem."

Kaaren nodded. "Mange takk, so many times over." She waved

one hand. "Thank you again for my life." Her voice choked on the last word.

Ingeborg strode along the grooves cut into the sod by the many passes of teams, wagons, and machinery. Soon they'd have to string the rope between the houses again, this time before a blizzard caught them. As Haakan said, there was so much to do.

The cold moonlight glimmered on the dew frosting the stacks of lumber set back from the barn. Paws greeted her, tail wagging and tongue lolling. Lamplight spilled from the window, losing the battle with the bright moon for a square of the earth. Ingeborg shivered, and while it was cold, she knew it wasn't from that.

"What will tomorrow bring, dear Lord?" She raised her gaze to the heavens, the blackness stapled in place by the myriad of stars. "Take care of Solveig and Kaaren and the babes. Father, I leave them in your hands, for mine are far too small and weak. You are God, and I thank you." She sniffed. Must be the cold that made her nose run.

As soon as she put Andrew to bed, she got down on her knees and dug way back under the bed for the carpetbag they had brought from Norway. She dusted it off and removed the carded wool all ready for spinning she'd stuffed inside. One more thing to do as soon as she could no longer work in the fields. She stroked the fine strands saved from the prime pelt of the merino sheep she'd paid such a high price for. This wool felt like the inner down of the goose compared to the wool from the other sheep. Her lambs, while crossbred, were showing the same length of strand. One of them, the male, she would keep for breeding.

Thinking of the dyes she would use on this fine wool, she stuffed it into a pillow slip and shook any remaining strands out of the bag. One corner looked as if a mouse had chewed it but had given up before getting through.

"Uff da." She got to her feet and set the bag on the table. What should they take? How long would they be gone? Questions continued to ripple through her mind like a field of wheat bending before the breeze.

It was a good thing she had just washed clothes a couple of days earlier. She folded underthings, a shirtwaister for her, a clean shirt for Haakan, and packed them in the bag. Her hairbrush and other things would go in in the morning. She rubbed the corner of her mouth.

"Mor?" Thorliff and Baptiste let the door slam behind them.

"Shhh, Andrew is sleeping."

"Sorry. Far said he'll be in pretty quick. Can we have some bread and sugar?"

Ingeborg nodded. Surely there was something she was forgetting. Towels, washcloths, and soap. She would pack a hamper of food in the morning. Even later in bed, her mind refused to quiet down and go to sleep. How badly was Solveig hurt? Instead of being a help, she would need care. *Uff da*. Ingeborg turned over for the third time.

"Cannot sleep?"

"Nei. What if we don't find the hospital? Chicago is a big place."

"The doctor gave us the name, and we will ask for directions." He turned to face her. "You are worried. That is not like you."

"I know. I just hate to leave Kaaren right now. If something happens to those babies . . ."

"You will not blame yourself. We believe God knows best, and He alone can give life or keep it. If He wants the babies with Him, there is nothing we can do about it. Nor blame ourselves."

"I know, but they are so small and helpless. Just keeping them warm enough—"

"Metiz is there. Penny will help, and the boys will do all they can."

Ingeborg reached over and laid her hand on his stubbled cheek. "You are so good to me, Mr. Bjorklund, calming me instead of sleeping like you need."

He turned his face and kissed the palm of her hand. "I thank God every day for you."

Ingeborg felt the tears sting her eyes. His words and actions again caught her off guard. What was she doing worrying when she was so blessed?

She laid her head on his chest and, with a sigh of contentment, fell into the peace of sleep.

After a flurry of chores, messages back and forth between the soddies, and final packing of food and necessaries, they made it to the rowboat in time for the second whistle. The captain had tooted the horn two miles or so downriver so they could get there in time.

Ingeborg made her way up the swaying ladder to the deck. Boarding from a dock was definitely easier. When Haakan swung over the railing, she waved good-bye to Lars in the boat and to the boys on the bank. Thorliff and Baptiste waved one last time and then ran back into the trees.

Haakan took her hand in his. No matter what lay ahead, they would meet it together.

## 9

W hat's that you are studying so seriously?" Ingeborg glanced at the page of numbers that captured Haakan's attention.

"The reorder for the lumber that was burned up." He traced a column of figures down and wrote the total at the bottom. "I'll drop it off while we're in Grand Forks, and maybe we'll be able to pick it up in Grafton soon as we get home." He glanced up at the drop in the thumps of the stern-wheeler. Water hissed off the slowly turning paddles as the boat nosed into the dock. A bump, followed by hollered instructions from the captain to the deckhands, and they were tied firmly. A man on the dock cranked on a wheel, and the suspended ramp began to swing out to the vessel.

As soon as the ramp was secured, the few passengers walked over it, and the stevedores immediately followed with trunks and bales and burlap sacks of grain.

The hubbub rose around them, and Ingeborg tucked her arm under Haakan's elbow. He smiled down at her, obviously still thinking about the lumber order.

"The barn can wait if it has to," she murmured, lifting her face so she could be heard.

"It don't have to. This way we won't lose too much time, just money."

"Uff da, as if we are made of it."

"If harvests continue like the last couple of years, it won't be long before that could happen." Haakan pointed toward the lumberyard down one side street. "You want to come with me? The captain said we would have plenty of time to sight-see before—"

"And turn in the lumber order?"

"Ja, that too." Haakan tucked the folded paper into his breast pocket inside the navy jacket he'd bought for the wedding. "Come on, wife, we have work to do."

By the time they caught the eastbound train, he'd ordered the lumber and learned of a man with a lumber mill for sale. "Just think, three days and our wood will be in Grafton." He shook his head in wonderment. "I had them send a message back with the riverboat captain so that Lars will know that."

"But surely Lars won't leave Kaaren and the babies?" Ingeborg felt stabbed by a bolt of homesickness. She should have stayed there to help out.

Haakan shook his head. "But maybe Joseph and Petar could pick up a load each. We'll just have to see how it goes and be grateful God can see the whole picture."

Ingeborg nodded. Whether she was warp or woof in the tapestry, she wished for a chance to see it from above too.

Early the next morning, the conductor called from behind them, "Minneapolis, St. Paul."

"So much change," Ingeborg murmured when the train crossed the bridge of many arches over the Mississippi River into St. Paul. The conductor had visited with them for some time, answering all their questions about the new bridge, this one of cut granite blocks and a series of arches to support it. He'd said the bridge received national attention as a new type of architecture.

"There's where our wheat comes." Haakan pointed to the flour mills bordering the river. "I've heard they have a monopoly on buying wheat and ship flour all over the country."

Ingeborg shook her head. "That means they can control the prices we get, doesn't it?"

Haakan nodded. "Some of the Dakota farmers are talking of starting up their own mills."

"How do you know that?" Ingeborg left off staring out the window and turned to him.

"I hear things. The men don't just talk of plowing and planting after church, you know." He nodded. "There's lots of change in store, you mark my words. The railroad coming close to our farms will bring nothing but change."

Ingeborg agreed and turned back to the window. In spite of the sights that flashed past so swiftly, her mind returned to the soddy on the plains where Kaaren and her two baby girls struggled for life. Back at their homestead was where she really would rather be, not clacking along at this outrageous speed, fearing she'd be thrown right out the window were she able to open it.

"St. Paul," the conductor intoned as he passed down the aisle again. "This is where you folks change trains. Good luck to you on your journey."

"Thank you," Haakan said with a smile. "You've been most helpful."

The man touched a finger to the narrow visor of his hat and left their car for the one in front. The wind from the opening and closing door tossed the hem of Ingeborg's skirt and smelled of burning coal. A cinder stung her cheek.

"Uff da," she muttered, using her handkerchief to wipe the grime away. Trains might be fast, but they were certainly dirty. As the train slowed, Haakan stood to retrieve their carpetbag from the overhead rack. Ingeborg clutched the satchel that held the remainder of their food. Some of the people had eaten in the dining car, but when she heard the prices they paid for the meal, she shuddered, grateful for their own cheese and bread.

She took the conductor's offered hand as she stepped from the train stairs to the metal stool he'd set for them and down to the platform. "Mange takk." She started again. "Thank you." In spite of all their practice with the English language, it was so easy to forget to use it, especially like now when she felt strung tight as the barbed wire fence at home.

"You have a good trip now," he returned with a nod and a smile. "Hope you find your sister-in-law fitten for travel. Maybe I'll see you on your return trip."

She nodded, moving forward to allow other passengers to step down to the marble-tiled platform. Such a good man and so friendly. She thought of that other train ride and her fear of the man in the blue wool uniform, looking so like the policeman who'd yelled at her in New York. Being able to talk the language made such a difference. Why couldn't the new immigrants take to heart the admonitions to learn the American language before they crossed the sea? Hjelmer hadn't, but then to be honest, neither had they.

Hjelmer. Was he working here in this big city or out on the western prairies? How . . . when would they know?

"Come." Haakan took her arm, and together they made their way to the large boards that announced the times of trains leaving and arriving. People flowed around them, some dressed so fine she wanted to brush up her skirt and tuck the errant strands of hair back in their braids. Others reminded her only of that other train ride when she felt certain her eyes had held the same combination of fear and astonishment she saw now on people's weary faces. She recognized the German language one woman used to scold her children. Two men spoke Swedish, and a man in a black homburg hat and black wool coat reminded her of Mr. Gould, her New York angel, as she still thought of him.

She would like nothing more than to sit and watch the crowds go by, but Haakan hurried her over to a ticket window. While she'd been gawking, he'd been studying the boards. He bought their tickets, and she smiled at a boy who looked much like Thorliff, only missing the deep blue Bjorklund eyes. A pang shot through her heart. How he would love to be with them. Her ears would be tired by now from his unending questions, but to see the delight on his face would be worth the questions.

"We have two hours to wait." Haakan picked up the worn carpetbag again and led them to a high-backed wood bench that reminded her of the carved pews in the churches of Nordland.

"I will use that time to write a letter to our families at home then." She sat down and leaned back.

"Our families on the plains of Dakota Territory or the ones on the mountains of Norway?" Haakan teased her as he sat down next to her. "Would you like something to drink? I could buy us each a cup of coffee before I go send the telegram to the hospital." He nodded to an area of table and chairs where folks sat eating, reading a newspaper, or visiting. The fragrance of coffee had already tickled her nose and made her stomach rumble.

"Such an expense."

"I *can* afford a cup of coffee for myself and my wife." Haakan jingled the coins in his pants' pocket. His attempt at a stern face failed as she drew herself up like a rooster going into combat. "Oh, Inge, you should see the look on your face. You'd have thought I uttered blaspheme or some such."

Her smile won out. "Coffee would taste good, but we could share a cup."

Haakan got to his feet, shaking his head. "I'll be right back."

Watching him make his way through the crowd still set her heart aflutter. To cover the reaction, she took out the piece of precious paper she'd found on the train, the bit of pencil she'd borrowed from Thorliff, and began to write.

"My dear family. We are well and I have much news." She slipped back into the familiar Norwegian and pictured her mother's face as she'd read this aloud to family and neighbors. While her mother had surely aged, she could only think of her as she'd been when they left that life, what seemed so many lives ago. "Kaaren has had her baby, and to our joy, she had twin girls, naming them Sophie and Grace. We pray for their lives, as they came early and are so tiny you can hold one in the palm of your hand, almost." She put the pencil in her lap. *Dear Lord, how are they? Please let them grow stronger and please be with Kaaren to heal her also. Give her plenty of milk and . . ."*

"Here's your coffee." Haakan held out a heavy white mug.

"Mange takk." Ingeborg eyed the words traveling across the page. She sipped the coffee, inhaling the aroma as she would that of a rose on a warm summer morning.

Haakan dug in their food parcels and brought out a slice of bread and a piece of cheese. Folding the bread in half over the cheese, he handed it to her and started one for himself.

"I should have done that."

"No mind. You write your letter. I'll make sure you don't pass out because of hunger."

A surge of warmth flashed from her belly to her cheeks at his teasing grin. Such a man God had sent her. Had she even begun to tell her family what a fine man he was? Probably not. She'd rather be breaking sod than writing letters, and her mother would never understand that. So she let Kaaren do most of the letter writing. But today was different. She could take out her knitting or watch the other travelers or—she returned to her letter as she alternately chewed her sandwich and sipped her coffee.

"We are in the train station at St. Paul on our way to find Solveig. Our sad news is that she was hurt in a train wreck, but we do not yet know how bad." She continued on with news of the farm—how many acres they had broken, what had been planted where, and how all the animals were doing. She knew her father wanted to know about the machinery, so she tried to describe the thresher and explain what harvest had been like. Closing with news of Thorliff and Andrew, she signed her name in tiny letters down in one corner. She'd put the sentences so close together that it would be hard to read, but she had too much to tell and so little paper.

"I could buy you more paper, you know." Haakan leaned close, his breath tickling her ear.

"Uff dah. You startled me." Ingeborg patted the area above her heart, calming now from a trip hammer beat. "Why would I need more paper? I am done."

Haakan shook his head. "Oh, Inge, if pennies had voices, all you owned would scream loud enough to be heard a mile away."

"That is why we have a few, both at home and in the bank."

"I know, and why we can buy new machinery and pay it off early." He rose, brushing the crumbs off his trousers. "You wait here. I'm going to the telegraph office down there." He nodded to the far end of the cavernous building. "I'll send that telegram off to the hospital. You all right?"

She nodded and turned from watching three children playing a jumping game on the patchwork tiles.

When he returned, he stopped to listen to the announcer's voice. "There, that is our train. We will get an envelope and stamp for your letter in Chicago." He took her arm to help her stand and bent down for their two bags. "This way."

To her own surprise, Inge fell asleep shortly after the train pulled out of the station and woke just in time to fix her hair and smooth her clothing before they pulled into the Chicago station. The squares of black-and-white marble that covered the floor looked familiar. Thorliff had played jumping games on them when they came west. She also remembered where the necessary was and how sick she had been.

"We will have breakfast here." Haakan stretched and yawned.

"Surely there must be someplace less cheap."

"More cheap, less expensive." His smile took any criticism out of his words.

She shrugged and laughed. "That's what I said. Let's go find such a place."

Guilt at spending so much money on food assailed her as they devoured their bacon and eggs and pancakes. "We should have finished our bread and cheese."

"Ja, we will do that for dinner." Haakan finished his last slice of bacon and eyed the one remaining on her plate. He leaned forward and whispered so only she would hear. "Our bacon is much better."

"Ja, you can have this last piece." She pushed her nearly empty plate toward him. "All you had to do was ask."

His eyes twinkled when he took the offered bacon and crunched it down. "We cut ours thicker too."

Ingeborg shook her head and rolled her eyes toward her eyebrows. Such a man.

But their teasing died an hour later, when, after a buggy ride and traversing the hospital halls, they followed a nurse into a long room lined with beds on both sides. When they stopped at the bed that the nurse said belonged to Miss Solveig Hjelmson, Ingeborg kept her hands from covering her mouth only through sheer will.

⁂

"Tant 'Ren, Andrew hungry." The grubby-faced child stood next to the bed where Kaaren and the babies in their sling lay sleeping.

"Shush." Penny swept him up before he could repeat his plea. "Let Tante Kaaren sleep." She whispered in his ear while carrying him back to the table. "Dinner will be ready pretty soon. Can you wait?"

He shook his head. "Want Mor." His lower lip pushed outward.

Penny shot a questioning look at Metiz, who stirred the stew bubbling on the stove. At the old woman's nod, the girl crossed to the bread box. "Now, you stay right here while I cut you a piece of bread."

Andrew nodded solemnly, all the while twining his fist in her skirt. "Bread and honey."

When she shook her head, he asked, "Jam?"

She handed him the crust and scooped him up to his boxed chair at the table. "Now, you sit there and eat your bread while I go ring the triangle for Mr. Knutson and the boys."

"Me ring." Quick as a river otter, he turned and scooted, rear first, off the box.

With a defeated shake of her head, Penny lodged him on her hip and carried him outside the door. She handed him the cold metal bar and held him so he could bang the triangle suspended on a chain from an iron bracket set into the sod wall. When his banging failed in carrying quality, she held his fist and together they hammered out the dinnertime signal. She grinned back at his delight in the noise. "You are a rascal, you are. How your mor gets anything done and keeps track of you, I'll never know."

She shaded her eyes to see if Lars had turned the horses toward home. Off in the distance she heard the shrieking whistle of the riverboat churning its way upriver. Was that the signal that meant the captain had something for the Bjorklunds, or was he just warning any craft going downriver that he was coming around the bend?

Metiz shook her head no when Penny asked if they needed to

go to the river. "Make three short hoots, like owl."

Penny set Andrew back on his chair and looked across the room to see Kaaren struggling to open her eyes. At her signal, Penny went to the bed to help settle the babies so their mother could sit up. Laying the sling so the tiny bodies slept side by side, she covered them with the quilt and gave Kaaren a hand.

"I feel if I don't get out of this bed right now, I might never make it."

Penny made a face and looked to Metiz, who nodded once. "Okay, but you must be careful. You want I should put the two in the box on the oven door?"

When she got there that morning, the first thing she did was line a box Lars had brought in with a quilt and sheet for the babies to sleep in when they weren't with their mother. Keeping them warm enough was the biggest problem. She and Kaaren had laughed about doing the same thing for baby pigs, only then the lining was straw.

"Help me to the rocker first, please."

Penny chewed her lip. Her aunt Agnes always said those Bjork-lund women were some stubborn. "You sure?"

When Kaaren nodded, Penny leaned over the edge of the bed. "Wrap your arms around me, and I'll do the same to you. Then we can pull together."

"I should wait for Lars, but he'll get all upset, so . . ." She did as told.

"On three." Penny braced her feet and knees against the pole side of the bed. She counted and together they heaved. Or rather, she lifted and Kaaren bit back a whimper. "See, I told you."

"These beds are hard enough to get out of when you feel strong." Kaaren took a deep breath and with great effort swung her legs over the side. "Now."

By the time she stood swaying, totally dependent upon Penny's strength, Kaaren wondered if staying in bed hadn't been a better idea. She heard a cry from the tiny mound under the covers. All the rocking woke Grace, and at the stronger, slightly deeper second whimper, Kaaren shook her head. "Now they are both awake. Let's get me to the rocker." The four-foot distance looked more like an acre.

Penny grabbed the pillow off the bed and put an arm around Kaaren's waist, helping the new mother hobble and sink down into the now pillow-padded rocking chair.

Kaaren leaned her head back with a sigh. "I don't remember being this tired and sore before."

"You never had twins before."

Penny brought a quilt over and tucked it around Kaaren's legs. Then she fetched a shawl and wrapped it around the woman's shoulders. She stepped back. "You want a footstool?"

The whimpers from the bed grew louder.

"What a wonderful sound." Kaaren tucked the ends of the shawl back under her arms. How could she be so tired from just crossing three or four steps? Of course, it had taken *her* more than that since she shuffled but . . . she looked up to see Penny waiting for an answer. "Yes, that would be nice. Then I'll have more of a lap for the babies."

Thorliff and Baptiste burst through the door, wiping their hands on their pants, their faces showing the effects of splashing water on streaks of dirt. "Lars said give him a couple more minutes. He was just finishing taking the harness off."

The two in the bed started crying at the sound of his voice.

"Oh, sorry." He toned it down, the look on his face saying "sorry, I forgot" plain as the streaks of mud said he'd been in the fields.

Penny pointed to their places, shaking her head. "You ever hear of a washcloth for your faces?" She smiled at their chagrined expressions. "If you ain't just like the boys at our house."

"How come they didn't come with you?" Thorliff slipped onto his chair.

"They're too busy splitting shingles. And besides, with Pa and Petar out in the fields, they got all the chores to do."

Thorliff and Baptiste swapped looks that said they had the same.

Metiz dished up the plates and handed them to Penny, who put them in front of the boys. Lars entered at that moment. "Did you already say grace?"

Thorliff put his fork back down. He shook his head.

Lars crossed to pat his wife's shoulder. "Good to see you up, but you could have waited for me to carry you." He looked toward the bed. "Who told them it was eating time?"

"Babies know." Metiz set a bowl of biscuits in the center of the table, fending off Andrew's reaching hand. She looked at Kaaren. "You want eat? Or feed them?" She nodded toward the bed.

"Them." Within moments Metiz had positioned a baby at each breast and helped Kaaren arrange a blanket to cover them. "Good." She took the last place at the table.

Kaaren let the noise recede as she concentrated on the tiny mouths pulling at each breast. Pains in both her breasts and belly made her breathe deeply. This was normal, she remembered from her earlier stints at motherhood. *Thank you, Lord, they are able to nurse, that they are strong enough. Such a miracle you have made happen.* She prayed for Solveig, for Haakan and Ingeborg's safe trip, and thanked Him again for those at the table. To think Penny arrived on one of the Baards' mules with some clothes tied in a bundle behind her, ready to stay however long she was needed. *Thank you, Father, for her, too, and for the Baards who surely are a gift from you. Please care for these your children—your babies—your gift to us.*

The sounds from the table intruded on her reverie.

"Andrew's almost asleep," Thorliff announced.

"Oh my." Penny's chair scraped back. "Here, den lille guten, let's put you to bed."

Andrew tried to argue, but his no came out so sweetly that everyone laughed.

"Just put him in the other bed. He sleeps there often." Kaaren shifted her arm. Tingles shot up it. A baby on each arm could put both arms to sleep, let alone her.

"Are they finished?" Penny asked a few moments later.

"Sophie is. I don't think Grace ate enough, but she is so weak in comparison. Maybe I should feed her more often since she can't seem to nurse very long."

Metiz joined them. She picked up Sophie and rocked the infant in her arms, crooning in her own language.

Kaaren put Grace up to her shoulder and patted the baby's back until a burp came.

Penny took that baby over to the waist-high chest of drawers that Lars had finished just before the babies came. They'd padded the top for a place to change diapers. Once both babies were dry again, she set the box on a chair in front of the open oven door and placed the sleeping girls side by side, closely wrapped in their flannel blankets. Draping a towel over the top, she stepped back, one finger to her chin. "I can't put it any closer, the oven's too hot."

"Put hot rock in box." Metiz turned from ladling stew onto a plate for Kaaren. "Wrap it up."

"Where would I find a rock?"

"At river. Ask Thorliff and Baptiste."

Penny nodded. "Metiz, you think of everything." She was out the

LAURAINE SNELLING

door in an instant, calling the boys as soon as she was beyond range of waking the babies.

The old woman snorted, but her eyes sparkled when she gave Kaaren her plate. "Penny good girl."

For the first time since her labor began, Kaaren appreciated the taste of food again. When Metiz handed her a cup of dark water with steam rising, she drank that right down, too, making only a small grimace at the taste.

"My mor always said to drink lots of milk with new babies to feed. Would you mind heating some for me? Cold things just don't sound too good yet."

Metiz nodded.

Kaaren felt herself dropping into a drowse while she waited, finally forcing herself to mop up the gravy with her last bit of bread. She was as bad as the babies—eat and sleep. She drank the warmed milk and didn't argue when Metiz and Penny helped her back to bed.

The next two days and nights passed in a haze of feeding, eating, sleeping, and longer spells at a time in the rocking chair. The afternoon she stepped outside and felt the sun warm her face, she knew for sure she was on the mend. When the steam whistle tooted three times, she sent Penny down to the landing.

"Either there's a message or someone is coming and will need a ride." Her heart leaped at the thought it might be Ingeborg and Haakan with the injured one, but she ignored it. There was no way they would be returning already.

"The captain said the lumber will be in Grafton day after tomorrow," Penny told Kaaren when she came puffing back to the soddy. "Sure is nice to get messages that way." She put her hand to her chest to catch her breath. *Just think, Hjelmer could come home that way. So much faster than walking or even a horse.* She shut off the "if only" before it had time to sprout into words. All she needed to do was keep busy. At least that was Aunt Agnes's remedy for an aching heart.

That night while Penny and Andrew slept in the other bed and Metiz kept to her pallet on the floor, Kaaren whispered to Lars that she felt like a sow with piglets that wanted to suckle all the time.

"Prettiest sow I ever saw," he whispered back, his breath tickling her ear. "And the prettiest pair of piglets too."

She joined the family for dinner at the table on the third day. When Lars offered extra prayers in gratitude for her growing strength and for the babies, who were still alive, she felt the tears that seemed to hover endlessly on the tips of her eyelashes leave their place and trickle down her cheeks. She brushed them away before the others raised their heads.

Thorliff and Paws announcing that company was coming woke her from a sound sleep a bit later.

"Who is it?" she asked.

The boys shrugged. "One man walking," Baptiste offered. "Pack on shoulder."

Kaaren yawned and stretched. "Go call off Paws so the man feels welcome."

"I'll put the coffeepot on." Penny headed for the stove.

A minute later, Thorliff darted back in the house. "He says he's your onkel, Tante Kaaren. Do you have an Onkel Olaf?"

O nkel Olaf! We thought you died years ago."

The oak-tree solid man removed his hat and held it in front of his chest. He had set his bundle down outside the door when Penny invited him in. "Ja, I was afraid of that. But as you can see, I am still alive. When I heard you was moved to America, I made up my mind to come looking for you."

"How did you hear?" Kaaren tried pushing herself up on the pillows, but her sling full of babies got in the way. At her look of helplessness, Metiz crossed the room and gave her a helping hand. Kaaren waved to the rocking chair. "Sit and be comfortable. Penny will have the coffee ready in a few minutes."

"Well, I finally sat myself down and wrote a letter to my home in Nordland, and my older brother—he inherited the farm there— he wrote me a long letter back. He told about you people homesteading out here and doing such a fine job in spite of your many tragedies. So I come to see my nearest relatives."

"Ja." Kaaren nodded. "Well, thank the Lord. Can you stay? I mean, would you like to work for a while? I mean, we would pay you wages for working." She stuttered and stammered a bit, not quite knowing how to proceed. It wasn't good manners to ask a guest to help, but she could only think God had sent them another pair of hands. Joseph sent his boys every day or came himself, but she knew he had plenty of work of his own.

"You sure? Without asking your husband?"

She smiled. "Things are some different out here. I know Lars will be overjoyed."

"Then I will work for my board and room." The words sounded like a pronouncement with no chance for argument.

Kaaren kept her arms under the warm little bodies in the sling and began the rocking motion that soothed them back to sleep after one whimpered. When she noticed his perplexed look, she shared a smile with Metiz. Yes, things were surely different out here on the Bjorklund farms. Babies in a sling around their mother's neck, boys or women doing man's work when needed, and a husband who even helped with a birthing. Uncle Olaf would have lots of surprises coming his way in the days to come.

"In case you are wondering, my twin baby girls are sleeping here." She gestured to the blue sling. "They were born so tiny that this was the best way we could think of to keep them warm enough. Sometimes we keep them in a box on the oven door."

"How are they now?"

"Getting stronger." She shrugged her shoulders to shift the weight. "Now, tell me what else you learned of home and where you have been all these years." Olaf was the next older brother of her mother, and Kaaren remembered the sadness when they no longer heard from the man. "Does my mor know about you now too?" At his nod, she smiled again. "She must be so happy. Strange that you got a letter before I did."

He only nodded at her many questions. "Mange takk," he said to Penny when she handed him a full coffee cup, and then again when she set a plate of bread and cheese in front of him. With a few terse words he told of his life aboard a merchant marine ship that took him all over the world before it sank on a reef off Florida, his rescue with a few of the other sailors, and then the various jobs he'd held traveling around the country. "I been a cooper of both barrels and buckets, built barns and stores in Wisconsin. Anything of wood, I can make, you know."

Kaaren itched to ask him more about his adventures, but the babies were stirring and she knew that meant feeding time. So she bit her tongue for the moment and looked to Penny.

"Would you please take my onkel out to the field to meet Lars and then show him the other bed in Ingeborg's soddy? The boys will have to sleep on pallets on the floor."

Penny nodded. "You want he should store his bundle over there too?"

"Ja."

"Now, I ain't got to have a bed. Been known to sleep real good in a barn or some such. You know, I ain't saying I have to stay here. I don't want to put you out."

"There's always room for one more." The whimpers turned to the creaks that would soon turn into full-fledged wails. Sophie knew how to get one's attention already. And she always woke up ready to eat—immediately if not before.

Olaf slapped hands whose very scars told of his many kinds of labor, from the missing little finger on his right hand to the bent index finger on his left. Ridges, valleys, gnarly knuckles, a black-and-blue fingernail, all spoke of well-used hands.

"Mange takk for the coffee and bread. I'll be going with the young miss here." He crossed to the bed and stood looking down at the babies, smaller than many baby dolls. With one nicked finger, feather-light, he touched Sophie's cheek. She turned in that direction, lips already circled to suckle. Olaf chuckled. "She be a smart one, that. Takes advantage of anything comes her way." He smiled directly into Kaaren's eyes. "They be something, all right."

She watched him leave the room, feeling as if he'd seen more in her baby than she. She looked up to see Metiz nodding.

"That one wise man." She lifted the sling from around Kaaren's shoulders and helped settle the two to nursing. As usual, Sophie sucked greedily while Grace was still searching. Metiz braced Sophie while Kaaren helped the weaker one. With both of them content, the two women exchanged looks of relief.

"How many children did you have?" Kaaren asked, brave enough at last to ask the old woman a personal question.

"Two man childs, one girl—all gone now. Baptiste born, mother die. My girl."

"Oh, Metiz," Kaaren answered with a heavy sigh. "So much you have borne."

"Life hard. Be born, grow, die. All up to Great Spirit."

Kaaren dropped light kisses on the downy heads of her babies. *Please, God, hold these two in your hand, like you said, in your victorious right hand.* She blinked against the burning at the back of her eyes, sniffing at the same time. Living in the right now meant letting go of both the memories of the past and the fears for the future. Someone had once said there was no room in God's hand for the past or the future, only the now. She nodded, grateful for that memory.

She watched Metiz put more wood in the firebox. "There's a smoked venison haunch in the smokehouse that would be good roasted for supper. We could cook the potatoes and rutabagas, carrots, too, in the same kettle."

"Onions." Metiz dusted her hands. "I get."

They spent the evening getting to know one another. Olaf, much to Kaaren's surprise and delight, was a master storyteller, keeping them entertained until she caught Thorliff bumping his chin on his chest. Andrew had crawled into his warm spot behind the stove hours earlier. After everyone was in bed and the others asleep, Lars whispered in her ear.

"God surely sent us a gift direct from heaven in that man. And to think he came right now when we so needed the extra hands."

"Ja, God is good." Kaaren shifted her sling so she could lie on her side, leaving the twins tightly bound in their blankets and lying close like two of the same piece. She laid her arm over Lars' chest, comforted by his steady heartbeat. God is good, and that said it all.

"Tomorrow Olaf and I will take the two wagons to Grafton to pick up lumber for the barn. The boys will stay home to help you."

"Will Joseph go too?" She felt him nod. "Good." As she'd said, God is good.

Ingeborg swallowed once and yet again. Praying for strength, she crossed the room to where the injured woman lay sleeping in the bed nearest the door of the eight-bed ward. *Ah, Solveig, once so fair, how will you learn to live with that scar?*

The oval face with a straight nose that looked so much like Kaaren's now wore a stitched line slanting from temple to nearly the point of her chin. The bones of her face looked to be poking holes through her skin. Hair, once so full and golden, now hung in strings, showing an area above her left ear that had been shaved so the doctor could stitch a cut that looked to be healing well. While a blanket hid her legs, the extra size of splint and wrappings showed which one had broken.

Ingeborg looked up at Haakan, who nodded sadly from across the bed.

She took in a deep breath, disinfectant with a trace of fleshly putrification stinging her nose. "S-Solveig?" When there was no response, she tried again, louder. "Solveig. This is Ingeborg. We have come for you."

The woman's transparent eyelids rose slowly. "Ingeborg?" The blue eyes focused. "Ingeborg, is it really you?" A tear slipped from one eye, ran over the shaved area and into her hair at the back. She reached out a trembling hand. "You got the message then."

"Ja, I am sorry it took so long." Ingeborg took the chilled hand in both of her warm ones. "But Haakan and I are here now, and in a couple of days, we will have you at the farm. Soon all will be well again."

"All?" Solveig blinked. "Never will *all* be well again."

Ingeborg knew she was referring to the livid scars. Seeing the stubborn set of the woman's chin, so much like her sister's, Ingeborg changed the topic. "How is your leg doing?"

"I can walk with crutches but not very well. That is why the doctor sent you the telegram to come get me. I didn't remember anything for some time, and since my baggage was lost in the wreck . . ." Her voice clogged and she cleared her throat. "They didn't know who I was."

"You are most fortunate to have remembered."

"Am I? I don't care if I never remember that terrible time. They say twenty people died right then and more later. Oh, Ingeborg." She closed her eyes at the painful memory. "I could never explain the horror. Having no memory at first was such a blessing, but then at that time I was so afraid." Her voice dropped to a whisper.

A cough from another patient, and a groan from the person in the bed across the narrow main aisle only magnified the silence around the bed. A metal pan clanged on the floor.

"Terror lurks everywhere if you don't know who you are."

"Ja, that must be so." Ingeborg beat back her pain for the starkness of the words. "But God is good, and . . ."

Solveig shook her head. "Nei."

"And He is making you well and . . ."

"Is He? I should be *thankful* for the doctors who sewed up my face into a horror mask and fixed my leg so that I will hobble for the rest of my life? Nei, Ingeborg, I don't see how I will be of much use on your farm. But I have no money to return home."

"I will go find the doctor and nurse to see what must be done for us to leave. You get her ready." Haakan turned on his heel and strode out of the room.

"He is angry."

Ingeborg shook her head. "No, but concerned. We hope to catch the evening train bound for St. Paul."

"I can't even leave here."

"Why not?"

"I . . . I have no clothes. Only this hospital gown." She plucked at the plain cotton garment.

"Oh, if I'd known, I could have brought some from home." Ingeborg thought to her meager belongings in the carpetbag. Not much help there. "Perhaps the hospital has a store of clothes for a time like this."

Solveig shrugged.

A woman in a white dress and a hat starched stiff enough to fly in a wind stopped at the end of the bed. Her hat reminded Ingeborg of a sailboat in full rig. "I am the head nurse, Sister Gordon. I see we are ready to leave." She nodded, setting her sails to flapping. "Mr. Bjorklund is signing the papers now." She turned to look directly at Ingeborg. "You brought her some clothing?"

Ingeborg shook her head. "I did not know."

"Ah. You did not receive our letter?"

"No, only the telegram."

"Ah." The wings flapped more gently this time.

"We will go buy some things and come right back."

"No." Again flapping sails. "I will find you something." She spun and, born on the wind of her hat, flew out the door.

Haakan and a bearded man in a white coat entered the ward.

"Sister will be back with some garments for you momentarily, Miss Hjelmson. You must be very glad your family has come for you." The doctor spoke slowly in German so Solveig and the others could translate.

"Ja."

When Solveig said nothing further, he turned to Haakan with a shake of his head. "She has been like this much of the time." He had switched to English since he now knew Haakan spoke the language. "There is nothing further I can do for her. The compound fracture in her leg is healing poorly, but she won't need a cane or crutch to get around on later. She is slow on crutches now, but that is to be expected."

"What about the bill?" Haakan said to the doctor, but with one eyebrow raised looked over at Ingeborg on the opposite side of the bed.

Ingeborg knew the silent question he asked. Had Solveig been like this the entire time since they'd arrived? The nod she sent back might merely have been a twitch to someone who didn't know her well. She closed the door of her mind to the questions that bombarded her. They could be dealt with later. Right now they needed to get Solveig on her feet and all of them on their way home. Perhaps the trip home would help make her feel more hopeful. Ingeborg's nose wrinkled at an odor that drifted by. She glanced down the row of white-covered beds to where a doctor and nurse were working on a patient behind a cloth screen. The patient bit off a scream that sent chills up and down Ingeborg's spine.

She brought her attention back to the discussion between Haakan and the doctor, who was speaking. ". . . and they have agreed to pay all the medical bills of those injured in the train crash. Your sister or relative here is one of the fortunate ones."

Solveig's shifting on the bed showed that she was listening and probably feeling frustrated that she didn't know what they were saying. Ingeborg laid a hand on her shoulder and smiled down at her. Solveig just stared back, her face revealing nothing.

*Ah, Solveig, this is not the end of the world—or your life. I know it seems that way, but the scar will fade with time, and a limp isn't such a terrible thing. Ask Lars. He'll tell you.*

The sister returned with clothes over her arm and carrying a pair of shoes in her hand. She waited until the doctor finished speaking.

When she cleared her throat, he turned. "Ah, there you are. Sister will see to you then." He extended his hand and Haakan shook it. "Good luck to you all." He nodded to Solveig. "You will do fine, my dear." When she tendered no response, he started to say something more, then nodded to them all and left the room.

"Now then, Mr. Bjorklund, if you will leave us, we will get our patient ready to go." As she spoke, the nurse ushered him out to the aisle and pointed to a screen, two beds down. "If you would be so kind?"

While Haakan brought back the two folding screens and set them around the bed, she laid out the garments. "Now, these might be a bit large, but you will gain some weight again once you are feeling better. If the shoes are too big, we can stuff paper in the toes."

With never an extra motion, she folded the covers back and helped Solveig to sit up and swing her legs over the side. Because of the splints on either side of the leg, the right one failed to bend properly and the splints stuck up above the knee.

She looked up at Ingeborg as if to say "see," but Ingeborg ignored the plea. They would have to do with what they had and make the best of it.

When Solveig was finally dressed in a plain waist and a black wool skirt over petticoats—the pantaloons had proved impossible—

Ingeborg picked up a comb and tidied Solveig's hair. By looping strands down on the sides, the wound on the side of her head nearly disappeared.

"Ah, that's better," Sister Gordon said, standing back, the easier to see the whole picture. "You will be looking good again without fail."

Solveig ignored her.

The nurse helped the young woman to her feet, handed her the crutches, and stood aside to let her patient take her tentative steps.

Removing the screens to let them pass, she pointed in the direction they should go. "I have a wheelchair coming so you won't use all your precious strength walking to the front door. You had them call for a horsecar, did you not?" she asked Haakan when he met them at the door.

"It is there now. I just checked."

"Mange takk," Solveig murmured when the nurse stopped the chair at the curb a few minutes later.

"Go with God," the nurse said. "He will be your strength in the days ahead." She held the chair while Haakan helped Solveig to her feet.

Haakan and Ingeborg both thanked her, then Ingeborg helped Solveig into a dark wool coat, as short in the arms as the skirt she now wore was overlapped at the waist to keep from falling down. When Solveig picked up her crutches, Haakan shook his head. "I will lift you into the cab so you do not stumble." He suited actions to his words, then gave Ingeborg a hand.

"Thank you again, Sister."

She turned with a waving of her sails and headed back into the three-story brick building.

After they were under way, Ingeborg asked, "Solveig, would you like us to stop at a shop and buy anything for you?"

Solveig shook her head. "As the nurse said, these will fit better eventually. I can sew a new dress when we get to the farm." She paused. "If you have any cloth, that is."

"We can get that in Grand Forks," Haakan said. "And maybe some boots that will be more appropriate for the Red River Valley. I'm sure whoever gave those shoes to the hospital never walked across grass with them, let alone into a barn." His smile showed his gentle humor with her. The shoes they all looked at might have graced a dance floor at one time. Low cut, shiny black, they looked more like slippers than real shoes.

Ingeborg wanted to laugh at the thought of those shoes being worn in the chicken house or out feeding the pigs. But she didn't. It didn't seem that Solveig remembered how to laugh. Ingeborg thought back to Nordland and the times she remembered Solveig teasing her brothers, beating them at foot races, and tenderly caring for her lambs. The two pictures didn't fit together, as if she had a puzzle with missing pieces.

Could the train wreck alone have caused the anger and bitterness she saw in this . . . this stranger?

Ingeborg prayed silently while the buggy carried them through the crowded streets, ever closer to the train station. Like in New York, angry drivers shouted at others more slow. Steam whistles blew from the factories bordering the street, wheels rumbled and squealed, and horses whinnied. From the sidewalk a dog strained at his leash, barking so hard his front legs left the ground with each yelp. The girl gripped his leash with both hands to keep him from running under the wheels of the passing dray wagons.

Ingeborg sneezed in the sooty air. "How do they stand it here, the filth and all? I can hardly breathe with all this smoke."

Haakan nodded. "Ja, give me our clean prairie air anytime."

Their driver joined the cab line that snaked its way to the marble portico in front of the brick station. When he stopped, Haakan handed him some money and stepped out, first to help Ingeborg alight and then to lift Solveig down.

"I can carry you into the station to one of the benches, you know."

"I would rather walk myself. I have to learn to get around with the crutches sometime, and at least here the way is smooth."

"As you wish." But Haakan and Ingeborg took up positions on either side of her to make sure no one knocked over the struggling woman.

Slowly they made their way to a long high-backed bench made of dark walnut. Solveig positioned both crutches in front of her and, using them as support, lowered herself to the seat with a sigh of relief.

"You did good." Ingeborg perched on the edge of the seat beside her. "Can I get you anything?"

Solveig only gave an abrupt shake of her head and leaned her crutches against the bench.

A little boy stopped in front of them and stared, first at Solveig's face and then at the wrapped leg. He stuck one finger in his mouth, his eyes round. When his mother called him, he blinked and trotted off.

Ingeborg could feel the anger radiating off her seatmate, like the heat from a well-stoked stove.

"He was only a little boy." She tried to bite the words back, but they raced out of her mouth.

"You think I don't know that?"

The words slapped Ingeborg about the ears. She started to say something else but this time got her thoughts in motion before opening her mouth. What was life going to be like in the soddy *this* winter?

## October 1884

Paws' barking snapped Kaaren out of a fitful nap.

Penny laid aside her mending and rose from the rocking chair. "I will see who it is." She pulled the door open and a gust of rainy wind blew her skirts straight back behind her. "Onkel Joseph, what are you . . . is Tante Agnes all right?" Her questions tripped over each other. "Put the horse in the barn and come on in."

She shut the door on his answer and hurried to the stove to bring the coffeepot to the fore. "He looks like a rain-soaked rooster."

Kaaren chuckled. "I wonder how Metiz is? Thought she'd be back by now."

"She said today would be a good day for catching fish. I think she trusts me to take care of you more now."

"She knows I am stronger. I'm just afraid that any day she'll leave for her wintering place. How I wish we could convince her to stay here." Kaaren patted the squirming bundle she lifted from her neck and shoulders. Squeaks, yawns, and other waking sounds came from the sling.

"They are hungry again already?" Penny shook her head. "All you're going to do for the next few months is feed babies."

"Thank you for enlightening me." Kaaren's smile said she was teasing as she reached up to tuck several strands of hair back into the braid she now wore in place of the bun for ease of care. She then wrapped the braid in a coil around the back of her head and tucked the end under. Salvaging one of her precious hairpins from the hair at the side of her face, she stuck it into the thick golden rope in the hopes of keeping the mass in place.

"I know, I just never thought two babies at a time would be more than twice the work. After the birthing, Tante Agnes just gets up and makes the next meal unless I order her back to bed. The new baby fits in with all the others, and whoever is closest when it cries picks it up."

While she talked, she cut slices of bread and set jam and butter in the center of the table. "I should have baked some cookies or something."

"Thorliff will let you know that he thought so too. But washing the diapers was much more important." A thin rope stretched from the back of the stove above the reservoir to the wall and back. White flannel squares hung folded over both lines.

Penny reached up to check if they were dry. "The rain sure didn't help."

Joseph knocked on the door and stuck his head in. "Where's the menfolk?"

"Over at Ingeborg's barn. They're all splitting shingles." Penny set the stack of bread in the center of the table and set coffee cups around. "You want to call them?"

"Ja." Joseph closed the door, and a second later the triangle rang.

When he came in, he slapped his brimmed hat against his thigh before hooking it on the peg by the door. "Thought to bring the missus in the wagon, but she ain't feeling too chipper. Best she stay off them feet of hers. She sure do miss you, Penny. I sent one of the boys in to help her, you'd of thought he were being told to take a bath in a snowbank."

"I suppose she sent him right back out."

Joseph shook his head. "No, she didn't."

Penny felt a cold hand clutch her stomach. "Is she that sick?"

"Says she ain't, but I don't know what to think on it." He shook his head, the few wisps of hair that covered his spreading pate bobbing with the motion. "She ain't never been like this before."

"If Penny is needed at home, we can manage here," Kaaren said, her voice gentle so as not to disturb the little ones.

"We'll see."

Laughter from outside caught their attention. "You didn't play fair." Thorliff's voice preceded him through the door.

"I did too," Lars answered. "Because I have longer arms, I can reach farther to touch the door." He swung a chortling Andrew to the ground as they ducked through the low door. "Someday your arms will be this long and you can beat boys at foot races."

Andrew bypassed Penny and leaned into his aunt's lap. Already he'd learned not to throw himself at her skirts as he used to. The babies were changing all of their lives.

Penny scooped him up and tickled him as she carried him to the washbasin.

Olaf and Lars hung up their hats and joined Joseph at the table. After the introductions, Lars leaned forward. "What brought you over here in the middle of the afternoon? Especially on such a good field day as this?" He smiled at his own small joke.

"Good for splittin' shingles like you been doing, ja. Me and the boys decided about the same thing. Winter be coming soon, cold as this rain is." Baard smiled his thanks up at Penny for the cup of steaming coffee she set before him.

They talked about the weather, about the loads of lumber they'd hauled and restacked out by the sod barn away from the one remaining haystack, and about the land. Then Joseph cleared his throat. "I been thinkin'." He nodded as he spoke between blowing on the coffee surface. "All that lumber out there is going to waste, far as I can see. Me and Johnson thought maybe we should all show up here bright and early day after tomorrow and just see how much of that barn we can get raised in one day—or maybe two, if need be."

Lars swallowed and both took in and expelled a deep breath. "That ain't necessary, you know."

"Oh, we know that, but we ain't had a good time all together since the schoolhouse went up. Seems you folk got enough to worry about without the barn too. So, if'n you don't mind us barging in like this . . ."

Penny bit her lip. *Leave it to my onkel Joseph and the others*. She checked the meat in the oven and forked the potatoes to see how long until they'd be done.

"Me hungry." Andrew planted himself in front of her.

"I know. How about some bread and jam? Supper won't be for a while yet."

"Chores first." He sounded just like his father.

"Yup. You want milk too?"

He nodded.

"Go ask Thorliff to bring in a jug then."

Andrew scampered to the door, but when he unlatched it, the wind blew it out of his hands and knocked him back on his posterior. Instead of crying, he scowled. "No! Bad door." He hoisted himself to his feet again, rump first, and pushed against the screen door. "Open door!"

Lars looked up just then from studying his coffee mug and smiled at Penny. "He sure has got the ordering part down right. Pretty soon he'll be telling all of us what to do."

A chuckle rippled around the table as Lars rose and opened the door for the determined youngster. "Where you going, little man?"

"Tor get milk." He leaned against the wind that now only blew cold and damp, not drenching.

They could hear him calling, since Lars kept the door open to watch the child. "He don't let much get to him, does he?"

Kaaren shook her head. "One thing for sure, he don't take after his father. He's more like his onkel Carl." She let Penny take Sophie and put her against her shoulder, patting the tiny back to produce a burp. Grace nursed on after being awakened again by all the shifting around.

"So . . . what do you think?" Joseph asked, half turning so he spoke more to Lars.

"I think Haakan should be home tomorrow, at the earliest." He held the door open for Andrew, followed by Thorliff and Baptiste.

"'Lo, Mr. Baard." Thorliff set the jug of milk on the table, then he turned to look Baard in the face. "You need any more barn cats over your way? We got extras."

"They good mousers?"

Thorliff shrugged. "Will be when they quit growing."

"I heard Hanson, west of me, needs some. Coyote got his mother cat and the whole litter."

"Good. I'll bring a couple in a gunnysack next time we have church." Thorliff reached for the bread but backed off at the look on Penny's face and nodded Baptiste over to the washbasin.

"So, it's settled then?" Joseph held out his coffee cup when Lars raised the pot in the age-old question.

"Do we have any choice?"

"Choice for what?" Thorliff brushed a drop of water off his face with the back of his sleeve.

"Oh, our neighbors think we need help raising that barn since we've had a couple of slowdowns this season."

"Oh, great jumpin' frogs! When?"

Penny smiled at Thorliff's latest phrase. While her brothers could tease with the best of them, Thorliff was the one to play with words. The meaning was clear—there'd be no nay vote from him.

"What will Pa say?"

"Mange takk would be about the best."

Thorliff grinned at his uncle. "Thank you very much, too, huh?"

Joseph nodded and slapped his hands on the table as he got to his feet. "I'll be seeing you, then, near to sunrise day after tomorrow. Agnes said she was coming if she had to lie in the back of the wagon, so you'll have company too." He dipped his head to Kaaren. "You take good care of them young'uns now. I'll tell Agnes you're looking a mite peaked yet but doing well as can be expected."

"Thank you, kind sir. Maybe I can keep her in here helping me, and we'll let the other women take care of the food. Just think, maybe we can have a barn dance when it is finished."

"Sounds mighty fine." He removed his hat from the peg. "Got the roof to put on the school, too, before a week from Sunday. I heard we got a travelin' preacher coming by."

Penny followed him out the door after the good-byes were said. "You sure you don't want me to come home with you?"

"No, they need you here worse'n we do. You're a good girl, Penny. If'n you see Metiz, you might send her over our way, though."

She watched him walk off to the barn in that loose-jointed way he had. You could always tell it was Joseph coming long before you saw his face, just by the way he walked. If Aunt Agnes wanted to see Metiz, she must be a mite worried herself. Penny shook her head. How could she be in two places at once?

⚜ ⚜

"Now, is there anything else that you need?" Ingeborg turned to Solveig, who had just settled onto a bench outside the dry goods store in Grand Forks. At the flat look in Solveig's eyes, Ingeborg wished she could rephrase her question. She had heard Solveig groaning in the night whenever she tried to move in the bed. Not only was the leg so cumbersome with all its wrappings, but there must still be a lot of pain. But the young woman didn't complain; she just didn't say anything. Which was better—the anger earlier or the sullen silence now?

She watched Haakan stride down the raised boardwalk that joined store to store. He'd been up at the machinery sales lots, right where she had wanted to be. He and Lars had been talking about a steam engine for running the dreamed-of lumber mill in the winter and the threshing machine in the summer. When she thought of either taking out another loan or spending the funds she had hoarded in the bank, she could feel her stomach begin to flip-flop. Ja, they had a good harvest, so there was a bit of extra cash beyond paying back on their loans. But they would have to buy hay before spring, since theirs burned, or else sell off part of the stock.

She rubbed her belly. The thought of the boat ride on the river made her even more queasy. She closed her eyes and thought of Psalm 91. Surely they were being cared for under the pinions of God's wings. The Scriptures said so. As close as they were now to proving up the homesteads, nothing could be allowed to endanger that. If they had to go without new machinery, so be it.

"Are you all right?" Haakan stopped at her side, the words meant for her ears alone.

Ingeborg left off rubbing her waistline as if seared by a brand from the kitchen stove. "I . . . I . . . ja." She bobbed her head and tried to smile.

"You're worrying."

She made a negative face, but when she looked in his eyes, she could tell. He knew her too well.

"I did not buy anything."

Even though she tried not to react, she could feel her shoulders drop in relief.

"I just checked the prices and talked with the salesman. They don't have what we are thinking of here. It would have to come from Chicago. I wouldn't buy it without having either Joseph or Lars along, or both. Lars knows more what a threshing machine needs than I do."

"Will the same engine work for both?" She kept her hands at her side, despite the urge to clutch her middle.

"The salesman said it would. Could be used to turn a millstone, too, if'n we had one. If we ground our own wheat and oats, we could save money there, besides doing it for the others in our region. Would bring in either barter or cash."

He unfolded the newspaper he'd bought and began reading.

Ingeborg glanced at the headlines. "Strikes Flare in Chicago." She wished she could read English better, but talking it was hard enough. "What all does it say?" she asked softly, glancing at Solveig, who was sitting with eyes closed and her head nodding.

Haakan turned to her with a smile. "You sure you want to know?" At her nod, he began to read her an article about the campaign of Grover Cleveland. "He's running against James G. Blaine for president of the United States. Once Dakota becomes a state, then I will be able to vote in elections."

"What about the women voting?"

The look he gave her left no doubt in her mind what his thoughts on that subject were. "What else is happening?"

"There's lots of talk about statehood for the territory, but even more about splitting it in two. There would be North and South Dakota that way." He pointed to the articles on the second page. "Down in Spink county, way south of Fargo, they're having a fight about where to put the county seat. The courthouse is out in the country now in a place called Old Ashton, but the town of Redfield figures they should have it."

"Uff da, such a thing to be bothered about."

"Means lots of money for the town that is the county seat." He read to himself for a bit. "Says here that men are being killed in strikes across the country, but right now Chicago is especially bad." He shook his head.

"Why are they striking?"

"The article says unions are trying to come in so that the workers get better pay and working conditions. This man they quoted says all the money goes to the owners of the mills and not enough to the workers."

Ingeborg had heard of such things before, which made her even more grateful for their land and that no one could tell them what to do.

"How soon until we board the boat?" Solveig asked.

The question startled Ingeborg. She'd almost forgotten Solveig was still there, she'd been so silent.

Haakan glanced up at the sun playing hide-and-seek with the clouds. "Soon. Where are your packages?"

Ingeborg nodded to the bundles on the bench beside Solveig.

"Is that all?"

Ingeborg felt like hugging him right here in the middle of Grand Forks, right out in public. She knew Solveig had been fretting about the amount they were spending, but a warm coat and boots were absolutely necessary with winter coming on. They had also bought cotton yardage for underthings, besides a dress for church and one to work in. Trying to figure when they would have time to sew these things, along with the fall butchering, making soap . . . if she continued the thoughts, she knew they would show on her face. And on top of all that, she hadn't been hunting for weeks. They needed elk and venison unless they were to butcher one of the steers she planned to train for an ox team to sell in the spring.

Haakan picked up the bundles that didn't fit in their carpetbag, handed Ingeborg a couple of the lighter ones, and nodded toward the dock at the river. "Let's be going then."

Once they had Solveig settled on a bench on the lee side of the paddle boat, Haakan wandered over to the railing to talk with two men who leaned there, their cigars sending a curl of smoke into the air.

"Why don't you turn and lean against that wall and put your leg up on the bench here? There aren't enough passengers for the boat to be crowded." Ingeborg shuffled the packages around, placing some under the seat. One that contained the dress goods, she held to use as a pillow behind Solveig's back.

"I don't want to make a fuss," Solveig hissed between clenched teeth. The white ring around her mouth told Ingeborg the pain was bad.

"This is no fuss." With swift but gentle movements, Ingeborg soon had her reluctant patient more comfortable by tucking the wrapped package of cloth behind her back and propping her leg on the bench. "When we get home, Metiz has some remedies that will help take the pain away and make your leg heal better."

"Metiz?"

"Ja, she is a friend of mine—ours, I mean. She has taught us much about living on the prairie and using the things that grow and live there."

"That is a strange name." For a change a flicker of interest lit Solveig's eyes.

"Ja, it is." *Doesn't she know of Metiz? Kaaren has written of the old woman, I know she has. Do only the old folks listen to our letters?* Ingeborg watched the men in conversation, wishing she were there to hear what they had to say. Neither of them looked familiar. Perhaps they were from Canada.

When Haakan returned and joined her out of the wind, he wore a smile like Andrew's when he accomplished something new.

"Ja?" She knew it wasn't a woman's place to question men's talk, but at that point she didn't care. What had switched Haakan into such good spirits?

"They are from Chicago, selling machinery farther north."

She nodded, wanting to poke him to get the news out sooner.

He rubbed the bridge of his nose and nodded, at the same time leaning against the forecastle housing. He nodded again, this time pursing his lips and staring off at the Minnesota shoreline.

"Ja?" Ingeborg could have bet her petticoat he wasn't seeing the trees but visions of new machinery instead.

"Oh, not much." He chewed on his bottom lip off to the right side and nodded again.

Ingeborg felt like jumping in the middle of his chest and flailing him about the head and shoulders. *Was he teasing?* She caught a glint in his eye. "Haakan Howard Bjorklund, if you know what's good for you . . ."

He burst out laughing, bringing Solveig out from a doze and frightening a sparrow that had perched on the rail hoping for crumbs.

"Ah, Ingeborg, you should see your face. If looks could kill, I'd have drowned minutes ago." He turned to face her. "They know of a steam engine for us. Halverson, the one in the round black hat, said this engine has enough horsepower to do any of the things we want, and he'll even include the wheels to make moving it easier. I had thought we'd move it on skids, but this will be better. He said they have traction engines coming soon, if we should want to wait a year or so." He shook his head slowly while speaking. "But we don't want to wait."

"Traction engine?"

"It moves by itself. Can you believe that?"

"By itself?" *Come on*, Ingeborg ordered herself. *You sound as if you never heard of steam engines before, as if you're maybe hard of hearing too.* She cleared her throat. "You mean without teams of horses or oxen the thing just pulls itself across the prairie?"

"Ja. Halverson said this flatland was the best for the new machinery. He said pretty soon they would be pulling plows and all with steam engines on wheels." He stopped and stared into her eyes. "Can you think of that?"

Before she could answer, he added, "Ja, they probably have them on the Bonanza farms down by Fargo already."

Ingeborg tried to remember the name of the man Roald and Carl had spent so much time with on the train coming to Dakota Territory. He most likely had the latest machinery on his farm. She knew the Bonanza farm across the river from St. Andrew, where they delivered their cheeses and eggs and such, still depended on horses and mules.

"What is this world coming to?" Now she couldn't focus on the nearly leafless trees.

"Wait till Joseph and Lars hear about this." He stared at her through squinted eyes. "I could get off at our landing and then drive the wagon to St. Andrew for you and Solveig. We can't get her off the boat without a dock, since with her leg and all she can't climb down the ladder."

Ingeborg felt her stomach bounce down about her knees. If she let herself think about another few hours on the boat, she had to swallow more than once. Why hadn't she thought of that? This way they wouldn't get home until long after dark.

She kept her head straight, even though it wanted to droop like a pouting child. Solveig didn't need to know their dilemma. It might make her feel even worse. What about the babies? Who was helping Kaaren? Maybe Haakan should continue on the boat and Lars could take the wagon up. But Solveig needed a woman with her. "Ja, that would be for the best. I will tell her."

The whistle shrieked above them, causing them all to flinch. Sitting this close the blast hurt their ears. How did the crew stand it all the time?

Ingeborg sat back down on the bench at the end of Solveig's foot. "We are nearly home, but you and I will stay on the paddle-wheeler to St. Andrew where it will be easier to get off."

"Oh."

Ingeborg looked up at Haakan who had come to stand by her shoulder. "Please ask Metiz to send some of her medicinals along so Solveig can ride in the wagon easier. And lots of quilts and elk robes for padding."

Haakan nodded. "I will." He looked down at Solveig. "Would you like to come around the wheelhouse so you can see where our land is? Not much but riverbank to see, but . . ."

Solveig shook her head, leaned back, and closed her eyes again. A white line circled her lips, and her jaw remained bone hard, nearly visible through the pale skin. Cords stood out in her neck.

*The pain must be terrible*, Ingeborg thought. *How can I help her? Oh, Lord, how can I help?* "I'll be right back." She followed Haakan around to the starboard side and looked downriver to their landing where the raft was tied to a cottonwood tree. While she watched, Thorliff and Baptiste burst out of the trees, each waving with one hand as they untied the bobbing raft with the other. Baptiste shoved the raft away, and Thorliff dug in with the long pole to maneuver the cumbersome thing out to the paddle boat.

The captain tooted the whistle again, gently this time.

"I will meet you in St. Andrew then. Since you'll get there before I do, take Solveig to the hotel. Those chairs in the parlor will be more comfortable than the benches on the dock."

"Ja, I will." Ingeborg leaned over the railing to wave at Thorliff. "You did a fine job."

The raft bumped against the boat. One of the crew threw the end of the rope ladder over the side and opened the railing for Haakan to climb down.

"I will see you soon." His eyes matched the sky arched above them with twinkles like fireflies in the dusk.

"Mor, wait till you get home!" Thorliff fairly danced on the bobbing raft.

"Are the twins all right?"

"Ja, and Tante Kaaren too. Penny made Andrew take a nap. He weren't none too happy 'bout that. He's missing . . ." Thorliff clapped a hand over his mouth.

Haakan landed on the raft, ruffled Thorliff's hair, and took over the poling. They both waved when the whistle tooted again and the paddle-wheel resumed its slush-and-slap song.

Ingeborg waved back, wondering at the boy's obvious excitement. What was going on at the Bjorklund farms now?

I ngeborg collapsed in a velvet chair in the St. Andrew Hotel next to Solveig.

"I am sorry to be such trouble," Solveig said with her eyes closed.

"It can't be helped, and it is not your fault. God will work all this out, you'll . . ."

"God?" The derision contained in that one word stopped Ingeborg midblink.

In Solveig's spiteful tone, Ingeborg could hear herself that long winter of her soul. Knowing how she'd railed against those who tried to remind her that God did indeed love and care for her, she clamped her lips shut. Prayer now would be more helpful than argument.

Taking her own inward advice, she sent her thoughts and pleas heavenward. The only sound in the silent parlor was the ticktock of the ornately carved grandfather clock standing against the red-and-gilt striped wallpaper. By the time the clock bonged the next hour, she had prayed for everyone she could think of, including Hjelmer, wherever the boy was. Because of his actions, she had a hard time thinking of him as a man, size or no size. She opened her eyes and yawned, feeling as though she could sleep for hours. Glancing at Solveig, she saw the younger woman was sound asleep, her breath coming in little snorts, her chin resting on her chest.

Ingeborg rose to her feet as quietly as possible and tiptoed out the door. If she didn't get some fresh air, she'd be sleeping too. The aroma of coffee floating from the dining room made her stomach rumble in a most unladylike way. When Solveig woke, they would have to get something to eat.

After pacing the front porch a few times and waving at Mrs.

MacKenzie over at the Mercantile, she returned to her seat and picked up her knitting. While the sock she worked on was too large for Solveig's foot, once she finished this one, she could start a smaller pair. She was just tucking in the final yarn at the toe when she heard a wagon whoa'd outside. The voice could only be Lars'.

"Solveig, they are here." She repeated the words, but the sleeping woman, who now looked more like the girl Ingeborg remembered, failed to stir.

"Oh." A smile flitted across the scarred face before Solveig had time to remember what had happened. The memory obviously surfaced as her face fell into the familiar blank slate. She pushed herself erect and with both hands lifted her injured leg down from the needlepoint-covered footstool Ingeborg had placed under it. "Can we find the necessary before we leave?"

A short time later, with Lars promising them there was food in a basket in the wagon, they headed west along the Little Salt River. The temperature dropped along with the sun. Ingeborg made sure Solveig had a sandwich of sliced elk roast and cheese, along with the now cold coffee, and fell to her own repast. How long had it been since they'd eaten breakfast, anyway?

"So, what is the surprise?" She spoke around a mouthful of bread and meat.

Lars shook his head with a chuckle. "I ain't tellin'. You think I want them young'uns to skin me alive?"

Ingeborg made a tisking sound. "Afraid of those two young pups?"

"Forget it, Inge. I ain't telling."

"Can you tell me how the babies are, or is that a secret too?" She checked behind her to see how Solveig was doing. The half-eaten sandwich now lay on the blankets over her chest. But if her eyes were open or closed, Ingeborg couldn't see.

"Getting stronger every day. Kaaren too. Penny and Metiz keep both places going. That Andrew, he's a live one, he is."

"Now what did he do?"

"I ain't telling that either."

"Lars. What is going on?"

He shrugged and clucked the horses to pick up the pace. He wore that secret grin that meant he was enjoying this mightily.

"Did Haakan get a chance to tell you about the machinery men?"

"No, what?"

Now that she had his attention, and hoping to get him so interested she could slip in a question about the farms, she told him all they'd learned.

"So did he buy the steam engine?"

"No, not without you seeing it and saying it is right for what we want."

Lars shook his head. "Shoulda gone ahead. Time is running out."

Barely had the sky darkened when the eastern horizon grew light as morn. The rising harvest moon silvered the prairie and threw sharp shadows, lighting the road home. Ingeborg shivered in the deepening cold and drew one of the elk hides from the back and pulled it up and over her shoulders. Her teeth clattered from the jolting wagon, but she never suggested they slow down. If she dared, she'd have set the team at a gallop. What was going on?

As the Bjorklund farm came into view, Ingeborg could not believe her eyes. Tall rafters rose from the dark prairie like bleached bones in the moonlight. Ingeborg sucked in her breath and let it out on a sigh. "Oh," she whispered, "the barn. How beautiful!" She turned in her seat to see Lars staring straight ahead.

"I promised I wouldn't say anything."

"I know. Who did it?"

"All the neighbors. The last two days there been a crew here working hard as ants getting ready for winter. I never seen anything go up so fast in my life. Onkel Olaf, he . . ."

"Onkel Olaf?"

"Day after you left, Olaf Wold, Kaaren's mor's brother, turned up here. He emigrated years ago and kind of lost touch with home. They all thought he was dead. Been working like a fool ever since he arrived. I think he don't sleep, that's what I think."

"They all gave up their own work to give us a hand. I mean, I know you and Haakan planned a barn raising, but this is . . . is . . ."

"Kaaren said the barn is just another sign of God's love and care."

Ingeborg heard a snort from behind them.

"Ja, well He sure helps us stick together here on the prairie, don't you say?"

"Ja, some debts you just never can repay."

The barn grew larger as they drew closer. Paws ran out to meet them, his barks turning to yips as soon as he recognized who it was.

"Let's stop at your house so I can see the babies first."

"If'n you want. Olaf is bedded down in your barn, now that you and Haakan are home. Kaaren says Solveig will share the bed at our house with Penny." He drew back a bit on the reins as the horses, nearing home, picked up the pace. "We sure do need some additions on these two soddies."

"And before the ground freezes."

Lars halted the wagon, and Ingeborg clambered to the ground before he could come around to help her. She could feel the frosted grass crunching under the soles of her shoes. "I will return in a minute to help you out, Solveig. I just have to see how the twins are."

Ingeborg pulled open the screen door and, giving a quick rap, opened the heavy wooden inner door. The warmth from the inside made her face tingle. "We are home." She unwound her scarf from her neck and head even as she spoke, crossing the room at the same time. She greeted the three women.

"I been telling the young'uns their tante Ingeborg will be back soon, so don't go to sleep right yet." Kaaren held a well-swaddled baby in the crook of each arm. She lifted Sophie for Ingeborg.

"Are they both doing all right?" She smiled into the baby's eyes as she spoke. "I think she's grown twice her size."

"Grace here still doesn't eat as much, but she is getting better."

Ingeborg leaned over to check on the sleeping twin. "She's growing though, I can tell. Oh, Kaaren, I am so thankful. Sometimes I thought—well, no need to go into that." She handed the bundled baby back to her mother. "Penny, Solveig is worn to the bone. Let's get her to bed right away."

"She drink first." Metiz nodded to the pan she had simmering on the stove. "Me see leg."

"I hope so, Metiz. I'm afraid she has some funny ideas."

One side of the old woman's mouth twitched in a smile. "We fix."

Within a few minutes Ingeborg left Solveig in her loving sister's hands and let Lars drive her and the baggage across to the other soddy where a lamp shone in the window. After whispering her thanks to Lars, Ingeborg opened the door with barely a creak and set her packages on the floor by her rocking chair. She first checked on Andrew, who slept with a curly lock of hair over one eye and had the look of a cherub. She resisted the urge to lean down and kiss his rosy cheek, instead turning to find Haakan's smiling gaze waiting for her.

She gestured to the barn and shook her head.

"I know," he whispered. "When I saw that, I . . ." He closed his eyes for a moment and sighed. "Such a gift."

"Where are the boys?"

"Out in the barn with Olaf. Since he's been giving them carving lessons, they took over the job as his shadows. Poor man, guess he doesn't mind. He's got them helping him make new buckets, alongside splitting shingles. Those two are busier than bees on a honeysuckle."

"Any news of Hjelmer?" She moved the lamp to the table and cupped her hand around the chimney so she could blow out the flame.

"That'll be the day. I think that young man is long gone."

"Haakan, how can you say that?" She undressed, hanging her clothes on the pegs in the wall and pulling her flannel nightgown over her head. Then like any good wife, she slid under the covers and planted her ice-cold feet on his warm legs.

"Uff da." He jerked away before taking her feet in his hands and rubbing some warmth back in them. Some time passed before Ingeborg cuddled even closer to his warmth and laid her head on his shoulder. What a perfect ending to such an exciting, albeit at times frustrating, day.

❦

"Drink this." Metiz held out a steaming cup to Solveig.

"Do I have to?" She turned her head away, sending a pleading glance to her older sister.

Kaaren nodded. "She's not trying to poison you, you know. All of us at one time or another have submitted to Metiz' potions and always been the better for it." She sighed. This wasn't the way she had pictured Solveig coming at all. There'd already been an argument over letting Metiz examine the injured leg. What in the world had her sister heard about Indians that made her act like a frightened sheep?

Kaaren shifted the twins in her arms and nodded when Penny motioned that she'd take one. But when Penny changed Sophie and laid her in the box on the oven door, the infant set up a wailing that would fit one twice her size.

"They don't like to be apart," Penny said, picking the red-faced baby back up and rocking her in her arms.

"You'd think she's too little to know better." Kaaren tapped the cheek of the twin she held, encouraging her to wake up and finish eating. She glanced over to the bed where Solveig lay propped up on pillows against the sod wall. The face she made sipping the bitter brew caused Kaaren to chuckle. "I thought the same, sister mine.

But believe me, that concoction helps you sleep and keeps the pain down. Tried some laudanum one time and this is better."

Only Metiz' twinkling eyes showed her response. She sat cross-legged on her pallet on the floor by the wall, using a rounded stone in a carved wooden bowl to crush her dried herbs into powder.

When Lars returned from putting the team up, he stood by the stove, rubbing his hands in the warmth above it. "If it rained tonight, we'd have snow for sure."

"Snow at dying moon." Metiz continued to grind.

"You think it'll hold off that long?"

One nod was his answer.

"Then maybe we can get the lean-tos done. Once the roof is on that barn, we can side it when we have time. Onkel Olaf has become the boss on the job."

Kaaren reminded Solveig who Olaf was. "God surely sent him at the right time." At the glower that darkened Solveig's face, Kaaren exchanged a questioning look with her husband. When he shrugged, she turned back to Solveig. While she wanted to ask what was wrong, in her heart she already knew. Like so many others before her whom life had treated fairly easy, Solveig's faith had been tested and found wanting. Solveig's hand strayed often to the scar that still flamed on the side of her face. It would fade with time, but there was no getting around it. Solveig would never be the beauty she had been, and if she kept frowning like that . . . Kaaren shook her head. Compared to what it could have been, the scar and the leg were a small price to pay for life.

But Solveig wasn't ready to hear that.

"Is she full now?" Penny asked from the side of the rocker.

Kaaren held up the baby. "I hope so. While Sophie can go longer between feedings, Grace wakes her up no matter how quiet I try to be." Kaaren got to her feet, meeting Metiz at the edge of the extra bed. "Do you want me to unwrap it?"

Metiz nodded.

"Now what?" Solveig asked.

"Metiz has made a poultice to apply to the wound. It will help draw out any infection and soothe the pain."

"My leg is as good as it is ever going to be. The doctor said so."

"Nevertheless, we will do what we can." Kaaren laid her hand on Solveig's shoulder and pushed her back to the pillows. "You just lie back. Metiz has the most gentle hands of anyone I know." She smiled down into her younger sister's eyes, eyes now full of rebellion instead of the love she'd dreamed of.

She watched as Solveig finished drinking the tea Metiz had prepared. Even with the honey they'd added, she knew firsthand how bitter it tasted. Her mouth pinched at the remembered pucker.

Once everyone was finally in bed, she shifted gently so as not to disturb the sleeping babies. *Father in heaven, please look with compassion upon my dear sister. She is so different than I remember, and I fear the train accident is the cause of much of that. Please help her to not become bitter. I know the scar on her face will fade with time, but scars upon her soul are more to be feared. Help her remember what Mor taught us from your Word, that you are love and will see her through this. I know that ahead of her may lie worse trials. . . .* Her thoughts flew back to baby Lizzie and the emptiness after her three went to their heavenly home and left her behind. Her heart had been shattered and the pieces scattered, only to be mended through God's grace. She sighed. *Thank you, Father. I know you have a great design for Solveig's life as you have for ours. I trust you with the care of all of us, Amen.* With that, she sighed and drifted off to sleep.

The next day flew by as the lumber seemed to take wing and make itself into the shed-roofed sides of the barn where the livestock would be housed. The men worked in teams, with some drilling holes for the pegs while others held the beams and pounded in the pegs. A wedge driven in the end of the peg sealed each joint. The boys on the ground took turns stripping the bark off tree branches of the right size and carving the sticks into pegs or splitting shingles. Laughter rang out over the grind of brace and bits, the rasp of saws and thuds of hammers, and all the while the rich fragrance of freshly cut wood hung in the air.

Ingeborg had a hard time keeping herself at the cooking with the other women. She wanted to climb the ladders and pound home the pegs, to hold the board and batten siding in place for another to hammer home the nails. Her feet wanted to dance a jig in time with the rhythm of the construction.

Much against her will, Joseph had said, Agnes stayed home.

Ingeborg knew her friend must be really miserable to miss the party air at the Bjorklunds'. She promised herself to ride over to the Baards' as soon as she could. In the meantime, she took out a few moments to run over to the other soddy and check on Kaaren and her brood there. Penny walked back with her.

"So, how are things there?"

Penny shook her head. "That Solveig, she ain't too pleasant a company, but I figure she'll adjust after a while. Body got to do that or you'll go daft like that woman over to the north of us."

"Mrs. Booth is getting worse then?"

"Seems so. Even this summer she would hardly come out of her house. Kept talking about the wind when we went over there for a visit. And it wasn't even blowing that day; it was still as could be. Why, soon as we got inside, she just shut the door tight. Something strange going on there, that's for sure."

Ingeborg brushed a piece of something out of her eye. "Auduna is such a fine seamstress. Besides all the work she did on the quilt the women made for us, she brought us a pair of pillow slips, all embroidered and finished. Just beautiful." She paused to think a moment. "Maybe if the women get together again and someone went and got her, she would come. Might be enough to help her some."

Penny nodded. "Tante Agnes tries to help her, but you know, some folks just don't want to be helped." She turned to Ingeborg with a shrug. "I sure hope Solveig ain't like that."

Ingeborg kicked at a lump of black prairie dirt. "Me too, Penny, me too."

By the time the last wagon drove off, the sheeting had been nailed to half the barn roofs, the board and batten siding covered the upper walls above the shed roofs, the front and back walls, and one shed side. Olaf said he would start laying shingles soon as it was light enough in the morning. Thorliff and Baptiste dragged themselves in for supper and returned to the sod barn to collapse right after. When Haakan teased them about splitting more shingles, they just shook their heads.

"Wore them right down to a nubbin, din't we?" Olaf rocked his chair back on two legs and stretched his arms above his head. "Those two are good workers. Them Baard boys too. You found a good place when you stopped here. And the folks what come after, they be good too."

"Except for one or two," Ingeborg muttered, thinking of the Strands and the Polinskis.

The older man chuckled, his pipe smoke circling his head. "Ja, there always be them kinds of folk, but they prob'ly weren't Norwegian, huh?"

Ingeborg threw him a smile over her shoulder, as she had both hands in the dishwater on the cool side of the stove. "You're right there."

Haakan stood with Andrew, who'd fallen asleep on his shoulder, and crossed to the bed to lay the sleeping child gently down. He pulled up the covers and gave the boy a loving pat as the little one turned on his side, drawing his knees up to his chest.

Ingeborg felt a tightening in her bosom at the gesture. How blessed she was to have such a good man in her life and home. She thanked the Lord for him every day, still learning herself how to answer to Haakan's teasing and loving ways. If only her mother could meet this man and give her seal of approval. She pulled back her thoughts from their winging toward Nordland and scrubbed the last pot clean.

The next morning when she entered the barn attired in her men's britches, Olaf only raised an eyebrow and then winked at her.

"This way we can get some more sod broken while you men work on the barn." She pulled her wide-brimmed man's hat down tighter on her head to keep the wind from tumbling it across the prairie. "You want I should use the horses or the oxen?"

Haakan shook his head. "I want you should go about the things you have to do. You would do better to go hunting than break sod."

Ingeborg glanced at Olaf in time to catch only a raised eyebrow. This man would do well here, that was for certain. Nothing much seemed to shock or surprise him. "I can do that late this afternoon. Penny is watching Andrew and the boys are taking the sheep out."

"I will help you harness up then." Haakan lifted the leather harnesses down from their pegs. "You get the horses."

Ingeborg reveled in the pleasure of riding the sulky plow rather than walking behind the hand plow like the year before. As the sod lay over in straight rows behind her, she caught herself singing. She went from one hymn to another, the horses twitching their ears as if enjoying the symphony of human voice, creaking harness, thudding hooves, and squeaking wheels. The bite of the plow blade into the earth had its own kind of melody to add.

Ingeborg enjoyed the pull of the lines against her shoulders and the push against the foot pedals to raise and lower the share on the turns. As the team went up and down the field, a few snow geese flew over them on their way southward. The prairie wind whistled in her ears, a song of rejoicing in the late fall and of the coming winter, a song of freedom and the joy of the land.

She let her voice soar as she didn't dare in their church services, cautious of some who felt such volume would be unseemly. Out here she could worship as she pleased.

Bagging a spike elk that evening put the finish on a perfect day.

On Saturday every available body met at the school to shingle the roof so they could have church there the next morning. "Our first service in the new building," sighed Mrs. Johnson from west of the Baards. "And to think we will have a pastor here to celebrate with us. He took the night at our house, you know. Said my raised biscuits was the best he ever tasted."

"Ja, Reverend Hostetler said he might consider remaining here with us if we were to ask him," said Mrs. Valders.

"You asked him?" Ingeborg could feel the furrow deepen between her eyes. "When did you meet him?"

"He was to our house the night before. But my husband didn't really ask him, just sort of hinted around to see if the good reverend might be open to such a thing. You know some of these itinerant preachers think stopping in one place is a terrible idea. Don't go along with what God called them to do."

"That's cuz they got the wanderlust like half the men here," muttered one of the women whose husband already had itchy feet to go farther west.

Ingeborg felt sorry for her. She knew the woman wanted to send her roots deep into the prairie soil like the rest of them, not pick up and move on.

About noontime, another wagon drove up. Ingeborg shaded her eyes with her hand and then let out a groan.

"What is it?" Penny appeared at her elbow.

"The Strands are here."

"Ach, I'm glad Tante Agnes is at home. She might tear that hussy, Mary Ruth, arm from shoulder." Penny bit her lip. "I don't think I can stand to be polite to her."

"You don't have to be polite, you can ignore her all you want," Ingeborg said for Penny's ears only. She handed Penny the bucket with a dipper. "You go offer a drink to the men on the roof, then I think you better go home to check on Agnes."

"And then to Kaaren's too?"

"Ja, that's a good idea. Take Bell over there, she rides well." The two shared a secret look, and Penny went to do as told.

Mr. and Mrs. Strand walked around greeting folks as though they'd just seen them all a week ago. Mary Ruth leaped nimbly from the back of the wagon bed and joined the group of younger women, some of whom kept an eye on a favored man.

*She's no more in the family way than . . . than Metiz is.* Ingeborg kept the observation of the young woman's slim waist and hips to herself. Surely she would be heavier by this time. After all, she would be four months along by now.

"That . . . that flaming hussy," hissed Mrs. Johnson. "And to think she accused young Hjelmer of being the father of her child. I'd bet my one and only Sunday dress she made it all up."

"You truly think so?" someone else asked. "Could be she . . ."

"Could be, nothing. She's a liar through and through. Poor Penny, the heartache she been through. I tell you someone oughta . . ."

The grumbling continued as the women put out the last of the food and called the men to eat. Ingeborg didn't have to say a word. All the other women said them for her. But what could they do? Short of chasing Mary Ruth and her family out of the area at the point of a rifle, that is. How could they possibly get hold of Hjelmer now to tell him to come home when they hadn't heard from him in months?

Poor Penny. What would she do when she heard this?

I could tear all that red hair right off her head." Penny spit out each sound.

"Don't blame you one bit. But that won't solve the problem for now. How do we find Hjelmer?" Ingeborg looked over at Haakan. The three were the only ones still up in the southern soddy. The shingling, bench-making, feeding all the workers, and the general merriment of the day at the schoolhouse had worn them all out. Only such an important discussion could keep them up.

Haakan shrugged. "Maybe you should send a letter to each of the train lines, asking if any of them have hired on a man named Hjelmer Bjorklund. You could include a letter to him to be sent on."

"How do we get an address to send letters to?" Penny looked as bewildered as Ingeborg felt.

"I would think all of them have offices in Fargo."

"Do you know the names of the railroads?"

Haakan sucked in a breath that lifted his shoulders and let them fall again. He closed his eyes in thought.

When he opened his eyes, he stuttered over three or four names, shaking his head the while. "Not sure what they are all called." He corrected one or two and watched as Penny wrote them down. "Other than that . . ." He shrugged. "Perhaps after the snow sets in Petar could go looking for him."

"Where?"

"Out west, far as the new lines are going. But, you know, when the weather gets too bad they shut down, and perhaps he'll come home by himself then."

"If he can." Penny gripped the back of the chair till her fingers turned white. "Maybe he doesn't want to come home again. Maybe

he built himself a whole new life and just . . . just forgot about us."
Her voice dropped to a bare whisper. "About me."

Ingeborg ached to comfort the young woman, but what could
she say? "God knows where Hjelmer is."

"Ja." Penny nodded. A heavy sigh accompanied the final motion
of her head. "But God isn't telling." She stared down at her whitened
knuckles. "I better get back to Kaaren's. At least there I am needed."
The unspoken "and wanted" echoed in the quiet soddy.

Ingeborg chewed on the side of her lower lip. "Remember you
and Kaaren talked about my writing to Mrs. Johnson at the hotel in
Fargo? Why don't I go ahead and do that? You could work there and
go to school. If nothing else, that would make the waiting easier."

"Sometimes I wonder why I don't do as Tante Agnes says and
just accept the attentions of Modan Clauson. He's been asking me
to go out riding with him, and he's a good man. At least that's what
Tante Agnes believes, and I do too."

"He has a good reputation with everyone. Comes to church regular as we have it," Haakan said. He thumped the front legs of the
chair back on the hard-packed dirt floor. "And he needs a good
woman to take care of his two children. They need a mor bad."

Ingeborg studied the girl's downcast face. "But you are in love
with Hjelmer."

"Ja, for whatever good that does me." Fire flashed again in
Penny's eyes. "Please, go ahead and write to your friend. Hjelmer is
not going to come home, and if and when he comes, he will not find
me mooning around here like a lovesick heifer. I've always wanted
to get more book learning, and I will." She straightened her shoulders as she spoke. "Good night to the both of you, and thank you
many times over." She strode out of the soddy as if a full marching
band played at her heels.

"That young man has some real accounting to do if he does come
home." Ingeborg blew out the lamp. Haakan had the wisdom to not
say a word, only folded her in his strong embrace when they settled
into the corn husk bed.

While the men were doing the chores in the morning, Ingeborg
wrote her letter. Perhaps someone from the church meeting would
be going to either St. Andrew or Grafton on Monday and could mail
it for her.

Several hours later the Reverend Hostetler stood at the door to
the sod school and church greeting all the arriving families. Taller
than the soddy doorway and possessed of a deep voice that could

call hogs five miles away, his piercing eyes quailed the hearts of the most stalwart, let alone the children.

Andrew buried his face in Ingeborg's shoulder, and Thorliff stood closer to his father's side. Even hat veils dared not rustle as the people took their places on the benches that had been finished and set in place at twilight the day before. At the front of the dim room, a narrow table covered by a white cloth held a lighted kerosene lamp, an open Bible, and a pair of gold-rimmed spectacles. In spite of the glass chimney, the flame above the wick flickered in the breeze from the open spaces planned for door and windows. The overcast day did nothing to lighten either the room or the atmosphere. Soon people were standing around the sides of the room, since all the benches were taken. Several men got up and gave the women their seats. At a glare from his wife, one man hastily snatched his hat from his head and held it in front of him.

All seemed to hold their breath as the frock-coated preacher strode down the center aisle and stopped in front of the table, bowing his head for a long moment before turning to face the congregation.

"We will start with the singing of 'O God, Our Help in Ages Past.' " His Norwegian words rang loud in the muffled room. He hit the first note and everyone joined in, singing as if to burst off the roof of shingles so recently nailed in place.

When he picked up the Bible from the table, his long forefinger trailed down the page before he began reading. "Thus saith the Lord our God: 'they that plow iniquity and sow wickedness, reap the same. By the blast of God they perish and by the breath of his nostrils, they are consumed.' " When he finished, he let the silence stretch. "We will now sing 'I Lay My Sins on Jesus.' " The people joined in after the first note.

Ingeborg held Andrew on her hip. When she glanced at him, his eyes were stretched wide and he carefully didn't look toward the front. She smiled at him but received no answering grin in return. They sat at the finish of the hymn, clothing rustling, throats clearing. The silence fell again, a silence that vibrated with tension.

"Welcome to our Father's house this Lord's day."

The softness of his voice let Ingeborg take a deep breath. She could feel her shoulders let go. Andrew sat straighter, beginning to look around.

"God said we are sinners. We are sinners." He paused. "You are sinners!" His words thundered in the tightly packed room. Andrew let out a shriek and buried his face in his mother's shoulder. A baby behind them wailed, and another small child began to cry.

"Hush, hush. You are all right." Ingeborg comforted the shaking child.

The man continued to thunder hell and damnation upon the people.

Ingeborg tried to close her ears against the ranting voice that now settled into a pattern. He would drop his voice down to a near whisper, shake his finger at them, then thunder again. According to Hostetler, they were all on their way to hell, some of them maybe faster than others, but all included. By the time he got around to telling them that Jesus died for their sins, Ingeborg's ears ached.

No one met the Reverend's eyes when he shook their hands after the benediction and final hymn. Once outside, the people congregated in groups far enough from the door so as not to be heard.

"He will not be our minister if I have anything to say about it," Joseph Baard muttered to Haakan.

"I feel the same." Haakan wore the tight-jawed look that said he'd had enough.

The crowd dissipated quickly, no one stopping to visit. Ingeborg had thought to invite the man home to their house for dinner but followed Haakan to their wagon without a backward glance. Andrew still had not left her shoulder nor Thorliff her side. Joseph's family stayed around him like a clutch of ducklings obeying their mother. Within minutes, the yard cleared, the creak of the wagons and thud of horses' hooves fading away. Many unspoken prayers that the preacher would move on filled many thoughts.

Halfway home, Haakan began to whistle under his breath. Andrew peeled himself off his mother's lap and, with her assistance, climbed into the wagon bed to be with Thorliff. A familiar giggle soon arose from the back, and Ingeborg exchanged a smile with Haakan.

"I gave my letter to Mary Johnson. She said her husband was going to St. Andrew."

Haakan nodded. "Good."

That night snow capped the fence posts and bent the remaining grass. When the sun finally came out about dinnertime, the snow disappeared like cookies in a crowd of children.

"We'll butcher tomorrow," Haakan said over his last cup of coffee. "The more shingles we can get on today, the better, but with November nearly upon us . . ."

Ingeborg knew what he meant. Last year the first heavy snowfall had hit before now, and a blizzard followed soon after.

After clearing away, Ingeborg bundled Andrew up and crossed to the other soddy to check on the babies. The ring of hammers for nailing shingles on the barn roof accompanied her. If the men would allow, she would have joined them, but she knew that was a futile thought.

Penny met her at the door with a finger to her lips. "They're all sleeping. Metiz went out for a final willow bark gathering."

"Good. Then I will put Andrew down for a nap at home and go hunting."

"You want to leave him here?"

Ingeborg shook her head. "He'd wake the babies."

Once out in the woods along the riverbank, Ingeborg drew in a deep breath of the crisp air. Soon Thorliff would have to set his snare line for rabbits, and as busy as he had been, they didn't have as much dried fish as usual. But after they slaughtered the two hogs they should have enough for the long winter. Another deer or elk would be a bonus.

But the elk bounded away before she got him sighted in. She settled back along the game trail for the deer to come down to the river to drink. With one shot she brought down a buck. The does following him scattered faster than she could blink.

Ingeborg approached the fallen animal carefully as she'd always done, watching to see if there was any motion. Blood pulsed from the neck wound, making her more cautious. Usually she got a head shot. She started to lean over to slit the throat when the animal threw up its head. The antlers snagged her pants.

She stumbled back, feeling a searing pain in her leg. She leveled the gun and shot again. This time directly in the head. The buck collapsed.

She sank to the ground, her heart pounding as though she'd run for miles. So close. "Dear God, thank you, thank you." She let her head fall forward to quell the nausea roiling her stomach. It wasn't that she hadn't been careful. She had. Each movement flowed through her brain as she checked her actions to make sure she hadn't been careless.

"Merciful God, thank you." She opened her eyes, feeling as if an hour had passed. She needed to make sure the deer bled out. When she got to her feet, her pant leg pulled away and she could feel the warm blood on her leg. She looked down, then bent over and examined the wound. A slash above her knee still oozed blood, but she could tell the worst was over. She dug in her pocket and withdrew a square of cloth to tie around her leg. With that in place, she hobbled back to the buck, slit his throat with her hunting knife, then leaned against a tree. Could she carry the deer carcass home?

By the time she'd finished gutting the deer and had tied it up to carry, the short dusk had turned to dark. She sighed. Should she fire the two shots that signaled trouble or make a travois to drag the deer home?

She didn't bother to glance down, she could feel seepage from below the wrap. She'd have Metiz sew the wound up when she got home. But for now, getting home was the immediate problem.

Taking the knife out again, she slashed at the base of a willow sapling. When it fell, she started on the next. Her leg burned as though someone held a hot poker against it. Hacking free several smaller branches, she used them to tie the sapling's branches together, giving her a web of limbs on which to lay the deer. She rolled the carcass over onto the travois from her knees, then using a tree by her side, she pulled herself to her feet. She needed a third hand to grasp a walking stick to keep herself upright.

Ingeborg tied the rifle along one of the willow poles, hoisted the two ends, and ordered one foot to place itself in front of the other. With each foot requiring a command of its own, she started up the game trail. One step, two, three and pause. The fire in her wound grew, working its way up her leg. Step again. She stumbled over a root and crashed to her knees. Cutting off the scream that made it past her lips brought blood to the end of her tongue. The pain brought tears to her eyes. Sucking in control as a drowning man gulped air, she pushed herself to her feet. One step, two . . .

"Ingeborg!" The shout came from a distance.

"Mange takk again, Lord." She then raised her voice. "Here! On the game trail!" Leaning against the trunk of an elm tree, she answered the call again, grateful the voice was so much closer. In a minute Paws leaped at her side, yipping his joy at finding her. After she ruffled his ears and thumped on his sides, he left her to sniff the deer, his tail wagging all the while. She could see a lantern glow faintly through the brush. Never had light been so welcome.

"What happened?" Haakan set the lantern down and wrapped his arms around her.

Ingeborg leaned against him. The thudding of his heart in her ear against his chest felt like a welcome home. He had come for her.

From the safety of his arms she told him what had happened. "Olaf will be here in a few minutes with a horse. Something told me you were in trouble over an hour ago. I should have come sooner."

"You are here now. That is all that matters." She shivered when he drew his arms away.

He leaned back, his eyes drilling into hers. "Ingeborg, why didn't you fire off the two rounds to say you were in trouble? We would have come immediately."

"I . . . I . . ." She couldn't stand the intensity of his gaze. Plain as if he were standing right behind her, she heard Roald's order. *Do not waste any shells.* "I . . . I couldn't waste the shells."

"Don't you know you are worth more to me than thousands of cases of shells?"

Tears started and flooded her eyes before she could stop them. She wiped them on the front of his shirt and leaned again into his warmth. One of his hands cupped the back of her head as he brushed the remaining flow away with his lips.

Chin quivering, she reached up to kiss him back. "Mange takk, my husband."

They stood close for a long moment before Haakan gently said, "Let's get to the open. Can you walk if you don't have to drag this?"

She nodded, then picked up the lantern. "Let's go."

After pouring some of the precious whiskey over the wound, Metiz sewed up the slashed leg without a word. Ingeborg clenched her teeth against the fire of that assault and dug her fingernails into the chair seat as the stitching progressed. Maybe she should have had a swig of the liquid herself as Haakan suggested. When she finally collapsed in bed, she fell asleep as if she'd been struck on the head by a rock.

Haakan postponed the hog butchering.

🙙 🙚

Each day Kaaren felt stronger. "I don't do anything but feed babies," she said to Penny. "I cannot tell you how much I thank you and Metiz for all your help. I know the babies wouldn't have made it without you, or perhaps me either."

Penny looked up from diapering Sophie. "I am glad I could help. I know Metiz will leave for her wintering grounds as soon as she feels we can manage on our own." She glanced over to where Solveig washed the dinner dishes at the stove. As long as she stood in one place, Solveig could do any number of things. But still, she never spoke unless to answer a question.

Kaaren followed Penny's gaze and shook her head. What to do about Solveig? She had made no effort to go out of the house, even though there was no mud to speak of. When others came to visit or check on them, she drew her silence around her as if she'd climbed in the trunk and shut the lid, just as they did as children. Had she lost her laughter and ready smile in the train wreck? And her faith?

As if she could feel them studying her, Solveig looked up from the dishes. She brushed a hank of hair off her forehead with the back of her hand, then deliberately turned away and resumed her chore.

Penny and Kaaren exchanged looks of consternation.

Kaaren knew her sister's actions weren't because of pain in the leg any longer. The wound had healed well, and the leg seemed to hurt only when Solveig put too much weight on it, so the break must be nearly healed also. The train wreck had been almost a month earlier now that November was upon them. Kaaren looked down at the baby sleeping in her arms. One tiny fist had managed to get out of the blanket wrapped so firmly around the little body, and it lay curled against Kaaren's apron bib. Grace still needed to nurse more often than Sophie, but both were growing. She could hear Penny talking to Sophie and the baby gurgling back. Strange, but Grace made no sounds yet except to cry when hungry.

Metiz entered the soddy. "Deer antler cut Ingeborg above knee."

"Oh no. How bad is it?"

"Sewed up." Metiz dug in her pack for her simples. "Lose blood."

"Can she walk on it?" Penny asked.

"Tomorrow." Metiz headed for the door again.

"Then we better make supper for everyone." Kaaren rose to her feet and put the still sleeping baby into the lined box by the stove. "I'll peel the potatoes. Penny, would you bring in an elk roast from the smokehouse. I think there are two large ones left out there. Get some turnips and onions from the cellar too. Solveig, do you know how many loaves of bread we have? Let's see." Kaaren laid a finger on her chin as she marshaled her troops. "I had planned we'd have krub tomorrow after they butchered the hogs, but I hope the men put that off for a few days now. Uff da." She shook her head. "What next?"

Stiff and sore as she was the next day, Ingeborg hitched the team to the plow and cut sod for the lean-to on the soddy while the three men shingled the barn. Thorliff and Baptiste split shingles and ran them up to the men as soon as they had half a bundle. Lowering clouds constantly reminded Ingeborg that Metiz had predicted snow on the dying moon. Tonight's moon, if they saw it or not, would show only a thin slice. No matter how much her leg throbbed from pushing the pedals, she kept going. If the ground froze deep, there would be no lean-to for a bedroom for Olaf and Thorliff, or for Baptiste if Metiz could be persuaded to stay. The deer she'd shot the night before hung in the sod barn, waiting to be cut up and either smoked or dried. But the weather was cold enough to keep the meat. Haakan had salted the hide and rolled it, hair in, so Ingeborg could tan it later. So much to do.

Penny served them all dinner and supper each day.

"I could split shingles," Solveig said during a lull in the conversation one afternoon.

Everyone looked at her, the boys with open mouths.

"Ja, I guess you could," Haakan said with a nod. "Have you ever done so before?"

She shook her head. "Thorliff will teach me."

Andrew banged his spoon on the table. "Me spit single."

Thorliff and Baptiste crowed with laughter.

Andrew watched them for a moment before the set of his jaw said he didn't think the joke so funny. He leaned over and banged his spoon on Thorliff's head. "Me spit single."

"Ouch." Thorliff rubbed the top of his head.

"Andrew." Ingeborg took the spoon away before he could repeat his action. She tried to look sternly at the two older boys. "You know he doesn't like to be laughed at like that." She rolled her lips together.

"But he's funny."

"I know." She handed Andrew back his spoon. "Eat your stew, den lille guten. You can split shingles when you get a bit bigger."

"Ride horse?" He gave his mother a hopeful look, accompanied by a wistful smile, the one that earned him extra cookies at times.

"We'll see." She finished her plate and looked at Kaaren. "Where is Metiz?"

"Packing her things." Kaaren sighed and shook her head. "I tried to talk her into remaining here for the winter, but you know Metiz."

"Ja, I know."

"But Baptiste can go to school with me all winter, soon's Tante Kaaren can start teaching." Thorliff turned to the sober-faced boy at his side. "Don't you want to go to school?"

Baptiste nodded. "But Grandmere needs me."

"Mor," Thorliff pleaded.

"I'll try talking to her tonight."

⁂

But talking did no good. Metiz just shook her head.

"I'm sorry, Thorliff," Ingeborg said when her son told her good-night before he followed Uncle Olaf out to the barn. "You know, you could have your place back in the bed with Andrew."

"I know, but Onkel Olaf would be lonely."

"It is here anytime you want it." She smoothed the straight blond hair back from his forehead.

Tonight, since he was alone, he tolerated her fussing, even moving closer to her side.

"Have you seen Wolf lately?" she asked.

"No, but then we almost never see him anyway. Only when he wants us to. Why?"

"Sometimes when I hunt, he appears. He knows I will give him the insides, but I haven't seen him for some time."

Haakan entered the soddy from checking on the livestock one last time. "Brrr, the temperature's dropping out there. You feel up to butchering day after tomorrow?"

"Ja, will you ask Joseph to help?"

"I will. Then we'll do his the following day." He hung his hat and coat on the wall pegs. "That Agnes, she don't look too good."

"Night, Mor, Far." Thorliff headed for the barn.

"I should have gone over to see her. I meant to." Guilt jabbed Ingeborg with its barb.

"We'll be there in a couple of days." He waited by the lamp. "You want I should wrap that for you?"

Ingeborg looked up from unwrapping the strips of cloth tied around her leg. Rusty looking spots stained the layer closest to her skin. The paste that Metiz spread over the slash crumbled like dry leaves, but the stitches held firm and now there was no seepage. "Would you hand me that pot please? Metiz said to use her medicine again."

Haakan stared down at the wound. "Looks good. No sign of infection."

"Thank the Lord for that." She smoothed the cool salve over the injured area. "Such a stupid move. Never should have happened." She took the new strips and rebandaged her leg, tying the ends in a knot on top. "Sure will be stiff by morning." She pulled her nightdress over her head. "But it could have been so much worse."

"Promise me that anytime something like this happens, you will use the rifle to signal me."

"Ja, I promise." Lying flat by her husband's side, Ingeborg laid a hand on her belly. Was there a child growing there as she suspected? Should she tell Haakan now or wait until she was sure?

Soft snores answered her question. And besides, what if she lost this one as she had the other? She snuggled against her husband's broad back with one arm over his ribs. As Kaaren had said, "What next?"

"No, you hold the froe this way, then hit it with the mallet." Thorliff demonstrated the action for splitting shingles again.

Solveig nodded and grasped the vertical wooden handle. With the blade of the froe set half an inch from the split edge of the butt, she tapped it with her mallet.

"Hit it harder."

She slammed the mallet downward but accidentally let the froe lean toward her. The froe bounced on top of the butt. She glared at Thorliff, almost daring him to say something.

He just nodded. "You'll get it."

She set her tools again, slammed the mallet down, and the shingle split clean away, falling between her knees on the pile Thorliff had started.

"You did it!"

A corner of her mouth tipped up in a near smile. When she hit the next one cleanly, too, Solveig let out a whoosh of held breath that dropped her shoulders several inches. "I think I got it."

"Ja, you do." Thorliff sat down on the other three-legged stool and picked up his own tools. With a smooth motion born of long practice, he set the froe, and the pile of shingles at his feet began to grow.

Solveig watched him for a moment longer, then set her froe, slammed the mallet, pulled the froe toward her so the shingle finished splitting, and set it again. When her pile reached ten, she laid the tools down and picked up the shingles to set them in the frame for tying. With each bundle, she felt an increasing sense of satisfaction.

She was doing something new, something useful, and it didn't matter that her leg wasn't quite straight or her face bore the reminder of the terrible accident.

When Thorliff flashed her a smile, she smiled back before she thought to keep a sober face. Maybe just getting out of the soddy helped her feel better. Much as Solveig hated to admit it, Kaaren had been right in encouraging her to do just that.

Paws leaped to his feet and darted around the corner of the sod barn. When Thorliff heard Baptiste greet the dog, the boy dropped his tools and ran outside.

"Baptiste, I thought you'd already left."

"I come to stay." The two boys entered the barn.

"But, Metiz, is she here too?"

Baptiste shook his head. "She gone. She say I must follow my vision." He pulled the pack off his back and set it off to the side. "I can still stay with you . . . go to school?"

"Ja." Thorliff danced in place, his feet refusing to stay on the ground with the news.

"You want your place back?" Solveig asked.

"No, I'll set up another."

By the time Ingeborg rang the dinner bell, Solveig could hardly lift her arms. With each slam of the mallet, her left shoulder burned like a poker had been laid to it. She'd tried shifting arms and that helped for a time, but the end result was a heavy aching in both arms and across her back. When she stood, her good leg nearly gave way. If she hadn't propped the crutch first, she would have tumbled into the bundling frame.

The boys grabbed the twine handle of a bundle in each hand and hauled them out to stack by the barn wall. One side of the upper roof was finished and the bottom three rows on the other. The newly shingled roof glinted nearly white in the sunlight.

Solveig leaned on her crutch and lifted her face to the sun, eager for any warmth. She breathed in a deep breath of wood-scented air, the smell reminding her of her father's workshop at home. When she opened her eyes, a pang of homesickness caused her to look for mountains and pine trees. The flat land that stretched as far westward as she could see seemed ugly in comparison.

Surely she had made a big mistake in coming to America. Not for her would there be the handsome husband and the white frame house she'd dreamed of. She clamped her lips together and limped toward the soddy that wore a crown of dried prairie grass. Now she understood why Ingeborg liked to work the fields. Anything to get out of the dark, close cave they called home.

They had just sat down to dinner when Paws announced they had company. They heard a horse coming in at a dead run. Haakan leaped to his feet and got to the door as young Knute Baard bailed off the heaving horse.

"Mor says she wants Ingeborg to come quick, and Metiz, too, if she is still here."

Ingeborg dashed outside. "What's wrong?"

"It's the baby. Mor's in big trouble." His lip quivered. "Please hurry."

Haakan was already at the corral to catch one of the horses.

"You go get Penny while I get ready." Ingeborg spun around back into the house and knelt in front of the trunk where she kept her medicinals. While her hands sorted through the packets, she spoke over her shoulder. "Thorliff, you'll have to watch out for Andrew. Solveig, can you manage at Kaaren's?"

"Ja, I can. You want Andrew should come there too?"

"That would be good. You'll have to make supper. Thorliff can help if you need him." She pulled the strings tight on her deerskin bag and got to her feet. Dropping a kiss on Andrew's forehead, she reminded him to be a good boy and, snagging her coat and hat off the pegs, out the door she went, just in time for Haakan to boost her up on the mule.

"One of these days we have to buy a saddle," he muttered as he smoothed the wool blanket he'd folded for a pad. "You be careful now. You fall off or something and who'll be there to help Agnes?"

Ingeborg leaned over and kissed him quickly. "Mange takk." She pulled the reins and Jack wheeled around, breaking into a lope before he'd taken three steps. Her sharp commands and the drumming of her heels in his ribs convinced him she meant business.

Ingeborg's pleas for God's help for her friend kept time with the pounding hooves of the mule.

⚶ ⚶

The baby girl, born just before dawn, lay inert in Ingeborg's hands. She handed the still form to Penny and shook her head. The baby had been dead for some time. She turned back to her patient. She had to keep Agnes in the land of the living, and with the flow of blood, she knew that might take a miracle of its own.

Palpitating the unconscious woman's belly, she prayed for the afterbirth to come quickly and the bleeding to stop. Agnes moaned but didn't open her eyes.

"How will we tell her?" Penny whispered, tears streaming down her face.

"I have a feeling she already knows." Ingeborg motioned for Penny to hand her some clean rags. "Make a tea out of the herbs mixed in the largest bag. Make it strong and put honey in it. Then start some beef to boiling, bones if you have them. We've got to get food in her, too, so she gets her strength back." She shook her head as her hands kept on with the kneading motion. "Why didn't she send for me earlier?"

"Because she's stubborn, just like the rest of us." Penny threw the words back over her shoulder as she left the soddy, silent but for her aunt's stentorian breathing.

"Come on, Agnes, you must try. Wake up and talk to me." But the thought came to Ingeborg that letting Agnes sleep and postponing the sad news might give her a chance to build some strength first.

They spooned the herbal tea into the woman's mouth, watching to make sure she swallowed. After several spoonfuls, Agnes's eyelids flickered.

"Is it over?" she asked, her voice a mere hint of its usual life.

"Ja."

"And . . . and the baby?"

"Was a girl."

"Was?"

"Ja." Ingeborg took Agnes's hand in one of her own, the other continuing with the kneading. At last check the bleeding seemed to be slowing.

"One more for the cemetery." Agnes kept her eyes closed. "Have you told Joseph yet?"

"No. Only Penny knows."

"I've been afraid for a long time." She shifted on the bed. "Something didn't seem right."

Silence again.

"Drink this." Penny returned and held the cup to her aunt's lips, slipping an arm beneath her shoulders to assist her.

A tear trickled from the edge of the sick woman's eye and into her hair. "A girl. A sister for Rebecca to have as a playmate." Another tear followed the first.

Ingeborg fought back the swell that gathered at the back of her throat. Agnes loved babies. She took good care of her older children, but babies were so special to her. Called them "little angels." Whenever someone gave birth, Agnes was the first on the scene with soup for the mother and a knitted bonnet or blanket for the infant. And if a baby was fussy, it quieted immediately once in Agnes's arms. Agnes loved them, and they always sensed it.

The thoughts made Ingeborg's eyes blur. "Do you want to see her?"

"Ja."

Penny brought the swaddled little body to the bed and folded back the blanket. She laid the baby in Agnes's arms and stepped back. Suddenly she whirled and fled outside.

Ingeborg continued with her massage, finally feeling the contractions beneath her palms. *Thank you, Father. Please continue with your grace, for this family needs their mother.* She thought of the little ones sleeping out at the barn with their father. Anji and Gus trying to care for Rebecca, and Joseph watching over them all. Had other babies died in those years between Swen and seven-year-old Anji? Did that make this any easier?

Why had they never talked about these things? Ingeborg looked down at her friend, one of those who'd tried to drag her out of the black pit after Roald died. Losing those you loved never got easier. Agnes had never seen this baby, only felt it grow inside, yet she had longed for the day she would hold the sweet newborn in her arms.

"She died some time ago." Agnes had unwrapped the quilt and was stroking the tiny body, the curved cheek, the eyes that would never light with laughter.

"Ja."

"Is Kaaren up to leading the service?"

"I think so. She will not refuse to do this for you, no matter what."

"Joseph could, but he has such a hard time with the little ones." Agnes folded the blanket back in place, covering first the feet, then one side and the other. She smoothed the soft flannel between each fold, adjusting the curve around the neck, tucking in the tiny fist. "I have a cap for her. It is on the top right side of the trunk."

Ingeborg fetched the finely knit bonnet. Agnes fit it in place and tied the strings beneath the dimpled chin. "Do you mind if we name her Elizabeth?"

Ingeborg shook her head. "We would be honored."

"We would have called her Beth." Agnes let her eyes drift shut.

"You rest now."

The woman on the bed nodded, a small motion that tipped loose the shiny drop hovering on her eyelashes.

The next afternoon they laid Elizabeth Baard in the square plot just east of the schoolhouse, next to the stakes that marked the foundation for the church. A rail fence surrounded the graves already dotting the mowed yard. For now, boards carved with the name and date marked those graves, with all hoping to one day set granite headstones. Too many of the graves were tiny.

Kaaren held her Bible in her hands, the wind ruffling both the pages and the clothes of those gathered. " 'Suffer the little children, and forbid them not, to come unto me: for of such is the kingdom of heaven.' " She turned the pages. " 'Nothing shall separate thee from the love of thy Father, neither life nor death . . .' " And again. " 'I will not leave thee nor forsake thee.' " The rich Norwegian words continued to roll over the assembled people, promises from the Father to the children. His children, no matter the age.

Joseph, his nephew Petar, and two older sons set the small wooden box down in the hole dug for it. With tears streaming down his lined cheeks, Joseph shoveled dirt on the box lid. The thud rang in the stillness.

"Let us sing." Kaaren's voice rose in the Doxology. The voices quavered, then climbed above and around the thudding dirt, gathering power as the people drew closer together, giving strength and promise for the days ahead.

Kaaren looked over to the two small graves next to one long one. She, like Agnes, would see her babies again one day. God had promised.

Since Agnes seemed to be on the mend, albeit slowly, Ingeborg left Penny in charge and returned home to find Solveig using one crutch so she could carry things with her other arm. Solveig and Kaaren cooked for both the families, took care of Andrew, and kept the twins fed and comfortable.

The barn was shingled, both the high center roof and the side additions. Uncle Olaf was finishing the board-and-batten siding on the eastern section, while Lars and Haakan had the soddy addition ready to add the shed-style rafters. Thorliff and Baptiste, besides, splitting shingles, had taken over most of the chores so the men could keep building.

"So, what do you think?" Thorliff asked when he took the mule's reins to put him away.

Ingeborg could tell he was dying to brag about all they had accomplished. "I think you have all been working night and day to get so much done. Let me see your hands."

He held them out with a questioning look.

"Ah, as I suspected." She turned them back and front, then smiled. "I thought so. Worked near to the bone. I think it is time two boys I know go fishing. How about if I ask your far if that would be all right? Maybe first thing tomorrow?"

While his eyes lit up, his head shook no. "Far says we butcher tomorrow, whether you got home or not."

"Ah. Which would you rather do?"

"Butcher the hogs. Me and Baptiste can make a ball out of the pig's bladder. Far said so." He cocked his head. "Did you ever do that?"

"My brothers did, and they kicked it around the yard for days."

"We have two pigs, so Baptiste and I can each have one." He paused for a moment. "Andrew is too little. He'd chew on it." He looked up at her with a hopeful expression.

"We'll find him something else for a toy."

"Thank you, Mor."

The next day Haakan started the fires under the scalding trough before milking the cows so the water that Thorliff and Baptiste drew would be plenty hot. The two hogs to be killed had been penned away from the others and not fed for the last twenty-four hours so the intestines would be easier to clean out for sausage casings.

Joseph Baard, his nephew, and two elder sons arrived before the sun.

"How's Agnes?" Ingeborg asked, handing them each a cup of coffee, the two boys' well-doctored with milk and a bit of honey.

"Somewhat better. I'll be thanking the Lord to see her smile again. Don't know what we'd do without Penny. And thanks to you, my Agnes will pull through."

"We'll just thank the good Lord for sending us Metiz who has taught me—all of us—so much. If it weren't for her, there'd be a lot less folks still alive around here. My mor knew much about herbs, but things are different here." She turned at Andrew's insistence, handing him another biscuit. "You want some breakfast? I got plenty."

"Thanks, but we already ate." He stepped back outside where the cold turned his breath to a cloud of steam. "Good day for butchering."

Olaf had all the knives sharpened and lined up in a slot at the top of the cutting table. A tripod of poles held a chain to attach to the hocks. Ingeborg looked around a final time to make sure everything was in readiness.

After one shot Haakan and Lars dragged the dead animal to the tripod, hung it, and began the butchering process. Once bled and gutted, the animal was lowered into scalding water just long enough to loosen the bristly hair, then hung again to be scraped.

While this was going on, Ingeborg, Thorliff, and Baptiste ground potatoes and mixed them with flour and salt and pepper for the krub, or blood sausage. With one kettle simmering over a low fire, they mixed the blood and potato mixture, formed it into hand-sized balls, and stuffed a piece of salt pork or bacon from last year's butchering in the middle. Then the balls were dropped into a net in the kettle to simmer for several hours.

Once skinned, with the scraped hide wrapped for later tanning, the first pig was laid on the cutting table, and the process began again with the second. Everyone worked like a well-trained team, doing their assigned jobs with speed and skill.

Ingeborg set the heads to cooking in another kettle, to be turned into headcheese another day. A third fire held the rendering pot where all the fat was thrown. Joseph's boys were in charge of maintaining the fires and keeping the lard from burning.

"Do we have to wash the guts out?" Thorliff made a face when his mother began that smelly job.

"You like smoked sausage, don't you?"

He nodded.

"No sausage casing, no sausage." She stripped the contents into a feed bucket by squeezing the long small intestine between two fingers and pulling it through. She plopped the flat white tube into a pan of clean water. "Here you go."

Over at the cutting table, Olaf wielded the largest knife and Joseph handled the saw. Together they turned the carcass into shoulder roasts, pork chops, salt pork, and cuts for hams and bacon. All the trimmings went into another bucket to be ground for sausage, both smoked links and patties.

Krub became their dinner, along with potatoes roasted in the coals and squash baked the same way. Eating outside, the sun shining but giving little warmth, it seemed more like a party than work.

Ingeborg missed Agnes and her hearty laughter. She missed Kaaren's gentle smile and teasing, too, though Kaaren and Solveig had come over for a short time to see how things were going.

The boys carried the sausage bucket back for them to begin the first grinding. They would make patties from the seasoned meat and store them layered in crocks sealed by a covering of lard. Sausage stuffing would happen the next day.

Come winter, all this work would be more than appreciated. As the fat melted to clear lard, Ingeborg dipped it out and filled the bread pans. Once set up solid, the lard would be stored in bricks or buckets in the well house until they had a spell cold enough to freeze it.

Ingeborg set the haunches to cure in salt water in preparation for smoking. While much of the work would be done today, things like smoking, tanning, and making headcheese would wait until after they butchered at the Baards' tomorrow.

"Okay, boys," Haakan said after they had sluiced down the cutting table and resharpened the knives. "I have here two clean bladders. Now we can blow them up if we have enough wind, or we can fill them with water. Either way, they need owners who will care for them and not treat them too rough, lest they break and Paws eats them." The dog perked up one ear at the mention of his name.

Thorliff stood before his father. "Me and Baptiste will do that." He stopped and scrunched up his face. "But I think Knute and Swen should have one."

"Good thinking, son." Haakan handed him the two skin sacs. "Now you tie off this end and blow through this one." He showed the boys what he meant. "I remember playing ante-over the house, the barn, haystacks, whatever."

"You could maybe do that with us?" Thorliff looked up, his eyes begging more than his words.

Haakan shook his head. "I don't know. These things look pretty flat to me."

"We could take turns blowing."

Haakan ruffled the boy's hair. "You blow first, each of you, and we'll see if they need stronger air." He winked at Olaf.

Within minutes, the boys wore red faces but only slowly the bladders swelled. Knute blew till his eyes bulged.

"Not full enough." Haakan turned to Lars. "You next?"

Each man took a turn, the bladders expanding. Haakan held one out to Ingeborg, who shook her head with a laugh.

"I don't have enough breath to laugh and blow too." She giggled. "You should see your faces."

"Now, ma'am, we take our bladder blowing seriously." Lars waved the swollen bladder in the air. It slipped from his fingers and shot across the yard, Paws right after it. The dog chased the shrilling bladder, the boys chased the dog, and Ingeborg wiped the tears of laughter from her cheeks with the heels of her hand.

This time the blowing up didn't take quite so long, Haakan refusing to let Lars help.

"You can't hold on to the thing." He shook his head and glanced down at the boys. "Can he? We won't even give him another chance." They too shook their heads, giggles escaping from between clenched lips.

It took a full-grown, well-muscled man to heave the bladder over the two-story barn roof, and boys swift of feet with lightning reflexes to catch it on the other side.

"You can't make it!"

"Ante-over!"

"That's mine!"

Shouts and laughter punctuated the teasing. Twelve milk cows and four oxen lined up along the fence, heads hanging over the bars to watch the crazy humans at play.

Thorliff slid in a fresh cow pie, missed his catch, and skidded flat out on the ground. Paws ran over, jumping between the boy's flailing arms to get in a nose and chin lick.

"Pee-uw." Swen held his nose with one hand and pulled Thorliff to his feet with the other. "How can we win if you just go lying on the ground?"

Ingeborg went inside to put the coffeepot on and make sure the reservoir held plenty of water.

That night they had fried pork chops with sliced potatoes and another fire-baked squash. Along with the pork chops, Kaaren served applesauce she'd cooked that afternoon.

They repeated the entire process the next day for the Baards. Much against Ingeborg's advice, Agnes sat on a stool, taking over the krub-making.

"Don't fret, Inge. If I don't have something to do, I will pull the covers over my head and not come out until spring."

Ingeborg looked her friend in the eyes and was afraid she meant it.

"Very well, but you will go rest in bed in a while." She handed a freshly brewed cup of Metiz' herbs to the woman whose skin still wore the pale drawn look of one who'd been through a terrible ordeal.

Agnes made a face. "I know this works, but must it taste so terrible?" When she winked, Ingeborg knew her friend was on the mend. *Thank you, Lord, for small favors that loom so large.*

After krub dinner, Agnes went back to bed without a word, only raising an eyebrow in Ingeborg's direction.

Snow fell that night and continued to blanket the world in fat flakes for the next two days. When the sun peeked out on the third day and set the world on diamond fire, Ingeborg took Andrew out to see the top hats on the fence posts, the sheep who wore new coats, and to hear the snow whoosh off the steep roof of the new barn. Icicles hung from the ends of the shingles. She picked several and together she and the fatly dressed little one sucked on their treats.

"Good." Andrew waved his in the air.

"Ja, all is good."

"Make snow angels, Mor." Thorliff came running around the corner of the sod barn.

Baptiste joined them as they all lined up.

"On three," Ingeborg said after telling Andrew what to do next.

"One," Thorliff called.

"Two," Baptiste shouted.

"Three!" Ingeborg let herself fall backward in the soft snow. With arms and legs fanning wide, she called encouragement to Andrew beside her.

"All right now, everybody get up easy so we can see who did theirs the best." She got to her feet, and after lifting Andrew up, they stood to admire the four angels carved in the fluffy snow.

"Again." Andrew patted her face with his mittened hands.

And so they did. Three different sets of angels now decorated and guarded the Bjorklund farm. When Paws set out with his welcoming bark, Ingeborg shaded her eyes with her mittened hand, the better to see across the sparkling prairie. Now who was galloping through the snow in their direction?

I t's Penny." Thorliff ran to meet her.

"Now what is happening?" A galloping horse usually meant disaster.

Penny pulled her horse to a stop, her grin wide as the Dakota skies. "Good morning, good morning. Isn't this a wonderful day?"

"Is Agnes all right? Joseph? What is wrong?" Ingeborg tried to match the joy on the girl's face with possible catastrophes.

"Nothing is wrong. Why?"

"You were galloping."

"Oh, I just couldn't help it. Such a gorgeous day, and Tante Agnes wants to have a quilting bee—tomorrow, if enough people can come on such short notice. Kaaren can bring the twins if she thinks they are strong enough, Solveig, too, and you. Then I'm to ride on and invite the others."

"She is feeling that much better then?"

"She says a party will help her feel even better. 'A good visit is what the body needs.' That's what she said."

"Such good news."

Andrew attached himself to his mother's skirt. "Penny, come play." He pointed back to the designs in the snow. "Me angel."

"That's for sure. Sorry, I have errands, Andrew. Maybe another time."

"You angel?"

Penny laughed. "That's not usually what they call me, but if you say so."

Andrew nodded, his cheeks red as his lips. "You angel." He grinned up at her. "Ride horse?"

"You little beggar. Sure, but only a short ride."

Ingeborg lifted Andrew and set him in front of Penny. "Have fun."

His deep belly laugh floated on the breeze when Penny trotted the horse back the way she'd come. "Faster! Faster!" His shriek of pure joy as the horse broke into a lope added music to an already wonderful morning.

Ingeborg caught herself skipping back to the house. Hammers rang from inside the barn now as the men erected stalls for the horses and oxen and stanchions for the milk cows. They planned to wall off part of the lower section for a workshop, but the animals had to come first.

She glanced toward the pasture when she heard a horse whinny. The four work horses and Jack the mule were racing around the fence line, bucking and kicking their heels in the air. Soon the cows put their tails in the air and raced after the cavorting horses. Even the oxen lumbered heavily behind.

Thorliff and Baptiste came running out of the barn at her shout, and the men followed. Paws ran barking after the animals while Thorliff tried to whistle him back. That took some doing because it was hard to pucker and laugh at the same time. In fact, the pucker didn't work at all, making Baptiste laugh so hard he rolled in the snow.

Haakan picked up a handful of the white stuff and formed a ball. It caught Thorliff full in the chest. With a shout, he scooped, formed, and threw. Snowballs pelted through the air, shrieks and shouts of "no fair," "got you," and "get Haakan" rang along with the snowballs.

Ingeborg made her way around the fringes of the fight, her own snowball formed solid in her mittened hands. "Haakan," she called when within range. Turning, he caught a faceful. The fight waged until all were panting and the boys dropped down in the snow.

Penny loped back after talking with Kaaren and Solveig, and Haakan lifted Andrew from the horse's shoulders to his own. "Looks like you had a free-for-all here," Penny said with a laugh.

Ingeborg shook the snow off her head. "I think I got the worst of it." She brushed white globs off her coat and skirt. "And to think I only planned on cooking and baking today."

"Mor, could you make snow candy?" Thorliff sat upright in his snow bed.

"Why not?" Ingeborg turned back to Penny. "You want to stay for dinner?"

Penny shook her head and turned her horse away. "I have to ride over to the others so Tante Agnes knows how many are coming. Then I plan to do the baking so she can rest again. You know her, sitting still is hard and lying down even worse. She's knit two baby blankets and a pair of long socks in the last two days."

Ingeborg waved again as the horse galloped off, its breath a steam cloud in the nippy air.

When sometime later she called Thorliff to bring a pan of packed snow, he hurried to do her bidding. The sugar and butter cooked to a thread spun fanciful designs of loops and curls in the snow-packed pan. Minutes later they all scooped out brittle caramel-colored pieces that disappeared in their mouths fast as a snowflake melting on the tongue.

Ingeborg spent the rest of the day cooking and baking as if she were feeding a threshing crew.

When she woke in the morning feeling as though her stomach wanted to bring up her toes, she knew for sure. She was pregnant again. Now she would have a daughter, or Haakan would have a son of his own. The dream made her smile to herself. When would she tell him? Would he be as happy as she was? She laid her hand on her belly, blessing the child growing within. "Thank you, Father, for your tender mercies." The thank-yous flowed through her mind while she cooked breakfast.

After they ate, she cleaned up the kitchen, set beans to baking, and reminded Thorliff he needed to make sure the fire burned hot enough to cook them for supper. Then she went to gather the pieces of material she'd been saving for a quilt: the back of a dress Andrew had both outgrown and worn beyond mending again, remnants from sewing the red-and-white checked curtains and tablecloth, a small stack of pieces she'd traded with someone else, wool from the worn coat of Haakan's she had ripped apart and used for Thorliff's jacket. She dug farther in the trunk, pushing aside the pieces of soft deerskin and several rabbit pelts she planned to use for a hood and mittens for Andrew. Finally she reached the dress goods she'd saved to work on during the long winter days. Since one was cut out, she took the leftover pieces. These she could trade too.

With her quilting materials in a basket, she wrapped up a loaf of bread and a hunk of cheese, then sugared the pancakes left from breakfast, rolling them in tubes, and added a jar of jam. All this would contribute to the noon meal for the ladies. With baskets in hand, Ingeborg headed for the barn to harness the horses. Kaaren and Solveig would ride in the wagon bed, well-padded with straw, quilts, and hides.

"Whoa." Haakan pulled back on the reins of the harnessed team, now pulling the wagon bed mounted on the heavy carved runners they used in the winter. Metal strips nailed to the runners squeaked in the snow.

"Oh, how nice." Ingeborg set her baskets in a corner of the wagon bed. Andrew crowed at her from the board seat beside his father. She shook her head, smiling up at Haakan and feeling a rush of tears behind her eyes. She swallowed, her smile wobbling. "You are the kindest, most thoughtful man I have ever known."

"All I did was . . ." Haakan stepped to the snowy ground and, with the tip of his finger, removed the drop that wavered on her eyelashes. He smiled, a slow widening of his lips that dented the curve of his cheek and filled his eyes. A smile of love meant just for her.

She would have to tell him soon.

He helped her up to the seat and placed the reins in her hands. "I'll see you before dark?"

She nodded, her throat too full to speak.

"Bye, Far. Bye cows, bye horses, bye Paws." Snugged against her side, Andrew kept up the singsong all the way to Kaaren's, laughing between each name.

Kaaren and Solveig came out of the soddy, each looking about to have a baby. They wore slings with a twin in each and coats buttoned over the precious bundles.

When Ingeborg made a laughing comment, Kaaren answered, "This is the only way I could be sure of keeping them warm enough. I probably should stay home, but, oh, I want to see a new face and hear all the news. They'll be all right, don't you think?"

Ingeborg looked up at the sunny sky. "No storms far as I can see, and we'll be home by dusk. It'll be noisy there with all the little ones, but you know everyone wants to see the twins and you."

"They are growing so fast no one will recognize them in a month." Kaaren set her basket in the sleigh bed and sat down on the open end. She turned and swung her legs up, inching her way to the mound of covers. "You can do that, can't you, Solveig?"

Solveig did the same, a grimace crossing her face when she banged her bad leg against the side. But she quickly joined Kaaren in building a cozy nest around them.

"Geeyup!" Andrew bounced on the sleigh seat. He shouted the

word again, and when Ingeborg clucked the horses forward, he shrieked in delight. "Faster, Mor, faster."

"He's a real speed hound, isn't he?"

"Like most boys." Ingeborg clucked the horses into a trot. The bells Olaf had fastened on the harness jangled even more at the quicker pace that ate up the distance to the Baards'.

One by one the wagons and horses arrived, bringing women who laughed in delight at having this time together. Over and over they thanked Agnes for inviting them. They cooed over the now sleeping twins, greeted Solveig with ready smiles when Kaaren introduced her sister, and right away set to piecing the new quilt. They were all careful to not stare at the scar on Solveig's face, having been coached by Penny when she invited them all.

"Where's Mrs. Booth?" asked one of the women of Penny.

"Her husband said she didn't feel up to coming," Penny answered, a frown crossing her brow. "I got the feeling things are worse than we thought out there."

"They ain't been to church, either, since I don't remember when."

"She had some trouble last year, remember? She turned quiet during the winter. Seemed to be off somewhere else, lessen you touched her arm or some such to get her attention."

Agnes nodded. "I remember. Maybe we can meet at her house next time, bring all the food and such. That might perk her up some."

"Oh, I had planned to go get her," Ingeborg said. "Why didn't I do that? Poor woman."

"We have to convince her we need her with us." Agnes motioned everyone to take their chairs. "Shame they have no children. The dark don't seem so bad with the noise and work of little ones underfoot all the time." She glanced toward the four playing in the corner and two others on the bed. "And then you can't hear the wind so either." A shriek came from the corner, followed by Andrew's chuckle.

"Ja, you are right there." Kaaren put one of the twins to her shoulder.

"It's the wind that gets to me," Hildegunn Valders said with a shiver that set her second chin to quivering. "That and the dark of the soddy. My Anner, he brought home some lime and we whitewashed the inside walls. Took some doing with the rough sod and all, but sure does make a difference. Them walls don't soak up all the lamplight anymore, and it looks so nice too." By the time she finished, her pointed nose seemed to be a bit higher in the air. She glanced at the dark walls around her and sniffed just a bit.

"What a good idea." Ingeborg felt the shiver run up her back, too, at the memory of former winters. She looked to Kaaren. "I'll bring some back from St. Andrew when I go to the Bonanza farm in the next day or so."

"Ja, if the weather holds. You'd best be careful." The circle of women, some in chairs, others sitting on stools or the edge of the bed, added their bits.

Needles kept time as the conversation ranged from how fast the children were growing to emphatic opinions on not hiring the Reverend Hostetler. Hildegunn sniffed again when her choice of a man of God was denigrated. Then Kaaren was asked when she would feel up to starting the school.

"I hope next week. Lars said the Johnsons donated a stove, and he and Haakan will hang the door and set in the windows before Sunday."

"Where is Mary?" Hildegunn asked immediately.

"She and the mister were going to Grafton today, early, so she couldn't come. She was real disappointed," Penny responded.

Kaaren glanced over at Solveig, who, though sitting just outside the circle as if she didn't belong, feasted on every word and laugh.

"We doing our service like usual then?"

"Ja, that seems best for now." Kaaren nipped her thread with her teeth, to the tisking of the woman next to her.

"You think you can manage the babies and all our children too?" Slender to the point of her clothes hanging on her frame, Dyrfinna Odell asked the question. Four babies in three years sometimes did that to a woman.

"Solveig will come with me to watch them while I teach. Then she will help the children with their lessons while I feed my two hungry sparrows." Kaaren hid her concern behind a smiling face. She hoped this would meet with everyone's approval. "I know this isn't the most perfect way, but . . ."

"But we all appreciate you being willing to take on such a big job." Ingeborg looked around the circle for heads nodding in agreement. "Might not do it like this in Nordland, but here in Dakota Territory we make do with what we got. And we got a fine teacher here, thank the Lord. If you ain't been doing any better than me at schooling your youngsters, Kaaren's got a whale of a lot of catching up to do."

Chuckles met her sally. Fitting in time to help their children with the three R's was hard for everyone. There was always just too much to do.

"Schoolteachers are supposed to be paid, but we got no cash money or nothing to pay you with," Hildegunn said, a bit of a bull-dog note in her voice. The two starched women on either side of her nodded.

"Lessen you'll take a stewing chicken or some such." These first words from the mouth of Brynja Magron on the left brought a *look* from Hildegunn. Brynja melted back into her chair and stitched faster.

"As if they need such a thing," Hildegunn hissed.

"I know you can't pay," Kaaren answered, her voice gentle. "I don't expect anything. I want to teach, and your children need a teacher. As Ingeborg said, we make do with what we got out here."

More nods and a few "mange takks" answered her.

Ingeborg watched the women's faces. Across the circle, Hildegunn said nothing more, but her eyes flashed her thoughts. She was not about to be happy with this arrangement.

The bits and pieces of cloth turned into bright jewels of the wedding ring pattern as the women's needles kept time with their visiting. Penny took the little children out to play in the barn after dinner and before their naps.

"This quilt should be for her," Agnes whispered when Penny was out the door. "Don't you think?"

"Ja, if that Hjelmer ever shows his face here again."

"It ain't just him, mind you." Agnes threaded her needle in the light from the lamps. "Mr. Clauson—the farmer south of here who lost his wife last winter—has been sniffing around. He would have made his intentions known months ago if Penny had given him any encouragement. He'd make her a fine husband."

"Ja, and he is here."

"Handsome too."

Chuckles met that comment.

With the children bedded down and everyone's coffee cup re-filled, the stitching and visiting continued. One would be hard pressed to say which flew faster, the needles or the tongues. When they finally began folding things away and waking the children to go home, they promised to meet at the Booths' house next and before Christmas.

"Or we could go to the schoolhouse in case there are more who would like to come. Just like we used to meet at the Stavekirke at home."

"Not much comparison between the Stavekirke and our school-house-church combination." Head shaking and chuckles met that comment.

"But one day we will have a church, too, right by the cemetery." Agnes leaned back in her chair with a sigh. "And even confirmation for the older ones."

"We need a pastor for that."

"Ja, he will come when God thinks we are ready for one," Agnes said.

Ingeborg was the last one to go out the door. "You take care of yourself, now, you hear?"

"Now, if that ain't the kettle calling the pot black." Agnes patted her friend's arm. She glanced over at Penny, who was buttoning Andrew's coat. "That one, she don't let me lift a finger."

Penny snorted.

"You think you could come help Kaaren tomorrow or the next day? If the weather holds, I need to make a last run to the Bonanza farm. I'd like Solveig to come with me."

"Sure she can," Agnes answered right quick, in case Penny tried to say no.

After the final good-byes, Ingeborg turned the sleigh toward home, thanking God for such a time as they'd shared. An idea popped into her head halfway home. They would have a barn dance in the next week or so at the first wood-framed barn in the area. She hoped Haakan would agree. She felt another surge of queasy stomach with the rocking of the sleigh on the way home. Tonight she'd better tell Haakan their wonderful news before he caught her throwing up and figured it out for himself.

⁂

"When?" he asked after stifling a shout of joy and hugging her hard. He'd propped himself up on one elbow so he could look down into her face. The bed creaked and rustled as he shifted his weight.

"Somewhere late in the spring or the beginning of summer." She paused, loving the intense look she saw in his eyes. "If all goes well." Her thoughts had swung to the baby they so recently buried.

Haakan nodded. "Agnes is doing better now?"

"Ja." *How did you know what I was thinking?* She kept the thought inside. So often he knew, just as she did with him. She reached up and stroked her fingertips down the side of his face. "You are pleased?"

"Oh, Inge, you have no idea." He quivered under her loving fingers.

"Ja, I do." She lifted her head to meet his lips. "This baby is a prayer answered for me too."

The weather held still and cold so the snow stayed on the ground, but not so cold so as to be confining. The men finished off the roof of the soddy addition, cut a doorway through the sod wall to the main house, and built two sets of bunk beds along the walls. Olaf immediately began working on cupboards with real doors that closed for the third wall and nailed a board of pegs along the other. Shelves fit below that.

"I'll make a cupboard for your kitchen this winter," he promised Ingeborg. "You need more storage places that the mice can't get into."

"You do such fine work, I can't imagine how we ever got along without you." She fingered the leather hinges he'd attached to the doors.

"One day I'll get time to pound out some iron ones, but these will do for now."

"You want I should buy you some in St. Andrew?"

He shook his head. "No sense spending money for that. I can make them just as well."

That afternoon Ingeborg took the three mattress tickings she had sewn out to the straw stack and, burrowing under the wet, pulled out dry straw and stuffed it into the mattresses. *One day*, she promised herself, *we will all have feather beds to sleep on.*

They had the sleigh loaded long before dawn lightened the sky. To the north the aurora borealis danced on the horizon and far into the heavens. Their breath made steam clouds in front of them.

"I could go, you know." Haakan swung one of the smoked haunches into the straw-lined bed.

"I know, but I can do this, and that will leave you free to work on the barn or your workshop. Think how it will feel to move the milk cows into that bright building. Line them all up at once instead of them taking turns." She eyed the stack of cheese rounds. "With that many cows, we sure have been able to turn out the cheese and butter. You know, if we had some goats, I could make gammelost."

Haakan's laugh exploded on the frigid air. "And if you had herring, you could make sur sild. Inge, will you never quit?"

"Not as long as something can bring in money to pay off the land and our bills. Just think, only a few more months and the homestead will be proved up. The sooner I can pay off the note on the half section Roald bought, the sooner we can buy more."

"And a steam engine for the lumber mill."

"I know, I know. And it will be used for threshing too." She tucked the edges of the hides in around their wares. "Perhaps I should take Andrew with me."

"Let him sleep. You know he loves being in the barn with us men. I swear that if I gave him a hammer, he'd help put up the stalls for the horses."

"He can't begin too soon. That's what my far always said."

"He was right. Now you be careful, you hear? If the temperature drops or that north wind starts to blow, you stay somewhere warm."

"I promise." She held up her hand. "But I'll be back after dark, so leave a light in the window."

"If you're not, I'll come looking for you."

With those words ringing in her ears, Ingeborg let him assist her up to the seat and slapped the horses' reins. Solveig had better be ready.

"But I don't want to go." Solveig turned back again at the door, sending a pleading look to Kaaren. "You need help with the babies."

"You know Penny is coming to help me." Kaaren tucked an oven-heated rock into a sack. "This will keep your feet warm." With that, she threw her heavy wool shawl around her shoulders and pushed her sister out the door. Solveig drew her muffler over the side of her face and across her mouth, effectively hiding the scar.

"See you tonight." Ingeborg clucked the horses forward and waved to Kaaren.

Solveig didn't say a word until after the sun was well up.

Ingeborg gave up trying to talk with her, wondering if this hadn't been a bad idea after all. Thorliff and Baptiste had clamored to go. She should have let them come and left this unhappy soul at home.

The ford at the Little Salt River was frozen solid just as Ingeborg expected. With the water so low in the fall, it didn't take too many days of real cold to cover the sluggish river. The river looked more like a good-sized creek at this time of year.

The horses stepped out tentatively, but when the ice held, they trotted on across. Bob only slipped once and that did nothing more than kick Ingeborg's heart into a fast tempo. She glanced at her companion to see Solveig clutching the edge of the seat with both hands.

"The Red won't be frozen yet, so young MacKenzie will have the ferry running. His far owns the Mercantile. You'll like the missus. She's the one gave me that slip of geranium growing in my window."

"Do they sell dress goods at the Mercantile?"

Ingeborg clutched at the reins, causing the horses to toss their heads and set the bells to ringing even more. Solveig had actually asked a question. "Why yes, and about anything else anyone needs. They bring their supplies in on the paddle-wheeler, you know, the one we traveled home on."

"That seems like years ago." Solveig shifted her injured leg.

"Ja, it does."

By the time they reached St. Andrew, Solveig was looking around with interest and commenting on the things she saw. Ingeborg figured that a definite improvement. Perhaps there was hope for the young woman sitting beside her after all.

What Solveig didn't yet understand was that as soon as the word got out there was a woman of marrying age at the Bjorklund farm, suitors, however suitable or not, would come calling. Had she thought to give George Carlson, manager of the Bonanza farm, an unexpected advantage? She shook her head at the absurdity of the idea. But the scar wasn't nearly so noticeable now as Solveig thought, since time and the concoction applied by Metiz had done their healing work. Solveig was still a beautiful young woman.

MacKenzie's son pulled the ferry, really a large raft, across the Red by way of the rope that lay on the bottom of the river until needed. The paddle-wheeler had stopped running for the winter several weeks before. The slow moving, mud-colored river flowed low like the Little Salt.

"Why do they call this the Red River?" Solveig relaxed again once the sleigh reached the Minnesota shore. The horses dug their feet in to pull the sleigh up the sloping bank. While wheels might have done better here, the mud allowed the runners to slip fairly easily.

"I wondered the same thing. Someone told me it's because the river looks red when the sun hits it just right. The silt in it causes that, I guess."

Solveig gave her a raised eyebrow look.

Ingeborg smiled. "That's what I thought too."

When they arrived at the Bonanza farm, Mrs. Carlson, mother of the manager, George, came to the door as soon as the dogs heralded a welcome. "Why, Mrs. Bjorklund, how wonderful to see you. I was afraid our supplier was done for the winter." She beckoned with her hand. "Come in, come in. One of the hands will unload and take care of the horses for you. Surely you have time for something to eat, a cup of coffee, at least."

"It's good to see you too." Ingeborg swung down from the wooden seat, stamping her feet to get the blood flowing before she tried walking on them. In spite of the elk robe that covered their legs, her feet had gone somewhat numb. She came around the rig to help Solveig down. "Be careful. Your feet may be asleep."

"If not frozen off."

Ingeborg looked up in time to see a smile flit across Solveig's face. She was joking! Solveig was joking. The smile brought back memories of the laughing young girl she'd known in Nordland. *Thanks be to God.* "No, I can see them. They're still attached to the bottoms of your legs."

Another smile. This one stayed long enough that Ingeborg could see the scar disappear in the smile lines so seldom used of late. Actually, the scar made the dimple that lurked there more obvious. She handed Solveig the crutch when she stood on solid ground, and together they made their way up the walk to the back door of the two-story square house, hugged by a wide porch on three sides. Solveig negotiated the four steps with ease.

"Mrs. Carlson, I'd like you to meet Kaaren's younger sister, Solveig. She came to us from Norway a month or so ago."

"My land, child, whatever happened to your leg?" Mrs. Carlson spoke Norwegian, albeit not well.

Solveig sucked in a deep breath. "I was hurt in a terrible train wreck east of Chicago. Many people died, so I am lucky to be alive." She gestured to her leg. "It is healing. Soon I'll be walking without my crutch."

*Thanks be to thee, oh, heavenly Father.* Ingeborg wanted to shout the praise from the top of the porch. Instead she removed her coat and gloves, knowing Mrs. Carlson would take them to be hung up. Solveig watched her and did the same.

"You just go right on in the kitchen there. That's the warmest room in the house. I made a pot of soup this morning, and we will have a bowl of that. George should be in from the machine shed any minute now." The guests turned to the sunny room where geraniums bloomed on the windowsills and the fragrance of something baking beckoned all to make themselves to home. A white cat snoozed on the braided rug by the polished wood range, yawning and showing its pink tongue as the visitors entered. A canary chirped from a cage beside the window.

Solveig looked at Ingeborg with wide eyes. *If only she could see the rest of the house*, thought Ingeborg.

"Sit down, sit down." Mrs. Carlson, her black bombazine gown rustling with every motion, quickly set two more places at the round oak table, which was covered with a pansy embroidered tablecloth. The napkins wore matching pansies in one corner.

*Someday.* Ingeborg renewed the promise to herself every time she came to this farm. *Someday I will have a kitchen like this, a house like this. Someday.*

Boots being kicked against the stoop announced George's arrival. A smile split his tanned face and brightened the golden flecks in his hazel eyes.

"Mrs. Bjorklund, how good to see you." He hung his brown wool jacket on the oak coat-tree by the door, setting his muffler and hat on top. "We didn't think you would be coming again until spring." He crossed the kitchen to rub his hands in the heat above the stove. "And who is your assistant this time?"

Ingeborg introduced them, watching George's face. Sure enough, his smile broadened when he dipped his head in greeting. She was glad to see he suffered no pangs from Haakan marrying her out of the blue like he did. George had shown interest in her and had asked to come calling as a suitor.

"And how is your sister-in-law?" he asked of Ingeborg.

"She is the proud mother of twin girls born a little over a month ago." Ingeborg filled them in on the news of the settlement growing across the river. All the while Mrs. Carlson continued bringing food to the table. The kettle of soup, a plate of sliced bread, sliced cheese, pickles, jam, and honey. The coffeepot took up residence on a hot pad near her elbow. When she finally took her place, George bowed his head and said the grace.

Soon with everything passed around the table, they all fell to, the talking lagging for a few minutes at first. Fluffy dumplings floated in the chicken soup, probably made from one of the Bjork-lund chickens. Ingeborg savored every bite. Mrs. Carlson was a marvelous cook.

When they got ready to leave, the older woman asked for the total she owed them and went to another room for her pocketbook.

"I hope you will come again." George held Solveig's hand slightly longer than necessary.

"Perhaps you can join us for a barn dance to celebrate our new barn." Ingeborg swiftly figured out a date. "Saturday after next." She hoped Haakan would agree. He'd already said a celebration was in order.

"Do you want me to bring my fiddle?"

"I didn't know you played. Bring it if you like, but you needn't feel you must. If your mother would like to come, bring her too." As the words spilled from her mouth, Ingeborg wondered where she would house these people. They were used to much finer than the soddy.

"Thank you for the invitation. I will come for sure, and Mother . . . I don't know. She doesn't like long rides in the winter."

"Which reminds me, this all depends upon the weather, of course."

"Of course."

Mrs. Carlson returned with the cash for Ingeborg. "There now. I will look forward to your return in the spring. When all our hands come back to work, we depend upon your produce to feed them."

Once on the road home, Solveig sat silently, her feet warm now on the hot bricks Mrs. Carlson had insisted they accept.

Ingeborg ached to ask her what she was thinking but refrained at the expense of several tooth marks in her tongue.

The sun was sinking toward the west when they were finally loaded with goods from the Mercantile, including a potbellied stove for the shop in the barn—Ingeborg's gift to the men. The harness and bells jingled as the horses picked up the pace, knowing they were homeward bound.

Protected in her pocket was the most important packet—three letters from Norway and one from Fargo. Though she had asked, there had been none for Penny. Hjelmer still hadn't answered, and neither had any of the railroad companies Kaaren had written to. That was no surprise, since the letters hadn't been gone that long. But Hjelmer. Where was Hjelmer? What had happened to him? Penny wouldn't wait forever, would she? The letter from her friend Mrs. Johnson at the Headquarters Hotel in Fargo would tell the tale.

I'm going with you." Katja, the young washerwoman, tossed her bundle up into the open freight car.

"No, you're not." Hjelmer looked around to see who else besides himself and Leif were in the dark freight car. They had just swung aboard themselves.

"In case you haven't noticed, this is a free country. I can go where I want, just like you." She hoisted herself up into the open door and got to her feet. Ignoring Leif's stunned look, she turned her attention and her ire to Hjelmer. "You were going to leave without a word, weren't you?"

Hjelmer glared down at her, feeling like an idiot for being caught out in so transparent a web. "I ain't made you no promises."

"I know that. And I ain't making you none either. But they're closing up the camp, and I thought I might as well leave with the earlier ones than the later. Which don't make no nevermind. You could at least have come to say good-bye." She stamped her foot, setting her multicolored skirt in a swirl. The draft from the open door added to the motion, showing more than a glimpse of her calf.

Katja ignored the wind and her skirt, her entire attention focused on the man-boy in front of her. "And I thought we was friends."

"We . . . we are . . . were." Hjelmer hated himself for stammering. He sent a pleading look to Leif, only to receive a shrugged shoulder response.

"Then why not take me with you? You two are friends and you stay together."

Hjelmer stared at her. She knew the difference, of course she did. Didn't she? Had he been reading her signals all wrong? He rubbed his hands over his head, knocking his hat back on the floor. When he stooped to pick it up, he noticed a broad smile of white teeth from the far corner. Sam's face was too dark to see.

Great, now they had an audience. After all this time he'd tried to keep his friendship with the young woman a secret. Keeping a secret in a railroad camp was like pushing a water-soaked rope uphill against an avalanche.

With a jerk the train started forward, iron wheels shrieking against the track.

She clutched the front of his jacket for balance. "I won't be in yer way, I promise."

Hjelmer shook his head and shrugged at the same time. "Suit yourself." He pulled away, picking up his pack and carrying it back to the end of the boxcar. Then he and Leif pulled the doors closed, cutting off all light except the rays coming in from a few places where boards were missing.

The four of them sat close together for warmth, making desultory comments as the morning passed. Hjelmer leaned his head back against the car wall and let his mind wander. At least he knew where he was going, and that he had work when he got there. The big boss on the job had come to him several days before, just as they were putting their tools away for the day.

"You want a job for the winter?" he asked, standing close so his voice didn't carry.

"Ja, I do." Hjelmer tucked his pigskin gloves in the ties of his leather apron.

"We need some good men at the roundhouse in St. Paul. The pay isn't quite as good as out here on the line, but it's better than average. You ask for John Reggincamp when you get there and tell him I sent you."

"Can Leif come too?" The words surprised Hjelmer as much as the boss.

The big man squinted and ran his tongue over his lower lip. Finally he nodded. "He works hard, and there's no shortage of locomotives to repair. There should be a place for him too. But I want you back here in the spring. I'll let you know when."

Hjelmer nodded in response. "Thank you."

Leif let out a whoop when Hjelmer told him the news. "Thankee, my friend. I owe you for that."

"You owe me already." The two jostled each other on the way to the meal car.

"No, you owe me. Remember the night I saved your bacon with Big Red? That's worth lots of paybacks."

Hjelmer brought his mind back to the frigid railcar. They should have hoisted a barrel in here to build a fire in. He untied his quilt from his bundle and wrapped it around himself, then lifted the edge to let Katja, whose teeth were clattering in the cold, crawl under it too.

"Didn't you bring a blanket?"

She shook her head. "I was in too much of a hurry."

Warming each other, they fell into an uneasy sleep. The train stopped in Fargo before heading farther east. Leif jumped down and promised to bring back some food for all of them.

"How far you going, Sam?" Hjelmer asked.

"St. Paul, like you. Thought to go on home, but dey need money more'n dey need me."

*Home. Is the Red River Valley my home now? Is Penny still waiting?* He thought of heading north before he continued east, but what if the job disappeared because he didn't get there right away? He would write to her as soon as he had a place to live, that's what he'd do.

Pleased with that decision, he fell to the bread and cheese Leif brought back. Bellies full and the train again in forward motion, the four of them shared their blankets and took advantage of the chance for some extra sleep.

⁂

Once in St. Paul, the four pooled their resources to rent a small house not far from the roundhouse. With no furniture other than a cookstove, the men took over the main room and gave Katja the bedroom. Since they'd arrived on a Friday night, the men headed out on Saturday morning for the roundhouse to find Reggincamp.

"I will find us a table at least," Katja promised.

"Or some lumber so we can build one. And we need either coal or wood."

"We need everything."

"Ja, well, we will make do."

When they got home again, after being told to start work on Monday, the fragrance of simmering stew met them at the door. A kettle bubbled on the stove, now hot from coal chunks like those in the box beside it. One upturned box made a table, and three smaller ones served as makeshift chairs.

"How?" Hjelmer and Leif exchanged puzzled glances.

"I found the coal along the tracks and the boxes in a heap. There are more boxes there if you want. The kettle I bought for a nickel from a peddler and the meat and vegetables came from . . . well, you don't want to know where they came from." Katja gave the stew a stir with a scrubbed stick. "You want to eat first or go out and look for more? I heard there's some real fine houses up on the hill. Those folks usually throw good stuff away. You just got to be there at the right time."

Sam chuckled. "She be right." His soft southern accent rounded out the words.

"You could carve us some spoons, Hjelmer. I seen your animals and birds. You are some good with a knife." She fetched four tin cans she'd scrubbed clean and poured the stew into them. "Take your places." She set a loaf of bread in the middle of the table. "That'll have to do for spoons for now."

When Hjelmer smiled at her and shook his head, she grinned back, giving her an impish look. "Told you I wouldn't be no burden. Katja carries her own weight in this world."

On his scouting trips that day and the next, Hjelmer found himself thinking of the places he passed where he knew men played cards. He could be in there, warm and comfortable, making real money instead of searching the city for things they could use. His cold fingers itched to feel the crisp cards, to finger the ones he would keep and the ones to discard. He forced his mind back to the hunt. He'd sworn off gambling. *Remember that*, he ordered sternly.

The evenings were spent turning their finds into useful tools. They tore apart more boxes, carefully saving the nails to be pounded straight again. When Leif produced a hammer head he'd picked up in the camp out west, Hjelmer fashioned a handle for it. They nailed some boards over one window that had no glass and used others to make a chair. What was left they stacked in the corner to be used later. One box became their food store and another the kitchen counter and cupboard. Keeping things cold wasn't a problem; keeping themselves warm proved more difficult. They needed bedding desperately. If a real cold spell hit the area, they could all be frozen by morning. Roughing it in the camp was luxury compared to this. At least there they'd had plenty of hot food and heat.

Picking up coal along the railroad tracks became habit for all of them. No one went out without the bags that Katja stitched up from some ragged curtain material she found behind a house.

Hjelmer thought of all the wages he had sent to the bank in Grand Forks. How he wished he had some of it now. He'd paid off his chit at the company store and already spent the rest of his last pay. He couldn't get into a card game if he wanted to. He had no more cash. But after payday, that would change. Vow or no vow, he—they—needed money to live here in the city, and he knew how to get some fast.

He remembered the wood carvings he'd so carefully wrapped and stashed in his pack. "You think folks might be willing to pay for those carvings of mine?" he asked Katja after supper on Sunday night.

She thought a moment, then nodded. "I could sell them for you, if'n you want. Most likely get a better price than you would."

He started to take offense at her remark and then caught the laughter in her eyes. "You probably would." He went to his bundle and brought out the carvings, setting them on the table in the light of the candle Sam had brought home. An eagle in flight, another sitting on a rock, a grouse, a flying duck, and two geese in a piece together. A half-finished fox he set to the side.

"What do you think?"

"I think we'll eat fine this week." She stroked the feathers of the goose.

Sam picked up the eagle and turned it to see all the sides. "You done more'n I thought, dose nights around de fire. I got some leather I been workin' on." He laid finely braided thongs on the table. "Could be watch fobs for de gentry."

"You want them sold?"

Sam nodded.

"Good." Katja gathered in the treasures. "You go bend iron, and I'll take care of the rest."

The next Saturday night all three men turned part of their wages over to the young woman to pay for food, sent Leif to pay the rent with part, and after supper, headed for the nearest saloon and the card games.

Hjelmer fought down the guilt that rose with his decision to gamble again. After all, he *had* made a vow. He jingled the coins in his pocket, knowing if he didn't win quickly, he wouldn't be playing long. There was no time tonight to feel out the men at the table, finding their strengths and weaknesses. He needed a win.

But Lady Luck seemed to have deserted him, and with the

money quickly gone, he and Leif slogged through the slush in the street back to the shanty. Fat snowflakes settled on their shoulders and hats.

Hjelmer felt like swearing. Playing poker tonight had not been fun.

By the next week, with a bit more cash at his side, he threw off the need-to-win and settled back in his normal style. Lose one, win one, give another, win small, and then edge toward the bigger pots as those around him got drunker and his glass stayed about the same.

"You did it!" Leif thumped him on the shoulder.

"Ja, but I wondered there at first." Hjelmer hunched his shoulders against the cold. He could feel the temperature dropping as they walked along. "How'd you do?" They always played at separate tables.

"A bit above even. I ain't got the touch like you. I heard about another place where some of the railroad men play, if that be any interest to you."

Hjelmer stopped to look at his friend. When the wind whipped around the corner and slashed his face, he started walking again. "Where?"

Leif told him, but when after a block of rapid walking and Hjelmer had not said a word, Leif asked, "So what do you think?"

"I think I need a plan, and part of that plan will be to wear better clothes than these when I go there to play."

"Ahhh. That's wise."

After three weeks of Katja using their money to purchase all the supplies they so desperately needed to survive, the three men did as they'd done out on the prairie—sent most of their wages elsewhere. Sam sent his to his family, who, now that he could get mail at the post office, wrote to him once in a while. Leif and Hjelmer sent theirs to the bank in Grand Forks, Leif having decided he might look for land up that way one day. But since the wages were much less than out on the train line, the accounts grew slowly.

Hjelmer's gambling stash at the house grew weekly, even after he gave Katja money to buy extra blankets for each of them and an ample supply of coal. With the bone-breaking cold setting in, they all moved their pallets close to the stove, but even that wasn't enough to keep them comfortable.

Katja lived up to her part of the bargain, keeping hot food on the table most days. The day coffee appeared at one of the meals, the men raised a toast to her health. The fire the compliment sent to her face made her look feverish, but her laughter dispelled any such notion. She fixed dinner pails for them and scouted for coal and wood for the fire every day. One never knew what her collecting would bring in, but between the men's carvings and her nose for finds, the house began to appear like a real home.

She bought herself needle and thread, patching the garments she washed and dried for them on a line above the stove. Every spare moment the needle flashed, turning scraps into a quilt top and then a braided rug. She haunted the bins behind the woolen mill for left-over fleece for batting and bits of yarn that she used to tie the quilt.

When the new quilt appeared on his pallet, Hjelmer took it into the kitchen. "Why for me?"

"Can't a body give a gift if'n they wants?" She looked up from her stitching.

"Ja, but you need it worse. I heard you shivering in the night."

"Yes, and you spread your new wool blanket over me."

Sam chuckled from his place at the other side of the stove. "That weren't him, that were Leif."

"Well, then . . ." She paused for a moment. "Then he'll get the next one." She held up the piece she was working on, already grown to a yard square. "Won't be long till it's ready."

Trudging through the near dark of the early morning on his way to work, Hjelmer considered the gambling and his vow. Surely if God minded, he wouldn't be winning like he was. The thought blunted the guilt that gnawed at his belly when he took time to think on it, but something about it just wouldn't let go.

Once inside the great domed building, he pushed thoughts of his predicament aside and, ignoring the cacophony of sound, made his way down the rows to his forge and the day's work. With pulleys screeching overhead and the belts that brought the power to the blowers whining when engaged, the steady ring of his heavy ham-mers on forming steel seemed to disappear in the upper regions of the two-story building. Donkey engines pulled the cars to be worked on along the tracks that bisected the switching area. Leif and Sam worked on the section that removed broken parts from steam engines and replaced them with either repaired or new stock.

Hjelmer soon developed a reputation for forging parts that fit without numerous trials.

"You got a good eye, Bjorklund," Reginncamp said one afternoon on one of his walk-throughs. "You want to stay on here instead of going back out on the line, you just let me know. Men like you are hard to find."

"Thank you." Hjelmer bobbed his head and stuck the bolt he was grooving into the bucket of water, sending steam head high. But working in a fire pit like this in the soot-covered, crowded city held no draw for him. He'd rather work the forge on a flatcar where the clean wind blows away the stink of steel and coke. Besides, the prairie was closer to home—and Penny.

Hjelmer caught Leif watching Katja one evening. His gaze followed the girl's sprightly movements like a sheep dog guarding the flock. *Ah, so that is the way the wind blows,* Hjelmer thought. He looked up to catch a small nod from Sam. Now he had a new puzzle to work out.

He still hadn't written to Penny, but he began to mention her once in a while, talking about her as the girl waiting for him back near the Red River. He hoped to heaven she still was.

He passed Christmas Eve playing cards with a bunch of lonely men. Christmas Day Katja surprised them all with a dinner of roast chicken and potatoes followed by a real apple pie.

"I'm sorry I don't have any presents to give you," she said, her eyes sad instead of the normal sparkle.

"This is gift enough," Leif said with a slight bow. "I don't know how you feed us like you do on the little bit we give you."

Hjelmer wished he had made things for each of them, but his mind had only worked on his plan to learn more about the railroad men so he could finally join their gaming table. "Thank you, Katja," he said simply.

"Me too," Sam added. "Don't you worry yourself none, missy. You do more'n your share." He smoothed his hand down the tear she had mended in the front of his shirt.

One paycheck later, Hjelmer was ready. He brought paper-and-string-wrapped packages home with him containing new fawn pants, a black tailored jacket, and a white shirt. The boots in their box drew oh's of appreciation from his friends. When he was washed—he'd nearly scrubbed the skin off his fingers to get the black out from around the nails—and dressed, he stopped in the arch to the main room.

"Well?"

"Well, Mistah Bjorklund, suh." Sam pretended to doff his cap and bow.

"You look mighty fine." Katja walked around him and brushed

some lint off his shoulders. "If I didn't know who you was, I'd never recognize you."

Leif laughed. "That makes sense." He wore a clean white shirt, new black pants, and had polished his boots to help them somewhat. He didn't plan to play with that crowd anyway. He was going along to protect Hjelmer's back, if need be.

The two set out, the night air frigid, but the wind and snow had stopped.

"Should have caught a cab," Hjelmer muttered, his chin sunk down in his collar. "Or bought a warmer coat." But when they walked up the front steps of the hotel, he ignored his cold hands, stuffed his hat in Leif's jacket pocket, and threw his shoulders back. They made their way to the back room where the gaming could be heard from down the hall. Smoke hung heavy on air redolent with the smells of fine cigars and premium whiskey. Men with green eye-shades and black garters holding up their sleeves dealt at each card table, while another ran a game of dice.

Hjelmer looked around. Which table served the men he was searching for—the railroad men? He strolled through the room, pausing once in a while to pick up on bits of conversation. In the mirror above the carved walnut bar, he saw Leif take a seat and give his order.

"Can I help you, sir?" The floor-length red velvet dress fit the woman as though it had been sewn around her. Her voice held a hint of honey. Only with a supreme effort, Hjelmer kept his eyes from straying lower than her face.

"I am looking for a table to play at." His glance had just shown him all were filled.

"Follow me." He was sure men were willing to follow her anywhere.

She drew out a curved-back chair from a table in a far corner. "This is the only seat we have available right now. Best of luck. May I bring you something from the bar?"

If her voice wasn't invitation enough, her eyes said it all.

"Thank you." Hjelmer asked for a whiskey, although he only pretended to drink it—his usual practice since he needed a clear head and hated the taste of it anyway.

He took his seat and nodded at the five men around the table. The man with the green shade announced the game.

When one of the men asked where he was from, Hjelmer said, "Out west." He answered their other questions with similar short remarks, asking few of his own. He knew he'd learn more just by listening. That night he only came out even. But he was invited to come back again.

"Part of the plan?" Leif asked on the way home.

Hjelmer nodded.

Each week he brought home more cash, the amount doubling and sometimes tripling the week before. One day he took it all with him on his way to work, using his dinner break to open a bank account. Leaving that much cash in the ramshackle house was foolish, and foolish he did not intend to be. This was his land money he was playing with, money to start a blacksmith shop so he could ask Penny to marry him.

One night after he'd been playing with the same group for about a month, the talk turned to railway spurs—who was laying them and where. Mention of Grafton and Drayton caught his attention. When they talked about the right of way, Hjelmer realized it would go right across a corner of the Bjorklund land. He was pleased for Ingeborg and Kaaren, but the railbed before that and on the other side of the Little Salt meant more to him. If he could buy up some of that land and resell it to the railroad at a better price . . .

He lost a goodly amount on the following hand. His mind was too busy counting up the profit to be made in the buying and selling of Red River Valley land.

How could he make it happen without anyone becoming suspicious? And before the news leaked out to the general public?

The afternoon of the barn dance finally arrived.

When the dancing began, Uncle Olaf played the harmonica, revealing another surprising side to this man who Ingeborg was realizing hid many untold talents. Along with George's fiddle, Joseph Baard's fiddle, and two guitars, they had quite a good band.

While Solveig still couldn't dance, she never lacked for a male partner to sit with her. When he wasn't playing his fiddle, George sat with her and the others took turns: several farmers, a store owner from Grafton, Joel Gunderson, pastor of the Lutheran Church in Acton—the town upriver from St. Andrew—and a new immigrant who spoke only Swedish, which most of them understood anyway. His smile more than made up for the language.

"I told you so," Ingeborg whispered to Solveig as she passed one time.

Penny, too, as the only other female of marrying age, never sat still for a minute. Modan Clauson tried to monopolize her time, but she made sure she danced with all the others who asked. "If only Hjelmer were here," she said to Ingeborg when they met at the cider bowl.

"I know. I thought the same thing. We'll have to do something like this for your wedding."

"If there ever is one." Penny downed her cider as another young man tapped her shoulder.

"There could be one right soon if you wanted."

"I'd rather go to Fargo. We have to write and tell your friend when I am coming." She whirled off to dance the pols, followed by a polka, either of which would set a person to breathing hard.

Ingeborg glanced over to the area near the stove where the children played. The babies were over at the soddy with the younger girls taking turns watching them and coming for the mothers when the children needed feeding. A long table off to one side had nearly disappeared under all the cakes, cookies, candies, and pies the guests brought, but now it showed the ravages of the partying horde. The scent of fresh lumber still filled the barn, since the animals hadn't been allowed in it yet. Even above the music and dancing, she heard the thunder of feet on the bare boards and the shrieks of laughter in the haymow above where the older children played. Haakan had hung two thick ropes with a big knot at the end for swings, which proved a perfect entertainment for them.

The westering sun sparkled on the new windows along the side walls. Ingeborg sighed. She'd rather live in the barn this winter than the house. Every once in a while, she let herself regret talking Haakan into building the barn instead of the house this year. But with all the new stock, they needed the barn worse. Even so . . .

"Ingeborg, may I have the honor of this dance?" Haakan asked from behind her, his breath tickling her ear.

"Ja, you may." She smiled up at him, glad they were playing a waltz so she could be in his arms.

With the stove red hot and the dancers red of face, no one felt the cold outside. About halfway through the party, Ingeborg noticed the men slipping outside more and more often. They always came back slapping their hands against their upper arms and shuddering "brrr," but it wasn't long before they went out again. Usually one at a time, sometimes two or three.

When she changed partners in one of the pattern dances, she smelled something and sniffed again. Sure enough, the man had been drinking. So that was the draw to go outside. Someone had brought a bottle, or from the heartier laughter she heard frequently, more than one.

"I think it is disgusting," Hildegunn Valders said when she dipped a cup at the cider bowl again.

"I'm not happy with the drinking, either, but as the saying goes, men will be men," Ingeborg answered.

Agnes joined them. "Are you are talking about what I'm thinking about?"

"Our imbibing husbands?" Ingeborg saw Haakan leave by the small door too. How come she hadn't noticed the smell on his breath when they danced? Of course he could be stepping outside for another reason.

"Ja, Joseph has had his share, but I think Petar is too young. And he's been out several times."

"Keeping count?"

Mrs. Valders raised her chin and therefore her nose a bit in the air. "Well, my Anner would never do such a thing."

Ingeborg cocked an eyebrow at Agnes. Anner had been the man she'd danced with when she first noticed the smell. His nose shone red as a polished fall apple. She wouldn't want to be in his boots on that long sleigh ride home. His wife's tongue was sharp enough to filet fish.

*So what do I do? Ask Haakan to make them stop? Go out there and take away the bottle myself? God, your Word doesn't say people shouldn't drink, but it does say many things about getting drunk—and none of them good. Why did they have to bring something like this along? Who brought it?* The thoughts raged behind the smiling face she presented to the laughing people.

"Would you dance with me, Mor?" Thorliff appeared at her side.

"Ja, I will. You think you know the steps to this one?"

He grinned up at her, his eyes appearing more blue above the red of his cheeks. "If I forget, you will help me."

"I saw you dancing with Ingrid Johnson. You were doing very well."

His cheeks pinked even more. "She is a good dancer."

Ingeborg bit back a smile. Ingrid had eyelashes as long as a cat's whiskers and already knew how to use them.

When the women brought the hot food out from the soddy, the musicians put away their instruments amid applause from everyone. They had certainly warmed this barn up well. After everyone ate, the move began to head home for chores. Ingeborg, Haakan, Kaaren, and Lars bid everyone good-bye at the door and thanked them for coming. The last sleigh to leave held the Baard clan. Agnes was driving, Knute and Swen up on the seat beside her. Joseph and Petar sat in the back with the younger children, all buried up to their noses in elk robes and quilts.

Ingeborg quirked an eyebrow, and Agnes shook her head. There was no further need for speech concerning what had gone on. She waved them off and turned back to the barn.

After they cleared away the tables made of sawhorses and boards covered with tablecloths, Thorliff began hauling in straw for the cow stanchions. They would milk in the new barn for the first time. When all twelve milk cows were lined up, their heads facing the center of the barn, all the Bjorklunds stopped to admire the sight. Thorliff poured a measure of grain for each in the long manger in front of them, and the men began milking. With three of them at it, the women returned to the soddy. They now had all the milk cows in one place, and the sod barn at Lars and Kaaren's would be used to house the young stock and the bull.

"That was the best party ever, I think." Kaaren leaned over the bed and picked up the fussing Sophie.

Solveig propped her leg up on the stool in front of the rocking chair. She leaned forward and rubbed below her knee, nodding as she did so. "George Carlson is a very nice man, isn't he?"

Kaaren and Ingeborg swapped secret looks at the dreamy tone.

"Oh, really?" Kaaren said. "Guess I hadn't noticed."

The two older women chuckled. Ingeborg added, "What we're going to hear about is the goings-on outside. Hildegunn Valders will make sure of that, unless of course she kills her husband on the way home and has to leave the area."

"Even then, she will have an excuse for him and a scathing tongue for the rest."

"Why, Kaaren . . ." Ingeborg stopped from saying the rest of her thought.

"I know. Don't tell me." Kaaren held up one hand. "The Bible says to say no ill of anyone. Actually it says of no *man*, so I guess this is permissible." She shook her head. "Ja, I know that doesn't count, either, but that woman makes me mad. Her and her nose in the air. Whatever makes her think she is better than the rest of us? Or that she should be able to tell us all what to do? That man she thought should be our pastor?" She rolled her eyes. "If he was the only minister on earth, we'd do better with ourselves. Scared those little ones half to death with all that thundering and shouting. He think we were hard of hearing or something?"

Ingeborg kept in her mind that Kaaren hadn't even been to the service the day of the Hostetler preaching. Someone had sure filled her ears with all the news.

"Who told you about that?" Ingeborg paused. "Other than me, that is."

"Oh, everyone. Even Thorliff. He was furious that the man made Andrew cry."

Kaaren unbuttoned her shirtwaist and sat down to let Sophie nurse. After throwing a blanket over her shoulder, she leaned back in the chair. "Guess I was a bit upset there and spewed it out all over you."

"Ja, I'd say so."

"He asked if I'd like to go on a sleigh ride with him sometime," Solveig murmured.

Ingeborg and Kaaren looked first at the dreamy-eyed girl, then at each other. Laughter rang in the rafters of the soddy, setting the bunches of drying herbs tied there to rustling.

Ingeborg whispered from behind her hand. "We better get busy on that quilt we all started. I know Agnes thought it to be for Penny, but I have a feeling . . ."

"Me too," Kaaren whispered back. "Hope she waits until the twins are walking."

At church the next day, a few of the men were missing. There seemed to be a rash of headaches and stomach ailments.

"Must have caught something at your party," Agnes said once the service was over. Joseph didn't look too good, but at least he was there.

"Ja, my far used to call it the hops-n-barley sickness." Ingeborg looked around the room. The twinkle in her eye brought forth one from her friend.

"I know. Interesting who is not here today."

Penny joined them. "Ingeborg, would you write your friend in Fargo and tell her I am coming?"

"When do you want to go?"

"Today if I could." She flashed a telling glance at her aunt.

"You could just take the letter with you. Mrs. Johnson said you would be welcome anytime."

"Onkel Joseph said he would pay for my train ticket. I need to find out when someone is going to Grafton."

"I think I heard the Helmsrudes say they would be going some-time soon. Why don't you ask them?"

All during the discussion, Agnes kept her gaze lowered. When Penny left, she whispered to Ingeborg. "How I am going to miss that girl. I couldn't love her more if she were my own daughter." She shook her head, setting the slack skin under her chin to wobbling. "Sure hope she is doing the right thing."

Ingeborg knew Agnes's opinions about Hjelmer. "So do I. Seems to me that since she wants more schooling, this is good for her. In the years ahead, she will be grateful for that."

"Why? We didn't need more schooling. You learn how to be a

wife and mother from your mor and the doing of it, not from teachers and classrooms."

"Ja, I know. But things are different in America. Here women can teach school and own their own land. You know she dreams of having a store one day."

"Ja, she does. And Hjelmer, that . . ." She glanced out the side of her eye, stopping the words they both knew she felt. "Guess you just have to let these young'uns learn their own lessons."

"You mean leave them in God's hands?"

"Ja, that too."

Three days later Penny said good-bye to everyone and left for Grafton and the train to Fargo.

"Uff da," Agnes said, turning to Ingeborg, who had come over to make it easier for her friend. "She's never been on a train in her life." Agnes used the corner of her apron to wipe her eyes. "How will I answer to my sister in heaven if something terrible happens to her girl?"

## 18

The next Monday, Kaaren rang the iron bar for the opening of school.

"Good morning, Mitheth Knutson," lisped a slender little girl. With straight hair the lightest of towhead, she stopped in front of the high bench Kaaren would call a desk. "I am Anna Helmthrude." Her speech in English showed careful rehearsing.

"And how old are you, Anna?" Kaaren asked, also in English.

The child's eyes darted right and left. She looked up again, a combination of fear and questions darkening her cornflower blue eyes. When Kaaren asked the question again in Norwegian, the child breathed a sigh of relief and her smile reappeared from its hasty retreat.

"I am five." She held up as many fingers to accompany her Norwegian words.

"Well, Anna, the five-year-olds will sit in the front row." Kaaren came around her table and lowered herself to look eye to eye with Anna. "I am very glad to see you here."

The smile broke out in full force as the little girl nodded. "Me too."

Hearing only a few words in English as the children filed in, Kaaren knew she would be teaching mainly in Norwegian, but she promised herself these children would be speaking at least the rudiments of English by the end of the year.

She looked over her group of pupils as the last one to enter shut the door behind him. While she waited for silence, she counted them. Fifteen in all and they had benches for twenty. She nodded. Most of the children she knew at least by face if not by name from worship and soddy raisings, but several were strangers. She breathed a sigh of relief—the Strand boys weren't present. Either their parents didn't wish them to attend school, or there was one to the west closer to where they had finally settled. Kaaren hadn't been to their home, and she didn't wish to go. Sometimes she chastised herself for her unforgiving attitude, but most of the time she ignored it and the small voice that prompted her discomfort. Or at least she tried to. Deep inside she knew that one day God would call her to task over this attitude.

"Good morning, class." She paused.

A few of the children who had been to school before intoned, "Good morning, teacher."

"We will try that again, and my name is Mrs. Knutson. Good morning, class."

"Good morning, Mrs. Knutson." The response rang stronger.

"Now we will try that in English." She caught the look of surprise on Solveig's face at the back of the room. *Good, she* thought. *Solveig will learn the language, too, whether she wants to or not.* She repeated the greeting in English, then said the words one at a time. "Now repeat after me." She said the words again slowly. While they stumbled over the response, she nodded. "Good. Now, let's try it again." By the third time, they had it. "Now, we will start all over again." She switched to English. "Good morning, class."

They responded likewise, using her name in place of class. Smiles of pride flitted across the faces of those who got it right, and those who didn't corrected themselves. One more time through and Kaaren clapped her hands. "Well done. Every morning we will start this way and add new English words to your speech. As we go along, we will learn to use those words during the day too." She paused to smile at them all, her heart already swelling with pride for them. "Now we will read from the holy Bible and sing a song. Then I want each of you to stand and tell us your name, your age, and how much schooling you have had."

Kaaren turned and lifted her open Bible from the desk. As the year progressed she planned to have the children take turns choosing and reading the morning verses. So many plans she had for this group of children God had entrusted her with. "Please stand."

From Proverbs chapter two, Kaaren began to read verses ten and eleven. " 'When wisdom entereth into thine heart, and knowledge is pleasant unto thy soul, discretion shall preserve thee, understanding shall keep thee.' " She smiled at the children. "Those are wise words for all of us. Listen closely as I read them again."

After the reading, she lead them in a hymn and then asked them to sit down. "Now we will start with the back row so the little ones will know what to do when it is their turn."

A tall boy who said he was fourteen led off. He looked big enough to be working alongside his father full time, which made Kaaren doubly glad his family allowed him to come. She knew most of the young people that age were being kept at home to work, their parents thinking they were beyond needing such a frivolous thing as more schooling. Changing their minds would take some persuading talk, Kaaren knew. She also fully believed she was up to the job of convincing the parents that their children needed to learn to speak English, if nothing else. If they had remained in Norway, the children would be in school, so why not here in the new land?

As each child said his name, she asked for the spelling and wrote it in her book. She included ages and at what level she thought they might be. Testing would come next.

When the twins began to fuss, Kaaren dismissed her pupils for recess outside. Sending Solveig outside, too, for a breath of fresh air, Kaaren nursed the babies in front of the window so she could watch the children as they ran shrieking in a game of tag, their breaths floating in clouds on the clear air. Quickly they tramped a large circle in the snow to play fox and goose. When she closed her eyes, she could see swings hanging from a thick board between tall posts and children pumping higher and higher as if they would fly into the sky. The schoolhouse would have a bell in a belfry, real desks, and many books lining the shelves, some for study and others for the children to read for the pure joy of it.

"So many dreams I have," she whispered to her satisfied babies, breathing a kiss on each smooth forehead. Sophie smiled up at her, gurgling and making sounds with her fist waving in the air. Grace followed her mother's every action with wide blue eyes, her perfect little mouth also widening into a smile. But she still hadn't made sounds like Sophie did, those little babbling noises Sophie answered with whenever someone talked to her. The fist Grace freed from the blanket went into her mouth instead. Could she not speak or hear? The idea of either one made Kaaren's heart ache for her precious baby.

"Are you ready?" Solveig asked, shutting the door carefully.

"Ja, if you will change these two." Kaaren handed the squirming bundles to her sister, righted her clothing, and with a ready smile, opened the door and clanged the bar. When the children had all taken their seats again, cheeks ruddy from the cold, she announced, "Since I don't know how much you know, each of you take out your slates and chalk."

Two children wearing the most threadbare clothes of all raised their hands.

"We don't got no slates," the older boy said.

"I brought some because I thought some of you might not." Kaaren looked around. "Any others?" One more hand went up. "That is fine. Please come up here and pick one up." When all had slates, she continued with her instructions. "Those of you who have been to school before write the most difficult arithmetic problem you know. Then go to the bookshelf and choose a book that you know you can read, but not the easiest one." A boy in the back ducked his head. "Do you all understand?" At their nods and as they bent their heads to the assigned tasks, she began with the front row.

One of the young ones knew his alphabet and could count to ten, all in Norwegian. His English was nonexistent, other than the few words learned that morning. While Anna could say her rehearsed speech, that was all. No one had taught her anything else. Likewise the other one, so shy she never once looked up at her teacher. Kaaren had to bend close to hear the answers at all, the voice was so faint. When she leaned forward and cupped her hands around the child's upper arms, the little girl flinched away, her eyes hooded and her mouth quivering.

*Ah, dear Lord, let me make a difference in this one's life—and all the others. Give me wisdom and a heart of love for each, especially this little lost lamb. Don't fear, little one, I will not hurt you.* Right then she repeated her vow to herself. She would never strike the children, remembering the ruler that had raised welts on her hand those years ago because she didn't learn the lesson quite quickly enough.

She heard a rude noise from the back of the room. When she looked up, all the faces looked angelic but for Thorliff. His glower and eyes slanted left led her to believe the boy next to Knute Baard was the guilty one. Now, the ruler might be necessary for some of the older ones, but she hoped not.

She sent the child in front of her back to her seat and stood. "That is enough." Her stern voice rang in the room. "You will be respectful of those ahead of you, or . . ." She left the sentence dangling.

By the end of the day, she had all the children assigned according to reading and arithmetic abilities. Size hadn't much to do with knowledge, therefore she decided to start reviewing from the alphabet on, setting the ones who knew those things to helping those who didn't. With about an hour to dismissal, she called all the children closer to the stove where she set her chair. As they found places on the packed dirt floor in front of and around her, she smiled at each of them again.

"You have all done so well today that I thought we would finish with a story. This will be the reward for trying your best each day and treating your neighbors as you would like them to treat you. The golden rule says, 'Do unto others as you would have them do unto you.'"

Anna raised her hand. "That is from the Bible. Mor read that to me."

"Yes, Anna, it is. Starting tomorrow, we will all be memorizing that verse and others." She opened her book of Norwegian folktales and began to read.

The days passed swiftly, with school even on Saturday to make up for starting so late. The boxes of books sat on her table on Saturday morning because someone had been to Grafton and picked them up at the railroad station. She had ordered them by mail weeks before.

The children flocked around her, their eyes wide at the riches contained therein. She handed the books around so each child could share the thrill of smelling and feeling the new bindings and the pages that crackled when opened. When each held a book, she showed them how to properly open it and gave instructions on the care of books, after which they lined the precious treasures up on the bookshelves pegged into the sod walls.

Since all her summer egg and cream money had gone into purchasing the new books, she rejoiced at their delight. In addition to the books, there was black paint to make a blackboard. Olaf said that by Monday he should be finished smoothing and sanding the boards he had tongue-and-grooved tightly together to make a smooth surface. Then they could give it a couple coats of paint and they would have a blackboard. Next to the paint, they discovered a box of chalk, paper, and pencils, and at the bottom lay a round tube containing a map of the United States of America and the territories.

Kaaren set the oldest two boys to fastening the map to the wall next to the place where the blackboard would hang. The entire class gathered round to ooh and aah at the colors. Several could identify a state they had lived in before coming to Dakota Territory. Knute

Baard pointed out Ohio, but he couldn't remember where in that state they had lived.

When everyone finally resumed their seats, the teaching began again with Kaaren saying the lesson and the children repeating it. Until more of them learned to read and write, there was no other way to instruct.

Church that Sunday was conducted by Reverend Gunderson, the young pastor from Acton. From then on, he would come one Sunday a month and the pastor from St. Andrew one Sunday. The other services the homesteaders would handle themselves. When the people discovered Olaf's deep and resonant speaking voice, they asked him to take over leading the service when they had no visiting pastor.

The first time he read the Scriptures, one child said afterward, "He sounds like God, don't he, Mor." Chuckles flitted around the room, but many nods accompanied the twitter.

Mrs. Valders shook her head and whispered loudly enough for everyone to hear. "Children should be seen and not heard, especially in the house of God."

Kaaren and Ingeborg swapped rolled eyes and raised eyebrows. *That woman!*

"But this is our schoolhouse," a youngster said from the other side of the room, accompanied by a mother's shushing.

Kaaren swallowed a laugh.

Kaaren and Solveig kept up their routine of leaving before daylight in order to have the sod school warm in time for the children's arrival. The two women always brought extra food, too—usually bread and cheese or some leftovers from the night before—because some of the children came with very little to eat in their dinner pails. Both Solveig and the twins grew stronger; gains in strength that could be seen almost daily. Since Kaaren was frequently exhausted by the time they arrived home from school, Solveig took over much of the evening cooking. Ingeborg invited them all to eat at her house, but Kaaren said she needed the time to rest, nurse the babies, and prepare for the next day's lessons.

With the barn and the additions to both soddies finished, Haakan and Olaf spent as much time as possible felling trees in preparation for their lumber mill. While they were hard at that, Lars took the train from Grafton to Grand Forks and found one of the salesmen Haakan had previously met. He looked at the improvements made on the equipment since the days when he had managed a threshing crew, and liking what he saw, he took out another bank note and proceeded to buy a steam engine for the Bjorklund farm. It would be shipped the next day. That afternoon he climbed back aboard the train and returned home.

"You bought it?" Kaaren asked the next morning.

"Ja, I did." Lars grinned at her. "And I bought one slightly bigger than we need right now because that fancy engine will do more than we ever believed possible."

When he met the others the next morning, they slapped him on the back, asking many questions about the new piece of machinery. On the sledge ride out to where they were cutting, the conversation turned to the saws and equipment they needed for the sawmill.

"It's your turn this time," Lars said to Haakan with a laugh. "Go get the sawmill and let *your* wife glare at you for increasing the amount we owe at the bank."

"Ja, well, both these will pay themselves off in less than a year. You know that as well as I do."

Lars nodded as he looped the reins around the brake handle. "You tell them."

Ingeborg carded the wool she had washed and saved from the sheepshearing last spring. She and Andrew took care of the chickens, which now laid only enough eggs for the families because they had moved Kaaren's hens over to join the others, sending them into a molt. But it made chores easier for everyone. Every afternoon, the two walked over to Kaaren's and stoked up the stove to warm the soddy before the homecomers arrived. Many times Ingeborg started supper for them at the same time.

"So, how are things going at the schoolhouse?" she asked one afternoon when she hadn't left before the scholars arrived.

"So good." Kaaren unwrapped the shawl from around her head and hung the woven wool garment on the peg by the door. "I think it is better even than I dreamed. We are working on the Christmas pageant already, and you should see the way the children hurry to get their schoolwork done in order to have time to practice." She rubbed her hands over the heat from the stove. "Oh, Inge, I can't thank you enough for all you do so that I can teach school. All my life, I wanted to do this and now I am."

Ingeborg nodded. "You are welcome. I would much rather cook and wash and all the other things I do than sit those boys down and teach them myself. Besides, Thorliff already knows more than I do about too many things. I think he has read every book on those shelves already."

"And some of them twice. Wait until you see the pageant. He wrote most of the script."

Ingeborg stepped back from the stove. "Truly?"

"Truly." Kaaren took one of the twins from Solveig. "He has said again that he wants to write a book someday. I wish I could have saved one of the stories he told the little ones one afternoon. Inge, he is a good storyteller and a good writer."

"Ja, I know. He showed me one he wrote on paper. His penmanship is easy to read, and I would have thought someone much older had written it. One night he wrote the letter to Mor and Far for me while I carded wool. I just told him what to write."

Kaaren took her place in the rocker and set the babies to nursing. "I never have to worry about giving him enough work to do. When he finishes what I have assigned, he goes and gets a book and starts to read or else helps one of the others." She shook her head. "Not Baptiste, though. He and Swen manage to get in hot water every once in a while. They have such a hard time sitting still."

The next day Kaaren announced that in addition to working on the Christmas pageant, they would begin making presents to take home to their parents for Christmas. This meant everyone would have to work extra hard on their lessons. When she asked if anyone had any ideas of what they could make, she saw Baptiste's eyes light up.

"What do you think, Baptiste?" she asked before he raised his hand.

"We could make small willow baskets or fish hooks carved of bone."

"Oh, the baskets," one of the other children chimed in. "I want to learn to weave a basket."

"Or we could braid thin strips of leather for a belt. That would be good for our fars."

"And where would we get the willow?" Kaaren prodded him. "Or the leather?"

"From the trees and tanned hides." He looked at her as though she'd asked a particularly dumb question. "I will gather the willow."

"And the leather?"

"Don't everyone tan hides?"

"No, I don't think so. Metiz taught us, remember?"

"I will ask Thorliff's mor." He sat back on his bench as if all was decided.

Kaaren pinched her lips to keep from smiling. Baptiste must indeed feel like one of the family if he would dare do such a thing. He often took for granted that all the children knew about the things he had learned from his grandmother and other relatives. When she reminded him that they didn't, he looked amazed and puzzled.

One day he brought in a packet of rabbit skins that had been stretched and dried. "I will show how to tan hide and make mittens." He laid the skins, fur side in, on the desk.

"Weren't you going to sell these skins?" Kaaren asked softly.

He nodded. "But others need to learn."

In church that Sunday, Hildegunn Valders confronted Kaaren. "Just what are you teaching our children in this school of yours? How to become Indian?" She spat out the final word as if it were filth.

Kaaren cut off the smile she'd promised herself she would always give this woman. She gritted her teeth and counted to ten. "Why, Mrs. Valders, I thought your Hilde would love a pair of fur mittens. They are so warm and nice."

"I knit plenty of mittens for my children, and they don't need no fur." Her reddened nose raised.

"Then perhaps you can give them to someone else more needy." Kaaren thought back to her class and the delight Hilde had shown in working with the soft leather. "Excuse me, I need to talk with Mary Johnson." She brushed past the still glaring woman. *I hope her face freezes in that . . . that look of hers.*

"Why do some people love to start trouble?" she asked when telling Lars what had happened. "The children are enjoying making the baskets and tanning the rabbit skins. Their parents should be grateful to Baptiste and learn from the children how to do these things." She sputtered down to silence.

"Don't pay her any attention. She will always have something to jaw about. You just do what you know best and all will be well. The children are learning and that's what is important. Why, I heard you are even teaching them to speak English." He shook his head, eyes dancing. "I'm amazed she hasn't cut into you about that too."

"That brings up something else."

"Now what?"

"I think we should begin English-speaking classes for the parents too. Agnes would be the best for teaching that, just as she did those winters for all of us."

"I agree, and between the two of you, everyone who comes will be talking like Americans before they know it."

Kaaren laid her head on his chest, and his arms came around her. "Oh, Lars, you are so good." She stood on tiptoe to kiss him.

He glanced around to see that the twins were sleeping, then kissed her once again, harder and longer this time. "When will Solveig be back?"

"I don't know. George just whisked her away in his sled. Last I heard, she was laughing at something." She nestled against him, hearing his heart thundering under her ear. When he began to unbutton her shirtwaist, she looked up into his now serious face. "Lars, it is daylight still."

"Ja, and we are alone for a change."

Sometime later sleigh bells singing across the prairie announced Solveig's arrival. When she danced into the soddy, Lars and Kaaren were seated at the table, steaming coffee cups in front of them.

"Are those stars I see in her eyes?" Lars asked, his voice just loud enough for Solveig to hear.

"Ja, and wings on her feet," Kaaren tried to say with a straight face and failed happily. "Isn't Mr. Carlson coming in before he heads for home?"

"George is in a hurry to get back before dark." Solveig hung her coat on the peg and dropped her shawl in the rocking chair on her way out to the lean-to. She parted the curtain hanging over the opening and disappeared.

"No one would ever want to marry her, huh?" Lars grinned at his wife over the rim of his cup.

"He hasn't asked her yet."

"Ja, but he will. You mark my words, he will."

## 19

Penny had no trouble with the train trip, her nose pressed so close
to the icy window that her breath cleared away the frost, enabling
her to see clearly. The land sped by so fast she could hardly keep
up. Her thoughts kept time with the clacking wheels. *What if
Hjelmer is in Fargo? What if I see him on the street? What will I say?*
She scolded herself for such fanciful fears. If Hjelmer was in Fargo
and had neither written nor come home, she'd never speak to him
again.

Her heart skipped a beat when the conductor announced that
Fargo was the next stop. Had she made a mistake in coming here?
What lay ahead? "Dear God, please stay with me," she whispered.

"Penny. Penny Sjornson!" An arm waved above the crowd greeting the train passengers.

Penny gulped as all the eyes now turned on her when she waved
back. She turned and thanked the porter for handing out her bag,
then made her way to the area where she'd seen the waving arm.
Mrs. Johnson looked just as Ingeborg had described her—tall and
commanding, yet comfortably rounded. Her smile of welcome left
no doubt in Penny's mind that it was genuine. With graying hair
bundled in a bun and covered by a black felt hat, Mrs. Johnson came
forward with hands outstretched.

"Oh, child, it is good to meet you. Ingeborg said so many nice
things about you that I began to think I'd have an angel working for
me. Now, how was your trip?" They had a minor scuffle over who
would carry the valise, but Penny won.

"Don't believe I've ever been thought an angel, but I loved the
train ride. We went faster than our horses at home can run, I think."
Penny switched the valise to her other hand. How could the little

she had in there weigh so much? Then she remembered the two books and the cheese Ingeborg had sent. "I have a present for you from Ingeborg."

"She sounds well and happy up there on her homestead. Such a shock it was to hear of the men dying like that." Mrs. Johnson shook her head, setting jowls to swinging. She pointed across the street to a three-story building with a covered porch and white railings around the second story. A bank of twelve tall windows fronted the entire first floor, with another porch leading to the double door in the middle. "That's where you'll be living. The Headquarters Hotel used to house mostly railroad people, but now we get every kind of folk imaginable, from theater to business and back again." She paused in both breath and foot. "Right good place it has been for me."

"Do you run the whole thing?" Penny asked, trying to take in all the sights at once.

"No, no, of course not. I'm in charge of the kitchens and making sure there's plenty of good food when needed. We have a man, Mr. Dempsey, who manages the entire hotel, and Miss Brockhurst oversees all the rest—the rooms, the laundry, all of it. She has a job I would hate, but then she doesn't like to cook. Takes all kinds, as they say." She stepped down from the platform that fronted the meager station and crossed the street, Penny right on her heels.

"Won't be long until you will easily find your way around. Fargo is easy to get to know."

Penny secretly doubted she'd ever find her way around the city, what with all the traffic and buildings and people. She couldn't remember ever seeing so many people in one place in her entire life.

She swung her valise along, trying to keep up with this woman who seemed mighty spry for her age. Of course the gray hair could be misleading, but her face wore the tracks of life dug in deep.

"Do you speak English?" Mrs. Johnson asked while she held the door open for Penny.

Penny switched from Norwegian immediately. "Ja, we lived in Ohio before we moved west, and there I went to an English-speaking school. There were too many languages in that area for Norwegian to be the main one."

"That is good. You will do well with the guests at the hotel. Have you ever been a waitress before?"

"Well, if serving thirty men on the threshing crew counts, guess I have."

"You got spunk too. That is good." Mrs. Johnson led the way up carved-walnut stairs, sided with wainscoting of the same rich wood. The wallpaper above pleaded for Penny to stroke its red velvet embossed fleur-de-lis. "Your room is on the third floor. I was hoping to have you down with me, but Miss Brockhurst insisted you be up here." She paused halfway up the second set of stairs to catch her breath. "Hope you will feel to home right away."

*Home.* Penny felt a pang at the word. When would she go home again? Not at Christmas, for that was too soon. Would she be able to go home when school let out for the summer? How would she afford the ticket? She borrowed one of Kaaren's favorite expressions—"Let the day's own troubles be sufficient for the day." May was a long way off. Who knew what would happen before then?

That evening after letting Penny settle into her slant-ceilinged room, Mrs. Johnson showed her around the rest of the hotel. Since the young woman would fill in wherever needed, she started at the top and showed her the linen closets on each of the three floors, some of the empty rooms for guests, the bathing rooms and water closets on each floor, the parlor down next to the dining room, and the bar off to one side through swinging doors. They toured the storage rooms off the kitchen, the scullery where Ingeborg had begun her service at the hotel, and the office behind the reception desk.

"You'll meet Miss Brockhurst and Mr. Dempsey tomorrow. He lives over in Moorhead, and although Miss Brockhurst lives here, an emergency at home took her away for the last couple of days."

Penny could hardly take time to answer as she admired the wallpaper, different for each floor, and stroked the carved-walnut stair rail that felt like warm glass beneath her palm. The linen closets were fragrant with lavender sachets the housekeeper put there each summer, and the huge room for laundry and ironing smelled of soap and starch. A row of flatirons of every shape and size lined the side of a black stove now gone cold until the laundress started again in the early morning hours.

Penny hoped she wouldn't have to work in that cavernous room with the strange-looking contraptions that Mrs. Johnson said were gas-powered washing machines. "Sure be better than boilers, tubs, and washboards. My land, what a difference they make. I heard they even got a gas-heated iron to take the place of flatirons, but we ain't bought one of those yet." In the doorway she turned to Penny. "You heard about that new electricity they got some places?" When Penny shook her head, Mrs. Johnson continued. "Wires and glass bulbs instead of gas jets and flame. Uff da, what is this world coming to?"

Penny wondered the same when she fell into her new bed that night. She would be attending high school in the morning. The thought made her shiver.

She was up early so she could help with the breakfast preparation, mixing and setting bread dough to rise, slicing ham to fry, and whatever else Mrs. Johnson asked her to do. The two waitresses looked her over rather carefully, but their smiles appeared to be genuine.

"We been needing some more help back here," said Rosy, the one with dark hair. "Work hard and you'll get along fine."

"Just get our orders right," Mabel added. She wore her mouse-brown hair in a pompadour. "Slows things down somethin' awful when the orders come out mixed up."

"I'll try." Penny hustled off to stuff a bevy of chickens to set to roasting for dinner.

When Mrs. Johnson said she had only half an hour before they had to leave, Penny hurried through her toilet, letting her hair out of the net wherein she'd bundled her golden curls. She brushed her hair out, tied the top back with a blue ribbon, and dressed in one of the only two outfits she owned that she hoped were suitable for school.

Mrs. Johnson strode along sidewalks scraped free of snow by the shop owners, pointing out landmarks as they went. When they arrived at an imposing brick building with columns embracing the double front door, she took Penny to the principal's office to register. Once that was accomplished, they said good-bye, and Penny watched her new friend sail out the double doors and down the steps.

She had the silly urge to fly after her. Life at the hotel might be far easier than here in school.

But instead, she answered Mr. Brevick's questions as best she could. No, she hadn't had Latin, yes to arithmetic through to Algebra, yes to United States history, no to world geography. Yes, she had a fine hand for penmanship and could write essays. In fact, she had brought one with her just in case. She handed him the paper with her best work written in a clear hand.

He perused the essay, reading over the tops of his gold-rimmed glasses. "Very good." He sounded surprised. "And you are fourteen?"

"Fifteen next month."

"And you believe you can complete the program here in two years?"

"That is what my teacher at home thought. She said I may have to take some tests."

"That you do." He nodded, handing back her paper. "I am going to turn you over to Mr. Radisson, head of our English department. He will ask you questions and give you several tests before deciding where you are to be placed. Follow me."

Their steps rang in the empty wainscoted hallway and up the stairs. Arched windows let in the watery sunlight. Mr. Brevick opened a door and motioned her to enter. After introducing her to the bespectacled Mr. Radisson, who wore the look of a scholar with ease, the principal left. With each exodus, Penny was feeling more cut off from any world she had known. Whatever had possessed her to think she wanted to get more schooling? As Uncle Joseph had said, surely she knew enough to make a good wife already.

She turned back to face the man behind the desk. "Welcome to Fargo High School, Miss Sjornson." His smile set creases into his cheeks and warmed his brown eyes, taking away the fear from her heart.

By the time she left the school building when the final bell rang, she had met five different teachers with one more to go, realized she would need to sew some different clothes, and at least fifty times wished she had stayed home. When she finally climbed the three steps to the front porch, the hotel seemed like a friendly haven after her first day at school. She pitched into the preparations for supper, happy to be so busy she didn't have time to think.

By the next morning she had talked herself out of returning home and into braving the school again. But she left the hotel early to make sure she didn't get lost either on the way or inside the confusing building. To a girl accustomed to a one-room soddy with two lean-tos, the three-story brick building seemed bigger than a small town. The two side wings looked out on a courtyard where horses and wagons were held in stables for the pupils who came in from the surrounding country. Penny looked out upon the courtyard in time to see a big box on runners with a stovepipe coming from the roof pulling up. When the four-horse hitch stopped, a door opened in one wall of the box and young men and women stepped to the ground and hurried into the building. What a marvelous idea. She would have to write to Kaaren about it. When the bell rang, she crossed the hall to her first class, taking the seat toward the rear she'd been assigned the day before.

"Hi, my name is Becky. What's yours?" The friendly voice and tap on the shoulder caused Penny to swivel around in her seat and return the cheerful smile. The slim girl behind her wore her strawberry blond hair cut in bangs across her forehead and the rest rolled up somehow in the back. A wide smile showed one slightly overlapped front tooth.

"I am Penny Sjornson, new from up north near Grafton." She didn't say Grafton was ten miles from home. It sounded better to be near somewhere.

"I hope you like it here. Where do you live now?"

"At the Headquarters Hotel."

Just then the bell rang, and the teacher rapped on his desk. "Order, class."

Having Becky in three of her classes and walking her halfway home made the day go a whole lot better than Penny had dreamed possible. This was only her second day here, and she already had a friend at school. After she said good-bye to Becky where she turned to go home, Penny sent her thank-you prayer heavenward. Maybe this was going to work out after all. But . . . when was she going to find time to study? Or look for Hjelmer?

×◈  ◈×

"Kaaren," Solveig asked one Sunday afternoon, "have you noticed anything different about Grace?"

"Ja, but what are you thinking?" Kaaren looked up from putting on the baby's woolen soakers. She picked up the yawning infant and laid her against her shoulder, patting her back and assuming the side-to-side rocking motion that put the little one to sleep so quickly.

"I think she cannot hear."

The words hung stark between them.

Kaaren started to deny the possibility but couldn't. She'd been sure something was wrong herself the last two weeks, actually since the babies were only a few weeks old, but had refused to put a name to it and say the words out loud.

"Why do you say that?"

"Because yesterday she was lying with her eyes open, and I clapped my hands near her head. She never paid the slightest attention. When I did the same with Sophie, she flinched and turned to see what was going on."

"Do it again now before she falls asleep."

Solveig did as asked, clapping her hands right behind the baby's head. Grace never moved. They tried banging a kettle, tapping a cup, whistling. There was no response—no turning of the head, no startled jerk.

Kaaren held the baby even closer. "Ah, my little one, how are we to help you?" Her eyes filled with tears but she blinked them back. "I wonder if Lars has noticed anything." She laid the baby back in the cradle next to her sleeping sister. They had tried putting them in the separate cradles Lars had made, but both infants cried so pitifully, they put them back together.

Standing over the little bed, watching her two precious babies, Kaaren saw Sophie reach out an arm and place it over her sister's back. They both slept on.

That night in bed, Kaaren confided the discovery to Lars.

When she had finished talking, he lay beside her for a while without answering. Finally he sighed. "I never knew anyone who couldn't hear from the time they was born." He sighed again and turned over on his side, his back to Kaaren.

*Is that all you have to say about it?* Kaaren's mind raced with questions. What were they to do? What could they do?

A gentle snore told her Lars had fallen asleep already. Kaaren felt like poking him until he woke. Didn't he understand?

*December 1884*

M ore of our relatives want to emigrate." Ingeborg waved the letter from Nordland she'd been reading.

Haakan hung up his things and motioned for Thorliff and Baptiste to do the same. "Who now?" He stopped at his usual place, rubbing his hands over the heat of the cookstove.

"A cousin of mine and one of Roald's. His uncle Johann's second son—oops, no, his eldest. His eldest?" She looked up. "He'll be the one to inherit the Bjorklund land in Valdrez. Why would he want to come?"

"Because he can do much more here in America than on that small piece of land in Norway."

"It's been supporting the family for generations." Her gaze skimmed back to the letter.

"Ja, barely. I don't blame him for wanting to come here." He took an unopened envelope she offered him. "For me?"

She nodded, then looked up from her reading, her mouth open in shock. "Roald's mor, Bridget, wants to come. Now that she is alone, she wants to come see her children here. Nothing is said about if she will stay. She wouldn't come and then go back, would she?"

"Why not?" He smoothed the creases out of the paper now in his hands. "Other people do."

"That long hard trip? And so costly?" She could tell he was no longer listening.

"*My* brother and sister both want to come. They each have three children and would come together. They are asking if there is more land around here for homesteading. A cousin, a single woman, would come with them." He looked up at his wife. "What will I tell them? There is no more land to homestead around here, only land to buy."

"There is homesteading in the west of Dakota Territory, but you know we've heard the land isn't so good as this."

Ingeborg finished her letter, folding it carefully and placing it back in the envelope. She would give it to Kaaren to read in the morning. "What do you mean there is more land to buy?"

He waved his hand in a signal to wait a moment, finished reading the letter, and looked up. "What?"

"Land to buy?"

"Ja, the railroad has released several more sections. One is directly southwest of us and would connect at the corner. I think we would be wise to get it now. If we don't want to farm it, we could sell it to one of our relatives. Heaven knows we better buy everything we can. They'll be coming like herds of migrating reindeer." He stared a moment longer at the letter before putting it away. "If you agree to buy, then I think we should go talk with Lars and Kaaren after supper. If we don't do this immediately, there will be none left."

"Unless some who are already here want to move on. I think men like to get the itchy foot and the women have to go along." Ingeborg had heard one man telling another how there was free land in the Pacific Northwest, and now that the trains ran out there, he thought about moving on. There were trees there big enough to dance on the stump and no blizzard winters like in Dakota. Oh yes, there would always be those with a restless soul.

Haakan left the next morning for Grand Forks to take out another note and to buy more land. He planned to see if he could find a used sawmill they could mount on skids to bring home as soon as possible. Besides felling trees, Olaf and Lars had used the crosscut saw to form some of the trees into beams on which to mount the saw when they got one. It would have been easier to wait until the saw arrived, but it wouldn't work without mounting. They took some leftover beams from the barn raising to put up a roof frame, planning to side the north wall so they could work even in bad weather.

Ingeborg took Andrew in the sleigh with her to pick up Agnes to go to quilting at the Booth home. With Agnes's two little ones joining Andrew under the elk robes in the back, the giggles and laughter rang out with the sleigh bells, bringing smiles to the faces of the women bundled in front.

"You think she really wants us to come?" Agnes asked.

Ingeborg shrugged. "Don't know, but Mr. Booth said she did, and I guess he would know. Maybe if they would have had children, she wouldn't have minded the winter quite so much." She gestured to the youngsters in the back of the sleigh. Turning slightly to speak over her shoulder, she said, "Andrew, you stay covered up. I don't want any part of you to get frostbit." He crawled back under the robe.

"Sometimes even with little ones at my feet, I fear the wind." Agnes shivered. "Joseph says it will be different when we have a house with more windows, but I don't know. The wind will still shriek about the eaves and plead to be let in."

"I know. For me it is the long dark days. Think I'll move out to the barn this winter."

"Well, Haakan wanted to build you a house, but you insisted on the barn, remember?"

"I know, and I was right. The cows have to come first." She clucked the horses into a faster trot. "This way, when the house comes, I will appreciate it all the more."

Agnes made a rude noise.

As soon as they arrived, Mr. Booth unhitched the team and led the horses off to the barn. Several parked sleighs showed that others had arrived before them. The women greeted one another, settled the children to playing, and found places for themselves. Sitting in a chair by the stove, Auduna Booth just nodded when they greeted her. When Ingeborg brought her some pieces to stitch together, they eventually fell from her lap. Even sewing costumes for the Christmas pageant failed to bring any kind of response. She accepted a cup of coffee when Brynja Magron handed it to her but never answered when Hildegunn asked where she kept the sugar. Andrew brought her the plate Ingeborg fixed for her at dinner, but even his cheery smile brought no acknowledgment.

"Lady sick," he informed his mother in a whisper heard clear to St. Andrew.

Hildegunn nodded. "Out of the mouths of babes." Mrs. Odell and Mrs. Magron, who always took the chairs on either side of her, nodded in unison like puppets on a string.

The women exchanged looks of concern and confusion, and soon after dinner everyone gathered up their things.

The women left early.

"Mr. Booth, Hagen, why don't you let me take Auduna home

with me for a couple of days? Maybe a change of scenery would help her?" Ingeborg asked as she loaded their things back in the sleigh.

He shook his head. "Mange takk for the offer, but I don't think so. She hates to go anywhere, even out to our barn. She will be better when we get closer to spring again. The winters are always the hardest on her."

"But isn't she much worse this year?"

He shrugged. "Only God knows that. We will see you in church on Sunday."

Obviously dismissed, Ingeborg started to say something else, then thought the better of it. Surely this man knew his own wife better than she did.

But when she told Agnes what had happened, Agnes shook her head too. "Men can be so stubborn, as if asking for help was a mortal sin or something."

"I just wish there were something we could do." Ingeborg clucked the horses into a trot, and the jingle of harness bells rang across the prairie. "Maybe even a ride like this would help her." She turned to Agnes. "Should we go back and just throw her into the sleigh?"

"I don't think Hagen would like that, nor would Auduna. I heard of a person who did something like this. Heard it called 'prairie madness.' It's not uncommon, you know, and it ain't just women who catch it. Sometimes men do too." She shook her head and huddled farther into the furs. "Ain't no cure far as I've heard, except maybe to leave and go back somewhere else."

When she got home, Haakan had returned, jubilant with the news that he found a sawmill for sale. He and Olaf would take two sledges with teams of four, and since the river was frozen over, they could head due east to pick up their new piece of equipment.

"Should only take two or three days each way. If the weather holds, we'll leave on Monday next." Haakan rubbed his hands over the heat of the stove. "We have to go to Grafton to pick up the steam engine tomorrow. If we leave well before dawn, we should make it back in one day, but that will be heavy pulling, even on the snow."

Ingeborg smiled at the look on his face. She'd seen one similar when Thorliff pressed his nose against a counter window at the Mercantile trying to decide which candy he wanted. She stopped behind her husband and wrapped her arms around his waist.

"You are like a child with a new toy."

He turned and enclosed her in the circle of his arms. "You don't mind the extra borrowing?"

"Ja, I mind. But I know you are doing the right thing." She leaned her head against his chest, his heart thumping in her ear. "Just please be watchful of the weather. I don't want you caught in a blizzard again."

"Not to worry. I learned my lesson." He tightened his arms. "You know, you are becoming more of an armful."

"Ja, babies do that to their mothers." She looked up into his eyes and read there the deep love she knew lived in his heart. The lips she raised to meet his said it all.

Kaaren threw every bit of energy and talent she possessed into helping the children with their presents and preparing for the Christmas pageant. At the same time, she developed a routine so that all their subjects were covered and the children were learning not only reading, writing, and arithmetic, but geography, history, and English as well. Some were memorizing poems for the pageant, others were learning songs. Each child would have his moment of glory, or agony, depending upon whom you asked. The bigger kids helped the middle-sized, and the middlers helped the little ones. Since Solveig could now move around without her crutch, she helped, too, whenever the twins were sleeping.

Kaaren invited Joseph with his fiddle and Olaf on the harmonica to come and practice two songs the children would all sing together. The harmony of "Jeg er så Glad Hver Jule Kveld" soared along with the fiddle until Kaaren had tears in her eyes at the end.

"That was wonderful. You sound just like an angel chorus must. If you sing like that the night of the program, you'll have some mighty pleased parents." She blew her nose and led them into the second number, a Norwegian folk song, "Ingrid Sletten," about a little girl with a colored cap of wool. Then drawing the benches around the stove, they practiced all the carols.

"Oh, my," Solveig said on the way home. "I never thought those children could sing like that. You'd think you were a concertmaster and been working together for years. And the looks on their faces." She drew a square of cotton from her pocket and blew her nose. "This cold weather surely does make my nose run."

Trying to find time to make presents for her own family seemed impossible. She knew Lars was making something out in the barn, and Ingeborg had whisked something out of sight one afternoon when she stopped there. Even Thorliff and Baptiste snickered once in a while, their eyes on her. She wanted to give each of her pupils some bit of a gift too. As the days grew shorter and the cold deepened, she was tempted a few times to remain at home. But she knew the children would show up, and she needed to have the schoolhouse warm for them.

One morning Lars rode the horse over to the school to start the stove so she could rest a bit longer. "You're looking peaked," he said to her. "Maybe this teaching while nursing the twins is too much. We don't need no one sick here before Christmas, or after, either, for that matter."

She could tell he was worried about her and trying to hide it behind a gruff voice.

"If the weather does what it normally does, we probably won't have school in January anyway, possibly February too. I will get some rest then."

"Ja, and the Norwegians worship the Pope."

"Lars!" His grin returned at her shocked look. She shook her head. "The things you say sometimes."

⚜ ⚜

With the upright steam engine standing beside the barn, the men looked forward even more to the trip for the sawmill.

"We need to build a machine shed," Olaf said, looking at the engine still set on skids so they could move it to the river when they were ready. "Mighty expensive things to have out in the weather."

"Ja, so much we need to build. Will be easier and cheaper when we have our own lumber." Haakan watched carefully as Lars tinkered with the engine. "You sure you know how to get that thing running?"

Lars laughed. "I'm about as good with this machine as you are with an ax, if that answers your question."

"Ja, well, my ax is a lot cheaper to replace, you know."

"You just go get me a couple buckets of water and we'll have this thing chugging in a few minutes." Lars started the fire in the firebox, and with the water in the holding tank, soon the dials began to flutter and move steadily upward. "See, I told you." When the dial hit the correct pressure, Lars pushed the lever for the flywheel and it began to spin. Lars stood back with a grin that overrode his sigh of relief.

"That's all there is to it. Simple."

"Ja, when you know what to do." Haakan slapped Lars on the shoulder. "Now we got another mouth to fill with wood. Come on, let's get some more trees cut today. Then when we get back with the saw, we can go right to work."

The moon still hung like a silver sliver in the western sky when they drove out of the yard before dawn. With four up the long sledges pulled easily over the iced snow, and by sunrise they were already miles away heading east.

They spent the first night with a couple who owned twenty cows and supplied milk to a nearby town and arrived at the mill by the following evening. Loading the next morning took several hours, using a crane with four horses to lift the saw pieces high enough for the sledges to back under the load.

Olaf and Haakan admired the large new rig the man had bought to take farther north where the timber was more plentiful. After the man's wife packed them a box of food and filled a jar with coffee, they struck out for home, the horses leaning into their collars with the extra weight.

Haakan hunkered down into the elk robe he tucked around his shoulders. The wind blew up bits of snow and tried to tug the robe away. He looked up at the sky where mare's tail clouds dimmed the sun. He hated to admit it, but there could be snow in the offing.

Small flakes started to fall about dusk. The horses dripped with sweat from pulling the heavy load, their breath steaming in clouds.

"I think I remember a farm not far from here," Haakan shouted to Olaf. "We'll see if we can stay overnight there."

After about another mile, they saw a lamplit window off to the north and heard a dog barking. They spent the night at the home of two Norwegian brothers, who had more questions about homesteading than Haakan had answers.

"Why do you ask?" he finally said.

"Our brother wants to come from Norway, and one of us will go help him out in the beginning."

"Is there nothing left in Minnesota?" Olaf asked.

"Only far to the north where it is too marshy for good farming."

"Near as I can tell, the Red River Valley is all taken, but western Dakota has room. Just that the land isn't as good as what we got."

"Still better'n Norway, I bet." The brother with the full beard nodded.

"Ja, but with rocks and hills, and there are a couple of Indian reservations out there too." Haakan leaned forward in his chair. "You be sure to stop by our place on your way west. You going by train or wagon?"

"Wagon, so we got something to start with. We'll take some livestock too."

The brother who hadn't said much asked softly, "There any women of marrying age in your neck of the woods? They be scarcer than hen's teeth around here."

Haakan and Olaf exchanged glances of amusement. "I think maybe I should go back to Nordland and bring over a boatload of women. If they were saleable, we'd make more money than out west digging gold."

"Don't let Kaaren and Ingeborg hear you say something like that. You won't eat for a month of Sundays."

Laughter rang out from both the brothers Robinson.

"We will see you sometime this spring, then," the bearded one said early the next morning. Four inches of new snow lay on the ground, but the stars above again glistened in their assigned places. "Go with God."

The trip took two and a half more days. At one point they stopped and cut four small pine trees and tied them to the tops of the loads.

"One for each of our houses, one for the Baards, and the biggest for the schoolhouse." Haakan brushed his gloves off before picking up the reins. He reached back and dabbed a glob of pitch off the trunk of the nearest tree and stuck it in his mouth. *Better'n chewing tobacco any day*, he thought, enjoying the bite of the sticky stuff.

Ingeborg and Paws met them in the yard when they drove in. "Christmas trees!" She clapped her hands in delight. "How wonderful." She looked up at her husband with a catch in her throat. He certainly looked the part of a conquering Viking hero. "Good trip?"

"Ja." He climbed to the ground, stamping his feet to get the blood flowing again. "Is the coffee hot? We're about froze through."

Lars trotted up. "When I heard Paws bark, I thought it must be you. Go on in and get warm. I'll take care of the horses." He peered at Haakan's face. "Think you got frostbite on your nose. I'd take care of that if I were you."

The men didn't need to be told twice.

Four days before Christmas, Lars and Olaf showed up at the school with a pine tree in the back of the sleigh. They dragged it inside to the oohs and aahs of both children and teacher. Once set in a bucket of sand and water, it reached up through the crossbeams and nearly to the rafters.

"It ith tho big." Little Anna stared in delight. "What we gonna put on it?"

"We will have to make some ornaments. Ask at home if there is anything we might use—ribbon, colored paper, leftover yarn, bits of bright-colored material, pine cones, whatever you think might look pretty on our tree."

"We need a star for the top."

"And candles."

"I saw a tree once that had shiny balls hanging from the branches."

"Thank you, Mr. Knutson and Mr. Wold, for our tree," the children chorused when the men turned to leave.

"We could use some of that carded wool to lay on the branches. Would look like snow." Solveig stood beside Kaaren.

The next morning each child brought whatever they could, and before long the tree began to color. Squares of red-and-white gingham tied with yarn around crinkled paper looked like cheery balls. White paper cut into angel shapes hung from the branches, and popcorn strung on long double threads looped around the limbs. Baptiste and Thorliff had their heads together over some pieces of willow. When they finished, the star formed of straight twigs of the same length and tied at the points lay on the teacher's desk.

"Boys, this is beautiful." She held it up for all to admire. "We could whitewash it to make it stand out more. What do you think?" Kaaren asked. "You two are so clever."

Baptiste nodded. "White make it show up better."

"We could make more, small ones, if you would show us how," one of the middle girls said.

When they had hung all the whitewashed stars on the branches, the sight of the tree made them gasp, it was so lovely.

The afternoon of the last pageant practice would have tested the apostle John's patience. They hung a rope from wall to wall and hung sheets and blankets on it for their curtain to the improvised stage. Two boys got tangled in the sheets and tripped, ripping them off the line. Standing in front of the other children for the first time gave some such stage fright that one boy had to run for the privy. Lines floated out of memories, giggles attacked, and others couldn't say a word.

Kaaren patiently coached them through the whole thing twice, calling from the back of the room, "Speak up now so everyone can hear you," and applauding their efforts.

The wiseman's crown fell off when he walked up the aisle, and Mary tripped on her robe. An angel kept pushing her halo up with one hand until it was bent clear out of round. For families with so little, they had thrown themselves into creating costumes for the children for the first pageant to be held in this, their new land.

By the time the last practice was finished, Kaaren gathered them all around the stove and popped more popcorn for them to eat, although more than one morsel had been swallowed during the stringing.

"I want you to remember something. I will be sitting right in the front row to prompt you if you forget your lines. That means I will whisper the words to you so you can go on." Several of the children gave deep sighs of relief. "Now we will all pray that our pageant will go smoothly." She bowed her head and waited for silence.

"Heavenly Father, I thank thee for all the work these children and their families have put into making this program to tell thy story. Please help us all to do our best and give glory to thee." Everyone chorused the amen.

"There will be no school tomorrow so that you can all get ready for the pageant tomorrow night, Christmas Eve. We will be serving cider and cookies afterward, remember?" She glanced back just in time to see the rope holding the sheets and quilts that made their curtain slump to the floor. When she broke out in laughter, the children followed. "Guess we'll have two of the men hold that up, what do you think?" They laughed again. "Now you all know your parts and where your costumes are, so come early to finish getting ready. We will start our program right at seven o'clock." *And hope and pray one of the twins is sleepy enough to be baby Jesus without crying.*

After the children left, she eyed the hole in the sod wall where the pegs to hold the curtain had been driven. "Maybe Lars will play at being a post."

Solveig chuckled. "I never seen such excited youngsters."

"Most of them have never had a Christmas tree. In case you haven't noticed, this land has few evergreens. If Olaf and Haakan hadn't brought these back from Minnesota, we wouldn't have them now. It's our first tree since we came here."

The babies began to fuss, so she fed them again before starting home. When she closed the schoolhouse door on the tree and the warm room, she breathed a prayer of gratitude for the tree, for the joy of the children, and for their excitement for the program. All their presents, made with such love for their parents, lay under the tree ready to be given out.

The day of the pageant dawned clear and cold, taking one worry off Kaaren's mind. Now if the weather only made it through the day like this. She bustled around baking cookies, caring for her babies, cooking, and caring for her babies again. "Solveig, if you weren't here, I don't know what I would do."

"You'd manage." Solveig salted one of the three geese Ingeborg had shot, cleaned, and left outside to freeze so they could have roast goose for Christmas Day. They were fixing the goose, and Ingeborg was bringing the rest of the meal since she didn't have a pageant to worry about.

"Well, I tell you, I am thankful I don't have to try to do it all." Kaaren rocked Sophie, snuggled against her mother's shoulder. Instead of taking a nap as usual, the baby wanted to play. "How can you play the part of baby Jesus tonight if you won't sleep now?"

Sophie waved her fist and wiggled all the rest of her. She smiled back at her mother, making sounds and gurgles. When Kaaren tried tucking the baby against her shoulder, Sophie bounced back like a limber branch. "Uff da, you aren't making this easy. Why can't you be like your sister?" Kaaren glanced over to the cradle where Grace lay sound asleep.

"Gaas" and "goos" were the only answer.

The Bjorklunds took both sleighs to the school that night because Kaaren had to be there earlier than the others. Lars put the line back up and promised to stay right there to make sure it held. As the children arrived, their parents buzzed around the benches and an excited hum filled the room.

Behind the curtain, the children put on their costumes, some giggling, some white of face.

"Now, now, you will do just fine." Kaaren shushed some and comforted others, moving from the wisemen to the shepherds and then to the angels as needed.

"Mrs. Knutson!"

She was sure if she heard her name hissed one more time with a note of panic in the voice, she would break out in either laughter or tears, and from one moment to the next she was never sure which.

The baby fussing out front was definitely Sophie.

A hush fell when Olaf took his place in front of the curtain with his open Bible in his hands.

"Welcome to our pageant this evening, and God bless us every-one."

"Mrs. Knutson," the boy playing Joseph hissed just before Kaaren stepped through the curtain to take her place. "I can't do this. I can't." Raw terror whitened his face. Kaaren stepped back and put her arm around his trembling shoulders. "Reimer, you can play Joseph. You've been doing really wonderfully. Once you start up that aisle, you'll do just fine." She looked into his eyes, trying to give him the confidence he needed. "Besides, I'll be praying for you. All you have to do is lead the donkey."

As the school filled with the music of the first carol, she gave him a little push. "You and Mary get on outside now. Mr. Baard is waiting with the donkey." *And also the sheep.* The thought made her wonder why she had ever let the children choose to have live animals. *Please, God, make that donkey lead for Joseph—er, Reimer.*

She glanced over at Solveig, who had promised to stay behind the curtain and make sure the children got to the right place at the right time. Mary and Joseph slipped through the crowd that filled the benches and lined the walls. There wasn't a square foot of floor not occupied. Kaaren took her seat on the bench. Ingeborg was bouncing the now quiet but wide awake Sophie on her lap. Haakan held the sleeping Grace.

As the voices died away, Olaf began. " 'And it came to pass in those days, that there went out a decree from Caesar Augustus, that all the world should be taxed. And this taxing was first made when Cyrenius was governor of Syria.' " His rich baritone voice rolled across those assembled, the familiar Norwegian words perfect and clear.

Kaaren felt a draft, knowing the door had opened. She turned to look and caused all the audience to turn also. There they came, Mary sideways on the donkey and Joseph, staring only at the floor, leading them.

Kaaren breathed a sigh of relief. They had begun, and all would be well now.

" 'And all went to be taxed, every one into his own city. And Joseph also went up from Galilee. . . .' "

An indrawn breath came as one upon the people. "Look, Mor, a donkey," a little one said to the shushing of his mother.

The age-old words continued, and the donkey with his cargo disappeared behind the curtain. Kaaren let out a breath she hadn't known she was holding. Olaf signaled to Joseph Baard, who swung into the opening strains of "O Little Town of Bethlehem," and at his nod, everyone joined in. While they sang, the manger was set out and the sheep led into place, grain dropped in front of them and a bit of hay. The sheep began eating, and during the last lines of the song, Kaaren took the sleeping Grace back behind the curtain and handed the bundled baby to Ingrid, the girl playing Mary.

Olaf continued. " 'And so it was, that, while they were there . . .' "

Mary came out from behind the curtain and sat down on the stool by the manger, holding the baby in her lap, and Joseph, leaning on his staff, took his place behind her. Kaaren resumed her seat.

" 'And she brought forth her firstborn son, and wrapped him in swaddling clothes and laid him in a manger; because there was no room for them in the inn.' "

Mary did so. The babe slept on, and Kaaren breathed another sigh of relief.

" 'And there were in the same country shepherds abiding in the field, keeping watch over their flock by night.' "

The shepherds stopped halfway up the aisle, blinding their eyes when an angel met them. The other three angels waited near the scene in front.

" 'Fear not!' " said the angel, and the shepherds removed their hands from their faces. " 'For, behold, I bring you good tidings of great joy. . . .' " The angel led the four shepherds to the front where Mary had laid the baby in the hay-lined manger. They knelt and the angels sang their chorus, little Anna lisping her words but making sure they were loud.

The shepherds said their lines and sat down around the manger scene, Thorliff putting his arm around Sheep, his own ewe. He looked up at Mary and smiled.

Kaaren glanced over in time to see Ingeborg wipe a tear away from her cheek.

The words of the beloved story continued, pausing for the children to say their lines. Kaaren only needed to prompt one. As the shepherds rose to leave, Joseph slumped over his stick and slid to the floor. One of the sheep jumped up and bumped into the manger.

A horrified gasp swept around the room.

Thorliff leaped forward and grabbed the baby just as she tumbled out of the falling manger. While he handed the now whimpering child to Mary, another of the shepherds righted the manger. Joseph, sheepish of face, sat down beside Mary, his head on his raised knees.

Kaaren signaled, and all the children broke into their next song, accompanied by fiddle and harmonica. Kaaren watched Mary calm the baby and rock her in young arms. When the song finished, the shepherds moved off to the side, and after taking a deep breath and flashing Kaaren a look of relief, Olaf continued reading.

The rest of the pageant went off without a hitch, and Kaaren's heart finally returned to its proper place in her chest. *Thank you, heavenly Father*, ran over and over through her mind. She knew Ingeborg was saying the same thing, her moving lips a testimony to it. They closed with "Silent Night," everyone singing every single verse. The harmony indeed sounded like an angel chorus.

A silence fell, as if no one wanted to break the heavenly spell. Kaaren rose to her feet and turned to face the parents. "I think these children deserve a mighty hand of appreciation, don't you?"

When the clapping, stomping, and "here, here" died out, Kaaren continued. "We would like you all to keep your places, for the children have another surprise for you." As she called their names, each child went to the tree, found his gifts, and took them to his parents. "Mange takk," echoed around the room. When the last present had been given, Kaaren spoke again. "We have hot cider and cookies on the back table. The children will be serving."

"No, not yet!"

Kaaren turned to find three children bringing a wrapped present toward her.

The oldest girl, Beth Johnson, stepped forward. "Mrs. Knutson, we made you this gift with our thanks and grati . . ." She stumbled over the word, took in a deep breath, and said it again. "Gratitude for starting and teaching our school. We have learned a lot, and we want to say . . ." She paused again. With one breath all the children shouted, "Merry Christmas, Mrs. Knutson, and a blessed and happy new year!"—in English.

Kaaren blinked several times and had to start over again when she tried to thank them. She opened the gift, a beautiful quilt with a pupil's name embroidered in each plain white square. Bright strips of colorful patches were placed between the white squares and bordered the outside edges.

"Thank you, mange takk, thank you." She could barely squeeze the words past the lump in her throat.

The children clustered around her and their parents around them, all marveling at the wonderful evening. Olaf invited everyone to come to church at eleven in the morning, and after the things were put away, people began to slowly leave, as if not wanting the evening to end. Outside, the air crackled, and to the north, the blazing and dancing aurora borealis looked much like angels' wings. Jingling sleigh bells and "God Jule" put the final blessing on the night.

At church in the morning, all people could talk about was the wonderful program the night before. When Olaf pronounced the benediction after a gentle and loving sermon, all rose and as one voice sang "Joy to the World" as if they really meant it.

Back home, after enjoying the good roast goose dinner and opening their presents, talk turned to counting the good things that had happened in the last year.

"We are indeed blessed," Kaaren said, a twin sleeping in each arm. She smiled at her husband.

"Ja, with more things than we can count." Haakan bounced Andrew on his knee, causing the contagious belly laugh to bring forth answering smiles and laughter from the others.

Thorliff looked up from his pad of paper. "I can write a list."

"That would be a good idea," Ingeborg said. "Make two and we can have one at each house. Who knows when we will have to be reminded of the blessings we counted?"

## January 1885

The year of 1885 blew in on the back of a blizzard.

*Thank you, Lord, that we got the ropes strung before this hit.* Ingeborg stared out the window into total white. While the bit of daylight coming in the window told her it was not snowed over, she could see nothing else. The wind howled like the train on which they'd traveled west. It only changed pitch and whine at times, never slacking in intensity. She had laid sand-filled sacks sown in a tube at the bottom of the door to keep out both the draft and the drifting snow. But unless she worked right next to the stove, she felt the cold. At the table, Andrew played with the wooden puzzles Olaf had made for him at Christmas.

Ingeborg thought of Auduna Booth in her soddy all alone. Hopefully her husband had stayed inside with her, knowing how she feared the wind. If she feared the normal blowing, this must be terrifying her. "Please, Father, help her today and every day." She stirred the pot of venison stew simmering on the stove, finding it nearly done. The apple pie in the oven filled the house with a cinnamon fragrance. The bread was rising on the lid of the reservoir, for away from the stove was too cold for it to raise.

She took pencil and paper and sat down at the table, returning Andrew's sunny grin. Even with two lamps lit, the room was dim, but his smile brightened it.

He dumped the pieces out again, laughing at the clatter they made. When one fell to the floor, he climbed off his chair and retrieved it, chattering all the while.

"Dear Far and Mor and all my family," Ingeborg wrote.

"We are well here, and while a blizzard is blowing right now, we are safe and warm. I pray it is the same for you. As to your questions about available land, there is none for homesteading around here, but there is some to buy. The bank is very good about extending credit to both seasoned farmers and new immigrants. It will be so wonderful to see familiar faces from home. . . ."

She continued on, describing the Christmas pageant and telling about the used lumber mill Haakan and Olaf hauled on skids back from Minnesota, and the new steam engine and boiler brought from the train depot at Grafton.

"Although they want to finish setting the machinery up so they can begin sawing the stack of felled trees into boards, this weather is keeping them in the barn. Thorliff and Baptiste are there, as well, splitting shingles to sell in the spring."

She signed off with messages of love and folded it for the envelope. Paws barking at the door announced the arrival of the men for dinner. "Put your puzzles away now, Andrew. It is dinnertime."

"I knew we should have built a covered porch this fall." Haakan held the door from slamming while the others came in, Paws included. The dog looked up at Ingeborg, and when she said, "You can stay," he wagged his tail and shook off the snow clinging to his caramel-colored fur.

"Are you froze clear through?" Ingeborg asked, removing the pie from the oven and setting it in the middle of the table.

"No, that stove in the shop works real well. It's just between the barn and the house that there's a problem." Haakan sniffed and rubbed his hands some more over the stove heat. "You knew how wonderful apple pie would taste today. How good you are to us."

Olaf agreed. "Don't think I've eaten like this for the last five years. Never did like cooking for myself."

"Mor, Baptiste and I split two squares apiece this morning. Far said that was good as some men do." Thorliff wiped his nose on his sleeve, drawing a reproving look from his mother. "Sorry."

"Good, then you are ready for lessons this afternoon."

Both boys groaned.

"But I thought since we can't get to Tante Kaaren's very good . . ."

"I know what you thought." She pointed to their chairs. "But I thought to surprise you."

They groaned again.

After grace, with Andrew as always tailing with the last emphatic amen, they fell to their meal. Olaf and Haakan launched into a discussion about the lumber mill, which had become a daily occurrence. But when Ingeborg served the pie, no one said anything. They were too busy making their warm pieces disappear.

By the end of the second day of the blizzard, with the wind still howling at banshee levels, Ingeborg wanted nothing more than to get out. Crossing the field to see Kaaren would help, but Haakan discouraged her from taking the chance.

"Even with the rope, there is danger of getting lost should you fall down, and . . ."

"Be blown down, more likely." Ingeborg shuddered. Memories of the terrible blizzard of '82 still lurked in the dim corners and pounced on her when she least expected it.

Haakan put his arms around her and held her close. "I won't let anything happen to you," he murmured in her ear.

But Ingeborg had learned the hard lesson that some things were beyond a strong man's control, and life could change in an instant. She locked her hands around his back, praying that he was right.

That night the nightmares returned, those she'd thought banished and dead.

"Ingeborg, wake up." Haakan shook her shoulder gently. "You're dreaming."

"Wha—?" She sat straight up, her arms flailing, one catching him square on the jaw.

Her heart thundered and her lungs heaved, as though she'd been running and running.

"Ouch, you didn't have to hit me." He rubbed his jaw, fingers scraping against the stubble on his face.

"Oh, Haakan, I was so . . ." Ingeborg switched to Norwegian to find the words to describe her terror. She leaned against him, and he pulled the quilts up over them. Her voice came through the darkness, bleak as the wind screeching so close to their ears. "The black hole is back. What if I fall into it again and never get out?"

"Inge!" He grasped her shoulders and shook her. "Listen to me. You will not fall in the hole again. You—*we* will get through this winter, and by the grace of God, you will never spend another in a dark hole like this soddy. Tomorrow you are coming out to the barn where there is at least light and space."

"It is so cold." Far away, the tone of her voice cried. Far away. She shivered, her teeth clicking together. Like a lost child clinging to its mother when found, she hugged herself to Haakan's chest and tried to find sanctuary in his arms.

She put on a cheerful face in the morning, seeking her Bible for comfort when the men went out to milk and feed the livestock. But every verse she turned to shouted of the wrath of God on His disobedient people. Even the Psalms. The wrath of God might be in the blizzard that still howled outside their home.

She kept thinking about Mrs. Booth and wishing she had brought her home with her whether her husband wanted or not. Guilt at taking the easy way out stole into her heart, making the day darker still.

She went about her chores, but the laughter in their home had fled before the wind.

Even Andrew moped around and clung to her skirts, whining to be picked up instead of playing like he usually did.

When the blizzard broke early in the morning of the fourth day, Haakan loaded her and the children, along with Olaf, into the sleigh and trotted the horses across the frozen drifts to the Baards'.

Agnes took one look into Ingeborg's empty eyes and shook her head. "It is back." She wrapped Ingeborg in her arms and led her over to the stove. Sitting her down in the rocking chair, she took Ingeborg's hands in hers.

The children played around their feet as Agnes prayed for her friend.

"Mange takk," Ingeborg whispered when the silence between them had stretched for some minutes. "I don't know what's the matter with me. It's . . . it's as if the lights have gone out, as if God has gone away . . . again. Agnes, I thought I was stronger than this. Why am I sinking backward? I have everything I need and want." Tears filled her eyes. "Why?"

Agnes sniffed herself. "I wish I knew. But you are here, and you have Haakan who is so worried. We will not let this take over you again."

They heard sleigh bells jingling outside and a "whoa" as the sleigh reached the house.

At the knock on the door, Agnes rose and opened it. Hagen Booth stood there alone.

"Come in, come in before you freeze." She took his arm and drew him inside the warm house when he paused. He removed his hat and held it in front of him, turning it in his hands.

"I . . . I come to tell you some hard news." His eyes swam with tears he refused to shed. "Auduna, my wife . . ." His voice choked. "She done wandered off in the blizzard. I didn't think to tie her down, and . . . and . . ." He raised his face to look fully at Agnes. "I didn't hear her go. I slept through it all, and in the morning she was gone. Even the dog couldn't sniff her out after all that snow."

"Come, sit down." Agnes stuffed her handkerchief back in her apron pocket. "I have the coffee hot."

He pulled away. "No. I thought to tell the others." He turned and left, the door slamming behind him.

"Dear God, dear God." Ingeborg rocked forward and back against the rhythm of the rocker. "We let her die. All of us, we let her die. Oh, God, forgive us." Her hands hid her face, but the tears streamed between her fingers. Would that . . . could that happen to her, too?

⚬ ⚬

"I think it just crept up on me," Ingeborg said in answer to Kaaren's question the next day. They, along with Solveig, sat around the cookstove at Kaaren's, knitting needles clacking, Andrew and the twins sleeping. "I could find no comfort in my Bible either."

"I wondered how the black spell came on so fast." Kaaren looked up from where she was turning the heel of a long stocking. "But I can see that today you are better. Why, do you think?"

"Agnes prayed for me and wrote out two scriptures I'm to keep with me all the time." She dug in her apron pocket to produce the two bits of paper and read aloud, " 'The Lord is my shield and deliverer, whom shall I fear,' and"—she switched papers—" 'And lo, I am with you always.' They help, and the strangest thing now is that when I pick up my Bible, I can find many verses like this with promises to hold on to. I tell you, those verses I read in the days earlier put more than the fear of God into me."

"What about Mr. Booth? Such a tragedy."

"I think that is one of the things that helped me too. The thought of ending up like her frightened me so much that I stepped back from the black pit and have been stepping farther back every minute." She studied her swiftly moving hands for a moment. "I really think God gave me a miracle." Her eyes swam with tears when she looked up. "And I thank Him for it."

"We will too." Kaaren sniffed and smiled, though her lips trembled. "I am thankful to God that we have one another, that we live so close, and only in the worst of storms do we have to be separated."

"Ja, I think God is working all kinds of miracles." Solveig lifted her leg, no longer crooked but straight and true. At a baby's whimper, the three looked toward the cradle. "All kinds."

Another blizzard followed on the coattails of the first, but this one only closed them in for two days. From then on, each time a blizzard arrived with its yawning pit, Ingeborg clung to the verses Agnes had given her and to others she found herself. The louder the wind howled, the louder she proclaimed her verses, shouting them sometimes into the teeth of the wind.

When the sun broke through, the men again headed for the lumber mill set about a quarter of a mile upriver from the houses. Since they already had the saw and gears reassembled and set into a frame of tree trunks, shortly after dinner they had the steam engine skidded out and set too. They let the boys start the fire in the firebox and assigned them the job of keeping it going. The flames snapped and ate at the pitch wood they threw in, and soon it was roaring under the water tank, sending steam into the boiler. They watched the needle on the gauge wobble and begin to climb. When it reached the proper pressure, Haakan pushed the lever forward and the long belt strung between the engine and the saw began to turn.

Thorliff let out a shriek and the men a yell. As the gears turned beneath the saw, the great blade spun. Haakan ratcheted a trimmed tree trunk into the saw carriage and the blade bit into the wood. A ripping scream split the air, wood chips flew, and the saw cut off the first slab of bark-covered wood.

"That'll be used for firewood," Haakan shouted to be heard above the whine of the saw.

Olaf drove the team that dragged another log up the ramp, and Lars used his pike to push it onto the carriage where the log moved forward until its turn to become one-inch slabs of siding.

They reset the saw blade, and the next tree became four-by-ten beams. By the end of the day, they had also cut two-by-fours, beams, siding, and two-by-eights. As dusk fell, sending a rosy glow over the glittering snow drifts, they cut the slab wood into lengths for the stove.

"Why is the belt crossed over in the middle?" Thorliff asked when they shut the machinery down to go do the evening chores.

Lars walked to where the ten-inch-wide canvas belt crossed, making a long figure eight. "You know, Thorliff, you sure are observant." He laid his hand on the belt and pointed to the two drums at the ends. "If the belt went straight from one to the other, which is what you think it should do, as the drums spun, they would spin the belt right off. You want to be real careful not to get in the way of a flying belt. I saw it kill a man one day when it broke. But with the cross, the belt stays in place."

Thorliff nodded. "Did you think of that?"

Lars laughed and slapped the boy on the shoulder. "No, but I wish I had. The man I worked for taught me, and now I'm teaching you."

"And me," Baptiste added, matching his strides to that of the men as they walked back to the soddy.

"Now that we know it works, you have to come watch tomorrow," Haakan told Ingeborg. "All you women should come. Thorliff can stay with the babies for a little while." He shook his head in amazement. "It really worked and the first time we fired it up too."

"Must be another of God's miracles," Ingeborg said with a broad smile.

"Miracles?"

"Ja, we must watch for them so we can thank Him." Ingeborg patted his shoulder as his look changed from puzzlement to acceptance.

"If you say so."

The next morning Baptiste and Thorliff brought the sleigh around, and after dropping Thorliff off at Kaaren's, Baptiste drove the women and Andrew out to the sawmill. The shrieking whine of the saw blade cutting through the timbers made Andrew look up at his mother with wrinkled eyebrows.

"That's just the saw blade," she reassured him, wishing she could cover her ears with her hands herself. But as the logs slid into place, the saw bit into them, and the slabs of wood fell free. Andrew clapped his hands and crowed in delight.

"Now, you must always stay away from the saw," Ingeborg told him, holding tightly to his mittened hand. "This is no place for little boys."

"Baptiste here." Andrew looked at her, reproach darkening his eyes.

"Baptiste is a big boy now, and he helps a lot. When you get that big, you can help too."

"T'mor I be big?"

Ingeborg and Kaaren both smiled at him. "No, not tomorrow but one day."

Solveig sniffed the frigid air. "The wood smells so good."

"Ja, fresh cut lumber has a perfume all its own." Haakan stopped beside them. He nodded to the carefully stacked cut lumber. "That's as good as money in the bank. We'll sell some, but the first things built will be frame houses for the Bjorklunds."

Squares of shingles soon took up half the haymow as they split shingles whenever the weather kept them in. Some squares were marked with a T and others with a B in chalk. When sold, Thorliff and Baptiste had been promised part of the money since they split them.

One night before Olaf read the Scriptures for the day, Thorliff looked up from his book and said, "Think I'll spend part of my money on books. What about you, Baptiste?"

"I will buy a rifle when I have enough. Then I can help your mor and my grandmere hunt. I will be a good hunter."

"That you will, Baptiste," Ingeborg said. "If you'd like, I will teach you boys how to handle a gun and how to shoot straight. Once you can do that, I will teach you to hunt."

"Know how to shoot and hunt. Uncle taught me. Metiz' boys learn from little." He held out a hand to show how tall they were when they first learned to hunt.

"Why have you never told us you know how to hunt?" Ingeborg asked, laying her knitting down in her lap and looking over at him.

He shrugged. "You never ask."

Haakan let out a snort of laughter. "That'll teach us."

"Mor." Andrew leaned on her knees. "Make popcorn?"

Olaf laid down the spindle he was carving. "I will. Come on, boys, you help me." Thorliff and Baptiste each rubbed two cobs together to break the tight little kernels off while Andrew dragged a big wooden bowl out of the cupboard. Olaf dropped a bit of lard in a kettle, poured in the popcorn kernels, then put the cover in place and set the pan over the hottest heat.

Andrew ran in place as the pops could be heard ricocheting off the insides of the kettle. When Olaf poured the popped corn into the bowl, Andrew giggled. When one dropped on the floor and Paws snatched it up, he laughed some more. "Popcorn, popcorn, we have popcorn," he chanted.

Olaf set the bowl in the middle of the table and, scooping Andrew under his arm, set him on his box. "There you go, young feller." He laid some of the popped corn on the table in front of the beaming boy. "Since you asked for it, you get first taste."

*Another miracle*, Ingeborg thought when she took her place. *It takes so little to make them—all of us—happy, Lord. Thank you.* She thanked the Father again when Olaf picked up the big Bible and began to read. He made the story of David and Goliath come alive with his inflections and changes of voice. Andrew's eyes widened as Goliath shouted for David, and he clapped his hands when the giant fell.

"Why do you think God put this story in His book?" Olaf asked the children.

Thorliff narrowed his eyes in thought, then replied, "So we would know we don't have to be afraid of big things. God will take care of us."

"Right you are." Olaf nodded. "You are a good thinker, Thorliff, and you listen for the true meaning of things. That is good for a man to do."

They could have blown out the lamps, Thorliff's smile shone so bright.

❧ ❧

Every day the weather allowed, the men spent felling trees and feeding the lumber mill. Neighbors came from both sides of the frozen river, gazing in awe and delight at the noisy beast. Soon horses pulling sledges loaded with logs were lined up, waiting their turn at the mill. Since Haakan charged by keeping a fourth of the lumber sawed, no money changed hands, but the stacks of lumber for the Bjorklunds grew.

❧ ❧

With the weather holding cold but sunny, Kaaren sent out word that school would start again the first of February, depending of course on the daily weather. There would be no school if it was snowing or a howling blizzard.

The first day back, her pupils clustered around her desk, each one trying to tell her about their Christmas and the big blizzard all at once. They jostled and teased one another like old friends, and several showed her books they had received for Christmas.

"Pleath read mine to everybody," Anna begged. "I can't read good enough."

"That we will do," Kaaren promised her, bringing a smile to the pale little face. The teacher clapped her hands and everyone scampered to their seats. She greeted them in English, and they answered in English. She asked one of the older girls to read the scripture for the day, and they sang the folk song they'd performed for the pageant. When they sat down again, Kaaren looked out over her schoolroom. "I am so proud of all of you, I cannot begin to tell you how much. Your program was wonderful, and everyone has told me so again and again. Because you have done so well, this afternoon we will have a special treat."

They waited but when she didn't go on, one asked, "What is the treat?"

"It won't be a surprise if I tell you, will it? We'll begin with reading, as usual."

The day passed in what seemed like minutes, and when Kaaren made snow candy, everyone hurried to fill the two flat pans with snow. Some of the children had never had such a treat, their eyes growing round with delight when they tasted it. She closed the day with the first chapter of Anna's book, *Daughter of the Prairie.*

"Thank you, Mitheth Bjorklund," Anna whispered from her place pasted to Kaaren's right knee.

They went a week before a blizzard closed them down.

Kaaren accepted the time off gratefully. Why was she so tired? Surely teaching school wasn't any harder than cooking and doing the wash all day. Those things didn't wear her out like this.

Several children were missing when school started again the next week, and others had runny noses and deep coughs. Two days later, Grace woke everyone during the night with her raspy breathing.

Kaaren hugged the little one to her, feeling the heat through the blankets and gown. "She's running a fever." Fear, of the gut-wrenching terror kind, made her short of breath. The flu that took her little girls had begun just like this.

Lars added more wood to the low-burning fire and opened the draft so it would catch quickly. "The willow bark will help in a tea if you can get her to drink from a spoon or something. That's what Metiz used for me."

Kaaren nodded. She laid the baby on the table and unwrapped the blankets. "We've got to cool her down." Clad in her diaper and shirt, Grace coughed again so hard that her face turned dark red and she gagged deep in her throat.

Kaaren turned her over and patted her back to try to bring up what was choking her. The baby coughed again, her entire body seizing.

"Tip her upside down," Solveig offered. "Mor used to do that with this kind of cough. She made a tent of steam too. That made the breathing easier."

Through the night they all worked to help little Grace. Sophie woke and demanded a feeding, but when Kaaren tried to hand Grace to Lars, he turned to put more wood in the stove. Solveig took the sick baby and walked the floor with her, alternately rocking her and laying the child against her shoulder.

"What do I do about school?" Kaaren felt a new dart of panic.

"When it is closer to dawn, I will go and ask Olaf to take over for you," Lars said after a time of thought. "The children already know him, and if he cannot do it, I will go to the school and send them all home."

"Thank you." Kaaren traded babies with Solveig, who changed Sophie and took her back into bed with her. "Lars, I am so frightened."

"Ja, I know."

"I cannot let another baby die." She looked down into the eyes of her sick child.

"You did not *let* your babies die. The flu took them and nearly you too. You got to remember a lot of people died that year."

"Ja, I know. But my heart screams."

Grace went into a paroxysm of coughing and finally vomited. For a time, she breathed more easily.

"I'll try to feed her now, maybe that will help."

"Shouldn't we try the tea first?"

Kaaren nodded. "You are right. You hold her and I'll . . ."

"I have it here ready. See if you can spoon some into her mouth." Lars held out the pan, now cooled to warm. "I put some honey in it—quite a bit. Maybe that will make it easier for her to take."

Kaaren sat in the rocker, the baby in the crook of her left arm and the spoon in her right hand. When she touched the spoon to the baby's mouth, like a little bird, it opened. She tipped a tiny bit of the liquid in, only to see it run out the side.

"She didn't swallow."

"Try again. It is new to her." Lars' warm hand on her knee made Kaaren feel he was part of her, part of the baby. She pushed a recurring thought to the back of her mind. Once again Lars sidestepped holding Grace. Was this true or only her imagination?

*Dear God, please let her swallow. This could help her. Father, spare this child, I beg of thee.*

Finally, the sick baby swallowed, then swallowed again. After three spoonfuls, Kaaren nursed her until she let the nipple slip away. Kaaren's thank-yous became the song that sang both her and the baby to sleep.

When she awoke, stiff and cold in spite of the blankets that had been tucked around her, Solveig held the sick baby. Lars had already left to talk with Olaf.

Ingeborg arrived in a flurry of cold air and coat. "I brought some other things too." She held up a packet of crushed leaves. "Metiz said this is good for cough and sore throat." She laid the back of her fingers against the restless baby's cheek. "Still too warm. It's hard to believe someone could be so warm when it is so cold outside. "You want I should help you bathe her? She won't like cooler water, but it may help."

Kaaren nodded. "It is so hard to see her suffering like this."

"Ja, I know."

"I've held her in steam and that seems to help the breathing, but then she gets so warm again. I cool her down and she starts to cough. She spit up all her breakfast."

"If she can keep the willow tea and this mixture down, that may do her more good than milk. We can try an onion poultice too. Oh, I wish Metiz were here."

Sophie didn't like being separated from her sister and let them know her displeasure in no uncertain terms. She only settled down when they put the twins back together in the cradle. Grace seemed to breathe somewhat easier with the closeness of her twin.

Late that long afternoon, Thorliff blew through the door, a big smile on his face. "Tante Kaaren, Onkel Olaf is a good teacher." He paused and sent her a special smile. "Not as good as you, but—how's Grace? Is she better?"

"I pray so. You pray for her, too, all right?"

He gave her that child-to-adult look that wondered why grownups were so slow. "I have been . . . we all are."

On the third day, the baby slipped into a peaceful slumber for two hours without a cough or gagging. After nursing her, Kaaren collapsed on the bed, and Solveig drew the covers over her. Surprisingly, the babies slept for three hours before Sophie demanded that she be fed. Solveig laid the babies at their mother's breasts and they nursed, Kaaren mumbling something but never becoming fully aware.

In the days following, another blizzard brought more snow and intense cold, driving the icy pellets like javelins before it. Lars came in from chores, the bit of his face not covered looking scraped raw.

That night Kaaren kept the babies in bed with them, for no matter how hot they kept the stove, there was ice on the inside of the sod walls. A water bucket froze four feet from the stove. During the day, she kept them in their slings and wore a blanket around her body to keep in the heat. In the morning the tip of Solveig's nose had frostbite.

"Uff da. Thank God Grace was better before this storm hit." Kaaren warmed rocks in the open oven and placed them under their feet as they huddled by the stove. "I have never seen it as cold as this."

Solveig put more wood on the fire. "At least we haven't run out of wood, as I fear some have. You think Mr. Carlson and his mother are warm enough in that big house?"

"I am sure they are. They have a large furnace in the basement that heats the whole house, plus that big stove in the kitchen." She studied her sister, who pinked under the scrutiny. "You care for him?"

Solveig nodded. "And he for me." Her hand went to the nearly invisible scar. "In spite of all this." She raised sober eyes to her sister. "You don't mind, do you?"

"Why no. Why would I? George Carlson is a fine man, and he needs a good wife. His mother wants him to have one too. I think she wants grandchildren mostly."

"There's plenty of room in that big house for many children."

When the cold let up, Kaaren told Olaf that she felt she could come back to teaching the following week.

"That is good." He smiled as he nodded. "Thank the Lord the babies are better. Most of the children are back too. I think we all got off lightly this winter. Only one death that I know of, besides Mrs. Booth, and that was old Grandma Anderson. She was ready to go home. At least that's what her grandson said."

"Have you heard how Mr. Booth is doing without his wife?"

He shook his head. "No, he hasn't been at church, and I haven't had time to go out there. I'll ask around."

"Is there anything else I should know about the school children?"

"Not that I know of. I've left their papers and marks on the desk. Think I'll start making a real desk for the teacher. That bench isn't too good."

Kaaren drove to school in the morning, leaving the team in the shed like always. The children greeted her joyfully and gathered around her to ask about the babies and tell her how happy they were she was back.

One of the older boys shook his head. "My mor ain't going to be too happy about this. Mor and Far, they think it is better we have a man for a teacher."

Kaaren stared at him, her mouth agape. Were there others that felt that way too?

**22**

Kaaren taught through the week, having heard from two more families that a man should be teaching. Each report drove a spear directly into her heart.

"They got more nerve than sense." Solveig stomped her feet when she sat down in the sleigh. "To think after all you done for them, why I . . ." She spluttered to a close.

"It isn't everybody, but I guess we will have to put it before the church on Sunday. I don't know what else to do." Kaaren looked back to make sure the twins were secure in their basket and covered well, then clucked the horses into a trot. Even the jingling bells failed to cheer her.

*Lord, is this the end of my dream? I was so happy you gave me a place to teach, and you know how much I love it. Am I not doing a good enough job?* She sniffed and swallowed the moisture burgeoning in the back of her nose and throat. *I will not cry over this. I will not.*

"I'm tempted to speak my mind, surely I am," Solveig said.

"You'll probably get your chance. We have the quilting bee at our house tomorrow." Never had she wanted anything less. If only she could tell them all to stay home, or—she thought a moment. She could ask Ingeborg to take it. The thought pleased her greatly, but what would be her reason? Say the twins weren't up to it? But that would be a lie! She drew in enough cold air to make her cough. No, she couldn't tell a lie like that. The quilting bee would meet at her house as planned.

With her mind in such a turmoil, the trip home passed from one hoof beat to the next.

Praying for another blizzard didn't help either. The sun rose, turning the snowy fields to glitter and glass that smote the eyes and stole the breath from the soul.

When the women began to arrive the next day, Kaaren put on her best company smile and her warmest welcome, even for those at whom she wanted to scream "Why?" The women chattered and laughed as they laid out their treasured pieces of different-colored cloths. They admired the growing twins and passed them around so everyone took a turn holding them. Sophie gurgled and cooed, flashing her smile to them all, while Grace lay more passive, as if studying each of her admirers. The Christmas program came in for more praises, and Kaaren thanked them for all their hard work on the costumes. When the talk turned to Mrs. Booth and her fear of the wind, more than one shuddered, knowing and fearing they all could be as susceptible.

"We got to stick together," Agnes said, "and look out for one another. You know these men of ours, though they be good souls, they don't understand. Especially one like poor Auduna, who had no young'uns underfoot and making noise of their own. You can't hear what's going on outside so much that way, and when you need to touch someone, you just grab the closest and hug 'em. Children always hug back." She stroked the downy cheek of the quiet baby in her arms, drawing forth a smile in return for her own.

"Ja, though sometimes you pray for a few moments of silence." Dyrfinna Odell said, rolling her eyes upward.

The gentle laughter that circled the room knit them all closer together.

"I heard your baby was real sick," Hildegunn Valders said. "Don't you think it is hard on them to take them to school every day like you been doing? I mean, I know Solveig helps care for them, but when they get older and are awake more . . ." She glanced around the group for support.

Kaaren forced herself to look up and smile cheerfully. "We've been able to work it out so far, and I . . ."

"Ja, so far." The woman nodded. "Don't get me wrong, I, and all of us, we appreciate what you done for our children. We just don't want you to suffer for being so kind." She looked up, obviously pleased with herself for managing this so well.

Solveig, seated on one side of Kaaren, muttered under her breath, her needle flashing in and out of the bits of cloth in her hands.

Kaaren glanced to the other side to see Ingeborg tighten her lips.

*Oh, Lord, please, I don't want a division here.*

"So, we thought"—Hildegunn waited for nods from the women on either side of her chair—"we thought that since we have a man here to teach now, you would rather stay home and raise your little family without the pressure of teaching the school too." The words came out in a rush.

Kaaren nodded, trying to give herself time to think of the right words to say. "I see."

"You know, it *is* more appropriate for a man to teach a school, especially with some of our boys so grown already." Hildegunn's voice took on its usual bossy tone.

That did it.

"More appropriate?" Ingeborg spit out the *t*. "You weren't looking for appropriate when Kaaren volunteered to teach and use her own money to buy books and school supplies because some people can't afford to buy the books their children need. You were just grateful, some of you, for a teacher. In fact, although some of your children had a bit of book learning already, others didn't know the first thing about reading or numbers when they should have." The accusation caused two women to study the pieces of cotton goods in their hands.

"Now, Ingeborg, don't get your skirt in a twist. We don't mean no harm by this. We just want what is best for these two little angels here." Hildegunn frowned at Ingeborg.

Just then Sophie let out a wail as if she'd been poked with a needle. Kaaren rose to her feet, grateful for the break. If she sat there much longer, she might say something she'd be sorry for later. She picked up the wailing baby and took her to the other side of the stove to quiet her.

"Just who is this 'we'?" Agnes asked in a quiet voice. "I haven't heard any of this discussion before. I am more than happy with the way things are right now. Joseph is, too, and our boys always learned good, because for the last two years—before some of you even moved here—Kaaren has been teaching our families book learning. I tried, but she is so much better at it. If she wants to continue teaching, I say she should have that choice. If she wants to quit, then we can look for someone else to take over and we should count ourselves lucky she helped us out."

"But we have a man here who can do it now!" Hildegunn acted as if the matter were settled.

"Does anyone have some blue pieces?" quiet Dyrfinna asked.

"Blue would look so nice right about here." Someone handed her a piece, and after she expressed her thanks, the discussion returned to quilting.

When Hildegunn started to say something else, Brynja, the peacemaker, quieted her friend with a hand on her arm.

"What have you heard from Penny?" Ingeborg asked, her jaw relaxing.

"She is happy as a lark. She loves going to high school and loves working at the hotel." Agnes raised her eyebrows and shrugged. "And still loves Hjelmer."

"Has she heard from him?"

"Not one letter. . . ."

"You aren't serious?"

"I keep hoping."

"You and Penny. I think she should have let herself see if she could fall in love with Modan Clauson. He is a good man, but—"

"But he's not Hjelmer." Ingeborg laid down her row of squares. "I'm going to see if Kaaren needs some help."

"Thank you, but no." Kaaren had spread a white cloth over the table and was setting out the food the women had brought. As was their custom, the hostess provided soup or stew and the others brought the rest—breads, sweet breads, jam, whatever they had to contribute.

She checked the oven and brought out a basket of rolls. Laying a cloth over the top, she announced, "Dinner is ready. Come and help yourselves. Agnes, will you lead us in grace?" The women's voices rose in the song and harmonized on the "amen."

After dinner they matched pieces, cut out others, and stitched for another two hours. Then began the exodus. Within a few minutes the last harness bells jingled away and the house fell quiet.

"All right, you can scream now," Ingeborg said, placing her hands over her ears.

Kaaren let out her breath on a whoosh. "That old biddy has to have her nose in everybody's business. Trying to tell me they wanted a man teacher so things wouldn't be so hard on me. And Brynja and Dyrfinna, sometimes I wonder if they have a thought in their heads but what she tells them. One of them doesn't even have children of school age yet. Pious hypocrites." She ranted on for another minute or two, then slammed her hands on the table, only to lean on her straight arms. She shook her head slowly.

"Guess I did almost scream, didn't I?"

"Ja, but that is all right. If you didn't, Solveig and me, we was ready to scream for you."

"I was going to bring it up in church tomorrow, since three children have mentioned their parents would rather go on with a man teacher. Has anyone even asked Olaf yet? Does he want to give up the work with Haakan and Lars to teach school for nothing?"

"I don't know." Ingeborg laid her hand on Kaaren's shoulder. "But I will find out. I better get on home and rescue Thorliff. Andrew should be up from his nap by now." She gathered her things but turned just before opening the door.

"Whatever happens, we must remember that God is at work in this too."

"I know. Thank you for the reminder."

After supper that night, Ingeborg asked Olaf if anyone had approached him about continuing to teach at the school.

He nodded. "Ja, but I told them I would need to be paid. Figured that would change their minds plenty quick. I don't want to cause no trouble with Kaaren. She loves to teach and should be allowed to do so."

"I agree, but this might not be her decision to make."

On the way to church in the morning, she told Kaaren about her conversation with Olaf.

"Isn't it interesting that people have found time to get together to talk about this in spite of the blizzards?" Kaaren asked. "I knew nothing about it and wouldn't have if the children hadn't mentioned it. Were they that unhappy about me taking the babies to school? Or did they not like the way I taught? What was it?"

Ingeborg wanted to wrap her arms around this sister of hers and wipe the sad, defeated look from her face. "Kaaren, don't even think such things. We both know you are a fine teacher, and the way the children learn from you, why, it is nothing but a gift, that's what it is."

"Then why am I being asked to step aside?"

"Because some of these people think they are back in Norway instead of here in Dakota Territory where we are willing to try new things and new ways." She turned her face away from the greeting by Brynja Vegard.

Kaaren felt like saying, "Then they should go back to Norway," but she refrained. She did not want to be the cause of further contention.

"Just remember, Olaf said he couldn't leave off helping Lars and

Haakan to go teach until summer without pay."

Kaaren nodded. She had a hard time keeping her mind on the service led by her uncle Olaf. He had taken her place as leader of the services and now would take over the school too. In church, that was according to the Scriptures, but the school? What was wrong with a woman teaching the school? Other places did it.

Late that afternoon two men from the church arrived at Ingeborg's house. "We come to talk with Olaf," Mr. Valders said. "Is he to home?"

"Ja, he is out in the barn working on something."

"Working on the Lord's day?" He harrumphed and touched the brim of his hat.

"Looks like you and your wife were cut from the same mold," Ingeborg muttered as they left. How she wished she could hide in a corner in the barn to hear what was said. What were they up to now?

⚕ ⚕

A knock on the door brought Kaaren to her feet. She waved Solveig away. "I'll get it."

Olaf stood outside.

"Come in, come in. You don't need to knock. You are my family." She ushered him in, gesturing to the coffeepot.

"No thank you." He stood on the rag rug in front of the door. "I come with a hard thing to talk over with you."

"Ja? Well, we will talk better sitting down."

When they sat at opposite ends of the table, he looked at her with great sadness in his dark eyes. "Kaaren, I do not want to bring unhappiness to you, please understand that."

She reached across the table and touched his clasped hands. "You are my onkel. I know that. What is it?" *Oh, please don't say you are moving away, that you want to leave here, when the men depend on you so much. We all do.* "You aren't leaving, are you?"

"Oh no. Not unless you want me to."

"Why would I want that?"

"Ja, you might. Hear me out, please?" At her nod, he continued. "You know that I took your place as teacher only because you needed me?" She nodded again. "I did not ask to stay on there."

"I know that."

"The men have asked me to continue, and I said it was up to

you, but that I wouldn't work for nothing like you have been. You should have been paid in whatever they had if there was no money. That is only proper."

"Ja, well, that didn't happen, and I wanted very much to teach the children. I even thought maybe we would have classes in speaking English for the adults so that everyone can learn the language." Her enthusiasm made her lean forward, her voice speed up.

He nodded again. "That is a good idea." His shoulders drooped, then squared. "Today they offered me money to teach. Every family will pay something for each child."

"What about those who have so little? Some of them have barely enough food to send in the dinner pails for their children." Then the meaning of his words sank into her mind. They would *pay* Olaf to teach in her place. They wanted a man that badly. They didn't want her.

She waited, a great cloud of sadness trying to push her right into the dirt floor. When she could speak, she said, "Olaf, I have never been one to go where I am not wanted. Teach at the school with my blessing." Her voice broke on the last word. She rubbed her lips together. "But please, please be gentle with the little ones, Anna especially."

"Are you sure?"

"I am sure."

Just then Solveig and the two boys burst through the door, their laughter bringing in the crisp dusk air.

"I will be going then." He pushed his chair back and looked at her intently. "You are sure?"

She nodded. "With my blessing." As he closed the door behind him, she looked at Solveig. "Would you watch the babies for a while? I need a breath of fresh air." Turning down Thorliff's offer to go with her, she threw on her coat and draped the shawl over her head. Maybe if she walked long enough and hard enough, she could find God's voice in the storm raging in her mind.

That week she turned out the entire house, cleaning every inch. She washed clothes, sewed a dress for Solveig, baked bread twice, used up all the cream for butter, and against Lars' remonstrations shoveled out the chicken coop. Solveig decided early on that staying out of Kaaren's way was an act of wisdom.

Only when totally exhausted could Kaaren sleep. But even in sleep, her mind refused to let go of the fiercely burning anger. Frightful dreams plagued her nights, startling her awake with heart-pounding frequency. Her stomach felt like a bouncing ball.

Kaaren said she didn't feel well enough to go to church that Sunday.

"You want I should stay home too?" Lars asked, bending over her in the rocking chair.

"No, you and Solveig go on. I will try to sleep when the babies are sleeping."

Lars looked at her and shook his head. "This is not like you."

But when she bolted for the basin, he did as asked.

"Now I know why I've been so tired lately." She stared into the mirror above the basin where Lars shaved and saw the dark circles etched under her eyes and the colorless skin of her face. Her stomach had been roiling more often than just in the morning. How had she missed it? She counted the months. February, March, April . . . they'd have a baby in September or October, about the time the twins were a year old. Would that God gave them a boy this time, for Lars' sake.

She felt some better by the time the quilting bee rolled around again in March, but like for church, she refused to go. Thorliff kept her up-to-date on things at school, and between Solveig and the burgeoning Ingeborg, the twins received plenty of attention. Kaaren felt like a milk cow, an extremely ill milk cow, what with vomiting at all hours. When she finally told Lars about the coming baby, he breathed a deep sigh of relief.

"I thought something was really wrong with you, Kaaren. You scared me half to death." He lifted his hands heavenward. "Now I can rejoice."

"I am glad you can do that. Maybe when I feel a bit better I will rejoice too." But she didn't tell him about the anger that burned deep within her. Anger at their neighbors for telling her to give up the joy of her life and stay home. "I don't care if I never see some of them again," she whispered to wide-eyed Grace. The baby only blinked. "Oh, my sweet baby, how I wish you could hear. It seems God isn't listening to my prayers very much lately. I guess you could say He has turned a deaf ear." She tried to smile, but it never went beyond a slight lifting of the corners of her mouth. Grace remained sober, too, staring deep into her mother's eyes as if she could see clear to the wounded soul.

"God above, I am so tired," Kaaren murmured.

One morning the Norwegian Bible in her lap fell open to a different place. For some time now the words had been just that, flat words on a flat page. But this time the words seemed to leap off the paper. "My will is only good for you. . . ." How could all that happened be only good for her? She laid her head against the back of the rocker. Could she have taught school every day feeling as she did now? Would she have had enough milk for her two thriving babies if she were rushing to try to keep up with all she needed to do? The questions marched through her mind.

She turned to the New Testament to the book of Ephesians where she'd been reading. When she began on her chapter for the day, more words grabbed her attention and shook it. "Be ye angry, and sin not: let not the sun go down upon your wrath: neither give place to the devil."

How many suns had gone down on her anger? Had her sadness turned to bitterness and taken root deep inside her? What would it take to rip those roots out if that were so?

Solveig returned from Ingeborg's with a wedge of cheese and a loaf of fresh bread. "We had some of this with our coffee, and Inge thought you might enjoy it too. She makes the best cheese."

"Ja, that she does." Kaaren continued rocking, letting other verses she had memorized through the years bathe her mind in their healing power. God had not turned a deaf ear. He had been waiting for her to listen, as He always did. "And if you have been wronged by a neighbor, go to him and . . ." Had she been wronged? It felt that way at the time. Did God have her good in mind? It certainly looked that way.

"Thank you, Solveig. My belly says that cheese and fresh bread would taste mighty good for a change."

"Were you this sick with the twins?" Solveig handed her sister a cup of coffee on a plate with the bread and cheese.

"Not this long nor so violently. They say every baby is different. I know Ingeborg wasn't very sick with this one, but I remember the first time. Uff da. And on the train trip west too."

That Sunday she joined her family in the sleigh heading for church. She would have to ask for their forgiveness, those who wanted a man for a teacher. How hard that would be. But then asking God to forgive her hadn't been easy either—but it was worth it to have the peace she so loved back in her life.

She was greeted with cries of delight and questions about her health. The ladies cooed over the babies and couldn't say enough how much they'd missed her. Afterward she left Solveig holding the twins and made her way to the group of three women she had most hated.

"Oh, Kaaren, it is so good to see you out and about again. I have been so worried about you."

"Thank you, Hildegunn. Sometimes babies make their announcements in rather difficult ways."

"Oh, how wonderful for you." Brynja beamed and clasped one of Kaaren's hands.

"I have something to say, and please let me finish before you say anything." Their faces sobered. Kaaren took a deep breath. "I have come to beg your forgiveness for being so angry at you when Olaf was asked to be the teacher."

"Oh, Kaaren, it is we who must ask you the same." Hildegunn took Kaaren's hands in her own. "We . . . we handled that so badly. Yes, I forgive you, but only if you can forgive me."

"I already have." Kaaren took each of their hands and pressed them between her own. "I know now that this is what God had in mind for me, and I'm not sure I would have listened any other way."

"Ja, sometimes the still small voice of God is too still and too small." Brynja bobbed her head as she spoke. "Please, can we all be friends again and meet for quilting? I have sorely missed your gentle presence."

"Ja, we are and we will. I thank you for . . . for . . ." She swallowed and blinked. "The sun is so bright." She smiled. "Just thank you."

"And you."

When she returned to the sleigh where the Bjorklunds and Baards waited, she walked right into Agnes's embrace. "Lord love you, child, you have a bigger heart than me, that's for certain sure. I think we all need some fence mending and you begun it."

A sense of peace flooded Kaaren's heart and soul, making the sun shine warmer and the wind sing instead of howl. The jingling harness bells sang with the wind.

The next Sunday just before the benediction, Olaf motioned to Mr. Valders to stand. Anner turned to the congregation.

"I asked Olaf here for a few minutes of your time to rectify a wrong we inflicted on one of our own. Would Mrs. Lars Knutson please come forward?"

Kaaren looked at Lars, who raised his shoulders and shook his head. She stood and went forward as requested.

"Things happened a while ago that weren't done God's way a'tall. All of us here would like to make it up to you in some small way, so we took up a collection to repay you for the books you bought for the school and, while it isn't much as we'd like, to repay you for the many hours you taught our children. We thank you for all you did. The school would still be just a dream, I'm sure, if you hadn't wanted one so bad for all of us." He handed her a pouch that jingled when exchanged.

Kaaren took it and stared at him a moment before she could speak. "Schoolteachers are never supposed to be speechless, but I am. Thank you." She faced the congregation. "Thank you very much." She returned to her seat, fighting tears at the smiling faces she had passed. Afterward the children said how they missed her, but that Mr. Wold was a good teacher. The men and women shook her hand and thanked her again.

When she counted the money at home, she looked up at Lars, her mouth an O to match her eyes. "They couldn't afford this much." She shook her head.

"Oh, I expect some felt more guilty than others and made up for those without." His eyes twinkled. "Those without guilt or money, I mean."

"I knew what you meant." She dropped the bills and coins back in the soft deerskin pouch. "I'm just glad it is all over."

"I'm proud to have a wife who could go to those . . ." He stopped at the look of caution she gave him. "Those saintly women?" His left eyebrow cocked. "And do what you did. You set a fine example, my Kaaren." He rose and came around to drop a kiss on her forehead. "I have a wife like no other."

I n late March Hjelmer approached his boss at the roundhouse. "I need a week off so I can do some family business. It can't wait any longer."

The man, sporting a bent nose and the body of a wrestler, looked at him through squinted eyes. "You'll come back?"

"Ja, I'll be back."

"I don't usually do this, you know, but you been a good man. . . ."

"Thank you. I didn't think you did. And I wouldn't ask if it weren't important." He waited a moment before the man nodded. "Thank you, sir."

The next day he caught a train to Moorhead and then one to Grand Forks. He'd been to the bank in St. Paul and withdrawn all but a thousand dollars of his wages and gambling money in the form of a check to deposit at the bank in Grand Forks. With the map in his pocket that showed the proposed spur-line route, he headed for the courthouse first, where he made a list of all the landowners along the stretch he was interested in. The next morning, dressed in the same clothes he'd worn to the card games that were enabling him to make his fortune, he entered the bank.

"I'd like to talk to the manager," he said to the man at the teller window.

"I'll get him." The green eyeshade bobbled as he scurried off.

"Hello. I'm the owner and manager, Daniel Brockhurst." The man's dark three-piece suit matched his eyes. He held out his hand, soft from lack of manual labor. "How can I help you, Mr. . . . ?"

"Bjorklund. Hjelmer Bjorklund." Hjelmer shook the offered hand.

"You by any chance related to the Bjorklunds up St. Andrew's way?" he asked as he ushered Hjelmer into his office.

"Roald and Carl were my brothers." He sat down in the leather winged chair in front of the desk.

"Fine men. Even in the little time they lived here, they made their mark on the area. Their families all right?"

"I . . . I'm not sure how they are right now. I've been working on the railroad the last few months." Hjelmer kept himself from looking down at his hands. He leaned forward. "I have been sending all my wages here for deposit, so you have a sum of my money." He laid his check on the desk. "And here is more. I want to buy land in the valley."

Brockhurst turned the check so he could read it better. "You've done all right for yourself, young man."

"I have, and I want that to continue. As I buy up the land, if I need more than this and what I have in your bank, will you back me?"

"How much more are you thinking?" Brockhurst leaned back in his leather swivel chair.

"It all depends on how much I can buy, or what's available. I plan to go talk to the homesteaders in that area and see if anyone wants to sell. With this hard winter we've had, there might be some who want to leave."

"There's railroad land available, too, should that interest you." The bank manager steepled his fingers, elbows on the chair arms.

"Depends on where it is." Hjelmer, too, leaned back and crossed one ankle over the other knee.

"Your family know about this?"

Hjelmer shook his head. "I'll stop by there. Would like this to be a surprise."

Brockhurst drew a ledger out of the bottom drawer in his desk. He flipped the pages, stopped, and ran his finger down the lines. "Ah, here it is. You have a total of $2,380.78 in your account. How much do you propose to take?"

"I plan to take twelve thousand with me so that I can offer hard cash. Men are more inclined to make a quicker decision when you lay cash on the table."

"Right you are, but isn't that a bit dangerous?"

"I won't be gone long. You could help me by pointing me in the direction of anyone wanting to sell." Hjelmer narrowed his eyes. "And backing me with another five thousand should I need it."

Brockhurst studied the young man before him. "The land would be the collateral."

Hjelmer nodded.

"Will you be needing machinery and the like?"

"Not right away."

Brockhurst tapped a manicured fingernail on the desk blotter. "Done. Two point five interest for five years."

"Two percent for eight years."

"Young man, you trying to rob me?" His half smile showed he was teasing.

"No, sir." Hjelmer shook his head. "Just wanting to make the best deal." He sat waiting, grinding his toe into the carpet to keep it from tapping in impatience. *Remember this is just like a card game. Wait and watch and play your cards close to your chest.*

The bank owner smiled and nodded. "We have a deal. I'll have the papers drawn up, and we can get them signed. I assume you want to get on your way as soon as possible."

"That I do. I have one more question, though. Could you prepare me some blank deed papers? Then I can fill them in when I buy the land and will bring them back to town to file when I am finished. Would that be legal?"

"The signatures need to match those on the original deed, that's all. Usually we would ask both parties to come in, but since you are offering them cash, this should work. They would need time to get moved."

"That's no problem. I might offer some of them to stay on and farm through to the fall."

Brockhurst rifled through some files in his desk drawer and pulled out a sheet of paper. "Well, let's get the paper work filled out, then you can come back in an hour to sign it. I'll have your cash ready then too. How were you wanting that? Hundreds?"

An hour later Hjelmer had a packet of hundred-dollar bills, another with blank deeds, pen and ink, and he had rented a horse and saddle from the livery. He'd thought about a horse and buggy but knew he could make better time this way. He rode out to the southern most parcel and began to make his way north.

He would ride up to the house, in most cases a soddy, and ask for the landowner by name. He'd introduce himself, and by then the housewife would be offering him a cup of coffee.

"I'm looking for land to buy," he'd say. "Cash money. You know anyone who might be interested in selling?"

The wife, who usually looked about worn down to the nubbins with a babe in her arms and another twisting a hand in her skirt, would sigh. If he took a moment to look up, she usually wore a face colored in hope, perhaps the first in a long time.

The man would lean back—that meant he needed to be persuaded—or forward. That's when Hjelmer usually offered less cash than he had planned, because the man wanted out. But, to his own surprise, Hjelmer let himself be led by his conscience or a sense of pity for these folks with so little, and he never paid less than a quarter under the market value of $2.50 per acre.

As he rode the snow-covered prairie, Hjelmer realized how well his brothers, and then his brothers' wives, had done with so many acres planted and reaped after the hard sod-breaking. Their buildings were tight, they owned much livestock, and already they brought in money from the sales of produce to the store and the Bonanza farm. No wonder they had earned such a good reputation with Brockhurst. Hjelmer's respect for Ingeborg climbed with each family he met. She had kept them all from the defeated look he saw so often on the faces of both women and men.

By the end of the third day, he had purchased four sections and had one pair of brothers who wanted to think about his offer for a couple of days. With the weather holding sunny and cold, he made his way northward toward the spot on the map known as Drayton. When he spent a night with families in the soddies, he tried to offer them some cash for their hospitality. In spite of their protests, he tucked some bills under one of the plates before he left.

One farm he only found by the smoke curling up from a snowbank. A woman came to the door at the dog's barking, a gun in her hand.

"Good morning, ma'am. Are you Mrs. Peterson?" He tried English first. At the shake of her head, he switched to Norwegian and repeated his question.

She nodded, turning her head sideways a bit, and studied him. A child wailed behind her. A cow bellowed from the barn. The dog wagged his tail by the horse's knee, but the rising hair on the back of the dog's neck and shoulders warned Hjelmer he'd best stay where he was.

"Is Mr. Peterson here?"

She shook her head, tightening her jaw.

"Will he be coming home soon?"

She shook her head again. "He's out in the barn."

Hjelmer thought for a moment. Had she misheard his question? "Could I speak with him?"

"Mighty hard. He died three days ago." She raised her chin a bit and blinked.

"I . . . I'm sorry." Hjelmer thought a moment. "My name is Hjelmer Bjorklund and . . ."

"From the Bjorklunds up north some?"

"Ja."

She stepped back. "You come right on in." She set the rifle back inside the door. "Tie your horse right there to the house or take him out to the barn. We got some hay left. You can give him a bit."

Hjelmer looked at the walkway to the barn not shoveled out but marked by footsteps. He smiled and nodded. "Mange takk." He set the horse along the path to make it deeper and pushed open the barn door. In the dimness, he saw two sawhorses covered by two boards on which lay the frozen body of Mr. Peterson. How she had gotten him up there was more than he could understand. He led the horse into the vacant stall next to the slack-bagged cow, and after loosening the saddle girth and hooking the bridle over the saddle horn, he used the rope on the manger to tie to his horse's halter. He tossed a bit of hay to the cow, some to his horse, and on his way out checked the feed bin. Empty.

Back at the house, Mrs. Peterson had water steaming on the stove, heated by twists of hay.

"Sorry, I have nothing better." She set a cup of weak coffee before him, a small child clinging to her skirt. When he took a sip, he knew it to be made from roasted grain of some sort. "The cow went dry, so I hope black is all right."

"This is fine. Hot is what helps." He heard a weak cough from the bed on the far wall. At his glance in that direction, she sighed.

"That's Hans, my son. He has outlived his far, but I don't know . . ." She squared her shoulders that slumped for a moment.

Hjelmer thought to some of the stories Ingeborg had told him of the terrible life some settlers endured. This was indeed the worst he'd seen, and two of the farms he bought hadn't been a whole lot better. But at least there, those husbands were still alive.

"Mrs. Peterson, what are you going to do?"

She shook her head. The cough came from the bed again, deep and wracking. She got up and took the boy a cup of warm water, spooning it between his lips. The smaller child stared at their guest out of eyes sunk so far back in her head they looked black. Under the bulky sweater that covered her to her knees, Hjelmer was afraid she had arms and legs of sticks. Either she had been terribly sick or she was starving.

The woman came back to the table and slumped to the stool that served for a chair. "I don't know. S'pose I better butcher the cow before she dies, 'cause we been burning the hay. That'll at least give us something more to eat." She sighed. "I hate to butcher the cow. She's all we got left."

"You have any family to go to?"

She shook her head. "In Nordland."

Hjelmer studied the weak dregs in his cup. He couldn't leave these people here to die.

"I can pay you cash money for your land. How many acres do you have?"

"Half a section, 180 acres. Only busted about forty, though. My Elmer, after that terrible flu in '82, he weren't a strong man. We should never have come here." She wiped the child's runny nose with the edge of her apron, then looked across the table to Hjelmer. "What good would the money do until spring? I got no way out of here." She gestured to the boy in the bed and the child at her knee. "We can't walk through the snow."

"You won't have to." Hjelmer counted out the money and laid it on the table. "I have some supplies on my horse. You have enough hay to last for two days?"

She nodded, looking at him again out of the side of her eye. "Ja, why?"

"Give your cow a good feeding. And bring in whatever you need for fuel. Is there any wood?"

She shook her head.

"How about the sawhorses and planks in the barn, the mangers too?"

As if afraid to hope, she let her fingers reach out and touch the money. "I hate for the rats to feed on my Elmer."

"Okay. I'll put the body in the grain bin and make sure nothing can get in there." Hjelmer got to his feet.

"Where you going?"

"Out to the barn. If you want to come, you can bring in the beans, and—"

"Beans?"

"Ja, I have some in my saddlebag. You have any flour?"

"A bit. Been making gruel out of it so my children got something to eat."

Hjelmer closed his eyes for a second. Never in his life had he gone hungry for more than a day or so, and then it had been his own fault for not packing enough on a hunting trip. "Come with me."

"You mean it about buying my land?" she asked when they reached the barn.

"Ja, I'll buy it, but first we need to get you and your children out of here."

An hour later, Hjelmer declined her offer to share the beans she now had cooking and headed north for the Bjorklund farms. Ingeborg would take these poor souls in, and perhaps, if the boy made it that far, she would use her herbs and knowledge to keep him alive.

He passed the other farms he had planned to visit without a backward glance. With the drifts frozen solid, his horse trotted on, not even breaking through the snow. *Will they run me off?* he wondered as his breath plumed in the frigid air. *What if Ingeborg won't take these people in? What if they are sick too? How will I tell them where I've been? What do I say when she asks why I've never written?* The questions plagued him as the miles passed and guilt rode heavy on his shoulders like a yoke carved of green wood. They made good time and trotted into the farmyard with dusk turning the skies and snowfields luminous with lavender hollows.

Paws met him with a stiff-legged stance and the deep-throated bark that announced a stranger.

"Hey, Paws, you know who I am."

The dog changed to wagging from his nose to the tip of his tail. He whined in apology and darted toward the house, returning as if to say, "Come on, what are you waiting for?"

Hjelmer stared at the new barn rising like a monolith from the land. Here the yard was tramped solid and the front of the soddy cleared of snow. Sheep bleated from the corral of the sod barn and cows bellered from the big barn. Smoke plumed from the house chimney and one at the end of the new barn too.

"Who is it, Paws?" Thorliff called as he pushed open the smaller door on the front of the two-story barn.

"It's your onkel Hjelmer." He rode his horse toward the boy. "Things sure look good here."

Thorliff turned and shouted over his shoulder, "Onkel Hjelmer is come home!"

"Tell him to get his sorry hide in here before he freezes," Haakan called back. "Then go tell your mor to set another place at the table. The prodigal has returned."

Hjelmer had trouble swallowing.

"Here, I'll take your horse. Far and Onkel Olaf are milking." Thorliff reached for the reins. "You want I should feed him too?" He looked at the sweaty neck of the horse. "I'll give him a drink later."

"Mange takk, Thorliff." Hjelmer laid a hand on the boy's shoulder. "You look like you grew a foot while I was gone."

Thorliff stared up from eyes that crinkled when he grinned, so like Carl's. "We missed you."

Hjelmer nodded. "Me too, son, me too." He entered the barn, pulling the door shut behind him.

A line of cows stood in their stanchions facing the wide center aisle, chewing their hay. A shallow ditch to catch the manure had been dug in the dirt floor between the end of the stalls and the rear aisle. From the side of a cow up the way, Haakan rose, a foaming milk bucket in his hand. He reached down to grab the three-legged stool, stepped to the aisle, and setting both bucket and stool down, strode toward the guest with hand outstretched and a smile wide as the prairie creasing his cheeks.

"We were afraid we'd never see you again. Thank God, you are all right." When their hands clasped, he clamped his other hand on Hjelmer's upper arm and squeezed. "Thank God. Come, let me introduce you to Kaaren's onkel, Olaf Wold. He immigrated years ago."

They walked down the length of the barn to the last stanchion, where Olaf was milking. He looked up and nodded.

"Good to meet you."

At that moment the outer door flew open, banging against the wall and startling the cows, let alone the men.

"Hjelmer, you have come home!" Ingeborg ran down the aisle and threw her arms around her brother-in-law. "Uff da. I thought never to see you again this side of heaven."

Hjelmer, driven backward at the force of her greeting, planted his feet and hugged Ingeborg back. "I was afraid you would not want to see me," he whispered in her ear.

"Ja, well if you were smaller I would take you out to the woodpile and whale you good, but since you are a grown man, you have to live with the mistakes you make. That's sometimes punishment enough." She stepped back and looked at him, her eyes drilling into his very soul. "You are in trouble?"

He coughed out a "huh," all the while shaking his head. Laughter glinted in his eyes. "No, I'm not in trouble, but I came here earlier than I thought because there is someone in terrible trouble. Someone I hope you can help."

"What is it?" Her tone changed to concern. "Who is it?"

"Do you know a Peterson from south of here about half a day's ride?"

Ingeborg thought a moment. "Ja, I think we stayed there one night on our way to find our homestead."

"That explains how she knew you. She wasn't about to let me off my horse until I gave my name."

Ingeborg's brow wrinkled. "That doesn't sound right. They were very friendly and gave us a hot meal."

"Ja, well . . . things have changed there. Mr. Peterson died three days ago and the place was pretty run down, what I could see. Maybe he'd been poorly or something. Anyway, they are out of food, with no wood for fuel, so she was burning hay twists, and a cow she is about to butcher. I got the feeling that all the other livestock had already been eaten. Her older boy is terrible sick, and the little girl don't look much better." He looked down to see his one gloved hand pulling on the glove of the other and then up at Ingeborg. "Can I take a sleigh and go get them?"

"Ja, of course." Haakan and Ingeborg spoke at the same time.

"The moon's full tonight, I could— "

"We could leave right after supper." Haakan bent down to pick up his oak bucket. "I'll take this up. Olaf and Baptiste can finish in here. Do you think the boy will make it through such a trip?"

"I don't know," Hjelmer said with a shrug. "But he'll die there. I thought maybe some of Ingeborg's simples might help him."

"I will get some things ready." She strode down the aisle to the last two cows where Olaf sat on a stool, head against a cow's flank. "Supper will be on the table as soon as you are finished here."

Within two hours, the wagon sleigh was loaded with elk robes and quilts covering the straw that padded the wooden planks. They added a bag of grain for the horses. Ingeborg explained how to use the medicinals she included and wrapped several heated rocks for their feet.

"You can warm them again and pack them around the boy to come home. Remember, you have to keep him warm and the cold air out of his lungs. We will all be praying for your safe trip and for

God to heal that dear child. Poor Mrs. Peterson. Losing a husband is bad enough, but a son too? Uff da. We will do all we can."

Haakan slapped the reins, and the horses trotted off. "Thank the good Lord the thaw hasn't set in or we wouldn't make it this night."

Hjelmer nodded and pulled the elk robe closer around his head and shoulders. "This cold ain't fit for man or beast."

"Ja, I am sure that poor woman feels the same."

Miles later, Hjelmer finally worked up the courage to ask the question that had been pestering him. "How is Penny?"

"Good, I guess."

Hjelmer waited but nothing else was forthcoming. Haakan wasn't making this easy for him. "Is she . . . did she . . . ah . . ." He sighed a heavy sigh. "Are the Baards well?"

"Had a bad time of it earlier but they are coming back. Agnes had a stillborn baby, and they took it hard."

"Oh." Silence again but for the jingling bells and click of the horses' hooves on the solid snow. He took in a deep breath, the air torturing his lungs as the silence tortured his mind. "And Penny?"

"What's that you said?"

"How is Penny?"

"As I said, good, I think. Leastwise I ain't heard no different."

"You don't see the Baards?"

"Sure, we see the Baards, but Penny left for Fargo before Christmas."

"Fargo! What is she doing in Fargo?"

"Going to school and working for her board and room."

"Oh." What could he say? Silence again. "Is she . . . did she. . . ?" He felt like a blithering fool. *For goodness sake, just speak up! You're a grown man.* He made another attempt after taking a deep breath through gloved hands over his nose and mouth. "Is she walking out with anyone?"

"Don't know." Haakan turned on the seat. "Penny helped Kaaren with the twins and then did something she's always wanted to do, go to school. She threatened to go looking for you, but we talked her out of that foolishness."

Hjelmer felt his heart leap with joy. *Penny still wanted him. She even thought about looking for him.* "She wouldn't have found me. I'm in St. Paul now. Why didn't she never write after that first letter? I thought maybe she found someone else."

"You'll have to ask her, but it is my understanding she wrote to you every week, even after she never got more than one letter. She is a faithful little thing."

"I never got them!"

"Did you write?" The question froze his heart like the cold air paralyzed his lungs.

"No." He didn't make any excuses. Those he thought of never sounded worth the air it took to say the words. *I had thought to ride over to the Baards' tomorrow. Fargo. How will I get to see her there? No time now till spring when we head west again. Will I be too late by then?*

They arrived at the silent soddy as the moon melted to the horizon. *Are we too late here also?*

24

H e's still alive." Haakan lifted the bundled boy out of the wagon box.

"Put him right there." Ingeborg pointed to Andrew's bed. "How did he fare?"

"I dosed him good last night, or rather, early this morning and then again just before we left. He hardly coughed at all on the ride." Haakan laid the boy on the bed and unwrapped him. "Ingeborg, this is Mrs. Peterson." He nodded to the women on either side.

"Glad to have you here. Why don't you and your little girl go stand by the stove and warm up. I have hot soup and coffee." She felt the boy's forehead and laid a hand on his chest to feel his shallow breathing. Her hand barely moved. *Dear God, please, this poor woman doesn't need any more heartache. You who can heal anyone, please pour out your grace upon this child. Please, I beg of you. Grant me wisdom in the use of the medicinals you have given us. Father, we will give you all the glory. In the precious name of your Son, Jesus.*

She stood there a moment longer looking at the sick child. His pale skin was so translucent she could see the tiny veins underneath. The poor boy's cheekbones were far too prominent, and his ribs poked through the thin skin of his chest. "Oh, blessed boy, please try to fight this. Your mor needs you with her." She whispered the words before kneeling at his side to spoon a tisane compounded of several of her herbs and honey. The first spoonful leaked from the side of his mouth. "Come on, son, swallow, please swallow." She tipped the spoon between his thin lips, watching his throat intently. The prominent Adam's apple bobbed once, twice. "Thank you, Lord." He took five more spoonfuls before a tiny shake of his head.

"You did real good, son. I'll bring some beef broth to strengthen you up when I come back. You just sleep now." She got to her feet, rejoicing in the small victory. If they could keep him drinking, even in spoonfuls, there was a chance he'd pull through.

"If you would sit down to the table, Mrs. Peterson, I will bring you some of this soup. That ought to warm you from the inside out." She looked down at the little girl. "And what is your name?"

The child hid in her mother's skirts.

"She's some shy. Never did see too many folks outside her family." Mrs. Peterson crossed her hands over her child's back. "This here is Ellie, short for Elmira. I'm Gudrun, but most folks call me Goodie. I . . . I want to thank you, Mrs. Bjorklund. You and yours saved our lives." She took her indicated place at the table and set the girl on her lap.

"It wasn't us. It was Hjelmer who found you." Ingeborg set the steaming bowls in front of them. "Now, you just eat up and you'll all feel better. I'm going to give your boy—what is his name?—some of the broth."

"Hans."

"Good, Hans it is." By the time the boy took another five spoonfuls and shook his head, the bowls on the table were empty. "Would you like more?" she asked. At the woman's sheepish nod, Ingeborg refilled the bowls and put another plate of sliced bread on the table too. "Maybe Ellie"—Ingeborg paused and smiled down at the child—"would like some jam on her bread." She set the pot of jelly directly in front of the pale waif. The child's eyes lit up, and she gazed up at Ingeborg as if she'd just produced the sun and the stars together.

Ingeborg felt a catch at the back of her throat. Such a little one to have already endured so much. She took one of the slices of bread, buttered it, and spread the chokecherry jelly on, thick as it would stay. "Ellie, here's your bread and jelly, all right?"

The girl nodded, one bony little hand reaching for the treat. She kept her gaze on Ingeborg as she took the first bite. "Mange takk," she whispered around a mouthful of food.

"Velbekomme, Ellie." It was all Ingeborg could do to keep from scooping the child up in her arms and hugging her close. For just a moment she hated the prairie and the cruelty it inflicted on the innocent beings who tried to tame it.

She looked up to catch the steady gaze of the woman who wore the mantle of suffering with her chin out and jaw squared. Goodie

Peterson might have been the mirror image of herself two years earlier.

The child on the bed coughed and choked.

Mrs. Peterson leaped to her feet.

"You just sit and rest for now." Ingeborg waved her back. "I'll take care of him." She raced to the bed and held the thin body upright so he wouldn't choke on the phlegm he coughed up. He coughed and coughed, bringing up more. When he finished coughing, he looked at her for the first time.

"I'm hungry," he whispered.

She laid him back down. "I'll get the soup." She scooped up the soiled rags and dropped them in the stove. Then skimming off the soup broth into a bowl, she returned to the bed. When the liquid cooled enough, she spooned some into the boy's mouth. Not counting the spoonfuls, she kept up a soothing murmur, one that both encouraged and calmed. At the shake of his head, she set down the bowl. "You did real well, Hans. Now let me clean you up a bit, and then you take a good long nap."

"That was good. . . ." His whisper faded at the end.

Ingeborg patted his hand lying limp on the quilt and went for a basin of warm water, some soap, and a cloth.

When the boy lay clean again and sleeping, she gazed down at him. Gratitude flowed from her heart, rose to the Father, and returned as strength for the child. She watched as his cheeks pinked and his breathing eased. When she turned, she saw Mrs. Peterson with her chin on her chest and her sleeping daughter in her arms. Ingeborg went out to the lean-to, fixed a bed on the empty bunk, and returned for the child.

"Come, Mrs. Peterson, the two of you need rest as bad as Hans." Carrying Ellie close to her chest, she led the way.

"I . . . I really should help you." The woman sank down on the bed.

"No, you rest. You can help me later."

The woman and child slept through the evening, the night, and into the morning.

☙ ❧

"Mor, he sleeping." Andrew stood at the edge of the bed and peered into Hans' face.

"Shhh."

Andrew's whisper matched the first, only with more hiss.

Hans turned his head, eyes open.

"He wake." Andrew flew across the short space and grabbed his mother's skirt. "He hungry."

"How do you know?" Ingeborg looked down with a smile and continued stirring the cracked oats and wheat that had been simmering all night.

"I hungry." Andrew clamped his hands on his hips and stared up at her as if he couldn't understand why she didn't get the connection.

"Good. Get up to the table."

Goodie Peterson and Ellie blinked their way out of the lean-to. "Breakfast's ready."

Ingeborg fed the woman and children first, then the men and boys when they came in from chores.

Hjelmer was ready to leave soon after. "Thank you, Ingeborg, Haakan, for taking these folks in. I need to get back to St. Paul, but first I want to call on the Baards." He nodded to Haakan. "Thanks for the advice." With hat in hand, he shifted from one foot to another. "Ah, can you tell me where Penny is living and working so I can write to her?"

Ingeborg started to speak, shared a look with Haakan, and amended what she'd been going to say. "I think you need to ask the Baards about that."

"You mean Penny might not want to hear from me?"

"I just think you need to talk with Joseph and Agnes. After all, Penny is their niece."

Hjelmer nodded. "I'll be heading west again with the railroad as soon as the weather breaks." He nodded to Mrs. Peterson, who was rocking Ellie in the chair by the stove. "Good-bye, ma'am. I'll take care of that business for you. I hope your son gets all better and strong again."

Ingeborg and Haakan followed him out the door.

He stood by his horse. "Inge, did . . . what . . . ah . . . Mary Ruth?"

Ingeborg shook her head. "Slim as a stick."

Hjelmer sighed and seemed to gain three inches in stature. "I knew it wasn't mine."

"*It* wasn't nobody's 'cause *it* wasn't real." Haakan shook his head. "I sure as heaven hope you ain't getting yourself in more trouble."

Hjelmer stared a moment at the rein in his hand. He looked up, a smile and one raised eyebrow lighting his face. "I'm not, but I am getting the money together for my shop and Penny's store—if she'll still have me, of course." He mounted. "Good-bye, and thank you for taking those folks in. That Olaf, he sure does know his building. That barn is some wonderful." He turned the horse toward the west. "I'll be back."

Ingeborg cupped her elbows in her hands and shivered in the cold. Haakan put his arm around her shoulders. "Why do I get the feeling there is something going on that he isn't telling us?"

"You mean like that business for Mrs. Peterson?"

Ingeborg nodded. "He looks awful prosperous. You suppose he's gambling again?" They turned and headed for the house.

Haakan shook his head. "I hope not."

✕✖ ✖✕

No one answered the door at the Baards'. Hjelmer checked the out buildings, too, but all were empty save for the animals that lived there. No one was home. Ignoring the pang in his heart, he started to write a note and leave it on the table but changed his mind. Joseph and Agnes deserved a full explanation, not just a note. As he rode on, he felt the weight of sadness press him into the saddle. *Too late, too late.* The thoughts kept time with the trotting hooves of the horse beneath him. Why, oh why, had he not written again? What was the matter with him? He could no more answer the questions than he could keep the moon from rising.

By the time Hjelmer reached Grand Forks, he had eight deeds in his pocket and five hundred dollars still remaining of his twelve thousand. He filed the deeds, put the money back in the bank, and caught the train for Minneapolis. Two farmers would stay on through harvest, giving him twenty-five percent of the harvest as rent. The rest were planning to leave as soon as the weather broke, including Mr. Booth. While he'd asked them each to not say anything about the sale, he knew just the leaving would create interest and questions. But by then the surveyors would be through, and he'd have sold his land to the railroad. What they didn't take, he would keep or sell to some of the immigrants Ingeborg had said were coming from Norway. Either way, he would make money above what he paid.

"You're a day late," the boss growled the next morning. "Have half a mind to let you go."

"Sorry, sir, some things happened I hadn't planned on." Hjelmer held his breath. *If I get fired now* . . . The thought made his stomach flutter. He waited, forcing his body to remain still.

"Ah, get on back to work."

"Thank you, Mr. Reggincamp." He dipped his head and headed for his forge.

" 'Bout time you got your sorry hide back here," the foreman grumbled. "Work's getting backed up, got a couple sick men, and you're off seeing the country."

"I'll work over to make up if that would help," Hjelmer volunteered.

"Might have to. They're gearing up for the spring track laying. If the weather breaks, you could be leaving soon."

Hjelmer felt his heart leap. Perhaps they would go through Fargo and he could find Penny. That is, if Penny would see him.

## 25

Y ou look to be 'bout running out of hay," Joseph said one March morning. He pointed to the two-foot remains of the hay pile.

"We still got some over to Lars'. We shouldn't have to buy much."

"What if we have a late spring?"

"Then we'll have to buy more." Haakan leaned on the pole corral where the sheep were enjoying the sun, even though it had little warmth yet. The lambs cavorted around their mothers and played tag over the snowdrift in the far corner. The boys had already shoveled out the drift that had covered the corral fence so the animals couldn't get out.

"Nope, ya won't be buying any hay. When yours burnt we said we'd share, and you got to give folks the chance to do that."

"But we can pay for it. No one around here has got so much extra they can just give it away."

"Would you give it away if'n you had it?" Joseph shot him a sly smile.

"Of course, but that's diff—" Haakan clamped his jaw shut. When had he ever won an argument with Joseph anyway? Especially when the man knew he was right.

"I 'magine there'll be a few sleds coming over in the next couple of days. You just say mange takk very nicely and help them pitch it off, if'n you knows what's good for ya."

Haakan sucked in a deep breath, the cold going all the way to his belly, and let it out on a plume of steam. "Mange takk, you old fox."

Joseph laughed, a rolling-over-the-snowdrifts kind of laugh that set the crows to cawing. "Hard for those who give so much to take back, ain't it?"

Haakan just glowered at him.

Just as Joseph predicted, sled loads of hay made their way to the Bjorklund homestead, filling much of the center aisle of the big barn so they didn't even have far to fork it for feed.

✼　✼

"Dear Tante Agnes and Onkel Joseph," Penny wrote.

"Thank you for your letter. I'm happy to hear that everyone is doing so good. As for me, I too am healthy and happy, both with school and work at the hotel. I am learning a lot about life in a city and am grateful indeed for this opportunity. Please tell Kaaren and Ingeborg thank-you again.

"I have met a young man at the high school, and he walks home with me every day. We have a good time together. I have made friends with some of the girls, and Mrs. Johnson encourages me to invite friends over. Can you imagine that? She is more like an aunt to me than an employer, but I still work very hard here. Running a hotel like this one takes much time and effort. All the girls here work hard."

She chewed on the end of her pen before dipping it in the ink again. She wanted to ask about Hjelmer but decided not to. The less she thought of him the better. *But wouldn't I know somehow if he really were dead?* She listened in the silence of the night, wishing for a reply to her prayer, her plea.

She dipped her pen and continued. "I hope to come home for a time in the early summer, and the way time has flown, I know that isn't far away. Give the little ones kisses from me and tell everyone that I think of you often and pray for all of you every night. Your loving niece and cousin, Penny." As she signed her name, she thought of all the studying she had yet to do. "Uff da," she muttered, folding the letter. "I better take my books down to the kitchen where it is warmer and lighter."

With supper finished, the hotel had quieted down this Sunday in March. The snow had started to fall early in the afternoon, and now, here in her garret room, she could tell the temperature outside was dropping.

✼　✼

"So, did you tell Penny that Hjelmer had been here?" Ingeborg asked at the quilting bee one March Saturday. The women now met at the schoolhouse since their group had grown too large for anyone's house.

Agnes shook her head. "No, Lord forgive me, but she didn't ask and I didn't say nothing." Her needle flashed in and out for several stitches before she asked, "Did you?"

"No. I told him it was your place to tell him her address, and if he didn't stop at your house and ask, that is all his own fault."

"Don't think I would have told him anyway." Agnes bent closer to her work. With the most recently pieced quilt now stitched to the stretcher, the four women, including Solveig and Goodie Peterson, sat along the sides to sew the myriad stitches that would form a ripple design in the wedding ring pattern.

"Agnes!" Ingeborg looked up, her mouth curving in a teasing smile.

"Ja, well, she don't mention him anymore in her letters. In fact, she told me about a young man who walks home from school with her. As I always say, let sleeping dogs lie." She looked across at her friends. "And it ain't a lie either. He didn't ask and I didn't tell. Of course, I didn't see him, so it makes no nevermind."

"Will you tell him if he writes and asks?"

"Don't know. Mail doesn't always get through, you know. I'll just have to deal with that when the time comes. It's not like Hjelmer is in any position to marry anyhow—no money, no prospects."

"Don't be too sure about that. He was wearing real nice clothes, and I just have a feeling he is up to something. Nothing he said, but—" Ingeborg twisted her face into a think-hard form. Then she shook her head. "Not sure what it is, but something is cooking."

Agnes turned her attention to Solveig. "How's that Mr. George Carlson doing?"

Solveig turned a bright red, discernible even in the lamplight of the dim room.

"Ha! Look at that, if your face don't give you dead away. You kind of like that young man, don't you?"

Solveig ducked her head but nodded.

"You watch, when spring comes and the roads are passable again, you'll see a lot more of him."

"Probably by then he'll be too busy in the fields to make a trek clear over here," Ingeborg said with a straight face. "Don't you think?"

Agnes grinned back. "Then, Ingeborg, you better let her drive that wagon carrying all your cheeses and things over to the Bonanza farm. She and Mrs. Carlson need to get right acquainted. But don't you make it too easy for him." She wagged a finger at Solveig. "Men like to do the chasin'—till we catch them, that is."

"Agnes Baard, you old matchmaker you. What's got into you today?" Ingeborg bit off the thread from the spool. She shook her head. "I know. You don't have to say it; my mor did often enough. Those with good manners use a scissors, but the scissor's clear over there and my teeth were right handy here."

"Spring is coming, you just watch."

Ingeborg shifted on the hard bench. The growing baby made sitting without a chair back more uncomfortable now. She rubbed the small of her back with her knuckles and pulled her shoulders back. And with spring, summer wouldn't be far behind, and by then she would have a baby to hold again. She glanced over to where Kaaren sat nursing one of the twins in the rocker they brought.

"Say, Mrs. Peterson, I been meaning to ask you, how did Hjelmer happen to stop at your place?" Agnes looked up from her stitching.

Goodie Peterson stared intently at her hands and the busy needle that faltered only a moment. "I . . . ah . . . God's grace, I believe. I'll be forever grateful to Him and the Bjorklunds. They saved our lives." She looked across the stretched quilt. "But please, call me Goodie."

"You thinkin' on what to do, come summer?"

"Agnes, you sure are inquisitive today," Ingeborg said with a laugh. "I don't know what's got into you, but I hope Goodie will stay on with us, at least through harvest. We can always use another good pair of hands around there. With Hans so well after his sickness, you know how happy he is with the boys and with school—"

"Ja, I know." Goodie beamed a smile her way that lit the colors in the quilt. "I would love to stay. I ain't been so peaceful-like in a long, long time."

"By then some man looking for a wife will just snap you up. You won't have nothing to worry about."

"Time for dinner, ladies." Dyrfinna Odell gave the pot of stew on the stove one last stir. "If you bring your plates, I will dish up." She pointed to the teacher's desk. While crude by some standards, Olaf had planed oak for a top and set drawers into both sides to store things. "Bread and things are set out up there."

All the women stood, and Kaaren led them in the table grace.

The young children flocked to their mothers, and soon the conversation took on a more general tone. After all was cleared away again and the quilters changed places with the piecers, someone asked if anyone had heard anything more about the proposed railroad spur that was reportedly coming through the area.

Most of the women shook their heads. "Won't know nothing till spring and the surveyors come through. The sooner the better, I say. Won't that be something to take our grain to a local siding and not clear to Grafton?"

"Roald always dreamed of a town on the edge of our land," Ingeborg said with a faraway look in her eyes. "Wouldn't it be wonderful if there would be a water stop right out here? We could build a granary, a church, maybe Hjelmer's blacksmith shop, and a store—that's Penny's dream. I can see a white church with a steeple and a bell right next to the graveyard, some houses, of course one for the preacher, and . . ."

Someone else picked up the thread of dreams. "The store would sell all the things we have to travel to St. Andrew or Grafton for. It would be easy for the store to order from Grand Forks or Fargo, and the things would come in on the train within just a couple of days."

"I, for one, want a frame house. My Anner says that's the first thing he will build, either with lumber from the Bjorklund mill or that what comes in on the train. Says he's tired of living like gophers underground," Hildegunn pronounced.

The talk flowed into discussions of building houses before barns, how they would get lumber for the church, and who had seeds to trade for the gardens. Seeds and quilt piecings were about equal in trade value, although with more of the women saving both from their sewing and gardening, the demand had lessened. Ingeborg had already promised cuttings of her rose bushes and the geranium that had nearly frozen in her window until she moved it to the table during the blizzard.

"You know, I heard about a woman over to the south who has a canary that sings. Now, wouldn't that be something to lighten a soddy?—a singing bird. Would make winter not seem so long or so harsh." Her voice turned dreamy. "My bestamor had a yellow canary once. I could listen to that little bird by the hour."

"Now, Ingeborg, don't you go getting ideas," Kaaren said with a chuckle. "We got enough to take care of as it is."

"I heard the birds themselves did all the work. You get a pair and they raise their young. I'll bet Onkel Olaf would build a fine cage, and . . ." Ingeborg paused at the laughter she heard around her. "All right. I get the hint."

But the thought of giving Kaaren a canary next Christmas took up lodging in her mind.

⚶ ⚶

### Mid-April 1885

"Ingeborg, you're fidgeting bad as Andrew," Kaaren whispered.

"I can't help it. If this train goes any slower, I will get out and push."

Haakan turned from answering another of Andrew's questions and laid his hand on his wife's arm. "That won't get us there any faster." When she shot him a look of exasperation, he just shook his head and chuckled.

By the time the two families disembarked in Grand Forks with all the children, she felt as though she needed a long rest—alone. Her back ached and she thought sometimes of using a wheelbarrow to carry her belly. But none of that mattered. They were on their way to prove up their homesteads. Thorliff had Andrew's hand clamped in his and had given his busy little brother strict orders to not move without him.

Kaaren carried Grace, and Sophie was playing with her father's nose, giggling when his mustache tickled her fingers.

"The courthouse is this way." Haakan pointed up the street. Together they all set out on the wooden sidewalk that kept them above the mud thrown by the wagons, drays, buggies, and carriages that traveled up and down the street.

Quiet fell when they shut the door to the titles office.

"How may I help you?" asked a man wearing gold-rimmed glasses and gaiters on his sleeves from behind a high counter.

"We have come to prove up our homestead claims," Ingeborg stated. "I am Ingeborg Bjorklund and this is my sister-in-law, Kaaren Bjorklund Knutson. Our husbands were Roald and Carl."

"And what year did you file the claims?"

"1880. Five years ago yesterday." She withdrew the papers from her reticule and laid them on the counter.

The man looked over his glasses. "I take it you two gentlemen are not Roald and Carl."

Haakan shook his head. "They died."

"Do you have marriage certificates?"

"Ja, but what difference does that make? The land is in my name and in Kaaren's name." Ingeborg fingered the papers in front of her. She'd had the names on the papers changed deliberately after Roald's and Carl's deaths so that there would be no problem.

"Ah." He held up the papers so he could see better. "And you have met all the requirements?"

She pointed to the second page. "There is the list of acres now broken and seeded, the buildings we have put up, and an inventory of our livestock and machinery."

"I see." He read, nodding as he turned to the next page. "It looks as though all is in order. Do you have any liens against the land over at the bank?"

"Not any longer." She extracted the bank papers next and laid them on the counter. "What loans we have now are against the machinery itself, but they are nearly paid also."

"You have done well in five years." He smiled over the edge of the forms.

"Ja, God has been good."

With swift movements, he stamped each page with a round seal, signed on one line for each deed, and pointed to where they were to put their signatures.

Ingeborg could hardly hold the pen, and Kaaren not much better. But their signatures were legible, and the man dusted sand over the ink to dry it more quickly. Then opening a leather-bound book, he located the original entries and wrote in the new information. He handed the papers back to Ingeborg.

"It's all yours now."

Ingeborg could feel her knees turning to mush. She gripped the edge of the counter with one hand and picked up the papers with the other, all the while maintaining a smile and continuing to breathe, but with difficulty. The land was hers. And Kaaren's. She had won. *They had won.*

"Thank you very much."

The men shook hands. Kaaren and Ingeborg gripped each other's free hand with a strength born of the sorrows they'd endured together.

"It is ours." Ingeborg could hear the awe in her own voice and see it on Kaaren's face. As the strength returned to her knees, she felt like dancing and leaping, whirling around the wooden floor until she fell down in a heap. The land, the precious land, was hers.

Now, for certain, she could call it home.

"There is just one more thing." She looked at Haakan to catch his nod.

"We will wait outside for you," he whispered, snatching up Andrew, who was about to put a cigar butt in his mouth. "Ishda," he muttered and glared at Thorliff, who hung his head.

Thorliff picked up the butt and dropped it in the can by the door provided for such things as that. The grimace on his face brought a smile to Ingeborg's. Her son was realizing how different life was in the city from that on their farm.

She turned back to the man behind the counter. "Now, here is what I would like you to do." The bell above the door tinkled as the others made their way outside.

✕✕　✕✕

The next Sunday after church, the congregation buzzed about the new men in the territory, men surveying for the much antici-pated railroad spur between Grafton and Drayton. All they would say was that soon the men buying the rights for the railroad would be coming through. They would not comment on the price being offered, but when one man said he wasn't selling any of his hard-earned land to no railroad, they just shrugged.

Stories of the railroad forcing some to sell ran rife with the high prices the railroad was paying for the right-of-way. It was said they puchased whole sections, and others bought only a couple hundred feet on either side of the right-of-way. Some said they condemned the land and took it by force if necessary. Other stories said some land had already been bought up and the new owners were holding out for higher prices. Rumors abounded, one contradicting another.

The last rumor teased Ingeborg into remembering and ponder-ing on Hjelmer's visit in the winter. Why had he been back in the Red River Valley without coming home to stay? Had it been a sneak visit to find out about Mary Ruth? No, that didn't fit. He hadn't seemed at all concerned about that hussy and her manipulating ways, nor even overly wondering about Penny. When she'd told him to talk with Agnes, he hadn't even gone to the Baards.

One morning when Olaf and the boys had left for school, she brought the matter up to Haakan.

"I been wondering much the same thing," he replied with a nod to the outside, where Goodie Peterson had started the wash. "She ever said anything about Hjelmer offering to buy her land?"

Ingeborg shook her head. "Where would he get that kind of money, anyway?"

When he just looked at her, she turned her head, glancing at him from the side of her eye.

"He wouldn't." She shook her head slowly. "Haakan, you know he said he would never gamble again."

He sighed. "I hope not, but I can't get the thought out of my mind that something isn't right here."

"Me too."

"Mor!" Andrew catapulted into the kitchen, Ellie right on his heels. "Sheeps out."

"Andrew Bjorklund, did you open the gate?"

At his shamefaced look, she shook her head. "You know I told you not to open the gate."

"Wanted to show Ellie the lambs, my lamb." He raised a dirty face to her. "Sheep ran over me."

Haakan was already out the door calling Paws as he went. With the help of the dog, they rounded up the spring-mad ewes and put them back in the corral. Tossing more hay in from the small pile remaining, Haakan took Andrew by the arm. "I think it is time for a session out by the woodpile, young man. You were told not to open the gate."

Andrew sent his mother a pleading look, but she only shook her head. "You knew better."

Even when the boy's lower lip began to quiver, she steeled herself. The Bible said, "Spare the rod and spoil the child," and while she hated to see him spanked, Ingeborg knew Haakan was right. Andrew had to learn his lesson, as if being trampled over by escaping sheep wasn't enough.

When she thought of it, she shuddered. He could have been cut by their sharp hooves, and though he was big for his age, the sheep were much heavier. She turned to see Ellie's eyes fill.

"Please, I wanted to see the sheep. Don't spank Andrew. I done it."

Goodie turned from pouring water into the big tub that sat over a hot fire. "Then you should get the spanking too." She took the girl's still thin arm and followed Haakan and Andrew to the woodpile.

Ingeborg began sorting the clothes into white and dark piles. Even bending over the tub caused her back to ache. Sometimes she wondered if like Kaaren she would have twins, she was already so large. Less than a month to go. She looked off to the riverbank. *I sure hope Metiz gets home in time to midwife.* Memories of another baby never allowed to breathe the clear valley air assailed her. "Please, Metiz, come home soon."

## 26

"They won't be buying any of your land but will take some off the piece I bought from Polinski," Haakan announced after talking with the land buyers. "They're taking ten acres from the Baards, and they said that right near the schoolhouse will be a good spot for a watering station. They set them up every twenty miles or so."

"So, we will have a town around the schoolhouse after all." Ingeborg closed her eyes and let the motion of the rocker soothe her. The last few days had been rife with speculation as neighbors visited back and forth, impatient to know the exact route of the railroad spur and anxious for the land to thaw enough to get the spring work started. The Bjorklunds still hadn't sheared the sheep, a task that always seemed to end up at the bottom of the list of things to be done. Thorliff, Baptiste, and Hans were figuring to start on that soon as they got home from school.

She rubbed her mound of baby, especially on the one side where it liked to drum its feet, or was it elbows? Whichever, this baby sure was an active one. Agnes said it was certain to be a boy, busy as it was, but deep in her heart Ingeborg longed for a girl.

"Are you all right?" Haakan's tone spoke of love and concern.

"Ja, I am fine, this is normal for the last month or so."

"We're going to have a burying tomorrow after the service. With the pastor here from St. Andrew, they all think it a good time." He poured himself another cup of coffee and stood looking out the window.

"I imagine digging the holes was hard yet."

"Ja, but keeping the bodies was harder."

Ingeborg nodded and relaxed for a few moments in the quiet. Goodie had gone to help Kaaren and Solveig begin the spring-cleaning since they were already finished in this soddy. Ingeborg wanted it done early just in case. She never finished the *just in case*, but they all knew babies sometimes came early. Andrew and Ellie were both sound asleep after playing so hard they nearly collapsed into their dinner plates.

She glanced over at the bed. Andrew's cheeks had already lost their winter pallor, and the April sun had started on his hair, streaking the gold to near white. He seemed to be growing up right before her eyes. She rubbed her belly again. She sent a few thank-yous heavenward for the health of all, for the man at the window, for the coming of spring.

At church in the morning, everyone wore their most somber garments. Reverend Amundson from St. Andrew devoted his sermon to God's promises of life after death, reminding them that Jesus and loved ones waited for those who died and welcomed them to the kingdom. Ingeborg let her mind drift. *Had Roald found their baby that died? Did Carl and the two girls watch over the family below? Surely the mansions in heaven had more rooms than a soddy.* She smiled at that thought and swayed the tiniest bit to keep Andrew sleeping before he slipped off her somewhat limited lap.

After the benediction, everyone followed the pastor outside and over to the graveyard where the caskets rested beside the previously dug holes. The wooden boxes ranged from infant size, where Agnes and her family stood, to man length for Elmer Peterson. Haakan had gone down to the farm to bring Mr. Peterson back for the burying.

Mr. Booth stood a bit apart. For him there was no casket and no hallowed ground in which to set it. They'd never found any part of his wife's clothing or anything.

Ingeborg knew how he felt since she'd experienced the same. They all figured the scavengers of the prairie had done their job, as God ordained them to.

One by one the boxes were lowered into the earth. "Ashes to ashes, dust to dust," the words were repeated for each body. The prayers rose as incense on the spring breeze that rifled the clothing of the worshipers, then dried the tears and sniffles of those left behind. Kaaren began singing the final hymn, her voice rising sweet as the meadowlark's trill while the others joined in. "Blest be the tie that binds, our hearts in Christian love. . . ." The Norwegian words rolled across the prairie, as if a benediction of their own on the burgeoning land.

Mr. Booth came to each of them before they left for home. "I just wanted to say good-bye and God bless," he said as he shook hands.

"You are leaving then?" Haakan asked.

"Ja. Without my Auduna I just can't care about the land like I did 'afore. When Hjelmer offered me such a good price for it, I didn't feel like turning him down. With the cash I can buy something somewhere else or homestead again in the Pacific Northwest. There's land there."

Haakan and Ingeborg shared a private glance. So that was what Hjelmer had been up to.

Two other men pushed forward. "You sold your land to Hjelmer Bjorklund? Why didn't you say something? I'd of bought it." The belligerent tone made Ingeborg step back.

"Wasn't planning on selling, but when the opportunity rose, I took it."

"But ain't you mad at him? He's selling to the railroad now, and you coulda used that extra money."

Mr. Booth shook his head. "A deal's a deal, and I got a fair one. They wouldn't of taken all my land like he done, so I'd still been stuck. Well, it's been good knowing you folks. Now I gotta get about packing and such."

But the grumbling around them didn't fade away when he left. Some cast blaming glances in the Bjorklund direction, as if they should be held responsible for Hjelmer's actions, let alone the railroad's.

Once in the wagon, Haakan began. "What I can't understand is why he didn't tell us." He slapped the reins over the rumps of Bell and Bob, setting them to a trot. "Since he knew where the railroad was going . . ."

"How do you suppose he knew?" Ingeborg reached over and snagged the back of Andrew's jacket before he took a header into the bed of the wagon. "You turn around to climb over, son. Thorliff can't always catch you, you're getting too big."

Andrew grinned at her and turned around, slipping over the back of the seat like a river otter down a bank.

"I imagine there are rumors abounding whenever you work on the railroad. He was in the right place at the right time. Hjelmer seems to have a knack for that."

"Or the wrong place at the wrong time. He has a knack for that too."

"Ja, and this time there are some pretty unhappy folks around here—those that sold to him and those that think he should have shared the information. I wouldn't have minded buying some land along that right-of-way either. He probably made over a dollar an acre for doing not much of anything. What the railroad don't take, he can sell this summer to the immigrants coming in or anyone else who wants to pay his prices."

"He bought my land, but I don't begrudge him one penny. Hadn't been for him, they'd of found all our bodies in that soddy when spring came," Goodie said from her seat in the wagon bed. "I'm just sorry I didn't tell you up front and honest-like. But he asked me not to, so I didn't. He paid me more'n he had to, you know. I woulda sold for about anything at that point." She sighed. "Seems like another lifetime now, even with planting Elmer in the ground this day. If'n you was angry with me, I would understand. I could go on now with spring here and all."

Ingeborg turned as much as her girth allowed. "Why would I be angry with you? It's Hjelmer whose ear I'd like to twist. Don't know what it's going to take to get him to think about someone besides himself."

"He didn't have to come back for us."

The words lay like soot upon a fresh snowfall.

The horses leaned into their collars when they hit a spot thawed deeper than the rest. The gumbo came up through the dead grass and sod, clutching at the wheels and horses' hooves to make them lag with the sheer weight of it.

"Won't be using the wagon for a while again." Haakan clucked the horses into a trot once they were free of the mud. Black chunks spun up and out, splattering those too near the back. The three boys laughed as they picked dirt off their pants and pointed at one another's spotty faces, but they didn't leave off dangling their feet over the tailgate.

"I . . . I could leave if'n you want, you know."

Ellie and Andrew, as of one mind, let out a wail that could be heard clear to St. Andrew.

"Andrew, hush, they're not going anywhere." Ingeborg glared at her young son. "Now, Goodie, why would you want to leave? I thought you planned to stay through the fall, at least."

"I did. I do. But if having me there makes you think bad of Hjelmer, well, I . . ."

"Hog swill."

Haakan gave Ingeborg a double raised-eyebrow look.

"It's not your fault Hjelmer manages to offend people. He'll have to deal with that when he comes home."

But the next week at the quilting bee, she knew the subject hadn't been discussed enough for the women. Countless times Agnes was told to keep her nice little niece away from that Bjorklund scalawag, and each time she shook her head and tisked the admonisher away.

"If the quilting bees are going to turn into nothing more than glorified gossip sessions, think I'll stay to home from now on," she muttered for Ingeborg's ears alone.

"You better wait till we have Penny's quilt done first." Ingeborg sorted through the pile of piece goods for the blue that would go next on her ring.

"Ja, that's a good idea." The grin returned to Agnes's face. "With all the 'Donald Moen says this' and 'Donald says that' in Penny's letters, Hjelmer might not be the man lying under this here quilt with her after all."

"Agnes!" Ingeborg dropped a piece on the floor and groaned when she leaned over to pick it up. "This baby don't like no squeezing, that's for sure." Sitting upright again, she took in a couple of deep breaths to catch up. She grimaced and leaned to the side. "Now I got a cramp in my leg. If this don't beat all."

She heard one of the twins beginning to fuss and laid her sewing down and got to her feet. "Think I'll carry that little one around for a few minutes. It'll get me in practice for the coming nights." She waved Kaaren back to her chair. "No, let me do this. I need to move around some." She limped back to the pallet where four babies slept and picked up Sophie. "Hush now, baby dear. You let your mother rest for a time. She's busy, you know."

Sophie looked back at her, a grin curving her lips. She stuck a fist in her mouth, answering around it with words all her own.

"You know, child, you are really going to be a talker." Ingeborg nodded and Sophie copied the action, then flailed her hand, her legs pumping in unison before reaching for Ingeborg's mouth. Ingeborg pretended to chew on the questing hand, making the baby laugh and repeat the action.

"What do you mean 'going to be'? She already is." Kaaren reached for the baby. "I'll feed her before Grace wakes. After that they'll both want down. This crawling is such a new adventure for them." She shook her head at the earthen floor. "I surely hope we can put a floor in here soon. Lars is talking about doing that in our soddy for the children's sake." She settled into the rocker. "Pretty soon we'll be bringing this chair for you and your baby."

"Ja, we will need two then." Ingeborg kneaded the tightness from her middle back. She glanced around the room of busy women. Several others were showing babies on the way also. "Our group is growing."

"Ja, in more ways than one."

About a week after the first of May, Ingeborg was already in the walking stages of labor, trying to keep busy and yet having to stop for the cramping sometimes. A warm breeze was drying the earth as fast as possible, and Haakan had plowed and disked the garden spot the night before. The two women were planting peas, potatoes, carrots, and onions—things hardy enough to survive a late frost. The corn wouldn't go in until last.

Ingeborg sucked in a deep breath and watched the sky nearly darken with another wave of water fowl flying north, their songs a spellbinding call to join them. "I should be out hunting. We can use some fresh duck or goose, and the feathers always come in handy."

Goodie had long since given up being astonished at Ingeborg's varied skills. "Why don't you go cut those seed potatoes for a while, get off your feet, and keep enough energy to push out that baby?"

"Andrew, come here, please." Ingeborg waved to the two small children hanging over the rails of the corral to watch the sow and her piglets on their first day outside. They'd been warned and warned again about staying out of the pigpen, the mother pig being extra protective of her new litter.

"But, Mor, she likes me." Andrew had planted his fists on his hips. "I feed her."

"I know, but you give her a few days outside to settle down again."

"I want to play with the piggies."

"Andrew, stay out of the pigpen, you hear?" She had to put a stern tone in her voice, otherwise he'd set his chin and try to explain to her why he should do it anyway.

Andrew loved the animals and the land they lived on. He always found the first dandelion, the first ripe strawberry, the mouse nest in the corner under the manger. Each find was a treasure to share with his mother and now with Ellie.

The two children backed down the two rails and ran to the garden. "What?"

"You help with the potatoes. Mrs. Peterson will dig a hole and you drop the cut pieces in. Ellie, you can cover them up again and step on the top to pack the dirt."

Andrew looked up at her from under the brim of a straw hat, still two sizes too big. "How many pieces?"

"Two or three." She tried to take another deep breath, but the pain arced around her middle. At least they were coming closer together.

"Would you bring me a drink, please? Oh, and did you water the rosebushes this morning?"

He tipped his hat back in a perfect imitation of Haakan. "Mor."

"I know, you wouldn't forget the roses."

"I watered the cottonwood, too, but Thorliff said it had deep enough roots it didn't need water." He thought a moment. "How long is deep enough?"

"Long enough—to reach water." She paused for a quick breath.

"But, if I pour in water—"

"Don't ask me any more questions right now, Andrew. You go help." She pointed to the bucket of already cut potatoes.

Paws ran toward the river, his welcome bark in good volume.

Ingeborg shaded her eyes against the morning sunlight. "It's Metiz. She's home again." Taking off her apron, Ingeborg waved it over her head.

After the greeting and introductions, Metiz studied Ingeborg through eyes that shone from behind more wrinkles than could possibly fit on one face. "You in big hurry, hmm?" She nodded toward Ingeborg's protruding abdomen.

"Good thing you didn't wait until tomorrow to return." Ingeborg gritted her teeth. "This one gave up on waiting for you."

"Said would be here. You walk."

✵ ✵

"Is she all right?" Haakan asked from the doorway a few hours later.

Metiz beckoned him in.

Ingeborg opened her eyes enough to smile at him. "Come see your new daughter."

"A girl? We have a girl?" He knelt beside the bed, taking her hand in his and lifting it to his lips.

"Is that all right? I . . . I mean, I know sons are important to you."

"I have two sons. Now we have a daughter."

Ingeborg stroked his cheek with her fingertips. "Haakan Howard Bjorklund, you are an amazing man."

He turned a kiss into her palm. "I love you, Mrs. Bjorklund. Now, will you show me this daughter of ours so we can become acquainted? She needs to meet her far."

Ingeborg laid back the blanket that shielded the baby from the drafts. "Astrid, meet your far."

Haakan reached out a trembling hand and laid his finger beside the round, wrinkled little face. Holding his breath, he touched her cheek, the bit of fuzz on top of her head, then stroked across her clenched fingers.

Ingeborg watched as his eyes filled and swam with tears, darkening the blue and beading on his eyelashes. He shifted his gaze to meet hers. "She . . . she is perfect. I never saw a baby so new like this, not since I was a boy."

"And then you thought it was ugly?"

He ducked his head, but his hand never moved from the baby's head. "Ja, I did."

The baby curled her fingers around one of his. "But not now." He cleared his throat again. "Not now."

Ingeborg sighed and much against her will, her eyelids drifted closed.

"Sleep well, my Ingeborg" were the last words she heard for several hours.

Mother and daughter, Astrid Bjorklund, were still sleeping soundly by suppertime.

"Astrid so little." Andrew tried to whisper, but like a blizzard mimicking a breeze, he failed.

Ingeborg opened her eyes and smiled. "Isn't she beautiful?"

Andrew looked at his mother. He stared at the baby. He looked up at his father, then back at his mother. "No." He shook his head. "Astrid is ugly. Give her back. Get one bigger." A puzzled look settled on his face when everyone laughed. He glared at Thorliff, who collapsed on Andrew's bed in laughter. "C'mon, Ellie. Supper."

Two days later, Ingeborg felt more like moving around again. Metiz rang the dinner bell to call the men. When they had all gathered around the table, Ingeborg turned to the rosemaled chest that came from Norway those five years ago. She drew out a piece of paper and handed it to Metiz.

"This is for you."

Metiz looked at her, her white eyebrows turning into question marks. "Not read."

"I know. I will read it for you." Ingeborg took back the paper and read the official-sounding words. When she finished, she said, "This means that the three acres where you usually put up your summer tepee are now yours. This is a deed making you the owner."

Metiz studied the paper as if trying to divine the words herself. "Land for me?"

"Ja, and if you want more, I will deed you more."

"Why want more?"

Ingeborg shrugged. "I just want you to own the land your husband should have filed on. It is now yours, and no one can take it away from you."

Metiz stood unmoving but for her eyes. Her eyes spoke of gratitude, of something deeper. "Man not own land, land own man."

"Or woman."

The old woman nodded. "Thank you." She folded the deed and carefully stuck it in her backpack. "Mange takk." She nodded first to Ingeborg and then to Haakan.

"When we eat, Mor?" Andrew crawled up on his chair. "Ellie coming?"

"No, they are eating over at Tante Kaaren's."

When Haakan sat down, he looked again at Metiz. "We will help you build a permanent house if you like. It can be of sod or wood, whichever you want."

"I think about it." She sat down and joined their circle of hands while Haakan led them in grace. At the end of the Norwegian words, he added, "And thank you for bringing Metiz back to us after the long winter and for her helping our daughter into this world so safely. Amen."

⤙⊗ ⊗⤚

A couple of days later, Agnes and her two little ones came calling with a knitted bonnet and blanket for the new baby. "She is a beauty, look, not a mark on her." She touched the fine down on the baby's head. "So precious."

"Go get Tante Kaaren," Ingeborg said to Andrew. "Tell her Mrs. Baard is here." So while Ellie stayed with the two Baard young'uns, Andrew scampered across the center field.

By the time Kaaren and the twins arrived, Goodie had set out the coffee cups, given each of the children a cookie, and sent them outside to play. She called the others to come for coffee. When they sat around the table, she set a plate of cookies in the center and filled the cups.

"What do you hear from Penny?" Ingeborg asked after they talked about the gardens and how close to flooding the Red River came.

"She writes regular, that one." Agnes dipped her cookie in the steaming coffee. "I sure do miss her sorely."

"Have you told her that Hjelmer was here?"

Agnes shook her head. "She didn't ask, and I didn't tell her."

"Agnes!" Kaaren and Ingeborg blurted as one voice.

"Ja, well, she seems so happy with Donald Moen that I couldn't bring it up. I didn't lie."

"What if she had heard he'd been here?" Ingeborg adjusted the blanket over her nursing baby.

"Then I'd have told her. But he weren't here long enough to talk to many folks." Agnes wiped her brow. "That was a relief. Inge, you saw the light on her face that's been missing ever since Hjelmer left. She's happy in school and loves to work at the hotel and this young man is . . . seems so . . . so responsible. He's older than her other school friends, you know."

Ingeborg kept her opinions to herself and watched Kaaren do the same. If Hjelmer ended up with a hurting heart, it was his own fault. But he'd seemed so much more like a man when he came through during the winter. He'd taken care of the Peterson family. Didn't that show his maturity?

"There is no hurry, that's for sure. Hjelmer said he'd find Penny when he went through Fargo this spring, but we haven't heard from him either. I thought maybe he'd be working the spur line. Haakan said he heard they started it."

When the men came in for dinner, Ingeborg watched as Goodie served Olaf first. The smile he gave her brought enough pink to her cheeks, you'd think she was a young girl again. So that was the way the wind blew. Ingeborg leaned back in her chair. They probably should get another wedding ring quilt started. One finished and put away for Penny and another on the stretcher for Solveig. At this rate the women might have to start meeting twice a month.

In June, with the spring fieldwork done and the fields already sprouted, everyone joined together to raise the sack house, a warehouse for storing the hundred-pound burlap sacks of grain. Since school let out, Uncle Olaf had spent his evenings laying out the sixty-by-forty-foot building and hauling lumber to the site. While it hadn't seasoned like he wanted, everyone knew the building had to be ready for the fall harvest. Haakan and Lars helped him set the three rows of pier posts deep into the ground, then string beams from post to post and nail the two-by-ten flooring in place over the joists.

This year there would be no grain hauling to Grafton or to the paddle-wheeler.

"I thought sure we would be building the church next," one of the women said while they were setting up the sawhorses to make tables for the food.

"Me too," another answered, wiping the perspiration from her forehead. "Got hot awful soon, didn't it?" They all turned at a shriek from the group of children playing around the school. When one of the girls ran from around the school, Knute Baard behind her with a garter snake in his outstretched hand, the women turned back to their labors.

"Uff da. Don't boys never change?" Chuckles and head shakings greeted her sally.

"No, and they always think they was the first to dream up that mischief. I remember throwing a snake back one time. The boy didn't like that one bit." This time chuckles tickled the air like a breeze in a cottonwood.

"I'll take a water bucket around," Solveig volunteered.

"And Mr. Carlson's not even here."

Solveig brightened up like a bad case of sunburn. "Is he coming?"

Her question did it. Chuckles turned to outright laughter, but of the gentle kind that says, "I'm laughing with you and this is a wonderful day to be together and laughing."

"If you don't know, deary, how are any of the rest of us to know?"

Solveig fled toward the well in the school yard.

"On the count of three now." Olaf's voice could be heard above the sawing and pounding racket of building. "One, two, three." The men on the ropes pulled, and the east wall that had been framed on the floor rose slowly into its vertical position. With men holding ropes from both sides, others scurried about nailing braces into place and pounding pegs into the ground to nail to. By dinnertime, the four walls stood gleaming in the sunlight, all braced together and squared off by Olaf himself. When he checked his measurements and nodded, a great cheer went up.

When Lars walked by Kaaren, who carried a twin on each hip, he chucked Sophie under the chin, making her giggle and wave her arms. But he ignored Grace as if she weren't even there.

Ingeborg watched the frown deepen between Kaaren's eyebrows at the slight. Ingeborg shook her head. She'd been afraid of something like that when she never saw him holding the deaf baby, but this was too obvious to miss. What would happen when the new baby came? Should she say something to Kaaren? *Oh, Lord, here's another problem for you. I sure don't know what to do.* She thought a moment more, then crossed to take Grace from her mother's arms. "Come on, Gracie dear, let's go for a walk."

Kaaren stayed with her as they ambled toward the cemetery. "You saw?"

Ingeborg nodded but continued playing with the baby, making funny faces and blowing on the delicate hand.

"I don't know what to do. One minute I want to scream at him and the next, cry in his arms. What is the matter with a man who, just because a child is deaf, can't bear to touch her?"

"I've heard there are people like that. They can't abide something that isn't perfect."

"Well, if that's the case, all he needs to do is look within."

The bite of her comment made Ingeborg raise her eyebrows. "Ja, but in case you haven't noticed, some men don't do that so well. In fact, some women don't neither." She raised Grace in the air so they were looking face-to-face. "Now you, little one, I think you will not only look within yourself, but you will see deep within others. Your eyes seem to see so far."

Grace smiled and reached for her aunt. The sun kissed the baby's hair and turned the white down on her head to shimmering gold.

"Ja, I know you are an angel, and God gave you to your far and mor for a very special reason." She settled Grace back in her arm and kissed the rounded cheek.

"I don't know what to do." Kaaren stopped walking and jiggled Sophie on her hip.

"Me neither, but someone once told me that when in doubt, pray, for God knows the answers."

"Ja, well, it's easier to say to someone else than to do yourself."

"Really?" Ingeborg adopted a surprised look that quickly turned to love and caring.

"One day at a time is the way we will do this, just as we do with everything else. I imagine there will come a time when you have to say the same things back to me. Let's go eat." They continued on around the building and back to the party.

"That Olaf, he be one good foreman." Joseph Baard set his heaping plate down and, sticking his skinny legs under the table, took a seat on the bench.

"I'm thinking we oughta ask him to run this here operation when harvesttime comes. Someone has to be here to check the grain sacks in and see they get loaded on the train," said Eric Johnson from west of the Baards' place as he copied Joseph's movements.

"Then who will teach the school?" a man across the table asked. "Good as he is, even Olaf can't be in two places at once."

"Well, they ain't too far apart." Joseph measured the distance with his eyes.

"Mrs. Knutson?"

Lars shook his head. "She won't be teaching. She'll be tending a new baby and the twins. That's enough to keep anyone busy."

" 'Specially if Solveig happens to move on." Haakan nodded toward the approaching buggy. "How come he always knows when the food is on?"

George Carlson stopped his horse and buggy by the other horses and leaped to the ground. "I see I'm just in time for dinner." He tied his horse to the wagon next with a long enough lead for some grazing, just as the others had done.

"No dinner for one who ain't put in the morning working." The man stared the grinning George up and down. "And you ain't dressed for no building work. You look more like you come courting."

"I'll work for a while. Have to prove my worth, you know," George said, then ambled off to where the food-laden table awaited.

"She's hiding behind the schoolhouse," Ingeborg whispered. "She hates being embarrassed, and they been teasing her like—"

"Like they never saw a pretty woman blush before?" The look in his eyes let her know he knew all about the teasing and probably had done his share at times.

Ingeborg clutched his comment to her heart to share with Solveig later. If Solveig knew George saw her as beautiful, maybe she would quit worrying about the nearly disappeared scar and faint limp. But how could she not know? That thought came when George's face lit up at the sight of Solveig walking back to join the women, bringing another bucket of cool water from the well.

The joy on Solveig's face, no matter how much she tried to disguise it, said it all.

"If they wait until fall to be married, I'll eat my apron," Ingeborg whispered to Kaaren.

"Good thing the last letter said a niece of mine was hoping to come this summer. She can take Solveig's place." Kaaren carried a wide awake, smiling twin on each hip. "These two are getting much too big to carry together."

"Goodie will come help you."

"You seen the looks between her and Olaf?" Kaaren raised one eyebrow. "You ask me, falling in love must be in the water or something."

"Or something."

The summer chores of gardening, making cheese and butter, butchering the young chickens, and harvesting fruits and vegetables both for their own storage and for Solveig to take to the Bonanza farm kept everyone busy from before dawn to moonrise. When there was enough moonlight, the men continued to break sod until about midnight. Ingeborg wished to go to the freedom of woods and fields, but there was no time. Baptiste and Thorliff, with Hans tagging along to learn from them, became intrepid hunters and fishermen, bringing back deer, rabbit, ducks and geese, game hens, and fish. The smokehouse sent up fragrant smoke continually, and there was always another hide that needed tanning. In between their other chores, the boys continued to split shingles, still racing with the Baard boys as to who could produce the most.

By mid-July, when the corn was higher than the horses' knees, the cultivator could no longer work the rows, so anyone with an extra minute took out a hoe to chop weeds and loosen the soil. The rains came as if on demand, and with the hot summer sun, Ingeborg often said she could measure how much the plants grew overnight.

The chief topic of conversation at the quilting bees that summer was what to do about a school teacher. Olaf would be minding the sack house and making sure the water tower was kept full for the train. The only way he could teach school was to wait until after all the grain was harvested and shipped. That might be near Christmas.

Kaaren kept out of the conversations. Deep in her heart still dwelt a hurt feeling or two from the slight last winter. But she never thought beyond caring for her two growing daughters, rejoicing in the babe within. She continued to wonder why Lars not only paid no attention to Grace, but he seemed to deliberately ignore the silent child. Sophie had already decided she was her father's girl, turning on every ounce of charm in her wriggling little body when she saw or heard her father. Kaaren stroked the cheek of the silent baby in her arms. How would she help this one learn to talk when she couldn't hear? How could she forgive the father who ignored one of his daughters?

⚬

"So, how will I find her?" Far to the west on the railroad track-laying crew, Hjelmer sat in the open door of the sleeping car, swinging his feet and enjoying the breeze blowing through the house on wheels.

"You spent enough time in Fargo. You think maybe she ain't there anymore?"

"I even tried the school, but the old lady at the desk said they can't give out the names and addresses of their pupils." He mimicked the prim woman's tone.

"You wrote to her aunt yet?" Leif asked. When Hjelmer shook his head, Leif slapped him on the shoulder. "You stubborn Norwegian, you. Wouldn't that be the easiest way to find out where this wonderful young woman lives? I'm beginning to think you made her up. There can be no one as perfect as Penny."

"Not even Katja?" Hjelmer sent a sly glance to the side.

"That's different. She's at least here and engaged to me, no matter what those foul-minded fools around the camp say." He bumped shoulders with Hjelmer. "Took her a while to figure out who really was the best man, but I convinced her."

"Why didn't you just marry her and stay in St. Paul?"

"Can't afford a wife yet. I didn't make a killing on land sales like someone else we all know." Leif tipped his head back and rolled it from side to side to stretch out his neck. "Think I'll just buy one of those pieces of land from you and go back to farming like my father. If the land is as good as you say, we should make a fair living."

"The Peterson piece would be a good one, though no one is farming it now. The barn and house are both sod but they seemed sound. Sorry, but I already sold the Booth place."

"You told me all this more than once."

"Then you know that it is there for you. Brockhurst at the bank in Grand Forks will give you a loan with no trouble with the amount you got saved." Hjelmer jumped to the ground. "Think I'll take a walk before turning in."

"You better watch out for Big Red, he done heard you learned a mighty lot about poker over the winter." Leif headed for the tents where his laundress lived. "See you later."

"Uff da." One more thing to worry about other than where was Penny? Had she forgotten him? Perhaps she'd found someone better?

⚜ ⚜

"Why you wearing such a long face?" Mrs. Johnson asked Penny one hot and humid night in July. They were sitting in rockers on the back porch of the hotel, hoping for some stray breeze to waft by and cool them off.

"Huh?" Penny jumped in the near darkness. "I . . . I was watching the fireflies."

"Fireflies might be pretty, child, but they don't bring out such sadness in most people."

"Donald wants to marry me."

"So?"

"So." Penny sighed and propped her chin on the heels of her hands. "So . . ." Her voice dropped to a whisper. "What's happened to Hjelmer? Where is he?" Only the purring of the white cat threading its way between their legs broke the silence. Penny reached to stroke the fluffy head and down the back. "Is he still alive?"

"I thought you was falling in love with Donald Moen. Looks to me that way." Mrs. Johnson set her chair to rocking.

"I could be. I just don't know. How can I be sure until I see Hjelmer again?"

"Or find out what happened to him?"

"Ja, that too." Penny picked up the purring cat and nestled him against her chest. The cat licked her chin with a raspy tongue, then settled in for some serious kneading of the girl's thigh with feline front feet.

"Have you written about this to your aunt, asked her questions?"

"I used to, but she never had any answers for me. Now . . ." She stroked the cat, who purred so loud it drowned out the song of the crickets. "Now, I don't want to make any decisions yet. I just want to graduate from school and . . . and . . ."

"And find Hjelmer."

"Ja, I guess." The sigh she heaved nearly dumped the cat on the floor. He nipped her hand in protest.

I had so hoped yours would be the first wedding in our new church."

"Ja, well, it is not exactly new, but the schoolhouse makes a good church nevertheless." Solveig stroked her hand down the rose watered-silk skirt of the wedding dress Kaaren and Ingeborg had made for her. After the wedding it would be her good dress, but for now, it made her feel like a beautiful bride. The high neck, trimmed in cream lace, framed a face that glowed with joy. The lace flowed down the sides of the front placket, edged the leg of mutton long sleeves, and banded the skirt.

"I wish Mor and Far were here." Her voice sounded much like it had the nights long ago when the sisters had shared a bed in their parents' home in Valdrez.

"I wish they could see their grandchildren, our home here, and the one you will soon be head of."

"That . . . that house frightens me."

"Why ever? It is beautiful."

"I know. That's the problem. I'm not used to such fine things. What if I break something?"

"Just so long as it isn't George's heart, you needn't worry about it." Kaaren got to her feet, swollen in the summer's heat. "Uff da. September in Dakota Territory sure ain't the best time to be with child. Leastways this time I'm only carrying one. I looked like I was ready to deliver any day last time, and that was at only six months along." She rubbed her back with her fists, then stretched as high as she could reach, her fingertips brushing the herbs she had drying in the rafters.

"What did you think of the new pastor that preached last Sunday?" Kaaren asked.

"I like him, and I'm glad he agreed to stay over long enough to marry us." Solveig peered in the small mirror that hung above the washbasin. "Kaaren, answer me true."

"I always do."

"Do you notice the scar?" Her finger trailed the faint line from brow to chin.

Kaaren shook her head. "Not anymore. I think it always looked worse to you than it did to any of us." She paused. "I'm more concerned about any scars remaining on your heart."

Solveig whirled from the glass. "What do you mean?"

"You were very angry with God and everybody else when you came to us."

"I know, but I finally asked God to forgive me and I know He did. What with all of you praying for me to get well, how could I not? At first I figured it was all God's fault, with my leg so tore up and my face . . ." She fingered the scar again. "The meanness just slipped out, like if I didn't say things, I would blow up from the inside out. And then, little by little, like my leg healing, the awful feelings went away and it was like always, the way Mor and Far raised us. I think being away from God was the worst part." She scrubbed one hand over the other, then raised tear-bright eyes to her sister. "But I'm not away from Him any longer, thanks to you and Lars and Ingeborg and Haakan. Even Metiz made me remember how our Father takes care of us, how He healed me, and she doesn't believe in God the way we do."

"Don't be too sure of that." Kaaren crossed the room and turned her sister around. "Let's get you out of this before the men come in for supper and something gets splashed on it." She hugged her sister and unbuttoned the long row of covered buttons. "I am going to miss you."

Solveig laid her hand over her sister's. "I'll miss you, too, but at least you have Ingeborg close by and babies to keep you busy."

The sod walls of the school/church had been newly whitewashed the day before Solveig walked down the aisle on Lars' arm to stand beside George and say her wedding vows loud and clear. When she saw the love shining in George's eyes, the words came easy, and she meant every one of them. When Reverend Solberg pronounced the blessing, she heard a sigh and a few sniffles from behind them. The smile the pastor gave her made her heart bubble up and brim over, as if the blessing and smile had been from God himself. When she looked again at her new husband, the bubbling continued and flowed out to encompass all the people gathered.

"God is good," she whispered.

"He is indeed." George tucked her hand in his arm and led her back down the aisle and out into the sunshine where they could greet everyone.

"Why you crying, Mor?" She could hear Andrew's *whisper* from clear out the door.

"These are tears of joy." Ingeborg knew the futility of whispering to Andrew, who always replied with a gargantuan "huh?"

With Astrid in her arm and holding Andrew by the hand, Ingeborg looked the very ideal of motherhood. Solveig held out her arms to them all. "Mange takk, my family."

Andrew looked up at her, suspicion rife upon his face. "You crying too."

"I'm so happy." She bent down and kissed his cheek.

He shook his head in obvious bewilderment, shook hands gravely with George, and looked around. "Where's Ellie?"

Ingeborg shook her head. "Those children have become each other's shadow. Go with God, you two. You have been blessed indeed." She wiped away the tear that threatened to overflow. "Don't know why weddings always make me cry. My eyes can stay dry at funerals even, but not weddings."

Those around them laughed, the music joining in perfect harmony with the lark arias from the fields.

"Would you like to join us for a wedding feast?" Haakan asked the pastor.

He nodded, shook hands with another couple, and turned back to Haakan. "I would love to. Never have I met such a friendly group of people."

"Maybe it's because you bring out the best in us." Haakan pointed down the wagon track. "Just follow those to that barn over there. Now that the cows are on pasture, we cleaned it up for the party. There's plenty of food, and dancing will come later. We have some pretty good musicians around here, you know."

"I think you must have everything around here that makes life worthwhile." The sweep of his arm included the people, the sky, the sun, the land. "Thank you for the invitation."

Just before singing the grace back at the Bjorklunds', Mrs. Valders, self-appointed queen of the quilters, stepped forward with a radiant quilt draped over her arm. "Mr. and Mrs. Carlson, we give you this wedding ring quilt as a token of our affection and blessing on your marriage. May the almighty God fill your home with love and laughter, children that make your life richer through the years, and . . . and . . ." She sniffed. "Here. I run out of words." She laid the quilt over Solveig's outstretched arms.

Down in the corner were embroidered the words, "To George and Solveig Carlson on this their wedding day, September 15, 1885, Dakota Territory, from your friends at . . ."

"We don't have a name for our place . . . for our . . ." Mrs. Valders made a circular motion. "Not even for our school and church. When we get one, I will finish that."

"Thank you all." Solveig hugged the glorious quilt to her chest. "Mange takk."

After the bride and groom drove off in the buggy, Ingeborg noticed Haakan in deep discussion first with one group and then another. At least the groups parted with smiles on their faces, so the conversations must be about something good

"What is going on now?" she asked him when she caught him by himself.

"Just getting everyone's opinions."

She waited for him to continue. When he didn't she prodded. "Opinions on what?"

He grinned down at her. "Ah, Inge, you are a curious one."

Again she waited. Nothing. In fact, he leaned to the side a bit as if he were leaving.

"Haakan Bjorklund, I'm going to go over and tell that nice young minister that you have been cruel to your wife."

He threw back his head and laughed, drawing the glances of several of the neighbors.

"Have you been drinking?" she hissed.

He shook his head. "Not me and none others. I made sure that won't happen again, least not at our house. But this is all about the minister. Everyone seems to like him and he likes us, so I suggested we offer him the chance to pastor our church."

"But . . . but we don't have a church, a building, that is." She narrowed her eyes in thought. "What if he were not only the minister, but he taught the school too? I think he would be a good teacher, the wonderful way he preaches. We'd solve two problems with one man."

"And where would this one man live?"

Ingeborg thought again. "I've heard of places where the teacher boards at different homes each week. That way everyone shares in his keep."

"You know, wife, you have a good head on those shoulders . . ."

She started to smile her thanks. Until he finished, ". . . for a woman."

She shook her head. "You're impossible."

"Besides, he could take Olaf's bunk in our lean-to."

"Where's Olaf going?"

"Over to the sack house. He wants to build a house there. Says he could start with a walled-off portion of the big building until we either get a soddy up or a frame house." He leaned closer to her. "I think it better be big enough for four no matter which we build." He nodded toward the couple walking close beside each other toward the river.

"Nothing like a wedding to spark a little romance."

"Ha, that's been sparking since long before today." He ambled off in search of those he hadn't spoken with yet. By the end of the day, they had an agreement. Reverend Solberg could take over as both pastor and teacher if he would like. Several of the men approached the young man together, and amid a spate of hilarity and shaking of hands, the plan was agreed upon.

When Haakan quieted everyone to make the announcement, he introduced Reverend John Solberg as their new pastor. While nothing was said as to how they would pay him, the general assumption was to continue as they had for Olaf, with each family contributing an amount for each child. Those who couldn't afford the cash would give in kind.

"I want to thank all of you for the kind invitation," Reverend Solberg said. "I look forward to many years of service here. I get the feeling we're all going to be growing together." He stopped talking and smiled at the children gathered. "School will start a week from Monday."

The party only slowed down and came to an end after sunset, when people finally began leaving to do their chores. There would be bellering cows on many farms that night, impatient for milking.

"I know what they feel like," Ingeborg said to Kaaren back in the soddy. "The cows, I mean. I got enough milk here for three babies.

You want I should feed the twins too?"

"You might have to. I've been giving them well-mashed food from what I cook, but they both think nursing is the best way. I won't be able to feed three, that is for sure."

⚜ ⚜

It wasn't but two days later that Hjelmer rode a horse into the farmstead. He swung to the ground and tied the animal to a post at the corner of the house. Paws danced at his feet, yipping a high-pitched welcome. Goodie came to the door.

"Why, Mr. Bjorklund, what a nice surprise." She wiped her hands on her apron. "Ingeborg will be done feeding the baby any minute now."

Hjelmer held his fedora hat in his hands. "What did she have?"

"A girl. Named her Astrid. It means divine strength. Now ain't that perfect for out here?"

"Ja, strength is needed and much better from the divine." He waved at the three boys out at the barn. "School hasn't started yet, I see."

She stepped back and motioned him inside. "No, that will be next Monday. The new pastor, Reverend Solberg, will be teaching in place of Olaf."

"I saw him down at the sack house. Some building that is. Splitting shingles for roofs must keep those three I saw at the barn out of trouble." Hjelmer blinked in the dimness of the soddy. "Hello, Ingeborg."

"Hello to you too. Welcome home."

"I'm going out to check on the boys," Goodie said as she went out the door.

"Besides splitting shingles, the boys do chores, along with the hunting and smoking I used to do. Don't know how we are going to manage next week after school starts." Ingeborg held Astrid against her shoulder and patted the baby's back until a hearty burp made Hjelmer smile.

"Real ladylike, ain't she?"

"That'll come if her far has anything to say about it. So, how are you?"

"Good, good. Think to be coming home soon as the snow flies."

"Really? That's wonderful." Ingeborg stopped at the look on his face. "What is it?"

"Have you heard from Penny?" He traced a finger around the rim of the coffee cup Goodie had handed him before she stepped outside.

"Not for some time. She was here in June for a bit."

"Did she ask about me?"

Ingeborg shook her head. "But then we didn't see her for long." *Lord, please keep him from asking any questions I can't answer.*

"I see. Think I'll stop over to the Baards', then I got to head back right away. I spent two more days in Fargo looking for her. Agnes *has* to tell me where Penny lives. Or at least give me her address so I can write to her."

*No, she doesn't.* Ingeborg bit back the thought before it could become words. "Will you be back for supper?"

He shook his head. "I need to get to Grafton yet tonight so I can catch the train again. I'm working out west beyond Minot and with one day off a week—if we're lucky—I can't get back to Fargo until we shut down in the late fall." He turned to the door, then paused. When he spoke, his voice carried the uncertainty of a young boy. "You . . . you think Penny wants to see me, hear from me?"

"Ah, Hjelmer, how can I know what is in her heart now? She wrote to you faithfully for so long, and you never answered after that first letter. She believed in you, you know?"

"But I only got one letter." Still young, his voice now held the pain of unshed tears.

"I don't know what happened to them, but she sent a letter along to be mailed with anyone who went to town. And each time they didn't bring a letter back, I think the pain in her heart dug a mite deeper until maybe now it is too great to overcome or has formed a callous to protect her." Ingeborg wove her hands into the fabric of her apron. *Dear Lord, help these two young people come together again if it be your will.* "Hjelmer, when I don't know how to handle something, I ask God for help."

His shoulders sagged. "I been asking."

"Sometimes a sin in our lives blocks His answers." It took all her courage to say the words, soft words that came gently through the dimness.

"Ja." He nodded. "Mange takk, Inge. I will see you again when the ground freezes."

"Go with God, Hjelmer."

He nodded again and strode out the door. After waving to the boys busy with their froes and butts set up in the shade, he nudged his horse into a lope across the prairie.

Ingeborg watched through the window until he was a black dot against the setting sun. "Lord above, I know you have something special in mind for that young man, and I know that only you can bring it about."

orry, Hjelmer, I cannot tell you that." Agnes shook her head.

"Cannot or will not?" He immediately knew he had gone too far.

She seemed to grow inches taller, her jaw tightened, and lightning flashed from her eyes. "I think, young man, that is none of your business."

Hjelmer could feel his hat crushing between his fingers. He wished for a moment it was more than his hat. *How . . . why is she being so stubborn?* "Agnes," he paused. "Mrs. Baard, I love Penny and I want to marry her. You knew that."

"Funny way you have of showing you love her." The disdain in her voice matched the look she shot him.

He started to say something, then stopped. One finger stabbed a hole in the felt. He took in a deep breath. "What must I do to prove that I love her?"

Agnes stared into his eyes as if plumbing the depths of his soul. He forced himself to stand without shrinking away.

Again she shook her head, slowly this time, as if the weight of it were more than she could bear. "I don't know, Hjelmer. I believe you are too late."

"Has she married?" His voice squeaked on the last word.

"No."

"Is she engaged?" Again a shake of the head. "In love with someone else?" The silence answered him. He could feel his heart tearing, ripping, much like the shredded hat in his hands.

"I see." Two words. Two simple words but the end of a dream, of a plan, of a life.

"I'm sorry." *Lord, have I lied? Or did I just not tell the whole truth?*

But Agnes held her ground and watched him go out the door. The curve of his back and neck cried out to her. *How does one prove they love another without . . .* She cut off the thought and returned to slicing the meat for supper.

By the time Hjelmer had ridden barely a mile, he could feel the fire begin in the pit of his stomach. "What gives her the right to keep us apart?" he roared to the heavens. The horse flicked its ears back and forth and added a spurt of speed. "It is for Penny to say if she no longer wants to see me!"

A crow flapped, cawing into the air.

He felt like striking someone, something. "God, if you are listening, this isn't fair!"

He galloped a distance more, drumming his heels into the sides of the now lathering horse. "Why are you hiding Penny from me?" He shook his fist at the heavens. "Your face from me?" The shock of the words made him pull the horse down to a trot. What was he doing? His voice softened. "God, are you hiding your face, or have I not been seeking you?" He stared toward the clouds. "I've been begging for help. I didn't lie to Agnes." The only answer he heard was the air pumping in and whistling out of the horse's flared nostrils. He stopped and got off to walk. "Sorry, animal, I . . . I know better than to take my anger out on a poor, dumb creature like you. Far would take the buggy whip to me if he saw my horse lathered like this." As he strode across the prairie, more of what his father had said in the past came to his mind. *Do your best and a little bit more and you'll have the approval of others and most important, your own.* The horse's breathing quieted.

*Fear God and love the brethren.* Hjelmer snorted at the remembered words, laughing at himself. "I might not love *all* the brethren, since right now one of the sisters is standing in my way. But I sure do love one of the other sisters. Ah, Penny, does it take losing the dream to make this hard-headed Norwegian realize what a fool he's been? You're more important to me than the money. I can always make more money, but only God could make someone like you." He stopped and stared at the horizon, flaring orange and every shade of red imaginable, the clouds burnished by the master's hand. The horse rubbed his sweaty forehead on Hjelmer's back.

"Easy, boy." He stepped back and used one hand to scratch under the soaking forelock and up around the animal's ears. So, what was he going to do? What could he do? "I don't know, God. Guess I'm going to have to wait for you to tell me."

He mounted the horse again and trotted off to Grafton, where a train awaited, if he hadn't already missed it.

⚬⚬⚬

Toward the end of September, Agnes drove the wagon into the yard at Ingeborg's house. With harvest finished at both the Baard and Bjorklund places, the men had gone on with the newly purchased separator and the steam engine to thresh at other homesteads. After all the noise and commotion of harvest, and with the older children in school, Ingeborg and Goodie were enjoying a quiet cup of coffee when they heard the wagon's creaking. Paws barked a welcome and Andrew banged on the screen door.

"Comp'ny," he sang out. "We got comp'ny."

Ellie stood beside him, echoing every word.

When Ingeborg saw who it was, she pushed open the door and went to meet her friend. "What a nice surprise. You're just in time for coffee."

Agnes wrapped the reins around the brake handle, and after using the wheel spokes as stairsteps, she turned and lifted Gus down, her last chick at home. At five, Rebecca had trundled off to school with her brothers. "Now, you go play with Andrew and Ellie and let us ladies visit."

The children tore off laughing toward the barn where Olaf had erected a swing from one of the beams.

"Uff da, such energy. I must have answered a hundred, no, make that two hundred questions on the way over here. The only time he's still is when he's sleeping." She reached back in the wagon for a basket and followed Ingeborg into the soddy. "I could use a cup of coffee, that I can." She greeted Goodie, oohed over baby Astrid asleep in the cradle, and took a chair at the table. "My land, there ain't nothing prettier than this prairie cloaked in a fine Indian summer like we got now. You get such a sight with the trees by the river. Wish I had planted a tree by the house like you did. That shade will be welcome next summer, let me tell you."

Ingeborg set a cup of coffee in front of the chattering woman and took her chair. Something was surely on Agnes's mind.

"Haakan was hoping to have us in a board house by winter, but we shall see. That tree is getting too big to transplant now anyway. I went down to the river one day and chopped a circle deep in the dirt around another sapling. That way the roots will grow more around the tree, so next spring I can transplant it by the house. Should have done more than one."

They sipped their coffee in silence, broken only by the crunch of the cookies after they dipped them in their cups.

"Ingeborg, I need some advice."

"I wondered what was bothering you."

Agnes dug down in her basket. She retrieved some quilt pieces and scattered them on the table, brought out a jar of applesauce she'd canned, and at last laid a letter on the table. "Brought you some things."

"Thank you. I'm in need of new colors to piece a quilt for Reverend Solberg's bunk. We sent some things with Olaf when he moved to his house, and it seems there is never enough."

Agnes pushed the letter closer to Ingeborg's hand. "Read that."

After looking at Agnes with one raised eyebrow, Ingeborg complied. "There's a letter within this letter."

"I know." Agnes still wore the sad face she'd driven up with.

Ingeborg read the single sheet and read it again. She nodded. "I see. So Hjelmer begs you to mail this letter on to Penny and let her make the choice if she wants to write to him."

"What do I do?"

"What do you want to do?"

"Throw it in the fire and pretend I never got it." The smile Agnes tried on failed. She sighed. "I thought he was out of her life for good, you know? Then when he asked me what could he do to prove he loved Penny, I just ignored him. I didn't know what to tell him then. I still don't." She pushed the letter with the tip of her finger. "But that don't sound like the Hjelmer we knew, does it?"

"No, he sounds changed, but . . ." Ingeborg rubbed her forehead with her fingertips. "As he says, if God wants him and Penny together, who are we to stand in the way?"

"So I got to send it, right?"

"What did Joseph say?"

"Never showed it to him." Agnes appeared to be looking for the answer to life's mysteries in the dregs of her cup.

"Does he know Hjelmer stopped by that day?"

A headshake answered her question.

"Ah, Agnes."

"I know. It was easy for me to say you had to forgive Roald for leaving you and that you had to get yourself back close to God where you belonged, but . . ." She sniffed. "I ain't felt close to the

Father for some time, and I . . . I guess what He is saying is I got to forgive Hjelmer for breaking my Penny's heart and get over being mad at him for all kinds of things."

"Looks that way to me too."

"Forgiving is easier when the hurt's been done to you rather than to one you love."

"Forgiving isn't easy no matter what."

"Ja, that's right." Goodie got up to pour more coffee. "It ain't easy but it's always necessary."

"I read in my Bible this morning about having ought against any and saw Hjelmer's name as if it were written on the page. It was like the Lord God was hitting me over the head with it. Been that way since I saw Hjelmer." She pointed to the letter. "And now this. Joseph had it in his pocket and forgot to give it to me last night."

"So?"

"So." She slapped her palms on the table, making the cups bounce. "I'm gonna beg the Lord to forgive me, drop this letter off in the mailbag at the sack house, and leave it all in the Lord's hands like I shoulda done in the beginning 'afore I began messing around in things that were none of my business." A smile tugged at the corners of her mouth. "Our God, He do have strange ways of getting our attention, don't He?"

"Amen to that." Goodie laid her hand on Agnes's shoulder as she refilled the coffee cups.

"With that settled, how about we go over and visit with Kaaren a bit? And how's Metiz? I seen so little of her this summer."

They gathered the children together in Agnes's wagon and headed for the other soddy. After dinner at Kaaren's, Agnes set out for home. Even her back looked happier as she drove off toward the west.

❧ ❧

Penny smiled back at the postmaster when he handed her a letter. "From home," she said, another smile following the first. "Thank you."

"You greet Mrs. Johnson for me, young lady. Tell her I expect an apple tart one of these days." He looked at her over the tops of his gold half-glasses. "I should go claim another for myself, that I should."

"I'll remind her, but you need to drop by for a visit. Been some time since we saw you."

"I'll do that." He lifted his hand to wave her off, then turned back to his work.

Penny stopped on the plank sidewalk long enough to slit the envelope open. Another envelope filled the space. With a shaking hand, she withdrew the paper. The sight of Hjelmer's distinctive writing made her mouth go dry. She stuck the letter in her pocket and headed across the street, through the hotel door, and up the stairs. The closer she got to her room, the faster her feet pounded on the stairs. Once the door closed behind her, she withdrew the letter and sank down on the edge of her bed.

Her fingers refused to move. After all this time, did she want to hear from him? Her heart thundered in her ears. She could see Donald Moen's face as if he stood before her. Would the news in the letter change their growing friendship?

"Open it, silly!" Her words rang loud in the stillness of the third-story room.

She stuck a fingernail under the edge of the flap and pried the paper apart. Pulling the sheets of paper out, she unfolded them, took a deep breath, and began to read.

Dear Penny,

How can I begin to tell you how sorry I am for not having written to you like I promised. I have no excuses, only remorse. Just as I do not deserve God's forgiveness, I do not deserve yours. But I plead with you, please forgive me. If you have any pity for a fool, I am in need of it. Even if we can never go back to where we were, know that I love you and have never stopped loving you, even though it must have seemed that way.

If there is someone else in your life now—and I believe there must be from the way your tante Agnes wouldn't say anything—I will understand, but I sincerely hope he is just a friend.

If you can find it in your heart to answer my letter, I will rejoice. And if God gives you the grace to grant me a chance to call on you and see your face again, I will be the happiest man alive.

Penny wiped the tears from her cheeks for the second time. She read the news of his life on the railroad and sniffed at his signature, "Yours, if you so desire, Hjelmer."

Did she so desire?

"Heavenly Father, what do I do now?" She laid the letter in her lap and stared out the window.

�֍  ֎✧

At the end of October Kaaren had her baby, a boy they named Trygve after Lars' father. Since it meant brave victory, Kaaren felt it fit their son. She had thought to name him differently since they were in the new land, but Lars looked at her shocked when she mentioned it.

"Trygve is a fine name."

"Ja, it is." Kaaren looked down at the infant in the crook of her arm. "A brave name for a brave little boy to have two older sisters."

Metiz brought her a cup of her special mixtures. "Drink now. Need milk for new baby."

"I am glad you stayed to help me through this." Kaaren took her hand. "After that other birthing, this one was easy." She looked over to where the twins usually slept in the trundle bed that fit under the other. Ingeborg had taken them home when their mother went into labor.

Lars sat down on the edge of the bed. "How are you going to feed all three of them?" The looks he sent his son warmed her heart.

Kaaren shook her head. "Ingeborg volunteered to take turns with the girls. I think Sophie will soon be eating enough table food that she'll be all right."

"And Grace?"

She looked up at him, surprise widening her eyes. He so rarely even said the baby's name, and to this day he had never held her. One day soon, when she felt stronger, she knew she would have to approach him about it again. Couldn't he see what he was doing? "She will catch up soon."

Lars merely nodded. "May I hold him?"

Tears sprang into Kaaren's eyes at the look on her husband's face as he fairly glowed down at the infant in his arms.

"My son. I—we have a son." Reverence painted the last word in gold.

"Ja, and two daughters." Kaaren could feel herself slipping away into sleep. She felt him lay the baby back in her arm and tried to say thank you as she fell into the healing sleep she needed.

✖֍  ֎✧

A few evenings later the opportunity arose. Goodie had gone back to Ingeborg's after helping Kaaren during the day. They had decided the twins would alternate nursing, once with their mother and then with Ingeborg. Sophie had been with her aunt for the last several hours and would be coming home soon.

Trygve had just begun nursing when Grace set up a clamor. Lars sat at the table reading. Kaaren waited. Grace wailed.

"Would you pick her up, please, and walk with her or something until your son is finished?" Kaaren raised her voice to be heard over the lone twin's cries.

"She'll be all right. You won't be much longer, will you?"

Kaaren's jaw hit her chest. What could she do? "Then hand her to me and I'll let them nurse at the same time."

Slowly, with obvious reluctance, he rose to his feet, crossed the room, and stood looking down at the crying child. He rocked the bed, murmuring soothing words at the same time.

"You know, if you just pat her tummy that might help. She cannot hear you."

He whirled around, hands on his hips. "I know that!" The words stabbed through the air.

Kaaren stared at him, shaking her head. "What is the matter with you, Lars, that you cannot or will not touch that child? Just because she can't hear, she isn't a leper or something." She saw his head drop forward, the slump of his shoulders, the futile clutching of his fingers. *Oh, God above, how do I reach him? What is the matter with this man? What kind of sickness lets him ignore that poor baby?*

"Don't ask it of me right now, Kaaren, for I cannot. I will care for the others, but please, don't ask me to hold Grace. Maybe when she is older." His words nearly disappeared in his shirt front.

Kaaren pushed herself up from the rocker with one hand, cuddling Trygve with the other. She crossed the three paces and stood in front of her husband. "Oh, Lars, how can you?" She handed him the bundle in her arms and picked up Grace, who by now was red of face and sweaty from crying.

"Look at her." Her fierce tone snapped his head up. "She is perfect in every way but one. And you cannot even see that. This child needs her father just as much as the others do."

At the tone of her voice, both children screwed up their faces and began to cry.

"I . . . I'm sorry." At the look of despair on his face, she could feel her heart melting. She steeled herself.

"Lars, I will not let you do this to her. If you are a believer like you say you are, then you had better pray for God to teach you to love this baby, to let His love flow through you. Or . . ." She shook her head, patting Grace's back as the baby snuffled into her mother's shoulder.

The one word quivered on the air between them. The silence stretched.

"You think I haven't been praying about this? What kind of a man do you think I am?"

"I wish I knew." She returned to the rocker and set Grace to the other breast. Lars walked the length of the soddy to stand by the stove, out of Kaaren's sight.

The trickle of the lullaby he sang to Trygve shattered his wife's heart like nothing else. She let the tears roll down her cheeks unchecked. *Dear God, what is happening to us?*

The next letter Agnes showed Ingeborg revealed Hjelmer's creative use of language as he tried to say thank you forty different ways. Penny had written back, giving him her address in Fargo and permission to come see her. He would go there before coming home when the ground froze.

" 'I regret the pain I caused you,' " Ingeborg read, " 'but know that each day I pray for God to take away the fear I have that she will not see me after all. I know that I brought this misery on myself, but that makes it no easier to bear, in fact, it makes it worse. Please pray with me that God will see fit to work this out in His good time. Sincerely, Hjelmer.' " She looked up at Agnes.

"I know. Kind of takes you by surprise, don't it? Never in my life thought I'd see words like this from that young man."

"Haakan and I thought he had changed some. This just confirms it. Guess all we can do is do as he asks."

"You think I haven't been?" Agnes's eyebrows met her hairline.

"Ja, me too."

Several days later, Lars knelt in front of the rocker where Kaaren was again nursing Grace.

"I . . . I want you to know how sorry I am, that I . . ." He paused.

She could see his Adam's apple jerk up and down. "Please, Kaaren, will you help me?"

Kaaren studied the thick dark hair that framed his strong face. When she looked in his eyes, she felt she was drowning in pools of sorrow. "Ah, Lars, but of course." She cupped her free hand around his jaw and stroked his cheek with her thumb. Watching the life come back to his eyes was like seeing the sun return after a thunderstorm. First the dark clouds blew away, then the lighter ones seemed to shred so the sun could peek through before it burst forth in all its splendor and warmed the earth again.

He reached out with one finger and stroked Grace's cheek as she lay against her mother's breast. The little one turned, studying her father as if she had been waiting for him. When he touched her hand, she gripped his finger—and smiled.

"She bears you no grudge," Kaaren whispered, "and neither do I."

"I promise that every day I will do more for her." He looked up at his wife. "I promise."

⚐ ⚐

"Does she know you are coming?" Leif asked for the third time.

"Not the day." Hjelmer stared out the train window. The snowstorm from the night before had left the ground white. A few drifts blew up to the tracks, but not enough to slow the train. When the snow started coming down like the storm of the century the night before, he'd almost panicked. The snow couldn't keep him away from Penny, not one day longer.

"You think she'll . . . she'll . . ." Katja stumbled over the words. She felt an elbow poke in her side and looked up to see Leif frowning at her. "Sorry."

But Hjelmer knew what she'd been going to ask. He'd been driving himself crazy with the same questions ever since he got her letter. What if she had changed her mind? What if she wanted to see him to tell him off? While he'd written right back, there'd been no other word. Surely if she had fallen in love with someone else, she'd have said so in the letter. Wouldn't she?

He chewed the cuticle on his left index finger. Maybe he should just get off in Grafton and head on out to the Bjorklund homesteads. There was plenty for him to do there, since it was too late to cut sod for his own house. He could build the blacksmith shop out of wood, though, right near the sack house so that he could repair wagons when people came to pick up things delivered by the train. Surely just resetting wheel rims would keep him right busy.

He thought to the last letter Ingeborg had written, telling of the celebration when the first shipment of grain left the sack house, loaded onto the freight cars right through the building. He wished he'd been there. But then maybe it was better he hadn't been. There were still some hard feelings over his land buying and selling.

Leif and Katja planned to move to their new home in the spring. If he didn't go on to St. Paul with them and work in the roundhouse again, he'd see that whatever repairs needed doing on the Peterson place were finished before they came.

"Hjelmer?"

The tone said this wasn't the first time he'd been spoken to. "Ja?"

"She won't like you any better without one finger." Leif and Katja laughed softly.

Hjelmer saw the dot of blood where he'd chewed off a hangnail. He wiped it away.

Were they never going to get there? The heaving in his stomach had nothing to do with the swaying of the train. He repeated to himself the same words he'd been saying for weeks now whenever he thought of Penny, whenever he thought of seeing her. *I am leaving this in God's hands. If He wants me and Penny together, then we will be. He will work it out.*

But his stomach didn't believe a word of it.

When the conductor finally announced, "Fargo, next stop Fargo," he looked up at Leif, who had chosen that minute to whisper something to Katja. He could see on their faces the joy and love they felt for each other. It had been growing steadily between them since last spring.

Would he ever get to talk with Penny like that?

The train slowed and his stomach did another flip-flop.

"You want we should wait for you?" Leif asked when they stood on the station platform.

"No, you go on over to the cafe and eat. I'll be back here in time for the train to leave for St. Paul, either to go on with you or to say good-bye."

Katja laid a hand on his arm. "We are praying for you, too, you know. All will be well."

Hjelmer nodded, spun on his heel, and left the station. To think Penny had been at the Headquarters Hotel all this time. If he'd paid better attention back in Nordland, when his mother read the letters from America, he would have remembered Ingeborg had worked there. That was when Roald and Carl worked on the railroad till they could head north to find the land to homestead. He had walked by the hotel countless times the last time in Fargo on his hunt for Penny. He ducked his head against the wind that tugged at his coat.

But when he got to the hotel's front door, he stopped. What if. . . ? He refused to finish the question and pulled open the door of windows decorated in beveled glass and brass trim. She had said to come into the dining room and ask for her. He entered the room filled with white cloth-covered tables and oak ladder-back chairs. A fireplace on the far wall looked big enough to hold a tree trunk. Gas lights instead of candles graced the wall sconces. A young woman in a blue uniform backed out of the swinging doors and took her tray of cups over to stack on another on a table loaded with clean dishes.

He cleared his throat. "Ah, could you tell me where to find Penny Sjornson?"

"Mercy, I didn't see you there." She spun around, a hand laid to her throat. Her mouth dropped open. "Hjelmer?"

"Ja." He waited as if his boots had been pegged to the floor.

She gripped the table behind her with knuckles gone white.

She looked like a deer caught in a trap. His heart sank clear to his boot tops. He'd been right. She really didn't want to see him. He took in a deep breath, the better to bear the pain. "I . . . I said I would come and here I am." *Stupid, such a stupid thing to say.* He called himself one of the names his mother had told him never to use again. "But I won't bother you anymore." He turned to leave. What else could he do? It was his own fault he lost her.

"Hjelmer, don't go."

Hjelmer now knew what was meant by shackles dropping from a prisoner's hands and ankles.

She stepped forward, her eyes blue as the uniform and swimming in tears.

"Ja." He took a step forward, willing his heart to stay in his chest. "You've grown up."

She shook her head. Another step forward. He could see her hands trembling.

Their eyes sent messages their mouths couldn't form.

"Ah, Penny." His heart cried out, putting all the fear and worry and love that filled it into those two words. "I am so sorry."

Before he could move again, she flew across the room and threw herself into his arms. He clutched her close, breathing in the wonderful scent of her, feeling her trembling, hearing her sniffs.

"Ah, my love, are you crying?" He stroked the nape of her neck and let the curls that escaped her hairnet tickle his nose.

"N-no . . . y-yes." She drew back, tears glistening like sun-kissed snowdrifts on her lashes. "I . . . I thought to tell you I loved another." Her voice broke in the middle.

"And now?" His heart stopped. She had said "thought."

"Now that I've seen you again, I remember what love feels like and that wasn't it."

Her simple words, the tremble of her lips, and the light in her eyes made him catch his breath. "Thank you, God, thank you." He felt like shouting, but instead he whispered the words again against the sweetness of her lips.

Later, after he'd met Mrs. Johnson and the others on the staff, he and Penny strolled arm in arm down the street to the cafe where he was to meet with Leif and Katja.

"Are you sure you won't come with me now?"

She shook her head, giving him a sad smile. "How I would love to, but I am committed to finishing this last year of high school. I will graduate in May." When he started to say something, she laid a gloved finger over his lips. "Hjelmer, this is very important to me, and I promised Onkel Joseph and myself. I will not let us down."

He took her hand in his and turned her to face him.

"I will come for you in May, when our house is built and your store and my blacksmith shop. We will be married in our church—"

"Have they built the church, then?"

He shook his head. "No. But who knows what can happen by then? We will have our own land to call home, but most important, we will have each other, with God's blessing."

"Ja." She looked up at him, her eyes dark in the dimness. "I pray God that spring will come soon." They no longer felt the cold wind of winter but instead the balmy breeze of summer when they shared the kiss of their commitment.

# Epilogue

*Late April 1886*

Paws announced a friend was coming. Ingeborg looked out the window of her new frame house, but seeing no one, she went on out the door. They had moved from the soddy only three days before. Metiz strode across the land already disked for the garden and the corn patch between the house and the river. Her step seemed a bit slower and her carriage no longer so erect. Was she limping too?

"Metiz!" Ingeborg shouted. "Welcome home. You are just in time for dinner."

The old woman waved and shifted the pack on her back. When they stood face-to-face, Ingeborg could tell the winter had been hard on her friend, but the black eyes still snapped, and while her smile pushed back more wrinkles, it still held all its warmth.

Metiz swung her pack to the ground and reached inside, pulling out a rabbit-skin jacket complete with hood. "For Astrid." A vest followed. "Andrew." Drawing out a soft doeskin packet, she handed it to Ingeborg. "For you."

"More simples?" At Metiz' nod, Ingeborg fingered the soft leather and the wonderful rabbit fur. "Thank you, my friend."

"Metiz, how wonderful to see you." Haakan set Andrew down after carrying him up from the barn on his shoulders. "Baptiste will be pleased when he gets home from school. He's been asking when you might be coming."

"Boy know."

"How would he know?"

Metiz waited for Ingeborg and Haakan to look back at her after sharing a questioning glance. "Me go by school." Delighted at their chagrin, she slapped her knee, the chuckles continuing to roll.

Andrew strode over to stand in front of the old woman. "You gone too long. You come back?"

She nodded. "I come back. Now I stay."

"So, we'll be building you a house?" Haakan asked.

She nodded.

"Wood frame or sod?"

She turned to give their new frame house a careful look. "Wood. Much windows."

The men finished the church on Saturday. When the bell that Hjelmer had donated rang for the first time that last Sunday in May, it was to announce the wedding of Hjelmer Bjorklund and Penny Sjornson to be held immediately following the church service.

The party lasted until dusk when people had to go home to take care of their chores. The main topic of conversation, other than the newlyweds, their store, and the shop that would open in a week, was one that had been bandied about for some time already. Now that they had a train stop for the sack house, the mailbag picked up and returned along with orders of machinery and other things, a school, a church and several other buildings, what could they call this town of theirs? The railroad referred to it as water stop number 342.

The men thought Nordland would be fine. Haakan suggested Bjorkton, but he was the only one voting for that. Others suggested various names but no one could agree. The women, after much discussion at the quilting bees, had decided on their proposal.

After church the next Sunday, Reverend Solberg called the group to order. "I believe we have a matter of business to bring up since you all decided this would be the day to vote on the name for our town. He turned to the blackboard and wrote five names on the board. Nordland, Bjorkton, Norville, Rivervale, and Blessing—the women's proposed name.

"Now we will vote by a show of hands," Solberg continued. "Or would you rather have ballots?"

"Ballots!" called someone from the back.

"All right." The preacher nodded to two men, who began handing out squares of paper with the names written on them. "You will vote for one, fold the paper, and pass the paper to the center aisle. I have pencils up here for those who need them."

Several hands went up. Women dug in their purses, shushed the restless children, and silence fell as the people made their choice.

With the ballots collected, three men—Haakan, Joseph, and Anner Valders—retired outside to count them.

People visited in the meantime, congratulating the families of the bride and groom on such a good time they'd had the week before. The men discussed seeding and fencing, the women the next quilting bee and their children.

Ingeborg bounced Astrid on her knee to keep her entertained, and Kaaren snagged Sophie back from crawling under the benches. Grace sat at her feet chewing on the hard crust of bread Kaaren had brought along for just that purpose.

"What's taking them so long?" Kaaren whispered. "Trygve needs to be fed, and I thought I could do that on the way home." When the baby fussed again, she handed him to his father, who looked a bit sheepish, but nevertheless rocked his son in his arms.

"They have to be sure." Astrid reached for the brooch at her mother's neckline. Ingeborg closed her hand over her baby's pointing finger and kissed the tip. Astrid poked her finger into her mother's mouth, her eyes dancing at the game she knew would come. Nibble and giggle it could well be called.

The men returned. Silence fell.

Haakan handed the paper to Reverend Solberg and took his seat next to Ingeborg.

"The name of this town is to be called . . ." He paused and looked around with a grin.

"Read it, Pastor."

"Blessing! A fine name for a fine town. And a good name for a church. Blessing Lutheran Church. Dear Lord, bless us all." While the clapping did not seem to be universal, the women applauded loudly.

"I like it," Kaaren said.

"You should. You thought it up," Ingeborg reminded her.

"You suppose it came from the Almighty?"

"I don't doubt it." Ingeborg closed her eyes. "Think of it. Blessing, North Dakota, for I bet you that's what we'll be called in the next few years. The state of North Dakota."

"Uff da. So much change."

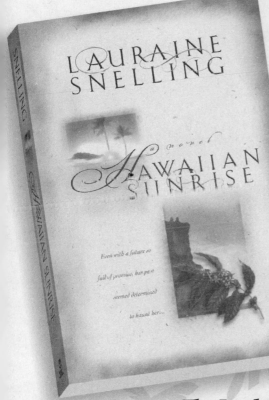